BRIGHTER
THAN THE SUN

MAYA BANKS

JOVE
New York

A JOVE BOOK
Published by Berkley
An imprint of Penguin Random House LLC
375 Hudson Street, New York, New York 10014

Copyright © 2017 by Maya Banks
Penguin Random House supports copyright. Copyright fuels creativity, encourages
diverse voices, promotes free speech, and creates a vibrant culture. Thank you for buying
an authorized edition of this book and for complying with copyright laws by not
reproducing, scanning, or distributing any part of it in any form without permission.
You are supporting writers and allowing Penguin Random House to continue to
publish books for every reader.

A JOVE BOOK and BERKLEY are registered trademarks and the B colophon
is a trademark of Penguin Random House LLC.

ISBN: 9780425277003

First Edition: March 2017

Printed in the United States of America
1 3 5 7 9 10 8 6 4 2

Book design by Laura K. Corless

BRIGHTER
THAN THE SUN

CHAPTER 1

ZOE. Your name is Zoe Kildare now.

Zoe mentally cautioned herself while she paced back and forth, her agitation only increasing as she stopped to check her watch. Where was she? Rusty should have been here by now. Zoe's mind raced with a number of gruesome possibilities. What if she'd been found out? What if she'd led Rusty straight into harm's way?

The door burst open and she barely managed to suppress her surprised cry of fright. She sagged with relief when her college friend Rusty Kelly hurried through carrying a stack of folders and loose papers.

Rusty dropped the load onto the coffee table and pulled Zoe into a fierce hug. The two women held on to each other for a long moment before Rusty finally pulled away, her gaze sweeping up and down Zoe as if assessing her condition.

"Are you okay?" Rusty asked anxiously.

Zoe swallowed and nodded though tears pricked her eyelids.

Rusty gave her another bone-crushing hug, and Zoe held on to her friend just as tightly. Then Rusty guided her to the nearby couch and urged her down, sitting diagonal to her and gathering her hands in her firm grip.

"Did anyone follow you? Did you see anything out of the ordinary or get a sense that anyone was watching you?" Rusty asked urgently.

Zoe shook her head. "No, I don't think so. I was careful. I did everything you told me. I made it appear as though I was heading west to California."

Rusty nodded approvingly. "That's good, but we can't afford to waste any time nor can we ever adopt a false sense of security. You went to college here and it's a city you're familiar with, so it stands to reason this is a logical place you'd go."

"I can't stay here," Zoe choked out.

"No, you can't," Rusty said calmly. "I need you to answer some questions for me, Stel—I mean Zoe. Damn it. We can't afford to slip. You've got to be aware and on your toes at all times. You cannot react to your real name. You can't flinch, show any awareness. You have to act as though you assume whoever is using it is calling someone else's name. And you absolutely have to be tuned in to your alias and behave as if it's the name you were born with."

Zoe nodded, clasping Rusty's hands more fiercely. Her heart felt as though it were going to beat right out of her chest. Not a minute had passed since overhearing Sebastian's—or whoever the hell he was—conversation six days ago that fear hadn't been a living, breathing constant for her. Her entire life had been upended the day she'd been crushed and had learned what a gullible, naïve fool she'd been. Had always been.

"Zoe is a name I'm intimately familiar with," she admitted, lowering her eyes in embarrassment. "When I was a child, I felt so isolated . . . so alone that I made up an imaginary friend. Zoe. Zoe Kildare. I had no other friends. I was a stranger in my own home. My father barely acknowledged my presence."

She broke off, tears threatening once more. Damn it. She'd shed no more tears over her father or a bastard like Sebastian. She'd never mattered to anyone in her life, so why should she have believed for a moment that she would matter to the man who became her lover? A man whom she'd overheard laughing and saying what a chore it was to have to fuck a loser like her. Just the memory had her cringing with humiliation.

"Oh honey," Rusty said, her own eyes going bright with tears.

Zoe shook her head, firming her lips. "They aren't worth your tears or mine. Now, what questions did you have for me?"

Rusty sighed but returned to the matter at hand. "Did you ever at any time mention me, my name, anything about me, to Sebastian, your father or anyone? Think hard, Zoe. This is important."

Zoe frowned as she thought back. But no. She hadn't wanted to risk Rusty in any way—Rusty was her first and only true friend. The only person in her entire life who was real and loyal. She shook her head in response to the question.

"Are you one hundred percent certain?" Rusty persisted.

"I wasn't exactly on speaking terms with my father," Zoe said bitterly. "And when I was with Sebastian we didn't talk about my life outside of our 'relationship.' I was too worried

he would find out about me . . . who I was . . . and that he'd
hate me, never knowing he knew all along."

Rusty looked relieved and then smiled, her eyes lighting
up with triumph. "I don't want you to worry. I have the perfect plan."

Zoe looked at her in confusion, but Rusty went over and
gathered the stack of folders she'd carried in with her. She
began placing items in front of a stunned Zoe.

"First, here's your driver's license. You're from Chicago,
by the way. Here's your birth certificate, passport and Social
Security card. Oh, and credit cards with an already well-
established credit history. You have a penchant for books
and wine, judging by the purchases. And clothes. I made you
a total clothes and shoe whore. You even have Facebook and
Twitter accounts that date back seven years—do you have any
idea how long it took me to make up and post inane details
of your life as well as establish fake friends for you? Oh,
and you also have a solid purchase history with Amazon,
including a Kindle and plenty of ebooks. You're a devoted
fan of cookbooks, romance and science fiction."

Zoe looked at her in utter bewilderment. Then she latched
on to one of the last things Rusty said. "Cookbooks?" She
broke into hysterical laughter. "I can't even boil water!"

Rusty shrugged. "Details. Not like you'll have to prove
your culinary prowess, and it was all I could come up with
on such short notice."

Zoe's jaw gaped in awe. "Rusty, how on earth did you
accomplish all this? Isn't this . . . illegal?"

Rusty didn't look overly concerned. "What can I say? I have
mad tech and hacking skills. I impressed even myself this time."

"I have no idea what to say. This is . . ."

Rusty gave her a cheeky grin. "Brilliant? Genius?" She
made a show of blowing on her nails, a devilish gleam in

her eyes. "Oh, and by the way, after you got your BA, you also graduated with an MBA from DePaul University. I didn't want any similarities to your past reality."

"I think I'm kind of afraid of you right now," Zoe said, though some of the panic that had been ever present since hearing of her intended fate from her scumbag ex-lover eased, and for the first time she began to feel . . . hope.

Rusty rolled her eyes. "It's just as well you can't tell anyone what I've done because it's not like my overbearing brothers would ever believe I was more tech savvy than my geek-god brother, Donovan. Not to mention a certain asshole sheriff who's the bane of my existence and hasn't missed any opportunity to demean and insult me over the years but then inexplicably decided to give me the most delicious kiss of my life. Not that there've been that many."

Zoe winced in sympathy. She was the only person Rusty had confided in about her love/hate relationship with Sean Cameron, the sheriff of the county she lived in.

"Apparently we both suck when it comes to men," she said lamely.

"No, sister. *We* don't suck. They do," Rusty said emphatically.

"I'll drink to that," she muttered.

Rusty leaned forward and squeezed her hands, sympathy brimming in her eyes. "He's an asshole, Zoe. And not worth your time or regret. You did nothing wrong. He played you. That's on him. Not you."

"Doesn't make me any less stupid," Zoe muttered.

"Well, join the crowd. I should have knocked Sean's teeth out when he pulled that stunt and especially since he apologized and said it *never* should have happened. But noooo. I stood there like a moron. God, I'm mortified to this day and avoid him at all costs."

"So you said you had the perfect plan," Zoe said, purposely turning the subject away from what was clearly a painful, embarrassing memory for Rusty.

Rusty's eyes lit up as she smiled. "I have the *perfect* plan. You're going to come home with me and stay for a while. You know. A friend I met at a conference while in college and kept in touch with. Marlene and Frank will love you and take you in just like family."

Zoe's expression became troubled. "That's not a good idea, Rusty. I don't want you or your family exposed to any danger. You've already risked far too much."

To Zoe's surprise, Rusty laughed. "I realize we've both kept our secrets during our friendship—you keeping the fact your father is involved in organized crime, and me? Well, let's just say that the very *safest* place for you to stay until we figure out a better plan or nail Sebastian's sorry ass to the wall is with my family. He doesn't stand a chance against my brothers, not to mention all the people who work for them."

Zoe's eyebrows went up in question.

Rusty held up fingers as she ticked off her points. "Apart from the fact that the asshole sheriff is exceedingly protective of our family and is an adopted family member much like myself, my brothers kick asses for a living. They're all ex-military and someone would be a fool to ever cross them in any way, and once you come home with me as a friend? Well, consider yourself a member of the Kelly clan. Their motto is 'no one fucks with the Kellys,' and trust me, sister, that isn't just an idle boast."

"What on earth do they do? I mean, apart from kicking asses for a living and being ex-military."

"They run an organization that takes a wide range of assignments from personal protection to hostage retrieval to messy jobs the government doesn't want to soil their hands on but don't mind throwing KGI under the bus for in order to achieve their purpose. They've done fugitive recovery, rescue missions, obliterated terrorist organizations, and that's when they aren't meeting their significant others while on a mission."

Zoe studied her for a long moment. "You're not joking, are you?"

Rusty shook her head. "Nope. When I say they are the ultimate badasses, I am not in the least bit exaggerating. Wait until you meet them!"

"Uh, maybe that's not a good idea," Zoe mumbled. "I'd feel better staying to myself as much as possible."

Rusty shrugged. "If you come home with me, it's inevitable you'll meet them at some point. Just be yourself and act casual. If you start acting all weird and jumpy then they're going to get suspicious, and that's the last thing we want."

"So you aren't going to tell them about . . . me? I mean, the truth?"

Rusty's eyes grew earnest. "I would never betray your confidence, Zoe. You're my friend, and as far as they're concerned, we're friends who met in college and you're visiting me while we decide what to do with our degrees and futures. The less they know, the better. In fact, no one but the two of us ever needs to know the truth. That's how fuckups happen. I'm going to keep you alive no matter what it takes. I won't let that asshole get his hands on you."

Zoe took a deep breath. "So when do we leave then?"

CHAPTER 2

"WE'RE almost there," Rusty said cheerfully as they crossed the bridge over Kentucky Lake.

"It's beautiful here," Zoe breathed. "It seems so quiet and peaceful. No hustle and bustle of a big city. Are the people here nice?"

Rusty wrinkled her nose. "For the most part. I mean, like any small town we have our share of nosy busybodies whose sole ambition in life is to make others miserable, but the Kellys are very respected in this area. Frank owns a hardware store in Dover, and as I told you, all six of his and Marlene's sons served in various branches of the military. I was on the other side of the fence growing up. White trash. Troublemaker. Loser. Pick your poison. My life changed when I broke into Frank and Marlene's house because I was starving and my asshole stepfather didn't give a shit about anything except where to score his next hit. He wasn't choosy. Alcohol, drugs, whatever would get him hammered the fastest. Taking care of a stepdaughter dumped on him by his slut of a wife wasn't exactly a priority. I wouldn't have ever stayed the first night with him, but I had nowhere else to go and I was too young at the time to pull off acting older than I was, so I would have just gotten hauled into the foster care system. At least my stepfather was the devil I knew and I learned to get around him." She grimaced. "Most of the time."

"God, Rusty. My life wasn't exactly wonderful, but I was never abused and I never went without. My father saw to it that I had the best of everything. Most likely so I wouldn't be more of an embarrassment to him than I already was. I mean, it was obvious that my own mother had no use for me. She left and couldn't be bothered to take her daughter with her."

Rusty scowled. "I don't see much of a difference in our situations. We were both unwanted, and that does a number on a child, as we can both attest to."

"That's true," Zoe admitted.

"I was so lucky," Rusty said, her features going soft, her eyes lighting with love and pride. "Marlene and Frank are the very best kind of people. Marlene took me in without question, even confronting my asshole stepfather and then permanently removing me from his custody. They even adopted me after I turned eighteen because they wanted me to know they truly did consider me a part of the family. Their daughter."

"They sound wonderful," Zoe said wistfully.

"Wait until you meet them," Rusty said, smiling. "I give it a day before Marlene claims you as family. My brothers give her shit about her propensity for collecting 'strays.' Strays being all the people she's adopted into the family over the years. It's impossible not to love her and Frank."

"They sound too good to be true," Zoe admitted.

"They're the real deal. You'll see soon enough."

Zoe twirled the ends of her long hair nervously through her fingers and glanced at her reflection in the side-view mirror.

"I don't know about this whole disguise, Rusty. It just doesn't feel like . . . me."

Rusty laughed. "That's the point." Then as if sensing Zoe's very real discomfort, she reached over and put her hand over her friend's and squeezed reassuringly. "You look stunning as a blonde. Going from red to black was too risky. The roots would be more prominent, though you're going to have to keep a close watch and touch up your color on a regular basis. You weren't a carrottop by any means, so even if your roots start to show it will be a lot more subtle."

"And the extensions?" Zoe asked doubtfully.

"Think about it. You had shoulder-length hair. What do most people do when they want to change their appearance? They cut it because they can't exactly grow their hair fast enough to complete a believable disguise. By making your hair a good eight inches longer it gives more credibility to your disguise, and no one can tell you have extensions in. It looks absolutely natural. That's why it took so long to do. I had to make it absolutely seamless, and again, this is something we have to stay on top of at all times. No slipups."

Zoe's lips curled into a glimmer of a smile. "You say 'we' as if you'll have my back the entire time."

Rusty's expression turned fierce. "If I'm able, that's exactly what I'm going to do until we figure out a way to get you out of this mess and get rid of that asshole trying to kill you."

"Still, I'm not sure I can pull off this sweet, all-natural, girl-next-door image you're trying to make me into," Zoe said.

Rusty's sigh was audible as she cast a sideways glance at her that was a mixture of rage and sorrow.

"Don't take this the wrong way, Zoe. This is not in any way a criticism of you," she said fiercely. "I'm well aware of the exacting standards your father forced on you and subsequently enforced your entire life. You were high-class, high-fashion twenty-four-seven. You were the epitome of wealth and posh. Hell, you never even set foot out of your apartment without makeup to conceal your freckles, because your father viewed them as an imperfection. Over time he made you feel the same way about them, about every single thing; he labeled you until you believed yourself that you weren't just fine the way you were. You said yourself the asshole you were dating had no clue you had freckles. You've never been allowed to just be you, and Zoe, listen carefully to what I'm saying. You, the real you? There is nothing wrong with her. You're beautiful, and you don't need clothes, makeup or jewelry to make you that way. But now your obsession with concealing what you were convinced was a flaw works in our favor because you're sporting a fresh face, makeup free, and you only have a dusting of freckles across your nose. They look freaking adorable. You look nothing like the high-class fashionista you've been your entire life. With the casual faded jeans, cute tops, and loafers and flip-flops, no one would ever look at you and see the person you were. You've simply allowed yourself to be who you were all along. Real and not some costume you were forced to wear for most of your life. Trust me, this look, the person you represent now, is a foolproof disguise because it isn't a deception in the least. It's one hundred percent honest and representative of the person you've always been."

Hot tears burned like acid at the corners of Zoe's eyes

and she blinked hastily to clear her vision as Rusty's impassioned words settled over her, sinking into places, vulnerable areas she'd never dared allow anyone to see.

"I sound vain and ungrateful," Zoe said, shame creeping up her spine. "I swear I'm not, Rusty. What I am is scared out of my mind, not only for me but for you. You've risked everything to help me and I can't help but wonder what happens if they find out about you or get to you. I could never live with myself knowing you were hurt or killed because you risked so much for me."

Zoe was gripping her hand so tightly that Rusty gingerly pried it from her terrified grasp and gave her a look of understanding, love and friendship that nearly brought tears to her eyes.

"You're my dearest friend," Rusty said sincerely. "There's no way I'd ever turn my back on you. Besides, I have mad skills. Not even my brothers would be able to uncover the truth of your past, and that's saying a lot considering what they do. It usually pisses me off that they either continually underestimate me or are so overprotective that they want to wrap me in Bubble Wrap like they do their wives and never let me out in the world on my own. God, you should have heard the objections when I wanted to move off campus and get my own apartment after my sophomore year. You would have thought the world had come to an end. Then there was the time when I was totally teasing one of my brothers and said that I was perfectly capable of defending myself and made reference to the fact that self-defense classes were a must for a woman going to university. He immediately demanded to know what assholes were giving me trouble and threatened to go kick some serious ass."

Rusty rolled her eyes, making her laugh.

"I don't know," Zoe said wistfully. "It must be so wonderful to have a family who loves and cares about you so much."

Rusty immediately looked chagrined. "God, I'm such a jerk. I didn't mean to make you feel like shit."

"Don't," Zoe said forcefully. "Do *not* apologize for having such a wonderful family just because for all practical purposes I had none. Besides, if what you said is true, then it looks like I'll get to experience what having a real family feels like while I'm here."

"Just remember," Rusty said in what Zoe thought had to be her best schoolmarm impression. "None of your usual makeup, no designer clothes. You have to act like what you look like. A fresh-faced, innocent, all-American girl next door who thinks a Jimmy Choo is a restaurant and not an outrageously expensive shoe."

Zoe burst out laughing. "That I can do. It'll be nice getting to be myself for once instead of some made-up Barbie doll controlled by my dad, who only remembered he had a daughter when he was telling her how to dress and act and where to go or not go."

"You're going to get through this," Rusty promised. "I don't have all the answers. Yet. But for now I want you to relax and enjoy hanging out with me and my family and try to forget about the asshole trying to kill you. He can't hurt you here, honey. That much I can promise."

They turned onto a winding highway that paralleled the lake, and a few minutes later, Rusty's Jeep pulled up to a huge security gate that had Zoe's eyes widening. When Rusty rolled down her window and faced the retinal scanner, Zoe's mouth fell completely open.

"I told you what my brothers do," Rusty said with a shrug. "They take the safety of our family very seriously. They've made some not-so-nice enemies over the years, and one of my sisters-in-law was even abducted from the compound before construction was complete, so believe me when I say no one gets in and out of here without them knowing."

For the first time since her entire world had fallen apart, Zoe began to feel hope. Maybe Rusty was right. This just might *be* the absolute safest place for her to lie low for the time being. As they passed an airfield, a shooting range, two buildings that Rusty explained were the war room and the infirmary, her belief was only cemented. Even her father didn't have the extensive resources the Kellys seemed to possess.

A few seconds later they pulled up to a large, two-story house that, while new, looked like a throwback to another era. The epitome of a southern, country home complete with charming dormers, a wraparound porch with rockers and a porch swing.

"This is Frank and Marlene's house," Rusty explained. "My brothers and their wives all have houses spaced out within the confines of the compound. It took a while for Sam, my oldest brother, to convince our parents to move, but here they are. They had an architect draw up an exact replica of their old place, the next best thing to plunking their old house right down on this plot of land. The only holdout remaining is Joe. He and Nathan are twins and the youngest. Well, until I came along," she added with a grin. "He's the only remaining bachelor, and he spends most of his time dodging Marlene's matchmaking efforts when he's not on a mission."

"Are they away often?" Zoe asked curiously.

"Depends," Rusty said as she climbed out and met Zoe around back to get the bags. "Right now things are pretty quiet but that could change at a moment's notice. They have three teams and are currently hiring new muscle and training. They usually rotate missions to give each team enough downtime between missions, but sometimes shit gets real and all three teams are involved."

Zoe's eyes went round. "I don't even want to know."

"You'll get used to it," Rusty said nonchalantly. "It's just a way of life around here. I guess for someone outside the family our setup appears bizarre, but it's just another day for us. In fact, it feels weirder when nothing is going on and we actually lead normal lives."

"Something tells me you have a lot of stories you could entertain me with," Zoe said, lifting an eyebrow in her direction.

Rusty laughed. "Boy, do I. I'll tell you all about them sometime. For now, let's get you settled in."

The sound of a door opening and Rusty's sudden joyous smile made Zoe turn in the direction of the front door. An older woman rushed out and Rusty dropped the suitcases on the ground and ran into the woman's arms. Zoe had never seen Rusty so excited before.

"My baby's home!" the woman she assumed was Marlene said as she enfolded Rusty in a fierce embrace.

A second later, an older gentleman also appeared and Rusty rushed into his massive embrace just as she'd done with Marlene.

"Glad to have you home again, girl," the man said gruffly.

Zoe couldn't control the surge of longing or the sudden tears that burned her eyelids. It was obvious these two people loved Rusty every bit as much as she loved them. What must it feel like to have such unconditional, abiding love? She suddenly felt completely alone and unworthy, casting her gaze downward, no longer able to take in the sight of all the things she'd longed for—and had been without—her entire life.

"Mom, Pop, I told you about my friend who's come to

stay with me for a while," Rusty said, heading back toward Zoe to grab her hand. "This is Zoe Kildare."

She pulled her toward the older couple, and Zoe was surprised to see the sincere, welcoming smile on Marlene's face and the instant affectionate expression on Frank's.

"It's wonderful to meet you, dear," Marlene said, shocking Zoe by pulling her into a hug every bit as fierce as the one she'd given Rusty.

For a moment Zoe held on, drowning in the sensation of what a mother's hug must feel like. God, she never wanted to let go. Almost as if sensing her need, Marlene tightened her arms around her and simply held her for a long moment. Then she stepped back and Zoe was at once swallowed up by Frank's huge arms as she was pressed against the barrel-chested older man.

"Any friend of Rusty's is considered family," he said in the gruff tone Zoe had already come to associate with Rusty's adoptive father. "Stay as long as you like. Marlene will be thrilled to have another person to fuss over."

Rusty sent her a smug "I told you so" look while Zoe could only stand there in utter befuddlement, unsure of how to react to their unreserved welcome.

Marlene grabbed her hand as Frank went to gather the bags. "Come inside, dear. You must be hungry and thirsty after your drive."

"Just go with it," Rusty whispered as she and Marlene passed them. "Marlene feeds everyone, and trust me, you've never tasted anything as good as her cooking."

Rusty led her up the staircase to a bedroom at the far end and the two women entered.

"This was the only modification to the original house," Rusty said with a soft smile. "Originally there were seven bedrooms, the master and then one for each of my brothers growing up. When I came along, only Nathan and Joe were still living at home, though they were rarely here because they enlisted in the army. They saw little point in buying their own place when they were only home on leave for short periods of time, so they stayed here. When I came along, Marlene just gave me one of my brothers' old rooms, but when they had the house reconstructed, she insisted on giving me my own bedroom even though there are now six unoccupied bedrooms in the house."

Zoe looked at her in confusion and Rusty laughed.

"I know, right? As I said, Joe is the only unmarried son left but he lives in my oldest brother's former home on the lake outside the compound. Everyone else has their own homes with their wives and children, but Marlene was adamant that everything stayed the same, everyone had their old bedrooms, right down to the way they'd been decorated with old trophies, awards, memorabilia, et cetera. It's kind of cool when you think about it. She said she always wanted a place for everyone to come 'home' to and gather for holidays and remember old times and happy memories. It was very important to her. And, well, I can't say I blame her. All her children have left the nest, and this is her way of holding on and keeping the family together and those memories alive. She wants her grandchildren to see where their fathers grew up, show them pictures and the things that belonged to their dads when they were younger. I guess you could say this house is a tangible link to the family history."

"I think that's beautiful," Zoe said, trying to disguise the ache in her voice.

"And," Rusty said, drawing out the word, "you're bunking with me. Not because there's a shortage of rooms, mind you."

The two burst into laughter before Rusty recovered and continued on.

"But because I want to be close to you at night." Her tone
sobered as did her expression. "You've had a hell of a scare,
girlfriend, and you haven't even had time to deal with it
much less process it. I need to be close so that if you have
nightmares or wake up screaming, Marlene and Frank won't
be alerted and we won't have to lie our way out of a sticky
situation. I realize I'm lying by omission to them, and I hate
the idea of lying to them at all. I'd never betray their trust
after all they've given me."

Very real pain shone in Rusty's eyes, mixed with shadows
from the past, and Zoe immediately felt a surge of guilt for
what she was making her friend do. They were both lying
to Rusty's adoptive parents and it made her feel like complete scum.

"Hey, don't look like that," Rusty said. "Sometimes we
have to do things we don't agree with or like, and in this
case, I'm okay with that. Besides, they'd never be angry with
me in a situation like this. I'm not lying to them out of mal-
ice or to get out of something I've done or a failure to take
responsibility. I'm doing this to save my friend's life, and
quite frankly, they'd be completely disappointed in me if I
turned my back on you and refused to help you or just looked
the other way. That's not who they are. Any of my family.
Frank and Marlene have always taught their children and
everyone they've adopted into the fold to step up, do the
right thing and be selfless. It's safe to say that they managed
to successfully instill those values into every single one of
their children, whether blood-related or not. It may have just
taken me a little longer to grasp the concept than the others,"
she added ruefully.

"Knock knock," Frank called out from the hall. "I've got
your bags. If you'll tell me where you want them, I'll get
you all squared away."

Rusty hurried to the door and swung it open and Zoe noticed already that any time Rusty so much as looked at her parents, her expression immediately softened into one of love and warmth.

"Thanks, Pop. You can just set them down here," she said, gesturing to the wall just inside the door. "We'll unpack later after we face-plant onto the bed for an hour to rest up. I swear the drive from Knoxville gets longer and longer each time I make it."

Frank kissed Rusty's forehead. "That's why you need to establish your career closer to home. It's not the same without you here, and your mother and I miss you. Would be nice to be able to see you more often and even better if when you marry and have children, you're right here with all our other grandchildren so we can spoil them rotten."

Zoe stifled her laughter at Rusty's immediate deer-in-the-headlights look at Frank's mention of marriage and children.

Frank turned to go. "I'll let you girls get unpacked. Again, it's nice to have you, Zoe, and if you need anything at all, you just let me or Marlene know and we'll fix you right up."

He had nearly disappeared from view when he suddenly turned back.

"Oh, I forgot to mention. Your mother wanted me to tell you that dinner will be ready shortly, so I'd put a rush on it."

CHAPTER 3

JOE leaned back against one of the desks in the war room and surveyed the loosely scattered teams, including the two new recruits, Ryker Sinclair and Allie Jacobs. Ryker had joined Joe and Nathan's team, a fact that made the twin brothers extremely happy. Ryker had served in the army with them, and Joe and Nathan both trusted him with their lives—and those of their other teammates, Swanny, Edge and Skylar.

Allie had been a surprise to say the least. She was an explosive fireball in a very small package. The look on Rio's face alone when he'd been introduced to his potential new team member had been worth the price of admission. Less than an hour later, after she had put not only Rio but Terrence—Rio's right-hand man and a giant of a bear—on their asses, Rio's skepticism had turned to respect in a nanosecond. And after her prowess at the shooting range and a demonstration of her ability to quickly and efficiently defuse explosive devices, everyone in KGI had been convinced that she was a superior recruit and grateful they'd snatched her up before another agency had.

All the elements of an awesome find were there, but there was some question as to whether she would be a match personality wise. Allie was stiff and seemed uncomfortable around the easy camaraderie of the KGI team members, but everyone was willing to give her the benefit of the doubt. It could be that she was simply nervous and ill at ease in her new surroundings.

Sam, his oldest brother and founder of KGI, looked at his watch with clear confusion.

"Anyone hear from Steele? Not like him to be late for a meeting."

The others appeared as surprised as Sam. Members of Steele's team shifted but remained silent, but concern clearly shone in Dolphin's eyes.

"What if something happened to him?" He asked the question most prevalent in all their minds.

In response, Sam picked up his cell and punched a button just as the door to the war room slid open and everyone turned to see Steele standing there, eyes glazed, appearing as though he didn't have one clue where he was or who he was.

"I was about to inform you worrywarts that Steele passed the security gate sixty-two seconds ago," Donovan, the resident tech guru, said dryly.

Joe's eyes narrowed when Steele continued to stand there, eyes fixed, seemingly unaware of anyone else's presence.

"Hey, man, are you okay?" Joe asked.

P.J. Coletrane stepped forward and put her hand on Steele's arm. "Hey, what's up, Steele?"

Cole moved behind his wife, P.J., also holding out a hand

toward Steele as if afraid his team leader was going to face-plant right then and there.

"Maren's pregnant again," he said in a dazed tone.

The room erupted into hoots and congratulations, and a round of back slapping knocked Steele back and forth between the many members of KGI as he drunkenly attempted to maintain his balance.

"Holy fuck," Steele breathed when the hoopla died down. "She's pregnant. *Again*."

Everyone laughed, but Steele's expression was one of complete seriousness and . . . fear. He rubbed his hand over his face as the others exchanged amused glances. Before Maren, Steele's nickname had been the Ice Man. Unemotional. Antisocial. Living only for his job and his team. Terse and not overly communicative in the least. He was more of an "actions speak louder than words" guy. Not an unappreciated quality in their organization.

"Hey, she's tough," Garrett, Joe's second-oldest brother, said in an effort to console the befuddled team leader. "After all she's survived, kicking ass while doing so, giving birth again will be a walk in the park."

"I don't think *I'll* survive another pregnancy," Steele burst out, the crazed look in his eyes intensifying.

Another round of laughter sounded but he was given looks of sympathy and understanding from the fathers in the room. And Jesus, but it had become a regular baby factory in the ranks of KGI. Joe sent his twin, Nathan, a nervous look, and Nathan, who would normally give him shit about being the last remaining bachelor and their mother setting her sights on him, shot him back an equally queasy look.

"Trust me, it doesn't get better after you're married," Nathan muttered. "I thought that would get Ma off my back and permanently onto yours until you succumbed and found 'the one,' but now she's dropping hints about when Shea and I will provide her with a grandchild. Geez. She already has nine by blood or adoptive family bond. I thought she'd lay off by the fifth at least!"

Joe gave his brother a disgruntled look. "Great. So you're telling me that in addition to Ma hounding me day and night about finding some nice young woman to marry, that once that happens, and I'm not saying it's going to occur anytime soon, she'll just move on to filling a fucking nursery?"

Some of his horror must have been reflected on his face because his twin laughed until he started wheezing. "Yeah, that's about the way it goes."

"And obviously it doesn't end after one either," Joe pointed out. "She was on Sam and Sophie to have another. She's already hinting about Sarah having another baby, and Kelsey is barely over a year old! Poor Sam and Sophie are probably hearing about baby number three now that Grant is fourteen months old."

"Oh, I don't feel sorry for Sam," Nathan said wryly. "Sophie gets my sympathy because there's nothing Sam would love more than for her to spend the next several years popping out babies. He and Ma probably coordinate their offensive and tag-team the poor woman."

"Maybe the news of Maren's pregnancy will appease Ma and distract her for a few months at least," he replied sarcastically.

Nathan scoffed. "As if!"

They tuned back in to the goings-on in the room just in time to see Steele slump into a chair that another team member, Renshaw, had hastily pulled forward and positioned near his team leader.

"She went through so fucking much during her first pregnancy," Steele said raggedly. "Kidnapped, intimidated, manipulated, controlled, living in fear for our child's life every single day of her captivity. She constantly feared the son of a bitch would rape her. She didn't eat or drink properly because she feared he would harm our baby. Then she damn near falls to her death from a helicopter and miraculously survives the ensuing helicopter crash. Then there's the fact she had me hovering over her twenty-four-seven after all of that because I was scared *shitless* if she was out of my sight for even a minute I'd lose her all over again. And the delivery. Jesus, the delivery took *forever*! She was in so much pain, and now she's going to go through it all over *again*? What if something happens to her or our child? I wouldn't survive it. She's my *life*."

The entire room was rendered incapable of speech and all stood staring agape at the team leader who'd often been deemed more robot than man. He'd said more in the last few minutes than he'd spoken in nearly the entirety of his leadership of one of the KGI teams.

"And you wonder why I avoid the fine institution of marriage," Joe drawled in a low voice. "Look at him. He's a fucking basket case and that man *never* loses his shit. Ever. Except when it has anything to do with Maren or Olivia. Who the hell would willingly sign up for a lifetime of constant worry, stress and anxiety?"

Nathan gave his brother a look that immediately made him feel inadequate, ignorant and, if he were completely honest, envious as hell.

"Because I can't imagine my life any other way," his brother replied simply. "The knowledge that Shea is mine, that she loves me and that I love her more than life? Well, it makes every worry, every fear, every paralyzing moment of terror worth it. If I had to do it all over again, I wouldn't change a single thing. I'd go back to hell and be tortured by those sadistic sons of bitches, because if not for that, I wouldn't have Shea now."

Joe went silent at his brother's quiet, impassioned vow. He had seen Nathan at his very lowest point and at his very highest. Shea had brought him back. Had given Joe back something priceless. His twin, that bond stronger than ever now, especially since the very special telepathic bond Nathan and his wife shared extended to Joe. It had startled the hell out of both Joe and Shea, but now he wouldn't have it any other way. It made him feel all the more close to his brother when otherwise he would have felt left behind, excluded from something so very precious and life changing. It comforted him to know that Shea could reach out to him if she or his brother were ever in danger or needed help.

"Maren's going to be fine," Ethan spoke up. "That woman is a fighter. All our women are fighters. You said it yourself. She's already survived the worst. Enjoy it, man. It only gets sweeter and sweeter from here on out. You can't dwell on the past or it'll eat you alive. Take it from someone who knows."

Steele looked up at Joe's brother, Ethan, understanding instantly flashing, his expression sobering at the remembrance of what he and his wife, particularly Rachel, had endured and where they were now. Stronger than ever. Rachel was a survivor. A fucking fierce survivor who'd refused to quit. Joe had never admired anyone in his life as much as he did his two sisters-in-law, Rachel and Shea. Both had endured the unimaginable for his brothers.

Steele's expression was pained when he glanced back up at Ethan. Another uncharacteristic display of his usually locked-down emotions. "God, I sound like such an asshole."

Ethan smiled. "No. We all need to be reminded how blessed we are and not to drive ourselves crazy with worrying about what might happen, or with mistakes or things we have no control over."

Sam cleared his throat. "If the morning meltdown is over, perhaps we can get to business?"

Steele shot him a glower but seemed relieved to have the attention diverted from him.

"Do carry on, oh lord and master," Donovan drawled irreverently. "I have a date with my wife and kids that I'd like to embark on before, say, next week."

Yep, business as usual once more. A sigh of relief seemed to settle over the room. Blowing shit up, bringing down the bad guys, being shot at, none of that was as uncomfortable as witnessing emotional meltdowns from men and women who made their living being ultimate badasses.

"As most of you know, or at least those who've bothered to pay attention," Sam said, making another amused dig at certain members of his teams, "we've hired two new recruits. Everyone's met Ryker Sinclair, Eden's brother, and Hancock's, as well."

A collective good-natured groan sounded at the name of their once archnemesis, who like Steele had done an abrupt about-face and gone from a cold, emotionless machine whose sole objective was to accomplish the mission however it had to be done to a man who lost his damn mind if his new wife so much as stubbed her toe.

And this is what Joe's mother and sisters-in-law wanted for him? On that, he'd take a rain check. A very extended rain check that he was in no hurry to cash in. He liked his sane life just as it was. *Sane.* Thank you very much.

"He'll be joining Skylar, Edge, Swanny, the team headed by Nathan and Joe."

Ryker cracked a grin. "Swanny, you should know that my sister has threatened to kick my ass unless I watch over her beloved husband and make sure he doesn't ever come home with any missing body parts."

Swanny rolled his eyes. "Yeah, well you got off light. She's told me in exacting detail what happens to *me* if her precious brother so much as gets a scratch. Pussy boy."

Allie scowled, scrunching her features into a ferocious expression of disapproval.

"Are any of you ever serious or did I sign on with a circus act? I thought this job was about being a well-oiled machine, training at the highest level and taking on missions that changed the lives of others for good."

More than one look of surprise was cast her way, but Rio just smirked, as did the rest of his team.

"Told you she'd fit right into you bunch of antisocial grouches," Sam said with no heat.

At that Allie's expression became even more outraged. Given the fact she'd already taken down half their asses in hand-to-hand, those closest to her warily backed off and eyed her cautiously.

"They're just shitting you, Allie," Skylar soothed, though Joe could tell Allie's remarks had annoyed her. "We can't be serious all the time or this job would eat us alive. I think you'll find that our sense of humor, or the lack thereof in a few select cases, in no way affects our ability to kick some serious ass when it's called for."

"Hooyah!" Ethan and Cole crowed simultaneously.

"I'm sorry if you took offense at our blowing off some steam," Donovan said seriously. "But what Sky said is true. When we face death on every mission we take, we learn to live for the moment and not dwell on the what-ifs. We know that every time we leave our wives, husbands or loved ones, it might be the last time we ever see them. Everyone deals with the pressure in their own way and we try not to judge unless it's completely out of line. Most of us have been to-gether for a long time and we've seen one another through shit that would destroy others or make them hang it up and simply walk away. We chose you because you're the best new recruit we've ever hired, with skills we not only need but that will make us even better as a team. Nothing in this organiza-tion is about one person. To borrow a phrase you'll hear often around here, we live and die by the team. And that means that not one of us is out for him or herself. So I hope we haven't given you the wrong impression. We certainly meant you no disrespect, and I do hope you'll choose to re-main on our side."

"Yeah, please do," Garrett grumbled. "You'd kick our asses if you were pitted against us."

For a brief second, Allie actually smiled. Wow, and her face didn't even crack. Damn, but when she wasn't so fuck-ing serious and wearing that pinched-ass expression, she was one beautiful woman. Straight midnight black hair, creamy skin and beautiful eyes, part of her Asian heritage. When she smiled, it was as though her entire face trans-formed, and Joe wasn't the only one affected. Others were similarly stunned as they stared back at their newest female warrior. Maybe there was hope for her yet. She was going to have to loosen up quick, or this job would eat her alive and spit her back out.

"Sorry," she said sincerely. "Let's just say my last team-mates weren't exactly an ideal set of people to work with. They talked too fucking much about shit they had no busi-ness talking about. If they'd talked less and actually did their fucking jobs, I wouldn't have gone down on my last job with them and then been forced to take an extended leave of absence that resulted in me never returning."

"That's just fucked-up," Terrence growled.

P.J. stepped forward and put her hand on Allie's arm, a surprising gesture since P.J. wasn't exactly known for being the warm and fuzzy type.

"Trust me, Allie. There are no better people to have at your six. I should know. They'll talk shit, yeah, but they will *always* have your back, and that you can trust if you trust nothing else."

Allie blinked at her ferocity but then studied the set of her jaw and gave a clipped nod that told Joe she was reserving judgment.

"I'll keep this short and sweet since we're long past short and sweet," Sam muttered. "Steele, I'd like you and your team to hang around base for a couple of weeks to assist with training the new recruits. Both Rio's team and Nathan and Joe's team will be conducting all training exercises here, and we can split off by specialty and get in one-on-one time in addition to team drills."

"We don't often get this much time off between assignments," Garrett said, picking up where Sam left off. "And I plan to keep enjoying my time with my wife and daughter as long as the calm lasts. To that end, we'll be reporting for training four hours in the mornings Monday through Friday, or at least until things go to shit and we get called out."

"Anyone ever tell you what an optimist you are?" Nathan grumbled.

"And," Sam said, a smirk forming on his lips, "I have a special treat for all of you. Allie will be heading up a training course on explosives: dismantling and disabling, how to tell when you're fucked and when you're not. Baker, you of all people should appreciate that."

"Oh, fuck you all," Baker growled. "For fuck's sake. It was one time and it was forever ago! Let it go already."

Allie's eyebrows lifted in question.

"I'll tell you all about it later," P.J. promised with an evil grin in Baker's direction.

"Hey, it wasn't all bad," Renshaw defended. "It did finally get boss man and Maren together."

"Why do I get the feeling this is going to be one long-ass story?" Allie asked in resignation. "Are you guys ever serious about anything?"

The room filled with laughter.

"They're all long stories," Skylar said, her eyes twinkling with merriment. "And I haven't even been here as long as most."

"We're serious," Joe said in an even voice directed at Allie. "We're serious about not fucking up and dying. That should be all the serious you need."

Her eyebrow went up and he could swear she sniffed at him in disdain. Skylar noticed the interaction and her expression darkened. P.J. caught Skylar's eye and the two women stood in silent communication for a long moment, their displeasure evident. Shit. If Joe was Allie, he'd be pissing himself right about now. Having one of the two women on his ass would be intimidating enough. But both Skylar and P.J.? If a grown man wasn't shaking in his boots over that double threat then he was a fucking fool. He hoped for Allie's sake that she lost the chip—or rather boulder—on her shoulder pretty damn fast or things were going to get ugly.

"Rio, you bringing Grace and Elizabeth for a visit?" Donovan asked with a grin.

Rio gave him a look that suggested he was an idiot. But then he didn't even dignify it with an answer. He motioned for his team to fall in and they simply walked out of the war room.

Joe chuckled. "You can't ever accuse Rio of not being consistent."

"She's good," Garrett mused, his gaze still on the closed door where Rio and his team, with their newest recruit, had exited just seconds before. "Damn good. She'll be a perfect fit for Rio's team. If the chemistry is right. When we hire a new recruit, it's a crapshoot as far as how well they mesh with their team. Their skills aren't in question—otherwise they wouldn't be hired. It isn't all about skills. A recruit has to fit seamlessly into their team or shit's going to go south damn fast. But I swear it's like fate or some hokey shit I don't understand because we couldn't have found a better fit for Rio and his team than Allie even if we'd created an entire checklist, personality profile, whatever. It's like a fucking gift got dropped right into our laps, and as freaky as it is, I'm not going to waste time pondering the statistical improbability of ever finding a recruit that would fit into a team that has no fucks to give and does it their way or no way but gets the job done every damn time regardless and just savor that we scored in a huge way. Like hitting the badass, take-no-prisoners lottery or something."

A series of chuckles rose and Joe rolled his eyes. "Um, dude? You just *did* waste a fuck ton of time pondering the statistical improbability of finding Allie."

Garrett scowled. "Fuck you. Are we done yet? I'd like to spend what's left of the day with my wife and daughter. She's already walking. Can you believe that shit? She's a genius. Clearly takes after her mother. Not a smarter baby in the world."

Groans replaced the earlier chuckles and several gazes rolled upward as if pleading for mercy. Joe was also ready to roll out, but not for the reasons everyone else was eager to race home. There was only so much home, hearth and domesticity laced with a fuck ton of mushy, embarrassing rhetoric a single man could take in a day. And yet the prospect of going back to the house he now was the sole occupant of held no real appeal. Maybe he'd go grab a beer, but then again, he'd be flying solo because all his brothers, not to mention the majority of the other members of KGI, were quite happily off the market and preferred ridiculous baby talk and boasting about their progeny being the most brilliant babies ever born to going out with the guys and having a drink. Or three.

Maybe Skylar and Edge would be down for a break from the display of grown-ass men losing their fucking minds during a meeting. And if not Skylar and Edge, Dolphin was always up for a good time. Like Joe, Dolphin was single and showed no signs of settling down . . . ever. Joe wasn't much of a party animal, preferring to spend his time with his family, even if they drove him crazy about his single status, but Dolphin's exploits were legendary and he kept his team, as well as the rest of KGI, regularly amused by his nights out.

He didn't even realize he was shaking his head until he caught Nathan staring inquisitively at him before asking, "Everything okay with you, bro? Why are you shaking your head looking like you want to go fuck up an entire terrorist organization?"

Right now taking down a terrorist group held more appeal than being subjected to the epic display of emotional meltdowns he'd just witnessed. Never before had he felt like an outsider in the organization founded and run by his three oldest brothers. He'd always known that after his final tour in the army was up he would join his brothers and had looked forward to it. He'd loved his time in the army. It had prepared him well to be on the level of the other members of KGI, but he'd been ready to move on to the next part of his life.

Now? He felt distinctly uncomfortable, and once again, a nagging sensation that felt strangely like envy tugged relentlessly at him. He wasn't jealous of his brothers. He was happy as hell for them. He didn't even *want* to settle down anytime soon. He had time. When he was ready, he was ready. All his brothers had known when they'd found "the one." Before that, they, like him, were perfectly content to be single and focused exclusively on making a difference and bringing justice to assholes who'd long escaped it. But the moment their wives had entered their lives, everything had changed.

Joe hadn't met "the one." Sure, he dated. His sex life didn't make him a man whore, but neither was he lacking for companionship when the mood struck. But none of the women he'd dated had stirred the fierce response he'd witnessed time and time again when his brothers had found their soul mates.

Sweet baby Jesus. Forget the beer. He needed something a hell of a lot harder. And he needed to get the hell out of here fast because he was actually standing around contemplating shit like soul mates and the fact that he hadn't found his. That wasn't even what he wanted right now. Was it?

CHAPTER 4

"ARE you sure this is a good idea?" Zoe asked Rusty in panic as she peeked from the upstairs window to see the dozens of people gathered below in the backyard.

When Rusty had told her that the entire Kelly family, even those considered family outside the bonds of blood, would be attending a barbecue at Frank and Marlene's home today, Zoe had been riddled with anxiety and . . . fear. She'd come here to hide, to be as unnoticed as possible. To be in a place where she wouldn't have to worry over discovery until she and Rusty came up with a plan for her next move.

Now she faced what looked to be at least thirty people, if not more, standing around smiling, laughing, having a good time. Children playing. Just what a real family looked like, or at least what Zoe imagined a real family to be. But what did she know? She'd had none of this growing up. Rusty was the first real friend she'd made, the first person who'd seemed to genuinely care about her, and Rusty had certainly gone to great extremes, with a great possibility of endangering her own life.

Not only did she feel terror over being exposed to so many people, she was also instilled with a fierce envy, something she hadn't thought she could even feel after long ago accepting her circumstances. What would her life have been like if she'd had . . . this. A loving, devoted family. Happy. Loving. Smiles and laughter. A far cry from the sterile environment she was accustomed to.

Rusty slid her hand over Zoe's shoulder and then turned her, pulling her into a hard hug.

"Stop stressing, Zoe. You know I'd never do anything that would put you at risk. This is my family. They're loyal to their bones. They aren't gossipers, nor do they pry into other people's business. You'll be welcomed as a guest, as a part of the family. No one will interrogate you, nor will anyone talk to outsiders about you or anything that happens within our family. We've well learned the necessity of discretion and keeping family business just that. Family business. By now everyone knows I've brought a friend home and it will be far more suspicious for you to spend the entire afternoon holed up in our room than if you come down and join in and, God forbid, actually relax and have fun for once. You need this, Zoe. You need to see that the way you were raised isn't normal—it isn't how families work. I can't think of a better way for you to see that than to spend the afternoon with my family, who will do nothing more than welcome you with open arms."

Zoe sighed. "I know you're right. It's just that I'm not sure I can pull this off without having a complete meltdown or looking so scared that everyone will immediately be suspicious of this 'friend' you brought home with you."

Rusty laughed. "Everyone is well acquainted with my . . .

well, let's just say I had a rebellious streak a mile wide in the early years, and I've always gone my own way. The difference is I always had a safety net to fall back on. And that's what I want you to have," she added in a more serious tone. "There isn't a person down there who wouldn't protect you with their life."

Zoe gave her a skeptical look. "I'm a stranger, Rusty. Not family, though you keep insisting otherwise. Why on earth would they risk anything for someone they don't even know?"

Rusty's somber expression disappeared as laughter escaped, her eyes twinkling in merriment. "Girlfriend, that's what they do. They risk their lives for people they've never even met before. I went over this with you already. The organization they formed is all about rescuing and protecting, exacting vengeance. They're the real deal, honey. But you won't know that unless you come out of hiding and join the festivities. And, well, I hate to pull out the big guns, but if you don't come down with me, then Marlene is just going to come up and drag you out, and trust me, no one tells Marlene no. She won't be mean—God, that woman is a saint—but suddenly you'll find yourself doing exactly what it is she wants and afterward you'll be puzzled because you won't even remember how she accomplished it, but you'll find yourself falling into line, just as the rest of the family does, and doing exactly as she determines."

Zoe's eyes closed a brief moment and then she squared her shoulders. "You're right. I'm being stupid, scared and unreasonable. I'm tired of being a timid little mouse. God, I hate the person I've become."

"It's never too late to change, honey," Rusty said, her expression softening with love and understanding. "I know that better than anyone. You can become whoever you want. You just have to take that first step in taking your life back.

Make yourself into whoever you want to be. It's never too late to achieve your dreams and to live the life you've always wanted. You just have to let go of the past and stop letting it control the present. *And* your future. You're smart, funny and beautiful. You're compassionate, kind and selfless. You can't tell me that your father or that asshole who fucked you over are responsible for those traits. *You* made that choice, despite being shown no other way. You're your own person and nothing they've done will *ever* change that. Unless you *let* them."

"I think you can mark 'intelligent' off your list of my virtues," Zoe said with a grimace. "I'm an idiot. A complete idiot. And you're right. I just wish I had you as a friend growing up. Or maybe not, since that would have meant you were exposed to the life I had. But I'm glad we're friends now. I don't know why you haven't washed your hands of my whiny ass and walked away. You've taken so many risks to help me and I'm acting like an ungrateful child."

Rusty's eyes narrowed and Zoe could feel her about to launch into a stern lecture about being so hard on herself. So she just held up her hand to stop the inevitable tirade and then raised the other in surrender.

"I'm coming, I'm coming. Give me a minute to at least make myself presentable?"

Rusty eyed her doubtfully. "Okay, but you get five minutes. If you aren't down by that time, then I'm sending Marlene up after you, and God help you then. She won't care if you're in your underwear. She'll drag you down the stairs kicking and screaming and then proudly introduce you to every single member of her extended family and decree that *you're* family now."

Zoe's face must have reflected her horror because Rusty laughed. "I'm only slightly exaggerating," Rusty said between

giggles. "She would at least give you time to get dressed.
Everything else? Not so much, and she would drag you down
in the sweetest way possible, but you would be incapable of
resisting, so I suggest you get to it. Besides, with the new you,
all you have to do is pull on a pair of jeans, a cute top and
brush your hair. See how much easier I've made your life?
No more hourlong makeup marathons, perfectly arranged
hair and looking like a Wall Street broker's wife. You should
be done in three minutes, tops!"

"Get out of here before I strangle you," Zoe muttered. "I
said I'll be down." Then anxiety tightened her chest and she
bit into her bottom lip. "You'll wait for me, right? There's
no way I want to just walk into that crowd on my own acting
as if I belong. I'd have a heart attack."

Rusty's eyes shone with understanding and compassion.
"I'll wait for you at the bottom of the stairs, but if one of us
doesn't present ourselves stat, Marlene *is* going to come up
here to see why the heck we're up here when everyone else
is down there."

"Okay, get down there, pacify her. I swear I'll be down
in the three minutes you say it will take me to make myself
presentable. I refuse, however, to look in a mirror, because
if that happens, I'll go into meltdown mode when I don't
recognize the person staring back at me."

"The person staring back at you is beautiful, Zoe," Rusty
said softly. "You have a natural beauty that just shines and
stands out in a crowded room. The person you were before
was fake. A role you were playing, never allowing the real
you to be seen. I've seen that person and she's gorgeous.
Besides, no one here has ever seen you in full-on designer-
chic mode. Trust me. I wouldn't let you make a fool of yourself in front of my family. I wouldn't let you appear in a way
that embarrassed you or made you feel ashamed. Will you

please just trust me on this? You're not the emotionless, perfectly made-up doll your father insisted you be molded into."

Zoe gave Rusty one last hug, holding on to her tightly, tears burning the edges of her eyelids. "You're the best friend I've ever had," she whispered.

"Same goes," Rusty said, pulling back, her eyes suspiciously bright, though she quickly averted her gaze as if embarrassed for Zoe to see her emotion.

But then Zoe knew enough of Rusty's own past to know that Rusty had endured a much harsher life growing up, and it made Zoe ashamed that she was putting up such a fuss and acting as if she'd been sorely abused. It was rare that Rusty's true emotions were ever evident in her eyes or expression, but Zoe knew just how deeply her friend felt, how big her heart was and how loving and compassionate she was.

"Shoo," Zoe scolded, suddenly reversing roles and ushering Rusty out so she could finish dressing. "We don't want Marlene dragging us both down the stairs by our ears."

Rusty laughed but she didn't dispute that Marlene would do just that.

"I'll be waiting downstairs and I won't leave your side when we go face the firing squad, er, I mean family," Rusty hastily amended with a grin on her face.

Seconds later, Zoe was alone and she picked frantically through the clothes Rusty had bought for her. Then she thought back to what Rusty herself was wearing. They were roughly the same age, Zoe being two years older but close enough that she would be expected to wear what every young twentysomething would wear. Or at least she hoped.

It was sad that she had no real idea what to wear when so much of her wardrobe and appearance had been dictated for so long. She finally settled on a pair of jeans decorated with embellishments and embroidered designs and a modest top that was a step above grunge wear, as Zoe called it, meaning a T-shirt worn around the house when one wasn't expecting company. Then she slid her feet into a sparkly pair of flip-flops that she had to admit she liked.

Her toes were freshly painted, thanks to a late-night girl talk and nail-painting session between her and Rusty, and they gleamed a hot pink color that made her feel a little . . . daring.

She brushed out her much longer hair now, opting to leave it flowing down her back since she didn't have time to do one of those cute messy buns Rusty had taught her to fashion, and she chose a simple pair of cheap hoop earrings, laughing silently at the thought of the outrageously expensive jewelry collection she'd pawned to pad her stash of money, since leaving a paper trail, in Rusty's words, was just stupid.

When Zoe would have simply taken the items to a local pawn shop, Rusty had given a long-suffering sigh and then explained to her how easily her location could be found out and how identifiable the jewelry was since it had all been given to her by her father. Instead they'd made the long drive to Atlanta where they'd pawned the jewelry, and in an effort to further confuse anyone tracking Zoe, they'd bought her a bus ticket to New York, the opposite side of the country from the destination where they'd purchased the plane ticket in her name to. Rusty had explained that it would be a piece of cake to determine that Zoe had never been on that flight but it would delay her pursuers a little. However, her presence on a bus, especially given the fact Rusty had made her present her ticket and board the bus, only to slip off before it departed, would be a lot harder to determine, hopefully leading anyone looking for her to New York.

Zoe had to admit, Rusty had her shit together. She'd long

thought the other woman to be a freaking genius, but this cemented it. Rusty wasn't just street-smart or even academically smart, both of which she'd certainly proven to be. The woman had a computerlike brain, calculating every possibility and preparing for as many as possible.

Zoe considered herself an intelligent woman, even if current evidence proved that she was the dumbest woman to ever live, but she couldn't hold a candle to Rusty's sharp mind and impressive tech skills. Maybe she could learn by osmosis, absorbing as much of Rusty's knowledge as possible before it was time to move on.

The thought filled her with instant sadness. She hadn't even met Rusty's massive family, but already the thought of leaving her best friend and Marlene and Frank, who'd been so very kind and generous to her, made her feel alone and afraid.

Knowing that if she didn't get her ass down the stairs right now Rusty and Marlene would likely burst into her room to drag her down, she hurriedly gave herself one last glance in the mirror, despite her vow not to, and was stunned by the result. No, she didn't look like herself—her old self. She looked almost . . . pretty.

Wiping the shocked look of realization off her face and then planting a serene smile that gave nothing of her inner turmoil away, she hurried down the stairs, where she found Rusty impatiently tapping her foot.

"Thank God," Rusty muttered. "I'm only able to put Marlene off for so long, you know. Thankfully, another of her grandchildren just arrived, so that gave us a few moments' reprieve before she rounded up the last of the holdouts."

Rusty gave her an assessing look. "You ready?"

Zoe took a deep breath, positive that someone could see her heart beating rapidly against her chest, and nodded.

Rusty took her hand and squeezed. "You look gorgeous, Zoe. You look like . . . you."

"Well thank goodness," Zoe teased. "I'd hate to look like anyone else."

Rusty grinned and then tucked her arm underneath Zoe's and steered her toward the French doors leading onto the back deck.

"Remember everything we rehearsed. Keep it simple and light. Don't deviate from the script," Rusty murmured. "While you have nothing to fear from anyone here, they *will* pick up on any discrepancies in your story. That's what they're trained to do. They have an eye for detail and nothing gets by them."

Rusty had grilled her endlessly on the details of her new identity and made-up past. So much so that Zoe could recite them in her sleep. But now her confidence faltered as she listened to Rusty talk about how her brothers were trained to spot discrepancies, slipups, inconsistencies.

"Oh God, I can't do this," she said, pulling Rusty up short.

Her heart was racing, about to pound out of her chest. She could feel her airway constricting and knew if she tried to speak, all that would come out would be an inaudible wheeze.

"What if I screw up?" she asked in a garbled, panicked whisper, her gaze darting left and right to ensure they weren't overheard.

"Relax," Rusty said soothingly. "Keep it simple, remember? The more complicated you make it, the more likely you are to contradict yourself. Focus on generalities and no specifics. They value their own privacy too much to ever pry into anyone else's. Now come on. People are already starting to stare. I need to introduce you around."

Her pulse still fluttering wildly, she allowed herself to

fall into step next to Rusty, pasting the serene smile on her face she'd practiced countless times in the mirror until she knew exactly how it felt and could do it without seeing the results to know if it was convincing.

Marlene hurried over, beaming as she enfolded first Rusty and then Zoe into a huge hug. Zoe closed her eyes, savoring Marlene's hold and, for just a moment, fantasizing that this was her life. *Her* family. *Her* mother.

One would think Marlene hadn't seen them in weeks, much less an hour prior, but then she seemed to treat all her family the same and, well, with the stories Rusty had told her of all their family had been through over the last several years, Zoe couldn't blame Marlene for making each moment count. Who knew when it would be the last time Marlene hugged one of her sons, daughters-in-law, grandchildren or adopted "strays," as they'd been labeled, though Marlene vehemently disapproved of any of her "chicks" being called strays.

The Kellys obviously cherished every single minute of their lives and celebrated their happiness. Before her entire world had crumbled around her—her entire fake world—she'd taken getting up the next day for granted. But then she hadn't had much *to* take for granted. Not like this family did. She couldn't imagine the devastation they would feel if even one didn't make it back from a mission, much less several, and given the structure of their organization as explained to her by Rusty, it was certainly not in the realm of impossibility that an entire team could be killed. All it would take was one misstep, one wrong decision. An ambush or someone from their past with a grudge to bear.

She gave an involuntary shudder even as Marlene gently disentangled herself from her arms. Zoe blushed and looked away, embarrassed that while Marlene had instigated the hug, she had taken it over and had clung far too long to the older woman.

But there was only gentle understanding and a soft smile as Marlene took one of her hands and squeezed as if to tell her it was all right before turning her attention to Rusty.

"I trust you'll take care of introducing Zoe to everyone? I need to start bringing out the sides to put out on the table because Frank says the meat is just about ready to take off the grill."

"Oh, I'll help you, Mrs. Kelly," Zoe said eagerly before she realized that once again she was trying to avoid the sea of people all standing around in the backyard.

"Thank you, dear, and please do call me Marlene or Ma. Anything but Mrs. Kelly, as I've already told you on a dozen occasions."

She softened the rebuke with laughter, her eyes twinkling.

"But there's no need. That's what my boys are for. We've declared this women's relaxation day and so all the wives are taking a well-earned rest while the menfolk watch the children and tend to the task of food preparation."

Zoe frowned. "Then why aren't you taking a break as well? You've been working all morning preparing food and getting ready. If anyone deserves a break, it's you."

"She makes a very valid point," Rusty said smugly. "I know it slays the control freak in you, but you're violating your own rule. Therefore, I'm going to point you to the nearest chair where I'm sure your grandchildren will be thrilled to provide you with all the entertainment you could possibly want. I'll make sure the guys take care of the rest."

Marlene looked startled and then opened her mouth to argue. "But—"

"No buts," Rusty broke in, already herding her adopted mother in the direction of the nearest lawn chair.

The look on Marlene's face was priceless and applause broke out over the gathering. Zoe flinched, not realizing that everyone had obviously been privy to the entire exchange. Not only that, but they'd all gathered closer to Zoe, Rusty and Marlene and now stood only a few feet away.

"Wow, Rusty," a large, muscled man who had to be one of Rusty's brothers said. "It's always been Ma who instills fear in all our hearts, but now I'm beginning to think the real tyrant is you and that we should all be shaking in our boots."

Rusty rolled her eyes. "Oh please."

Then Zoe suddenly found herself thrust forward so that she was facing the impossibly tall, very muscled man.

"Garrett, this is Zoe, a friend of mine from college. Zoe, this is Garrett, the second-oldest brother in the cult."

He laughed and then extended his hand to her. Trying to control the betraying tremors that seemed to pervade every muscle in her body, she tentatively slid her hand into his grasp. To her surprise, his grip was extremely gentle and his smile was genuine.

"Glad to meet you, Zoe. And welcome to the family. I've no doubt that Ma has already indoctrinated you into the cult, as Rusty so irreverently deemed us."

"Glad to meet you too," Zoe murmured. "Rusty has told me so much about you all that I feel as if I already know you."

She instantly gave an inward groan. *Way to go, idiot. Do exactly what Rusty said not to do. Open yourself up for more than you bargained for.* But to her relief, Garrett's teeth gleamed all the more and he cocked an eyebrow in his sister's direction.

"I hope it was all good things. Like how I'm the best-looking and smartest brother."

There were muffled and some not-so-muffled choking sounds made in the group now surrounding Zoe and Rusty.

"I believe she mentioned that Donovan was the brains of the operation," Zoe said, unable to help herself, relaxing and returning his tease.

"That I am," another man said as he stepped forward.

To her surprise, he didn't shake her hand, but instead enfolded her in a gentle hug and then turned and introduced her to his wife and then to their two children, though Rusty had explained they were actually Eve's half siblings, Travis and Cammie.

Soon it became a muddled confusion as Zoe attempted to commit each name and face to memory. She had the names already, but now she needed to make sure she remembered which face went with each family member. Even before the introductions were complete, she was all but wilting. Never had she been made to feel so welcome or at home by complete strangers. Well, by anyone, anywhere, for that matter. It only brought home the fact that she was utterly ignorant of something as simple as family dynamics, and it brought an unassuageable ache to her heart.

But then she noticed another man standing just off to the side, one she hadn't been introduced to yet. She searched her overwhelmed brain for who this might be, but all the family names—and God, there were a ton—blended together and she could barely recall the last few people she'd been introduced to, much less the ones who had come first.

On cue, the man stepped forward, his expression more intent than those of the others had been. Almost as if he'd been studying her and had found a discrepancy. His welcome didn't seem to be as automatic as all the others', and she immediately tensed in an effort not to give in to the over-whelming jitters that threatened to make her muscles quake.

"And this is the last of my brothers," Rusty said cheer-fully, oblivious to the turmoil unleashed inside Zoe. "Joe is Nathan's twin, the older of the two by a few minutes or so."

His hand slid over her outstretched palm that she hadn't remembered extending. She was besieged with sudden aware-ness, an odd sensation snaking through every single muscle in her body. Though his expression was indecipherable, his touch was exceedingly gentle, almost as if he could sense her terror. And when he spoke, it was all she could do to suppress a full-body shiver.

"Welcome to our home, Zoe," he murmured.

CHAPTER 5

"WHAT exactly does anyone know about Rusty's friend?" Joe asked with a frown as he and Donovan stood to one side, watching Rusty and Zoe.

The two women were conversing quietly away from the others, but Zoe frequently allowed her gaze to travel over the rest of the assembled people, and it was what Joe could see in her eyes that bothered him. What he *couldn't* see reflected in her gaze bugged him even more.

Something seemed off, but he couldn't put his finger on what. It was obvious she was checking Rusty's entire family out, but instead of idle curiosity or even genuine interest being the most probable reasons for her scrutiny, he could swear he saw worry and fear. It was almost as if she were literally looking over her shoulder expecting some sort of surprise attack, which would be absurd given that Rusty would most assuredly have given her friend at least basic background information on her brothers. Then again, he might be seeing what he'd expected to see. What apparently, he, and only he, was projecting onto Zoe's skittish behavior judging by the fact that none of his brothers or the hodge-podge smattering of team members present from both his and Nathan's team as well as Steele's seemed to share the nagging in his gut, which was becoming more aggressive by the second. And if any one of his brothers or his teammates thought for a minute that there was a danger to the family, their wives, children and friends, they wouldn't stand idly by or wait for the appropriate time. Which meant that Joe was on his own with his scrutiny and suspicion of Rusty's friend.

Donovan chuckled and elbowed his brother. "Worried this is another one of Ma's plots against you?"

Joe made a sound of exasperation. That hadn't even crossed his mind, though now that Donovan had mentioned it, could that be all it was? Was this a setup? He nearly shook his head in denial. No, that wasn't what was going on here. That wasn't at all the vibe he was getting from Zoe.

"Can you be serious for once? From all accounts, no one has ever heard Rusty even mention this friend, and then sud-denly she calls Ma and says she's bringing her to visit for an indeterminate amount of time. I don't know, man. Some-thing's not right. She's skittish and seems extremely nervous. She barely managed to make eye contact during introduc-tions, and if she's supposed to be my downfall, she didn't seem in the least interested. In fact, she couldn't back away fast enough once she got through all the names and faces."

Donovan snorted. "Hell, can you blame her? Our family intimidates the hell out of me on a good day. Have you con-sidered she's shy and overwhelmed by being besieged by the entire Kelly clan all at once? It wasn't as if she was eased into this. I feel sorry for the poor woman. She was all but thrown to the sharks just a couple of days after she arrived."

Joe grunted. "I can't put my finger on it, but something isn't sitting with me very well."

"That wouldn't have anything to do with the fact that she's a beautiful woman, with a stunning smile, the few times she's let go of her terror at being surrounded by a horde of really big men, not to mention seeming to be utterly bewildered by all the children clamoring for her attention. To me, she just looks like a fish out of water. She's probably scared shitless, bro. Cut her some slack."

At his brother's soft reprimand, Joe felt like a first-class asshole. Van was probably right. She'd literally been thrown to the wolves with no advance warning. And Van was correct about another thing too. His family *was* intimidating. Loud, boisterous. Irreverent, and at times, downright obnoxious. But he wouldn't have them any other way. A stranger wouldn't likely feel as the rest of the family did and likely wouldn't deem this the average, normal family.

His thoughts turned to the observations he'd made—was still making—about her, even as his gaze found her once more in the crowd. She drew him like a magnet, and already he had an uncanny way of finding her, of knowing just which direction to look in order to see her again.

She was beautiful in a quiet, understated way. She looked natural, not made-up as someone she wasn't. Even the faint freckles that dusted her flawless skin added to her appeal. She appeared wholesome, innocent even, and as Van had inferred, way over her head. What was Rusty thinking tossing her into the deep end to sink or swim?

For some reason, she intrigued Joe, his curiosity piqued, not that he'd ever admit that to any of his brothers and *especially* not to his mother. They'd be all over him to move in, seal the deal, settle down, get married and start producing yet more grandchildren to add to the already growing numbers.

But it was the sadness in Zoe's eyes when she thought no one was observing her that made his chest tighten. The way she seemed to duck her head and attempt to remove herself from the focus of attention each time it was directed her way. No, this wasn't some scheme hatched by his matchmaking mother, because Zoe hadn't so much as looked in his direction the entire time she'd stood around, her body language broadcasting her discomfort.

It riled his protective instincts, and at that realization, he went rigid.

"Fuck me," he muttered under his breath.

He *was* attracted to her. And not just in a sexual way. His interest was more than simple curiosity. She was a puzzle, and he didn't like mysteries, especially one that existed in the midst of his family. Not to mention, his attraction was pointless since she'd barely spared him a glance and a timid hello when it had been his turn to be introduced.

What was her damage? Her story? She had the look of someone who'd seen the worst humanity had to offer, and God knew he'd seen that look often enough in his years in the army and now with KGI to know what stared him in the face. One thing he'd learned was that it wasn't the women one only had to look at to know they'd been broken who'd endured far worse than others. No, it was those who covered it up that broke his fucking heart. The ones who held themselves together only by sheer will and desperation and the vow to themselves never to give in that kept them from crumbling in front of the world. Women who looked a lot like Zoe, who from the outside one would never guess was anything but a beautiful, intelligent young woman with her

entire life ahead of her. But it was those few glimpses into
her eyes—they'd been a window straight to her soul—that told
him this woman had been to hell at some point in her life.

Denial rose sharply within him. No, he wasn't in the least
interested in her, beyond wanting to make sure she wasn't
a threat to his family. He was simply curious. When the
opportunity presented itself, he'd pull Rusty aside and ask
what Zoe's story was. Then his sudden fixation would be
resolved and he'd go back to exactly the kind of life he'd
outlined just a few days earlier when his twin was giving
him shit about being the next to fall. He barely held back
the snort over the absurdity of the idea that he was in any
way attracted or even emotionally invested in a woman he
knew absolutely nothing about.

So why the hell was he besieged by the urge to pull her
into his arms and offer comfort and reassurance? Let her
know that she was safe here? No one would ever hurt her as
long as she was firmly ensconced in the bosom of his family.

Clearly he'd been subjected to his brothers' nauseating
adoration for their wives and the fact that they were utterly
captive to their every whim and would move heaven and
earth—making complete asses of themselves in the process—
to make the women they loved happy. He wasn't ready to sign
on to that kind of commitment yet. He wasn't ready to give
up his freedom for any woman yet, but then again, no one
said displaying mild interest in a female or even contemplating what it would be like to kiss her was akin to his bachelor
days being over.

Kiss? Jesus. Now he was fantasizing about kissing a
woman he'd met mere minutes ago? He needed to separate
himself from this veritable lovefest going on around him.
That shit might be contagious. Once Ethan had gotten Rachel
back and then Sam had fallen head over ass, it had been a

domino effect with every one of his brothers, not to mention a good many of his teammates, quickly following suit.

He'd just make sure to steer clear of Zoe until her visit was over, and problem solved.

But there was still that nagging sensation that something was off—that things weren't at all as they seemed—and that bugged him. What if they had a threat in their midst? Separating himself and making himself scarce was pretty damn stupid if he so much as suspected anything was up with Rusty's friend.

Maybe he should make it a point to hang around more often. Hell, maybe even ask her out. A date hardly constituted a freaking marriage proposal, and well, in the meantime he could get Van to do a little digging on Zoe Kildare. Just in case any red flags popped up. After all, his first duty was to his family and their protection.

He glanced back in Zoe's direction to see that she was now standing alone, and though it wasn't glaringly obvious, she was agitated, panic flaring in her eyes as she turned her head in all directions as if searching for Rusty. Come to think of it, Rusty hadn't left her side for the entirety of the barbecue. So where the hell was Rusty now, and why had she abandoned her friend, who clearly wasn't at ease with standing alone among strangers?

For that matter, why did he even care? As soon as the thought occurred he was besieged by guilt. If it was one of his sisters-in-law or one of the team members' wives, he wouldn't have thought twice about walking over to ensure she wasn't standing alone. He'd ask her if she was okay or if she needed anything and then he would have busted ass to get her whatever she wanted.

But those women were taken. Off-limits. And he felt genuine love and affection for each and every one of them.

Just as their husbands would, Joe would do anything in the world for any one of the women KGI claimed as their own. Was he such an asshole that he could only bring himself to care about a select group of women and treat all other women with such indifference and disdain?

Before thinking better of it, Joe surged forward, grabbing a cup of lemonade as an excuse to approach her since she was no longer holding a drink in her hand. She didn't even notice his approach because she was so engrossed in studying her surroundings. *Study* was hardly an appropriate descriptor since *studying* implied interest or at least the desire to learn more about the goings-on around her. Zoe was constantly flitting her gaze over the crowd, moving quickly between groups, only to return seconds later, almost as if she feared missing something important.

He wondered if others could see the fear that seemed permanently etched in her brow and reflected in her eyes as easily as he could, or if he was the only one who'd bothered to look beyond the transparent mask she'd donned. Her entire body was a study in unease, and she was tense. Her fingers were curled into tight balls, pressed against her denim-clad thighs, and she appeared as though she were battling her fight-or-flight instinct. His money was on flight. She appeared far too fragile to fight anyone, and judging by the dismay in her eyes when she'd been introduced to all the hulking Kelly brothers, she realized that flight was her only viable means of escape.

Oh yeah. Joe was going to have a serious come-to-Jesus meeting with Rusty, but first he was going to do everything he could to assure Zoe that they—he—wasn't some monster lying in wait to blindside her.

His steps were slow and measured as he drew closer, and yet she still didn't register his presence. He frowned, because for a woman as terrified as she appeared, she was frighteningly unaware of the potential threat to her. She was too worried about the ones far enough away that she could possibly escape and was paying no attention to the fact that Joe now stood a mere foot away from her.

He cleared his throat, not wanting to startle her too badly. He instantly regretted not being more obvious in his approach. For not calling out to her when he was several feet away. Color leeched from her cheeks, leaving her deathly pale, and she flinched, stepping back so quickly that she nearly stepped right off the deck and into nothing but air.

Joe let out a string of curses even as he lunged to grab her arm before she plummeted to the ground below. It wasn't a huge drop, but she was so damn tiny and fragile-looking. Such a fall could easily result in a broken bone or bones. His relief was palpable when his fingers managed to curl around her wrist and he squeezed, hating her soft cry of pain, knowing he was the cause, but no way in hell was he letting go.

He hauled her back to safety, refusing to let go until both her feet were planted on the deck once more and he had positioned himself behind her, a barrier to any chance of her taking a fall again.

She looked at him in bewilderment even as she cupped the wrist he'd manacled and rubbed as if trying to alleviate the discomfort. He frowned, hating the thought that he'd been too rough, but damn it, she could have been hurt far worse if he hadn't caught her.

Slowly, so as not to alarm her, he reached for her wrist, and at first she resisted, her eyes going wide, but he persisted, gently tugging it free. He turned it over to see his fingerprints red against her pale skin. Already a shadow of a bruise appeared and he cursed violently under his breath.

"I'm sorry I hurt you," he said in a low voice even as he rubbed his thumb soothingly over the marks. "I wouldn't hurt you for the world, Zoe, but I couldn't let you fall."

She blinked in surprise and then slowly relaxed, her shoulders sagging slightly, and the tension left the wrist he held so carefully.

"It's nothing," she said huskily. "Just caught me off guard. I didn't even realize what I'd done. Thank you for not letting me fall."

Joe smiled. Really smiled. He couldn't remember the last time he'd actually smiled the way he did when looking at her. Her eyes widened a fraction as she studied his reaction and a light shiver stole over her body, chill bumps erupting beneath his fingers that still stroked her soft skin.

"You're more than welcome. You're safe here, Zoe. No one, especially me, will let you fall. I hope you believe that. If not, then I guess I'll have to prove it to you."

Her brow furrowed. "Why wouldn't I be safe?"

"That's a very good question," he murmured. "Perhaps a question only you can answer."

She frowned and withdrew her wrist from his grasp. He barely managed to suppress his protest at the sudden loss of contact.

"Have you seen Rusty?" she asked anxiously. "She's been gone forever."

Joe glanced around and then grimaced when he saw Rusty and Sean a distance away. Judging by Rusty's scowl, whatever the two were discussing wasn't pleasant.

"Uh, I think she's pretty occupied at the moment. But I'll stay with you, Zoe. We don't even have to talk. I'll just stand here until Rusty gets back. Whatever makes you comfortable."

She didn't immediately say no but neither did she look thrilled over the prospect. Her gaze swept the area for about the hundredth time and she seemed relieved when she found that no one was paying her and Joe the slightest bit of attention.

"So how long do you plan to visit?" he asked, purposely guiding the conversation into neutral territory.

Or so he'd assumed.

Once more her eyes grew wary, panicked almost, and she froze, going absolutely still. So still he wasn't sure she was even breathing. What the fuck was going on with her? And why did any question, no matter how innocuous, seem to send her into meltdown?

That conversation he planned to have with Rusty was going to happen immediately. Just as soon as he could maneuver his baby sister somewhere they wouldn't be overheard, and then she was going to damn well spill. Everything. Because something was very wrong with this situation. A simple visit from a college friend? He nearly snorted aloud. Zoe was scared—no, she was terrified—of something or someone, and she wasn't just staying a few days with her college friend. She was hiding, fearful of discovery at any moment, and that pissed Joe off.

He wasn't pissed at her. He was pissed at whatever or whomever had put terror in such beautiful eyes and made her jump at her own shadow. And he was going to find out the truth, the real truth, if it was the last thing he did.

"I don't really know," Zoe said softly. "It's been a while since I saw Rusty. I graduated ahead of her and we were so close at school. I missed her."

She said the last painfully. As though Rusty were her only friend and the only person who truly cared about her.

"So I was so happy to get to see her again, and when she suggested I come home with her and spend time with her so we could catch up, of course I agreed, but we really didn't talk about a timeline. I suppose we should have." Pain creased her forehead and her eyes became sad. "I don't want to impose or outstay my welcome."

"How about you and I spend the day together tomorrow," Joe said impulsively.

Even as the words escaped he cursed his lack of control. What the fuck was he doing? Had he seriously just asked her on a date? For fuck's sake. His first priority had to be finding out the real story and if his family was in danger because of her presence. All of which he could do just fine without going out on a fucking date with her.

But at the same time, something deep inside him seemed to settle and his initial reaction and rejection of his impulsive action subsided as peace spread through him.

She yanked her head upward to meet his gaze, her eyes rounded with shock, her mouth similarly forming a surprised O.

"What?" she croaked.

"I could show you some awesome places here. This part of the state is beautiful. There's a lot to see and enjoy. Ever heard of LBL?"

Her nose wrinkled and she shook her head.

"Land between the lakes," he explained. "It refers to a piece of land between Lake Barkley and Kentucky Lake. It's a beautiful spot. A protected refuge for wildlife like bison and even elk. We could go swimming off my dock or just sit and dangle our feet in the water and be lazy. We have some great hole-in-the-wall places to eat where the food is to die for. And the scenery is absolutely beautiful."

Shock was evident in her eyes, as well as the fear she worked so hard to hide. He didn't have the heart to tell her that she was a complete failure at maintaining a poker face. She'd get eaten alive in a high-stakes game.

"Are you asking me out on a date?" she choked out.

Taking a chance on her not immediately withdrawing and taking the fall he'd only barely managed to avoid the last time, he reached out and curled his fingers around hers, holding on loosely so she wouldn't feel threatened.

"I'd rather consider it taking the time to show you around the area we call home. You've been holed up in Ma's house with Rusty ever since you arrived, and today is the first day you've actually ventured out. It's obvious to anyone with eyeballs that you're completely overwhelmed by my loud, raucous family. I thought it would be good for you to get away for a while. Just you and me. I promise to be a perfect gentleman."

He flashed his most charming grin, one that had proved effective many times in the past, but apparently it was lost on her because she continued to regard him with suspicion.

"Zoe, I won't hurt you," he said gently. "No one here will ever hurt you. Every person here would protect you with their life."

She nibbled nervously at her bottom lip then briefly closed her eyes. "It's probably really stupid of me, but you know what, Joe Kelly? I think I believe you. So yes, I'd love to get a personalized tour of the area. I have been a bit stir-crazy cooped up in the house since I got here. A day out sounds nice."

He smiled then. "I'll pick you up at eleven. If I know Ma, she'll pack us a picnic lunch, so we'll leave early enough to find the perfect place to eat whatever she fixes us. After that? We can do as little or as much as you feel like."

For the first time, she actually smiled in return, her eyes lighting up, the shadows that seemed so permanently ingrained lifting and fading away. He stared a long moment, at a loss for words at just how much her smile transformed her features. She wasn't just pretty and wholesome and natural as he'd observed before. She was absolutely beautiful.

Fuck. He had a bad feeling about this. A very bad feeling that he'd just landed in the same exact position that all his other brothers had, and the hell of it was, he could no longer give them shit with a straight face, because now he understood their reactions to the women they'd laid claim to.

CHAPTER 6

ZOE seemed relieved when Marlene bustled over to see how she was faring, a frown marring her face as she scanned the crowd, obviously looking for Rusty and likely about to give her daughter a solid dressing-down for leaving her guest unattended for so long. But when she saw Rusty and Sean in the distance, a scowl covering Rusty's face and an exasperated expression on Sean's, she rolled her eyes heavenward and muttered something indecipherable under her breath.

"Thanks for keeping Zoe company, baby," she said, beaming at Joe. "I can take things from here." She made a motion with her head in Rusty and Sean's direction, a silent plea aimed at Joe.

He barely suppressed his smile but nodded and turned away before he made an even bigger fool of himself in front of Zoe, especially now that his mother would stand witness to the entire thing. Besides, Rusty and Sean butting heads was nothing new or earth-shattering. The day those two ever agreed on anything, the entire family might die of shock. Well, and he had his own motive for wanting to break up whatever spat the two were currently involved in.

He wanted information that only Rusty could likely provide, and he'd pry it out of her or threaten to sic Sean on her at every opportunity. Rusty didn't back down often, but when it came to Sean, she had no qualms about backing away as quickly as possible. He might be the only person on earth who actually managed to intimidate her, or at least infuriate her to the degree of her losing her composure, and she had learned at a very young age never to let her thoughts or emotions betray her. She was a lesson in stoicism. Joe admired her resiliency and her take-no-prisoners attitude but he hated the reason why those attributes had become necessary to her survival.

More than once he wished her piece-of-shit stepfather hadn't up and disappeared the minute Marlene and Frank Kelly paid him a visit and told him in no uncertain terms that Rusty was theirs now and if he ever attempted to get within a mile of her there'd be hell to pay. Joe—and his brothers, particularly Nathan—would have loved the opportunity to pay the bastard a visit and enact some old-school justice for all the abuse and neglect that Rusty, who'd been a mere child, had suffered.

Sean's back was to Joe as he approached, while Rusty was facing him, though she had yet to register his arrival. Her face was red, fury glinting from her eyes, and she'd just opened her mouth, no doubt about to turn Sean into a pile of ashes, when she suddenly looked up and saw him. She snapped her mouth shut but her stare was still mutinous as she glared at Sean, as if telling him they were *not* finished.

"Hey, Rusty," Joe called out, announcing his presence to the sheriff.

Sean hastily turned around, color scouring his cheeks, and Joe noted he didn't look any happier than Rusty had. He must have interrupted one hell of a pissing match. Not that it would surprise anyone present at the Kelly family gathering.

"I hope I'm not interrupting, but I wondered if I could steal Rusty for a few minutes," Joe said in an easy tone, as if oblivious to the obvious tension emanating from the two people standing a short distance away.

To his surprise, Rusty looked relieved. And grateful for the reprieve. Surprising, since she wasn't one to ever not have the last word. But at the moment she looked as though she wanted as far away from Sean as possible, while Sean looked pissed over the interruption.

"Sure, Joe," she chirped with far too much cheerfulness.

She was sharp as a tack, extremely intelligent, but she was also a sarcastic, mischievous shit stirrer who delighted in tormenting her many overprotective brothers. The only two people who escaped her brand of "charm" and sharp wit were their parents. For Rusty, the sun rose and set with those two people. She adored them when she had little reason to love or even like most people. She was protective and loyal to her bones and would take apart anyone who ever hurt or disrespected her adopted parents in any way.

"We are *not* finished," Sean bit out as he stared Rusty down, never once flinching from the scathing look she threw in his direction. A look that would wither a lesser man and have him clutching his nuts in an automatic measure of protection.

"Yes, Sean, we *are*."

"The hell we are," he barked. "You can't hide from me forever. I'll find you, Rusty, and we will finish this conversation once and for all. I'm a patient man but you would try the patience of a saint. Trust me, when you least expect it, I'm going to be there, and this time there will be no one to rescue you, no running and no hiding from the truth. You can take that to the bank."

Joe's eyes widened. One thing was certain: Shit never got boring around here. Thank God for that. His brothers, the other members of KGI, hell, even the wives wouldn't know what to do with themselves if shit didn't hit the fan on a regular basis.

Without giving her the opportunity to get in the last dig, Sean turned and stalked away, Rusty glaring holes through his back the entire time. Joe almost chuckled and would have had it not likely resulted in him having his balls rearranged—he liked them just fine the way they were.

After Sean disappeared from sight, she turned to Joe, her head cocked to the side as her gaze probed him inquisitively.

"What's up, Joe? Everything okay?"

And then she went pale and looked at her watch. "Shit! Shit, shit, shit! Fuck but that man makes me crazy. I can't believe I left Zoe to fend for herself this long. I had no idea I'd been over here with the caveman for half an hour. God, she has to think I'm the worst friend in the world when I swore to her I wouldn't leave her side the entire time."

He put his hand on her arm before she took off running back to where everyone was milling around on the deck, eating, talking, reminiscing about old times and cracking jokes.

"Zoe's fine, honey. I promise. I kept her company until Ma showed up to take over. No one is upset with you, and that includes Zoe."

She fidgeted uneasily. "Still, she's my responsibility and I should probably get back to her."

Since all the Kelly brothers were blunt and Rusty had

been around them long enough to adopt the same characteristics, he saw no reason to pussyfoot around the subject of Zoe forever when he wanted information and he wanted it now.

"What's her damage?" he said, crossing his arms over his chest so Rusty would know just how serious he was and that he wasn't in the mood for her to dodge his questions or pretend to misunderstand.

To her credit, she did none of those things. Her expression became troubled and she let out a long sigh, her eyes filling with sorrow. And anger.

"Look, Joe, I don't know everything. I don't even know a whole lot yet. I'm hoping that by bringing her here and making her feel comfortable and at home that she'll eventually confide everything in me. What I do know is that she got burned. Bad. I'm not talking about a boyfriend breaking up with her and her needing time to lick her wounds and feel sorry for herself until anger kicks in and then she wants his balls served up on a platter."

He had to force his jaw to relax because it was clenched so tightly that he worried he might break his teeth.

"What *are* you talking about then?" he asked in a dangerously soft voice.

She huffed out a breath. "Look, as I already said, I don't have all the details. If I did I would have already gone after the son of a bitch myself. But he did a real number on her. He fucked her over, pretended to have feelings he didn't so he could get close to her. It was almost as if he had access to her childhood and knew exactly what to do and say and how to act and how to give her the things she never had but always desperately wanted. He played her, and she fell for it because she had no basis for comparison. Not enough experience to be able to see through his act or the strange way he was with her or the fact that he was shrouded in secrecy. He had an excuse for everything, and he was convincing. And the only reason she discovered what a complete bastard he is was pure luck. Being in the right place at the right time and overhearing him on the phone talking about what an easy mark she was and how stupid, gullible and naïve she was."

Rusty broke off, tears shimmering in her eyes. Joe palmed her shoulders and gave her a comforting squeeze, waiting for her to look up at him again. He sensed that he hadn't even heard the worst of it yet and he was already ready to hunt the motherfucker down and beat the ever-loving shit out of the shithead.

"What else?" he asked quietly. "What else did he do to her, Rusty?"

"He humiliated her," she said painfully. "Not that he hadn't already done enough, but he devastated her. He destroyed her and stripped her of her self-confidence, her sense of worth. He made her feel expendable. Like she was dirt. Worthless. Unlovable. Not worthy of being loved. I've been her, Joe. I wouldn't wish it on anyone. You can't imagine how defeated and hopeless it makes you feel. And that no one will ever see inside you—her—and the beautiful, selfless, generous and loving woman she is. She didn't deserve that. She of all people didn't deserve what happened to her. He made her question everything about herself. He made her doubt herself as a beautiful, desirable woman. And I hate him for that, Joe. I hate him. I wish I could kill him myself. God help me, if I came face-to-face with him tomorrow, I'd kill him in cold blood and never regret it or feel remorse."

"What. Did. He. Do?" Joe growled. "Physically, Rusty. Did he put his hands on her? Did he hurt her? Did the son of a bitch rape her?"

She emitted a weary sigh. "He raped her emotionally. He pretended to be in love with her. Treated her like a queen. But then she overheard him talking to someone on the phone, and he was laughing at how pathetic she was in bed. How she was inept and clumsy and that sticking his . . ." She broke off, color rising in her cheeks. Then, defiantly, she continued as if pissed that she'd allowed herself to be embarrassed. "He said having to stick his dick in her frigid cunt was like fucking an iceberg and he'd be lucky if it didn't freeze off before it was over with."

Joe's brow furrowed. Part of the story he could absolutely see, having met more than his share of assholes who treated women like second-rate citizens. Hell, some of them didn't even afford women that much of an "honor." They were chattel, possessions, slaves whose only purpose was to please the man in any manner he deemed necessary.

But the part about this asshole complaining about Zoe's frigid cunt, how clumsy and inept she was . . . That didn't add up, and there were a hell of a lot of missing puzzle pieces to this story. If he was so dissatisfied with Zoe as a woman, further proving what a fucking idiot this pussy ass was, then why even bother? Why feel obligated to endure clumsy and inept sex with her? And the line about being lucky if his dick didn't freeze off before it was over with? What the fuck was that supposed to mean? It made no goddamn sense whatsoever.

But when he posed those same questions to Rusty, she shrugged and sent him a helpless look.

"Zoe is an extremely private person," she said in a low voice. "I'm surprised I got as much as I did out of her."

Then her entire demeanor changed and her expression became fierce and she closed the short distance between them and gripped his hand, holding tightly as she stared at him, eyes glittering with purpose and intensity.

"She's not someone to play around with, Joe. She's been hurt badly, and it's going to take her a long time to recover from this. She has to be handled with care, so don't make her fall for you. She's not the typical girl you date and then move on. Those girls know the score before you ever go out the first time with them. You have a good time. She has a good time. Then you move on because you've made it clear you have no desire to settle down anytime soon. Stay away from her, Joe. Don't send her mixed signals. She's too vulnerable right now and I'm not sure how much she can take before she completely falls apart."

It took every bit of his self-restraint not to lash out at her, to tell her he'd never hurt Zoe. But he could also understand where she was coming from. Hell, a day ago, he would have wholeheartedly agreed with everything she said, and if he'd heard Zoe's story then, he wouldn't have been able to get away fast enough. He didn't do commitment. Not yet. Not for a long time. He had plenty of time to consider settling down with the right woman and giving in to the domesticity that had plagued every single one of his brothers.

But he didn't want to walk away from Zoe and forget she existed. He didn't want to hurt her, didn't want to be the cause of yet more pain in her young life. He hated how vulnerable and scared and unsure she looked when she wasn't aware she was being observed. And protective instincts unlike any he'd ever experienced had come roaring to the surface. He was extremely protective of his sisters-in-law. The wives of the other KGI operatives. He'd give his life for any one of them without hesitation. But never had he felt such a personal vested interest in the protection of a woman he didn't even know and had no connection to whatsoever.

What the hell was he supposed to do with that? Even if he wanted to act on this insane attraction or curiosity or need to keep this vulnerable woman safe, it was obvious that she would run hard and fast in the opposite direction if he so much as tipped his hand.

What a fucking time to decide he might actually be interested in exploring an actual . . . relationship? Was that what he was thinking? Or was it simply the warrior in him, sworn to protect the innocent and the victimized, that had spurred his sudden interest in what had caused this fragile woman so much pain?

No, he knew that for the lame excuse it was the moment that thought entered his mind. KGI came across brutalized, helpless victims in eight out of ten missions, and while it enraged him that women would be treated so callously and used as pawns, things, possessions of men who thought themselves above the law, he'd never taken a personal stake in it. He went in, just as all his teammates did, and exacted justice for those victims and made damn sure they got a fresh start, a new lease on life, where they'd never have to worry about the predators they'd once been tormented by.

But he didn't want Zoe to be a KGI mission. He didn't want his team to close ranks and ensure she never looked at every single person with fear and apprehension in her eyes. *He* wanted to do that for her. No one else. And he felt fucking helpless as to how to accomplish that when it was clear she trusted no one, especially a strange man she'd been introduced to once.

Determination seized him. She had accepted a date of sorts with him, though he hadn't called it such. Even if it was damn well just that. Whatever she wanted to call it, if it made her feel safe and secure, he was fine with it, especially if it bought him time alone with her to carefully peel back the layers she'd wrapped herself in. One layer at a time. It would require more patience than he ever thought he'd possessed. He wasn't known for tact or patience. He was the hotheaded twin. The one who saw in black-and-white and didn't have much tolerance for excuses.

Much to his shame, those characteristics had nearly lost him the person he was closest to in the world. The other half of himself. His twin, Nathan. He hadn't understood the sheer hell his brother had endured. Maybe down deep he hadn't wanted to know or understand because then he would have had to face just how close he'd come to losing him. He'd wanted his brother back the minute he was rescued after months of horrific torture and inhuman living conditions.

He'd been an overbearing asshole who'd been angry that his best friend had been taken from him and had returned a very different man. Joe had just wanted to move on like nothing had ever happened. Nathan was home, alive, back with his family. He never considered the private hell Nathan endured every single day even after being set free. The demons he'd dealt with every waking hour and, worse, in his fractured sleep where nightmares plagued him.

He couldn't adopt that same attitude with Zoe or he would lose her and he'd never get her back. And as he knew next to nothing about her, if she disappeared tomorrow, he'd never know how or where to even begin looking for her.

For the first time in his life, he was going to have to go against his every instinct and force himself to be patient, understanding and willing to give Zoe all the time in the world. If that kept her here and not running to God knows where, then it would be well worth reevaluating every single thing that had made him the man he was.

"Rusty, I get where you're coming from. I know I'm seen as the last man standing and determined to remain that way. The ultimate commitment phobe. I have no plans to hurt Zoe. But I looked at her and saw someone who is scared, wary and has a hell of a lot of fear in her eyes. And I don't like that look in any woman. I'm not that much of a bastard."

When Rusty attempted to deny that she'd implied any such thing, he held up his hand to silence her.

"I'm not accusing you of anything, honey. What I'm telling you is that I only wanted to do something to make her feel more at ease, and she was standing there alone, looking scared to death and like someone was going to jump out of nowhere and attack her."

Again he had to halt Rusty when guilt crowded her eyes and she lowered her gaze.

"I'm not blaming you, Rusty. Just let me say my piece, okay? I brought her a drink and she had no idea I was even approaching her because she was too busy looking everywhere else. When she realized I was there, she damn near fell off the deck. And that pissed me off. That's why I came to you to see what you knew. I did my best to assure her that she was safe here and that no one would hurt her and that she was welcome here and would be considered family. Then I invited her to spend the day with me tomorrow so I could show her around the area. Check out LBL and some of my other favorite spots."

Rusty's eyes widened in surprise.

"It wasn't a marriage proposal," he said dryly.

"It may as well have been one," she muttered.

He rolled his eyes. "Look. I have no intention of playing her or having a fling and moving on. I wasn't planning on it before I talked to you but if I was, I sure as hell wouldn't now that I've talked to you. My stance on settling down with a nice girl, getting married and providing Ma with more grandbabies hasn't changed. But nothing says I can't be a friend to her. From what she implied and what you confirmed, you're her only real friend. No one can have too many friends. That's what I'm offering Zoe. Friendship. And maybe she'll see that not all men are selfish dickheads like her asshole ex. So I'd appreciate it if me taking her around for the day tomorrow doesn't become a big fucking deal, and I especially don't want Ma and the wives to start plotting to get me and Zoe together. And not just because it's what I don't want. If I had to guess, Zoe would run like hell if the entire family started matchmaking. So call off Ma. Tell her whatever, and make damn sure the wives don't make more of this than it is. Can you do that for me, please? If you won't do it for me, then do it for Zoe."

Her expression softened. "You're a great guy, Joe, and while I know how adamant you are about not settling down anytime soon, when that time comes, whoever the woman is will be a very lucky lady."

"Oh, for fuck's sake," he growled. "Can we stop right there?"

She laughed, her eyes glinting mischievously. "I won't lie, brother dearest. I can't wait for the day a woman knocks you on your ass and you become as pathetic as all our other brothers."

"That is not going to happen," he said, sending her a murderous glare.

"You know what they say," she said merrily. "Never say never. That's like throwing fate a direct, in-your-face challenge, and only a fool would ever do that."

CHAPTER 7

RUSTY finished towel-drying her hair and slipped into her faded pajamas, pausing before going back into the bedroom where Zoe was already in bed. Guilt flooded her and she closed her eyes. She'd made peace—mostly—with betraying Zoe's confidence, because, well, she hadn't told Joe much at all in the scheme of things. And it would have seemed suspicious if she'd told him nothing or claimed ignorance of at least part of Zoe's history, but she hated lying to her family. It was something she'd sworn never to do.

And it wasn't only Joe she was lying to. She was lying to Frank and Marlene and everyone. By omission. She sighed. Torn between loyalty to her adopted family and Zoe wasn't a pleasant place to be. But she also knew if Zoe even thought she couldn't trust her, she would be gone. Into the wind, and she'd likely end up dead. She *would* end up dead, and that's what bolstered Rusty's flagging determination to continue the facade.

Her family would understand. They'd understand better than anyone, but somehow that didn't give Rusty much consolation. With another heavy sigh, she squared her shoulders and opened the bathroom door to head to bed.

Zoe was nestled in a mound of pillows on her side of the bed, but she was very much awake. And pensive. She was so lost in her thoughts that she didn't register Rusty's appearance until she plopped onto the bed next to her. Zoe cast a startled glance in her direction.

"Those must have been some pretty deep thoughts for you not to have even known I was out of the bathroom," Rusty teased.

She purposely injected lightness into her tone in an effort to ease the obvious tension surrounding Zoe, because she knew all too well the kind of shit Zoe was thinking about. But when Zoe opened her mouth and blurted out her response, she said the very last thing Rusty would have imagined.

"I'm so stupid." She had a panicked look in her eyes. "God, Rusty. I'm such an idiot! Your brother asked me out and I said . . . I said yes! What the hell was I thinking?"

Rusty smiled and slid underneath the covers, reclining against the pillows as she lay next to her.

"It's not a crime to be a woman, you know. We all have those pesky little things called hormones."

"This isn't a joke, Rusty! He scared me shitless. He kept . . . looking at me."

Rusty arched an eyebrow. "I'd be more concerned if he hadn't, or at least I'd be questioning his sexual orientation. You're hot, sister. What unattached man wouldn't look at you?"

"You don't understand," she said in agitation. "He wasn't looking at me like that. He kept staring at me, and he wasn't looking at me like he was attracted to me. He looked . . . suspicious. Like he knew every single thing inside my head. I don't think he's buying our story, and he didn't seem thrilled over my presence at a family gathering."

Rusty stifled her grimace, because Zoe was partially right. Joe wasn't exactly buying their story, but not in the way Zoe was assuming. It only twisted the knife in her heart a little more over deceiving her family. She reminded herself that any one of them would do the same. Her brothers, the members of KGI, even Frank and Marlene, were born protectors. But even that knowledge didn't diminish the guilt that weighed so heavily on her.

"So why did you agree then?" Rusty asked with genuine curiosity.

"I was flustered. I didn't know what to say, think or do. If I said no, would that make it more suspicious? Especially since he was being nice and just offering to show me around the area. I mean, it's not like it was a date date, you know? He was just being friendly. I didn't know what else to say. If I said no, it would make me look like a bitch, but by saying yes, I'm scared to death I'm sending him the wrong signal."

Rusty's lips pressed tightly together to suppress the grin. *Nice, my ass.* Joe was the most commitment-phobe member of the Kelly clan, and while he would put his life on the line to protect an innocent person, he sure as hell wouldn't ask a woman out, even under the guise of being welcoming, if he weren't interested.

But then there was the fact that he obviously had his suspicions, as evidenced by his interrogation of Rusty. Only he hadn't questioned Zoe's character. He'd been far more interested in who'd hurt her. Her lips twitched with the urge to smile. Maybe Joe was a little more interested in Zoe than he'd led Rusty to believe. Or maybe he was in denial himself. Having him hover over Zoe was definitely not a bad thing because there was no way in hell he'd allow anyone to get to her.

"You said yourself he was being nice," Rusty said calmly. "Maybe he just wants to make you feel welcome and put you more at ease. Our family can be overwhelming, and face it, sister. You looked like you were in front of a firing squad for most of the day. Can't say I blame you. But I think you're reading more into this than you need to. There's no crime in having a life, Zoe. Friends. People who care about you. I get that you're freaking out because you've never had that before, but you do *now*."

Zoe flopped back against the pillows and let out a long breath. "You're right. I'm overreacting. Besides, why would someone as hot as him even look twice at someone like me?"

"Now you're just pissing me off," Rusty growled. "You're gorgeous and you need to stop letting the dickheads who shaped you control the way you view yourself. Have you even looked at yourself in the mirror, Zoe? Really looked?"

Zoe flushed and glanced away. It broke Rusty's heart that so much damage had been done to her friend's self-esteem. Hell, not damage, because she'd never had any in the first place. She'd never been shown what a beautiful person she was, inside and out.

To temper the rage that was boiling in her veins, she took the opportunity to tease Zoe. She sent her friend a sly look, nudging her arm with her elbow.

"So you think he's hot, huh."

Zoe looked mortified, her face turning completely pink. "Yes. No. Well, duh! I mean, have you looked at your brothers, Rusty? All of them? They have to be the most genetically blessed men alive because they're all mouthwateringly gorgeous."

Rusty shuddered and then covered her ears. "Stop. Just stop. Ugh. I'll never be able to sleep tonight thanks to you."

Zoe sent her a withering glance. "You can't tell me you didn't think they were hot when they weren't considered your brothers."

"What I thought was that they hated me and they scared the piss out of me," Rusty said honestly. "Nathan was the only one who was nice to me at first. Everyone else wanted me out of the picture."

Zoe grimaced. "That must have been hard."

She shrugged. "I got it. I mean, I couldn't blame them. I wasn't exactly the poster child for a nice young teenager since the first time I met Marlene and Frank came courtesy of me breaking into their house. Besides, that was years ago, and I've long since been indoctrinated into the clan."

"You keep saying that," Zoe said with a shudder. "Like you're all some religious cult that does crazy shit. Should I be worried that I'll never be seen or heard from again?"

Rusty laughed. "Would that be a bad thing?"

"Touché. Now, uh, can we get to more important matters before we go to sleep?"

"Such as?" Rusty inquired.

"Like what do I wear tomorrow so I don't look like a slob but I don't look like I think it's a date either."

"It's simple," Rusty said gently. "You just be yourself, Zoe."

"I need you to do me a favor," Joe said quietly into the phone.

Donovan's voice had an edge of concern when he replied. "Name it."

"Can you do some discreet checking up on Zoe? Just see if anything sticks out, doesn't match up or seem right?"

He could almost hear Donovan's frown through the phone.

"Any particular reason why?"

"Yeah. About a thousand shadows and secrets in her eyes and the fact that someone did a real number on her. She's been hurt. Badly."

Predictably, Donovan pounced on that. "What kind of hurt are we talking about here, Joe?"

"Rusty said her ex crushed her and I'd like to know more than the little she could tell me. Zoe hasn't said much according to Rusty, but she wasn't hurt in a way that makes a woman mad as hell and plotting to cut a man's balls off. She's scared to death, and that makes me uneasy. Especially when she's staying with Ma and Dad for the next while. I'd just like to know her history, or whatever you can dig up on her."

"Ever think about just asking her?" Donovan said dryly.

"If she's not talking to Rusty then she sure as hell isn't going to talk to me. Hell, I was lucky to get more than two words out of her today. She had a deer-in-headlights look when I approached her and spoke to her."

There was a long silence. "What exactly is your interest here, Joe?"

"The safety of my family," he snapped. "Which is exactly what your interest should be as well, or need I remind you that you have a wife and kids who depend on you to make damn sure nothing ever hurts them."

It was a low blow and he knew it. Even before Donovan could respond, he quickly apologized.

"That was way out of line. I'm sorry, man. Look. Something just seems off. My gut's nagging me and I'd feel a lot better if we knew exactly who and what Zoe is. It never hurts to be too careful."

"I can agree with that," Donovan conceded. "I'll see what I can do. I'll holler when I have any info."

"Thanks," Joe said quietly before disconnecting the call.

CHAPTER 8

THE next morning Joe pulled up to his parents' house and hesitated before getting out of his truck. Jesus, was he nervous? Shaking his head, he threw open the door and strode to the front door only to have it open before he reached the handle. His mother stood in the doorway, a smile on her face.

He groaned inwardly then he took a step back. "A word, Ma?"

She frowned and then did as he requested and stepped out, closing the door behind her.

"Look, this isn't what you think so don't call the entire family and tell them I've met my doom. Zoe's been hurt. Badly from what Rusty says, and she's scared to death. The last thing she needs is for the entire family to descend and start pressuring her. I'm taking her out today to show her around, hopefully make her feel more at home and at ease with us. Nothing more."

Marlene narrowed her eyes at him. "Anyone with two eyes can see that child has had a lot of hurt in her life, and

I can't believe you'd stand on my front porch and imply that I would add to it in any way."

He immediately felt contrite and his shoulders slumped. "Look, Ma. I wasn't trying to imply you would ever hurt anyone. You're incapable of it. I just didn't want you or anyone else to get the wrong idea and, as a result, make Zoe feel pressured or embarrassed. She obviously needs friends, support, and I'm offering her both."

Marlene smiled then, her features softening. She cupped his cheek and then leaned up to kiss the other. "I never doubted for a minute that you would turn a blind eye to anyone in need. Now, Zoe is ready and I have a picnic basket packed for you both. Go and have some fun. Make that girl smile, and for God's sake get her to relax so she doesn't think we're all overbearing ogres."

Joe caught her in a hug, squeezing her against him. "Love you, Ma."

"Love you too, baby. Now come on in so you and Zoe can hit the road."

He followed her into the kitchen where Zoe and Rusty were sitting on bar stools, finishing up glasses of juice. Rusty broke into a big grin when he made his appearance. Zoe, however, froze, panic and fright firing in her eyes. She was wearing a simple T-shirt and a pair of low-slung jeans with strategically placed cutouts and holes that Rusty insisted were the style, though it bewildered him that people would pay so much money for a pair of torn-up jeans. Hell, he could do the same with a pair of jeans from Walmart and a pocketknife. But he'd learned from observing his sisters-in-law that women's fashion trends were not only mysterious but apparently held sacred, with no two women's preferences being the same. He didn't even want to see what his brothers' credit card bills looked like each month.

Her hair was pulled up into one of those messy buns Rusty was rarely seen without, and he had to admit, on Zoe it looked damn cute. A few tendrils escaped here and there, giving it that mussed, just-out-of-bed look. He nearly groaned and yanked his focus back to the matter at hand. Taking Zoe out for the day. Oh, and saying hello and complimenting her would be a good start, though he purposely kept his distance, not wanting to spook her even more than she appeared to be.

"Ladies," he said, dipping his head in acknowledgment. "You both look beautiful today."

Zoe's face flushed, her cheeks going a delicate, feminine pink that seemed to make her features shine all the more, while Rusty snorted and rolled her eyes, glancing down at her sweats and T-shirt.

"What?" he asked innocently. "Is it a crime for a brother to tell his sister she looks beautiful?"

Rusty's eyes softened and she looked meaningfully at him, mouthing *thank you* from an angle Zoe wouldn't see. He knew she meant his careful handling of Zoe and not his compliment, but it only spurred his determination to get to the heart of what had hurt Zoe so badly. A woman as beautiful as she was should never be made to doubt her self-worth. No woman should, because at the end of the day, no amount of superficial beauty could make up for lack of a beautiful soul. And beneath Zoe's soulful eyes was a woman, though cloaked in sadness and fear, who was absolutely beautiful.

It should concern him that he was spending so much time reflecting on a woman who was a complete stranger. It was uncharacteristic of him. But he felt a pull he couldn't explain and that quite frankly terrified him. At the same time, it just felt . . . right. Was this what it had been like for his brothers? He almost shook his head. He needed to stop before he got in way over his head and remember the objective here. And it wasn't to find his soul mate and fold like every one of his brothers.

"Zoe?" he asked softly. "You ready to go?"

She sent a nervous look in Rusty's direction but then seemed to pull herself together and smiled at Joe. "I'm ready."

All the breath left his lungs in one forceful exhale. God almighty. If she was beautiful before, she was breathtaking when she smiled. Truly smiled. And it was the first time she seemed to lose the reserve she wore like a second skin. It felt like a punch in the stomach and for a moment he stood there like an idiot gawking at her, wishing for her smile to never end.

His mom handed him a large picnic basket, shaking him from his trance. Then he extended his free hand to Zoe, hoping she didn't reject his overture.

She hesitated a brief moment and then slid her palm over his and he laced their fingers together, pulling her closer into his body.

"I'll have her back for dinner, Ma, so don't worry. Just going to play it by ear today and let Zoe call the shots."

Marlene smiled, her eyes shining in approval. "You two have fun. And that goes especially for you, young lady," she directed at Zoe. "Relax and enjoy yourself."

He led Zoe out to his truck and opened the passenger-side door for her before putting the picnic basket in the extra cab. When he walked around and settled into the driver's seat, he glanced over at her and his heart softened at how nervous and ill at ease she was.

"Zoe."

He waited for her to peek up at him from beneath her lashes before he said more.

"I'm not going to bite you. Promise. I very much want to be your friend, and you can never have too many friends, right?"

If he thought the smile she'd bestowed on him in the kitchen had knocked the breath out of him, this one was a punch to his gut that nearly left him unable to breathe at all. Her entire face lit up and she looked shyly back at him, her cheeks a soft pink that just begged to be touched and caressed. God, she was beautiful. He couldn't recall ever meeting a more beautiful woman, and his sisters-in-law were all gorgeous women. But he'd never looked at them the way he was currently looking at Zoe.

He mentally kicked himself for even going there after he'd already lectured himself, convinced himself and tried to convince his mother that this was nothing more than a friendly gesture. The only problem was *he* wasn't so convinced, and it was huge.

"Thought we'd hit LBL first and then after that go where the wind blows us," he said, smiling back at her.

"That sounds so nice," she said wistfully. "I can't say I've ever just gone where the wind took me. It sounds poetic."

As if realizing she was divulging information she'd rather not, she clamped her lips shut and averted her gaze as they drove out of the compound.

Anger simmered in his veins because he sensed there was more going on than just a bad relationship. What had her life been like *before* she'd hooked up with that dickhead? Rusty had given him nothing on her past. Nothing but a relationship from hell. Where was her family and why weren't they surrounding her and smothering her with love and support like his family was?

It was on the tips of his lips to ask—he was dying to know all about her—but he knew she'd likely shut down and he'd lose the relaxed, sweet and shy Zoe who had greeted him this morning. And if it was as he suspected—bad—then he hardly wanted to bring back painful memories and ruin their day before it even began.

So instead he acted as though he hadn't noticed and gave her a warm, slow smile. "Well then, darlin', I'd say it's about time you did."

He did a mental fist pump when she relaxed and once more turned her baby blue eyes his way and smiled with more enthusiasm.

"Sounds like fun." Then she paused a moment and her cheeks again went that delectable shade of pink that damn near did him in. "Thank you, Joe."

Startled, he glanced fully at her, taking his eyes from the road for a brief second. "What on earth are you thanking me for?"

"For being my wind today," she said softly.

It was a damn good thing they were driving down the highway. It was a damn good thing he'd given himself the mother of all lectures regarding Zoe's status with him. Otherwise he'd spend the next hour kissing her. What man could resist a woman looking at him with so much vulnerability but at the same time like he was the hero of her universe?

I'm so fucked.

Fucked.

Fucked.

Fucked!

When he slowed to take the turn onto the main highway, he took out his cell and hastily texted Sam.

Unavailable today.

Then he did the unthinkable and shut his phone off, tossing it into the console. Never before had he taken himself out of commission with KGI. He had nothing to tie him down. No commitment to anything or anyone other than himself—and his family, of course. But if KGI got called out today, they'd have to work without him. Sam would have all sorts of questions. Questions Joe had no intention of answering. He was due a day to be off call seeing as how he'd never done so before, and that should be sufficient enough explanation to any of his nosy, prying, interfering brothers.

He just hoped to hell they didn't tell their wives or they'd descend much as they had with Eve, all wanting a closer examination than they'd gotten at the family barbecue to make sure she was good enough for him. He nearly snorted. They needed to be worried about *him* being good enough for her. He wasn't exactly known for his wit, charm or subtlety when it came to women, but he was going to need everything he could muster to crack this particular nut.

Oh God. He was losing his fucking mind. He hadn't even been out on an actual date with this woman yet and he was already making excuses to his family and plotting a game plan. It was time to slow the hell down before he got in way over his head. He should have never offered to show Zoe around. Should have kept his distance and let it be. But he hadn't, and now he was going to have to deal with the consequences.

CHAPTER 9

GRADUALLY Zoe relaxed under Joe's calm and easygoing manner. And to think she was worried that he'd been hitting on her when he was treating her in much the same manner as he did Rusty, who was his adopted sister. She forced herself not to feel humiliation that she'd panicked and misread the situation. Thank God, she hadn't made obvious what she'd assumed. Well, other than her blurting out the question of whether he was asking her out yesterday. Hopefully, he'd forgotten all about that, or just put it down to a simple misunderstanding. She'd taken all the embarrassment over rejection she could handle in this lifetime.

Still, a small voice in the back of her mind demanded to know what was so wrong with her that no one wanted her. Cared about her. Her father. Sebastian. Her mother even. No one wanted her. Stella Huntington. How could her mother have left her and never looked back? To a man who had no obvious love or interest in his daughter. Was it because he'd wanted a son?

Knowing now what she hadn't known then, that was likely the case. A daughter could hardly take over Garth Huntington's criminal empire. Had her mother always known? Was that why she'd left? But if that was the case, why hadn't she taken Stella with her? Wouldn't a mother want to protect her only child from such a dangerous environment?

Hot tears stung her eyelids and she inhaled sharply, blinking rapidly so as not to betray the sudden surge of emotion. *Damn it.* Now was not the time to be feeling sorry for herself and reflecting on the past. It was just that—the past. And there was nothing she could do to change any of it. If she had any desire to live, to be free of the life she'd unwittingly led, she had to move forward and reinvent herself. She was Zoe Kildare now, and Stella Huntington was dead. Just like Sebastian and likely her father had wanted. But why hadn't Sebastian just done the deed from the start? Why go through the farce of making her fall in love with him? Did he get off on humiliating her? Had he planned to taunt her with just how stupid and naïve she was before he killed her? For that matter, had her father hired him to get rid of her?

All the questions made her head ache vilely and she wanted nothing more than to crawl into her bed—Rusty's bed—and cry for a year.

"Hey, you okay?" Joe asked gently.

Mortification burned through her mind. She schooled her features and then turned, flashing her most convincing smile in his direction.

"I'm fine. Just excited to see the bison and elk. Do you think they'll be out?"

Joe studied her a moment, his slight frown telling her he

didn't buy her explanation a bit, but thankfully he didn't press her on the issue.

"Bison, almost a guarantee. The elk are a little scarcer. The best time to see them is in the evening, right before sunset and at dusk. If we don't have an elk sighting today, then I'll bring you back one evening and I'll see what I can do about rustling one up for you."

He grinned as he said the last and she couldn't help but grin back, the earlier heartache lifting beneath his friendliness.

"I thought we'd hit the Old Homestead while we're out this way too. It's a representation of the area in the 1800s with cabins and structures that existed in that time period. They have homestead days there and have people dress in period clothing. Folksingers perform, and they have refreshments, including watermelons chilled in the stream that runs right through the settlement."

"It sounds amazing," she said excitedly. "Too bad it isn't going on now. That would be fun to see."

She couldn't keep the wistful note from her voice and promptly shut up before she descended back into the dark sadness that had plagued her moments earlier.

"Maybe you can. You're family now," he said in a teasing manner. "You could come stay with Rusty the next time they have an event and I'll take you."

She flushed but wisely kept her mouth shut before she accepted an invitation she knew she'd be unable to take.

"It's beautiful here," she said as they drove into LBL. "The whole area is beautiful, I mean. You all live right on the lake, and I've never seen so many trees in my life."

"City girl, huh," he teased.

She flushed again.

"Hey, it wasn't an insult," he said softly.

"I never wanted to be a city girl," she said in truth.

He cocked his head, glancing at her as they slowly traveled the road farther into the preserve. "What did you want to be, then?"

She grimaced. "It sounds stupid."

"Try me."

She sighed and then shrugged her shoulders, bracing herself for him to laugh at her. "I always thought living in the country would be fun. Maybe even a farm. And fishing! Do you know I've never fished in my life? And it looks so fun."

"No!" he said in mock horror.

His eyes twinkled with merriment and she relaxed.

"This kind of place is exactly where I always thought it would be wonderful to live. Where people are friendly. It's quiet. People help one another. Life moves at a slower pace. It's so . . . peaceful."

"Something tells me you haven't had a lot of peace in your life," he said in a quiet, serious tone.

God, she had to shut up. What was it about him that made her just blabber on when she knew she had to be careful of every word that came out of her mouth? Rusty had reminded her about a hundred times that she had to be on guard every single waking moment, and yet she couldn't make it two days without messing up.

Hoping he'd buy her act, she nonchalantly lifted one shoulder. "Oh, you know how it is in a big city. Chicago is just so crazy. It's like watching a film in fast-forward. Everyone scurrying around, always on the move, never taking the time to just stop and . . . forgive the cliché . . . smell the roses."

"So move," he said as if it were the simplest solution in the world. "You graduated college and have a degree. You can move anywhere you want. Why stay somewhere you're unhappy?"

Why indeed.

"I don't plan to," she said with absolute honesty. "I just haven't figured out where I want to move to yet. I have an MBA, and, well, there isn't as big a demand for MBAs in rural areas as there is in more populated towns and cities."

"Start your own business. Pop did that when he got out of the service. Dover isn't exactly a metropolis but he started a hardware store and he's managed to not only stay in business for over thirty years but turn it into a thriving enterprise."

"That's what you and your brothers did too, right?" she asked, curious for more information on KGI. "Rusty told me you all served in various branches of the military but formed KGI when you got out."

Joe's brow furrowed as he slowed to a stop, but he didn't immediately speak. Instead he pointed. "Look. There's a bison and her calf."

Zoe whirled in her seat and made a sound of excitement as she saw the giant beast standing about a hundred yards away, her calf next to her, rooting to nurse.

"Oh my gosh! That's amazing!"

She pressed her hands against the glass as if somehow that would get her closer and stared in fascination as the mama bison moved away from her calf, leading it toward the cover of the trees. Her lips turned downward and a sound of dismay sounded when both ambled off and disappeared from view.

"Don't worry," he reassured. "It's actually rare to see so few at a time. They tend to move in herds, and LBL's is pretty large. We'll likely run into it before we get finished."

She perked up as she turned back to him. That is until

he didn't resume driving and instead regarded her seriously, his eyes flat and his expression much less warm than it had been.

"Just what all has Rusty told you about KGI?"

Zoe's mouth fell open. Crap. She'd probably just gotten Rusty into trouble. She knew Rusty wasn't supposed to talk about what her brothers did, but then she hadn't said that much! All the same, he didn't look very happy to know his sister had been discussing him and his brothers with her.

"She didn't tell me a lot," Zoe said defensively. "Don't be angry with her. She told me she couldn't talk about it much, that none of you did. All she said was that all her brothers had served in the military and that Sam, Garrett and Donovan formed KGI when they got out of the service, and that you, Nathan and Ethan joined later. She said that you protect people and go after bad people. That was it."

Joe quickly reached for her hand, giving it a reassuring squeeze. "Honey, it's okay. I'm not mad at Rusty. I was more worried about what she *didn't* tell you than what she did tell you."

She looked at him in confusion. "I don't understand."

He sighed. "To an outsider, the things we do . . . well, let's just say you might not think very highly of me if you knew some of the things we've—that *I've*—done."

Her forehead wrinkled. She didn't understand what he was trying to say. "But Rusty said you *help* people."

"We do. That's our top priority. There's a lot of bad shit in the world, as I'm sure you know. But we take measures that most would deem extreme. I've killed people, Zoe. But I've also helped people. We protect the innocent and take out the evil. We take out criminal empires. Eliminate terrorists. Drug dealers. Arms dealers. Kidnappers. Mobsters.

Human and child traffickers. Pretty much everything vile and evil. I have so much blood on my hands—me and all of my brothers and KGI members have so much blood on our hands that we very much exist in gray areas. And it's not always by the books or the . . . law. We will eliminate any source of evil possible. We all have stains on our souls, consciences to deal with, but we live with it and accept it, because at the end of the day, it's the only way we can live with ourselves. If we ever started turning our backs on the many victims we encounter, it would all be over for us."

He sucked in a deep breath and averted his gaze from her.

"It's a huge responsibility and presumption on our part to play judge and juror and take justice into our own hands. Not many would condone our actions or our mission. Hell, we don't always agree with what we know has to be done."

She could feel the blood drain from her face and she pressed her hands against the seat so as not to betray the trembling. Bile rose in her throat. Oh God. What would he do— *think*—if he knew who and what she was? What she came from? What her father was and that he—and she—*was* the very thing he fought so valiantly to rid the world of?

He would despise her. He would look on her with disgust. She wanted to cry because she was damned from birth with no way to change who she was—what she was. Her father's blood ran through her veins. Evil. Corrupt. Sins of the father for which she had no chance of ever finding absolution.

"I knew you would feel this way," Joe said grimly, his hands curled so tightly around the steering wheel that his knuckles were stark white. "I disgust you, what I do disgusts you. My family disgusts you. I don't blame you—"

"No!" she burst out, cutting him off midsentence. "You're wrong! I *admire* what you do, who you are. I was just . . .

shocked. How can anyone be so selfless? To make your life's work risking yourself for complete strangers? For victims and people who don't have anyone else to stand for them. How can you all do it? You have families. Children. God, it must be terrifying for your loved ones every time you go on a mission, not knowing if one or all of you won't come back. And that if you don't, it's because you were protecting someone you don't even *know*."

He gave her a peculiar look, warmth entering his gaze. Never had she felt more wretched about her deception than now. She was the epitome of what he risked his life to combat. Her kind. Her way of life.

Former way of life.

She gave herself a stern reminder that she wasn't what her father was. She wouldn't make the same choices. And no longer would she live under his thumb, obeying his rules. But she still couldn't hold back the fact that she felt dirty. Unclean. Not good enough for this warrior who stood for all that was good.

Then she almost laughed hysterically. *Way to get ahead of yourself, Zoe. This man couldn't be less interested in you. He's being nice. It doesn't matter if you're good enough or not. He's off-limits. He doesn't want you, and even if he did, he wouldn't if he knew the truth.*

To cover the lull and to escape the warmth that emanated from his face, wrapping her in its comforting embrace, she struggled to change the subject.

"So what do you do when you aren't saving the world?" she asked brightly.

He chuckled, but the warmth didn't leave his gaze. Far from it. It seemed to burn over her bare skin, and his smile . . . He had the most bone-melting smile. He was looking at her oddly and she didn't at all know what to make of it.

He started forward again, following the paved road through the park, but he kept his gaze on her from his periphery.

"I guess you can say that when I'm not out saving the world, I'm showing a pretty lady around my home turf."

Pleasure suffused her veins even as she argued that they were treading on forbidden territory.

"I'm sure that's a full-time job," she said dryly. "I can't imagine you ever lack for female company."

God, was she actually feeling him out? Asking him how many women he saw on a regular basis? Was the sudden burn in her chest *jealousy*? She needed to tape her mouth shut so she'd stop blurting out embarrassing things, and she definitely had to get a rein on her emotions or hormones or whatever the heck was making her think and act like a jealous lover.

His eyes gleamed now and a hint of laughter sparked as the corners of his mouth inched upward even farther.

"Only one," he said vaguely. Then he winked at her before turning his attention back to the road.

What the heck was she supposed to make of that? Rusty had made it clear that Joe was a very happy bachelor and had no plans to change his relationship status from single to not single anytime soon—if ever. It was a running joke in the family, and Rusty had told her that Marlene and the other wives had tried—unsuccessfully—for years to get him to settle down, get married and have a family.

No way she believed he was a tease or that he was leading her on or that he wanted a fling before walking away. Okay, so maybe she was being incredibly naïve. Her taste in men was horrible, but she just couldn't see Joe Kelly being anything like Sebastian.

And maybe that was what scared her the most. Because she had zero experience with good guys, and Joe appeared to be the ultimate good guy. Exactly the kind of guy she wanted and exactly the kind of man she could never have.

CHAPTER 10

"**THIS** is fun!" Zoe exclaimed as she waded barefoot into the shallow brook that cut across land that used to be owned by the same paper company KGI had bought the land for the compound from.

Though it was privately owned now, Joe knew the owner and he had access anytime he wanted, as it was one of his favorite places to go when he just needed peace and quiet.

He felt a smile crawl over his face as he watched her roll her jeans up a little higher so they wouldn't get wet and splash playfully, kicking water up so it skittered over the surface. Then she bent over and thrust her hand downward, retrieving one of the smooth stones from the creek bed.

"This is perfect for skipping," she announced, her face flush with excitement. "I bet it could skip forever across the lake."

"Well, why don't we find out in a little while?"

She cocked her head in question.

"How about we skip the Old Homestead and instead, I'll take you to my house. It's right on the lake and you can skip your rock from my dock. The water's calm today. Not a breath of wind and the surface looks like glass. Perfect skipping conditions."

She nibbled her bottom lip in sudden concentration as she studied the gurgling water.

"I'd better find more, in that case. What if I mess up the first time? I need more than one rock so I can practice if I screw it up."

"Haven't you ever skipped rocks before?" he asked with an indulgent smile.

He was sorry he asked when her smile faded and sadness entered her beautiful eyes.

"No, but I always thought it looked so fun," she murmured.

"Well, then, we need to stock up."

She looked at him in surprise when he removed his shoes and rolled the bottoms of his jeans up to midcalf and waded into the water with her.

"You going to make me do all the work?" he teased. "We'll need to hurry so we get back to the lake before it gets too dark to see your prowess at skipping stones."

She flashed a smile again, and his stomach did that lurch it seemed to do every time her face lit up.

For the next half hour, they carefully selected several dozen perfectly smooth stones, with Joe ferrying them back to the truck. After his last trip, he grabbed the picnic basket his mom had packed and carried it to the bank of the stream.

"You ready to eat?" he called out to her.

She turned from where she'd waded farther down the

brook, eagerness flashing on her face. "I'm starved! I got so caught up in the day's activities that I forgot all about food."

He clutched his chest and staggered back in mock horror. "That's a crime in these parts. Particularly when my mother has provided the food. You'll discover that food is akin to religion in our family."

She laughed and he absorbed the carefree sound.

"I'm already beginning to see that. At first I thought your mom had made way too much food for the get-together yesterday, but that was before I saw how much everyone ate."

"One thing no one does is turn down Ma's cooking. I'm pretty sure it's one of the ten commandments."

She laughed again and it made him want to continue to do and say things to make her laugh. Not only did she sound beautiful, but every time she did, her face lit up and her eyes shone. She glowed, and it was an enchanting sight to behold.

He quickly unfolded the blanket and spread it over the softest spot of ground and then motioned for her to come sit while he unpacked the basket.

"Hope you like chicken salad sandwiches," he said as he unwrapped them. "Ma's chicken salad is legendary and second only to her fried chicken, which Donovan asks for pretty much anytime she's cooking."

"I've never had one," she admitted.

He feigned horror once more and clutched at his heart. "You're in for a real treat then. But Ma being Ma, she packed options as well, because God forbid anyone ever goes hungry on her watch. We also have roast beef sandwiches, beef she slow roasted overnight with gravy on the side for dipping, served on homemade hoagie rolls. My advice is go for half of each because you haven't lived until you've tried them both. But save room for dessert, because she also packed pecan pie, triple fudge brownies and homemade peanut butter cookies. Hell, why am I even bothering to qualify the peanut butter cookies as homemade? Everything is homemade. Ma thinks anything store bought, ready to eat, is the gravest of sins."

"Oh my God," Zoe said, her eyes huge in her face. "I'll never eat all of that, Joe! And I don't want to offend her." Though she looked at the offering spread out like she wanted very much to try to eat as much of it as possible.

He laughed, reaching for her hand because he just couldn't help himself. If he held it a bit too long before retreating, well, he wasn't complaining. His thumb drew lazy patterns over her knuckles and it struck him that he hadn't been this content to take a day off and go where the road took him in longer than he could remember.

"The key is to sample everything. Then I take all the leftovers home with me. She'll never know we didn't devour it all, and then I eat like a king tomorrow as well."

"Oh, I see now," she said with mock sternness. "You get to hoard the leftovers. How is that fair?"

"Fair?" he sputtered. "You're staying with her and get her cooking every day. Me? I only get her cooking when I come over or beg her to take pity on her wifeless son who can't cook to save his life."

Zoe rolled her eyes, but he secretly delighted in the fact that she'd relaxed and lost her earlier reserve and unease.

"What's that?" she asked when he pulled out a large insulated drink container.

"Ah, this? Only the nectar of the Gods and the official beverage of the south. Sweet iced tea."

Her lips puckered and he purposely looked aghast at her. "Don't tell me you've never had sweet tea. My heart can only take so many shocks in one day."

She burst into laughter and he stared shamelessly at the sparkle in her eyes and the enticing shape of her mouth as it broadened into a huge smile.

"Does instant tea count?"

He arched an eyebrow. "Instant?"

She laughed and held up one hand. "Don't tell me. I already know the answer to this one. Instant tea is a sin. Am I right?"

"Got it in one," he quipped.

"Apparently I have a lot to learn about life in the south," she said in amusement.

He adopted a mournful look. "We'll make a southern girl out of you yet, Zoe Kildare. Before you know it, you'll be hunting and fishing and we'll have you out of those jeans and into cutoffs and flip-flops as standard wardrobe procedure."

He wondered if she knew how wistful she looked in that moment when he'd merely been teasing her. But hell, she'd already expressed a desire to fish. Maybe . . .

He shut his thought process down immediately. No, he damn well wasn't going to take her fishing. This was a one-time deal. He was being friendly. Showing her all men weren't assholes out to take advantage of women or out for a piece of ass.

But . . . they could be friends, right? No law against that. And Zoe definitely needed friends, as Rusty appeared to be her only friend and ally. Yep. He could definitely offer her friendship. His pulse sped up over the idea and he found himself smiling. It was the perfect solution.

"What are you smiling so big for?" she asked inquisitively.

Busted. He scrambled for a response and then decided what the hell. The truth was always the best idea.

"What *don't* I have to smile about?" he asked, sending her an even warmer smile. "I'm spending the day with a fun-loving, beautiful woman who has a great sense of humor and likes the same things I do. What's not to love about *that*?"

She looked rattled by his reply but he pretended not to notice. Instead he changed the subject. But not before he witnessed that despite her initial befuddlement, she looked . . . pleased with his reply.

"You full yet? We still have rocks to skip, and then I have to get you back home before Ma sends someone looking for us. She's very protective of those she takes under her wing, and there's the fact that missing dinner is a cardinal sin punishable by death in her eyes."

He didn't miss her flush of pleasure at the idea of having people who cared about her, and it pissed him off. Had she never had anyone who gave a shit about her? It was obvious she hadn't because she soaked in every bit of attention she received, savoring it like it was the most cherished gift she'd ever gotten. Hell, it likely was. Did she have no fucking clue just how precious *she* was?

She emitted a groan. "I'm way past stuffed. I may not be able to skip rocks. I'm not sure I can even walk at this point."

Warmth spread through his veins once more. Damn but he liked being in her company. "Lucky for you that you don't have to worry about that. I'll carry you anywhere you need to go."

Her face flushed a delightful pink and she ducked her head shyly in an endearing way. How the fuck was he going to keep this a platonic friends-only relationship? But then he didn't have a choice. Neither of them wanted—or were ready—for a romantic relationship.

He stood to his feet and groaned. "I take that back. I may need you to carry *me*."

She giggled, her eyes sparkling like a pair of gemstones. "Maybe we should just try to hold each other up on the way back to the truck. You'd flatten me if I tried to carry you."

"Good call," he said, grinning back.

He held out his arm, and after a moment's hesitation she came to him, fitting perfectly beneath his shoulder. He staggered in an exaggerated manner as they stumbled back toward the truck, laughing like two lunatics. It struck him as he opened the passenger door for her and lifted her into the seat that he was actually having *fun* just . . . being. Relaxing and forgetting about the rest of the world and the assholes who inhabited it.

He shook his head ruefully as he headed around to the driver's side. It was a good thing he'd set ground rules and established that he and Zoe would be friends only. Otherwise he would be fucked.

"Ready to go try your hand at skipping rocks?" he asked as he cranked the ignition.

She nodded eagerly.

He couldn't help himself. He had to touch her. He reached over and tousled her hair affectionately. Much like he would a sister or one of his sisters-in-law.

"Try not to kick my ass too badly. You might damage my manly ego too much if you make me look like an amateur."

She rolled her eyes. "As if. Are you forgetting I'm a complete newbie at this?"

"You know what they say about beginner's luck," he countered.

Even as he said it, he made a vow that no matter how badly she did, he was going to ensure he did worse. There was no way he'd take this moment from her. And if he was honest, he wanted very badly to see her excitement when she *did* kick his ass at rock skipping. Something that none of his brothers had ever been able to best him at.

"YOU ready?" Joe asked Zoe as they stood on the dock overlooking Kentucky Lake.

She gripped the smooth, flat stone in her hand, rubbing it with her thumb as she prayed not to make a huge fool of herself.

"Yep," she said, with more confidence than she felt.

But then who cared if she sucked at it? She sucked at everything else, and at least this time she'd have fun. She could barely contain her excitement as she considered the best technique. She cocked her head, studying which angle would give her a better chance at success, flexing her wrist as she prepared to make her first attempt.

As if he could read her mind, Joe spoke up. "It's all in the wrist. You want to turn your hand sideways and launch, not throw, the stone at an angle where it strikes the surface on the flat side."

He moved around behind her, sliding his hand down her arm to grip her hand, turning it and then flexing her wrist in a forward motion.

"Like that," he said. "Not too softly, but not too hard either."

She shivered, sudden awareness of his touch catching her off guard yet not alarming her. With him, she felt . . . safe. Which only proved what a naïve idiot she was since she'd thought the same thing about Sebastian.

She slammed the door on old memories before they took over and ruined what had been a spectacularly awesome day. Joe wasn't Sebastian, and this wasn't her being a clueless moron. Sebastian would never risk his life for a complete stranger. He wouldn't make it his life's work to help others in need. He was an egotistical, self-absorbed dickhead, and she had only herself to blame for not recognizing that a hell of a lot sooner. Certainly before she'd given him her virginity.

Wincing, she once again shut down her train of thought and instead focused on the here and now. She wasn't that person anymore. Stella Huntington no longer existed. Maybe she never did. She'd been molded to someone else's expectations since birth, never allowed to be who she wanted to be. Zoe Kildare was whoever Zoe wanted her to be, and right now, more than anything, she wanted to be the kind of woman who lived the kind of life she'd experienced today.

Realizing Joe was waiting on her to give it a try, she took careful aim, positioned her wrist just so and let it fly. She held her breath when it hit the surface, and then to her surprise, it didn't sink or make a huge splash. It skipped! And kept on skipping!

Once, twice, three times. *Oh my God! Four, five, six, seven!*

She threw her hands over her mouth and then jumped up and down like an excited two-year-old.

"I did it! I did it!"

Then she launched herself into his arms, nearly taking them both down in a heap on the dock. He steadied them, and she squeezed him as hard as she could.

"Thank you," she whispered. "This has been the best day ever."

When she pulled back, the corners of his eyes crinkled and warmth entered his gaze that she could swear she felt all the way to her toes. He had such beautiful brown eyes. Eyes that could be dark and brooding but also tender and funny. On the surface he seemed such an uncomplicated man, as if what you saw was what you got, but he was anything but.

"Now it's your turn," she said breathlessly, handing him one of the choicest stones from her stash.

"I dunno. You were pretty impressive. I don't want to embarrass myself," he teased.

She rolled her eyes. "Oh please. You'll probably skip it all the way across the darn lake."

He made a show of getting prepared and assuming the same stance he'd instructed her to take. Her breath caught in her throat and she softly counted under her breath as his rock followed a similar path to hers.

Then she plunged both fists in the air and twirled like an idiot. "Take that Mr. I've-been-skipping-stones-all-my-life. I beat you by one!"

She had no idea which was warmer on her skin, the sun or his gaze. Then he smiled broadly, teeth flashing, and it was no longer a question of what warmed her. Who needed the sun when all this man had to do was look and smile?

He held up his hand to high-five her then held up his other fist to bump knuckles with her. Pleasure suffused her face, soaking into her very bloodstream. For one precious, stolen afternoon she'd been allowed to retreat from the reality of her circumstances, and for once she'd experienced the joy of being a part of something bigger than anything she'd ever imagined.

Yes, Rusty had cajoled her with stories of her and her brothers and their lives in this small Tennessee town on the shores of Kentucky Lake, but in all honesty, Zoe had just never gotten it. Who really lived those kinds of lives? It had been so foreign to her that she'd assumed Rusty embellished those tales. After all, she was a good storyteller. In Zoe she found a captive audience because while the two women shared similar childhoods, devoid of any overabundance of love or caring, unlike Rusty, she had continued that existence into her adult life, never knowing that something so rare even existed.

A part of her had wanted Rusty to have been exaggerating the bond the Kelly family had because it brought home all too well the sterile, austere environment she'd been subjected to, thanks to a mother who'd simply walked away without ever looking back and a father who was more interested in a robot he could program than raising a child.

She sighed, turning once more to face the lake, forcing her hungry gaze away from Joe and everything she saw in his eyes that she lacked. She let out a wistful sigh and hugged herself, simply absorbing the splendor of early summer in Tennessee on the lake.

She went very still when a strong hand wrapped gently around her nape, offering it a gentle squeeze.

"Was it fun kicking my ass?" Joe asked lightly.

She was too afraid to look back at him, knowing how raw she must appear in this moment. The corners of her mouth tipped upward in a ghost of a smile as she attempted to lift the veil of melancholy that had slowly draped itself over her like an incoming fog. He would ask questions. Questions that required answers she herself didn't even know or want to know.

Then she turned her sad smile on him, the words pouring out of her chest despite her not wanting to speak.

"Does it make me pathetic that one of the highlights of my life has now been skipping a perfectly smooth stone that I found while wading in an ankle-deep stream with my jeans rolled up from a dock overlooking one of the most gorgeous views I've ever seen in my life? All after having the most wonderful entire day I've ever had?"

His hand stilled and then his thumb feathered over the sensitive skin behind her ear. She closed her eyes when he leaned into her side and pressed his lips to her temple.

"Does it make me any more pathetic that one of the highlights of my life was teaching a gorgeous woman in bare feet with rolled-up jeans how to skip that stone seven times across the lake all while enjoying one of the most beautiful views I've ever seen?"

Her eyes widened and she swiveled, staring up at him in shock. He was suddenly so serious when all day he'd been so lighthearted and teasing. Sincerity radiated from his expression and his eyes never once wavered from her profile, giving a clear indication of just what view he was referencing.

The warm imprint of his fingers on her neck remained long after he pulled away.

"I should get you back home," he said in a low voice as the sun dipped lower on the horizon. "Ma will have dinner ready soon and she won't be happy if I don't get you back in time."

He reached for her hand, much as he'd done at the beginning of the day, and they returned to his truck in silence. His easy charm and ready laughter, so prevalent all afternoon, were now replaced by a silent, almost brooding mood, though he made an obvious attempt to smile each time she glanced his way.

When they pulled up to his mother's house a few minutes later, a permanent ache seemed instilled in her chest. So lucky. These people were so lucky to have the lives they had. To have so many people who loved and cared about them. That the simple things evidently weren't taken for granted.

Life just seemed to move at a slower pace here, and that statement placed against Rusty's—and now Joe's—explanation of what he and his brothers did seemed laughable. No doubt they'd argue that dodging bullets and bombs, protecting people in danger and bringing justice to the people who would corrupt the very way of life the Kellys held in such esteem could hardly be considered a slower pace, but this place, these people, seemed to defy it, to send a message to the outside world.

And above all, they answered their calling without allowing the ever-increasing fast-paced corruption of the outside world and humankind's resignation and acceptance over the near extinction of core beliefs once valued by so many others in the world to infringe on the way of life they held so sacred.

People like the Kellys simply didn't exist outside of movies and popular fiction. People and places like the ones Zoe had come to experience in her short time here with Rusty were thought behind the times, not current or relevant. She herself would have likely laughed in disbelief over a description of what she was now witnessing firsthand, dismissing it as simple nostalgia for something created by people who'd lived decades ago before the explosion of modern technology.

In other words, places—people—like this were just myths.

Only now that Zoe had experienced it, had felt it, tasted it, seized upon it, she desperately didn't want to let go. When the real world intruded—and damn it, that time *would* come—she knew that if she survived that inevitable collision, nothing would ever be the same for her again. Nothing in her life up to now had ever been real.

She nearly laughed aloud as Joe halted them at the top of the front porch steps. Here she was offering somewhat sagely that people like the Kellys didn't exist outside fiction when her entire life had been nothing but a staged, made-up alternate reality, and as a result, she still didn't have the first clue as to who she was or what her purpose was.

"Thank you for today," she said politely as he turned to face her.

She held herself aloof, knowing she'd never experience another day like this one, and for that reason, she locked it away, determined to protect and cherish it. In the meantime, she wasn't about to broadcast the fact that she wanted to crawl under the covers and, after pulling them over her head, cry for what her life never was and could never be.

CHAPTER 11

JOE had only been home a few minutes when he heard a knock on his door. He let out a groan and dragged a hand through his hair. He was sorely tempted to pretend he was in the shower or indisposed or that he'd gone to bed and hadn't heard the summons. But if it was one of his nosy brothers they wouldn't give up. He might as well put the hammer down now before things got out of hand.

He strode to the door, wishing he'd at least had time to shower. He looked ridiculous with his pants still rolled up and his boots shoved on sans socks. The ends of his jeans were still damp from his wading around picking out skipping stones with Zoe, and he knew whoever was on the other side of the door wouldn't miss a single detail of his appearance.

He opened the door and was surprised when he saw Shea standing there, his twin, Nathan, pressed in close behind her.

Shea smiled up at him and he couldn't help but smile back. He adored his sister-in-law.

"Hi, Joe. I hope you don't mind that we popped over."

Joe pulled her into a hug and then picked her up and swung her around to the inside, depositing her in the entryway. He dropped a kiss on her cheek and then ruffled her hair as he drew away.

"Of course not, sweetheart. I'm always glad to see my favorite sister-in-law and her pain-in-the-ass husband."

Nathan snorted, and as soon as Joe turned to greet his twin, Nathan slugged him in the shoulder with his fist.

"Knock off the flirting. Or find someone else's woman to flirt with. She's taken."

Joe rolled his eyes. "As if everyone in the world doesn't know that. In case it's escaped your notice, the poor misguided woman only has eyes for you, though it makes me question her judgment in men. Clearly I would have been the better choice."

Shea laughed and slipped one slender arm around Joe's waist, squeezing him affectionately. Nathan scowled and gently pried his wife's arm free of Joe and then proceeded to wrap both arms around her, holding her so she couldn't escape.

"Y'all come on in," Joe said as he ambled toward the living room. "Can I get y'all anything?"

"Shea wanted to come visit," Nathan said.

Over Shea's head, his gaze connected with Joe's, sending a silent signal to have a care. Joe rolled his eyes again. As if he wouldn't handle Shea with the greatest of care. He would always share a special bond with his twin's wife, and he was grateful for it, as inexplicable as it was.

Shea was gifted with extraordinary talents. Abilities that had made it possible for her to connect telepathically with Nathan when he was imprisoned in the Afghani mountains undergoing horrific torture. Not only had she kept him sane, refusing to let him give up hope, but she'd also taken his pain and torture as her own. She had siphoned it from him and, as a result, had suffered it for him, a fact that still caused Nathan to nearly lose his mind when he thought back on it.

She was one of the strongest women Joe had ever met in his life, and that was saying a lot given the strength of all his brothers' wives. And his teammates' wives. The men of KGI had been blessed beyond measure to find women every bit as fierce as themselves, all possessing wills of steel and a fierce refusal to ever stay down or quit. He had no doubt that these women had saved his brothers and teammates every bit as much as they asserted that their husbands had saved them.

Without Shea, Nathan would be lost to them. As would Swanny, who had been imprisoned with him and who had suffered every bit as much as he had. Joe would never be able to repay her for the gift of his brother. Back home where he belonged. He thanked God every day for her and he prayed that the woman he one day settled down with and married would possess even a fraction of her spirit, fierceness and generosity.

"I knew you couldn't stay away," Joe teased. "Has my brother been an overbearing grump ass lately? Want me to rough him up for you?"

Shea rolled her eyes and laughed. Then she dropped her gaze and twisted her hands nervously in front of her. He immediately picked up on her unease and he lifted his gaze in quick concern to Nathan, asking without words what the fuck was going on.

Nathan's lips compressed into a grim line and he shook his head, nodding toward Shea, and then he simply shrugged, telling him that whatever it was that was bothering his wife, she hadn't told Nathan yet. The fact that she'd asked to come here, to talk to Joe, worried the fuck out of him because Nathan and Shea were tight. Two halves of a whole. True soul mates, and Joe had never believed in that concept before her, even having already witnessed Ethan, Sam and Garrett fall hard for their wives.

Joe went to Shea, taking her hand and uncurling her fingers before wrapping his hand around them. He guided her toward the couch and sat her down beside him. Nathan settled on the other side of her, his hand going immediately to her shoulder.

"What's wrong, sweetheart?"

"I know you took Zoe around today," she said hesitantly.

Joe's brow furrowed and he once again looked at his brother in question. Why on earth would his taking Zoe anywhere cause Shea so much distress?

"It's none of my business what's between the two of you," she rushed to say before Joe could interject his questions. "That's not why I'm here and I don't want you to think I'm butting in or being nosy. I wouldn't do that to you. I may tease you about your eventual downfall but I know how much you value your privacy and how much it bothers you when everyone starts harping on you about finding the one, and that's why that's all I'll ever do is just tease you in passing."

He was growing more confused by the minute, and Nathan didn't look any more enlightened than he did.

"Honey, I know you wouldn't pry and I know you're just teasing me when you nag me about finding a wife and settling down," Joe said in his most gentle tone. "Besides, of anyone, you know I feel closest to you and Nathan. How could I not? And for that reason, I would never mind you or Nathan butting in, nor would I mind you knowing about any relationship I may one day be in. Now what's going on here, sweetheart? You're worrying me, and if you keep on this way, Nathan is going to come unglued over there. As it is, he looks like he's about to rearrange my living room because he's worried to death about what's bothering you right now. And so am I," he added softly.

"Have you told her anything about me?" she blurted out. "About my abilities?"

"Of course not. You know I'd never expose you or Grace to an outsider. No one in the family would. I hope you're not worried about that."

She shook her head. "You don't understand. I needed to know if she already knew because if she didn't, I don't want you to say anything to her because . . ."

She broke off and looked down, an unhappy frown marring her delicate features.

"Because why, baby?" Nathan asked, sitting forward so he could look back at her. He was about to fidget right off the couch, and Joe knew that his twin's patience was waning. When it came to anything that upset Shea, Nathan would tear down the damn house to get answers so he could fix the problem.

She sighed, her expression dimming, her eyes looking more and more unhappy. "I connected to her at the cookout," she whispered. "Or at least I think it was her. It had to be, right? I mean, I've never been able to connect to anyone else in the family except the two of you, and she was the only one there I hadn't been around before."

Joe and Nathan exchanged sharp glances and Joe sucked in his breath.

"What did you see, honey?" Joe asked, trying to keep the sudden surge of anxiety from his voice.

His pulse had immediately quickened and sweat formed on his brow. He realized he was . . . scared. Scared of what Shea might tell him but at the same time, if she had seen into

Zoe's thoughts, then she'd be able to tell him what he wanted to know. Most importantly, she'd be able to tell him what the hell Zoe was so scared *of.*

"I didn't see anything," she said, her shoulders sagging.

Nathan pulled her into his arms, his gaze full of worry and concern for his wife. "How bad was it? And why didn't you tell me when it happened? Damn it, Shea. You should have told me the minute it happened so I could get you the hell out of there."

He could understand Nathan's point. It was never easy for Shea to connect to another person. It was an enormously draining experience, one that sapped her strength and left her extremely vulnerable. Not to mention the pain it caused her if she attempted to help the other person in any way.

"But I felt . . ." She broke off, and her eyes were troubled as she looked up at Joe. "I felt her fear, Joe. It was overwhelming and so suffocating I thought I was going to pass out."

Nathan's grip tightened around his wife and his expression was a mixture of fear, anger and worry.

"I didn't want to intrude or invade her privacy," she said quickly. "I hope you know that, Joe. I would never do that to family or someone who was a guest of the family."

Joe reached out to touch her cheek. "Shhh, honey. I know that. We all know that. You've said it yourself. You can't help who you connect to. It's random and beyond your control. But why were you so worried that I had said something to Zoe about your abilities if you didn't see into her mind?"

Shea reached for Joe's hand, holding it so tightly that her small nails dug painfully into his skin. He doubted she even realized the urgency that was radiating from her. He and Nathan could both feel her agitation. It was the first time in a long while the mental pathway between him and Shea had been open. He doubted she was cognizant of that either, and it bothered him that her experience with Zoe had messed with her so badly that she didn't even realize she was broadcasting loud and clear to both the brothers. Nathan was understandable. The pathway was always open between the two of them, and as a result, Nathan always knew if Shea was in any sort of pain or distress, if she was afraid or in trouble. But that was not the case with Joe.

Except . . .

"Wait a second," Joe said, glancing quickly at his brother to see if he'd already picked up on what he had. Judging by the tightness of his expression, he had. Or he was getting there at least.

Shea glanced up at Joe in question.

"Why didn't Nathan know when this was happening?" he asked.

"That's a damn good question," Nathan growled.

Color rose in Shea's cheeks and she dropped her eyes so she wasn't looking at either brother.

"Shea?" Nathan prompted. "Baby, why would you hide that from me? I don't like the idea of you experiencing something like that, when that was the last place you expected something like that to come at you, and especially when you just said you felt like you were suffocating and were worried about passing out. Why would you close yourself off to me like that?"

An edge of hurt tinged his brother's voice and Joe's chest tightened in response. No one but Joe and Shea knew the battle that Nathan still fought with his demons. That there were still nights he didn't sleep and nights when he did that were haunted by nightmares. One of the biggest nightmares being that of losing Shea. It was why he needed her near at all times, even when they were physically separated. The telepathic connection they shared meant she was in his head at

all times just as he was in hers. It kept Nathan grounded and
secure, as he needed to know at all times that the woman
he loved more than life was safe, especially when he was
on a mission and was away from her for an indefinite period
of time.

The fact that she had closed herself off from him would
feel like a rejection to Nathan, and Joe worried what that
would do to the battle that still raged within him. And what
it would do to his brother and sister-in-law's relationship.
God help them all if Nathan ever lost Shea. He wouldn't
survive it. What a bunch of fucking terrorist bastards hadn't
managed to do to his brother, break him, prevent him from
coming home, end his life . . . would be accomplished if he
had to ever live without Shea.

Joe found his grip tightening around Shea's hand, whereas
until then she'd been the one with the death grip. When she
winced, he promptly let go, cursing under his breath.

"Sorry, Shea. I didn't mean to hurt you. You're broadcasting, sweetheart, and it's pretty intense."

She frowned and then suddenly he no longer felt her. It
was always abrupt and not a pleasant sensation when she
suddenly ended the communication, even if it hadn't been
conscious. Joe could well understand Nathan's dependence
on Shea as a constant shadow in his mind and why it would
worry him that she'd closed off that intimate pathway at the
moment she'd felt Zoe's emotions. He only hoped he hadn't
given Shea the wrong idea with his gentle pointing out of
her communicating down his mental pathway and not just
Nathan's. In truth he'd wanted her to pull away before she
saw and felt the force of his own thoughts.

"I never meant to hurt you," Shea said softly as she turned
to Nathan, her arms wrapping around his neck.

Nathan crushed her to him, burying his face in her hair.

"I know, baby. It just makes me crazy to think of you hurting or suffering and me not knowing or sharing that with you."

"I didn't want to make a scene," she said, her voice still hushed. "And most of all I didn't want Zoe to know or for anyone to have to explain it to her. I still don't want her to know. She's so frightened, Joe, and if she knows that I now have a pathway into her mind, it might frighten her even more and I think she'd run."

"Did you pick up on anything other than her fear?" Joe asked carefully.

She withdrew from Nathan and shook her head as she turned her attention back to Joe. "I haven't felt that kind of fear since what happened when I was taken from . . . here," she said, her voice knotting as she invoked the memory of her abduction. "And when I was hooked to those horrible electrodes and unable to talk to Nathan or you. I have no idea what she's so terrified of, but she was paralyzed with it. She was broadcasting so powerfully that I was helpless to do anything until I finally managed enough strength to break away from her. It was . . . crippling."

Nathan swore and Joe added his own silent barrage of curses. Both that his sister-in-law had suffered for something she didn't ask for and couldn't control and also that his assessment of Zoe had been spot-on. She was fucking terrified. So scared that her fear had been the only thing Shea had picked up on when she'd been assaulted by the force of Zoe's mental overload.

Joe's cell rang, and he reached to silence it but saw it was Donovan calling. "Give me just a second, Shea. Try to relax for me. We'll figure this out, honey. I don't want you to worry. It's Van on the phone."

He stood and purposely put several feet of distance between himself and Nathan and Shea so as to give them privacy. Nathan would be shaken by what Shea had related and he'd need a few minutes to collect himself.

"Hey, Van," he greeted as he answered the call.

"I did as you asked and did some digging on Zoe's background," Van said, his voice betraying nothing, which should have comforted him, but in light of what he'd known already and Shea had just confirmed, he was anything but at ease.

"And?"

"Not a damn thing out of the ordinary, though it would help to know what I'm supposed to be looking for other than her being screwed over by some jerk ex-boyfriend."

"Tell me what you *did* find," Joe said impatiently.

"Nothing. She's the poster child for a quiet, not very colorful life. She's twenty-six years old, no family, lives alone, graduated from DePaul University a year ago with a master's degree in business management. She paid for school like a lot of students who have no family support or scholarships do. With student loans, which she'll start repaying in a couple months' time. She held a wide range of part-time and weekend jobs throughout school. Enough to pay her rent and get by but not much else. Not very active on social media. From what little I've managed to pull up, she doesn't seem very active in much."

Joe frowned. "I guess that answers the question of why we'd never seen or met her before. We assumed when Rusty said she was a friend she met while at university, that Zoe had gone to UT also. But if she went to school in Chicago, then apparently they had a long-distance friendship."

"It would also explain why Rusty would have invited her home with her to stay an indefinite time. I don't imagine they've seen a lot of each other, and if Zoe just got out of a bad relationship, it stands to reason she would need a friend like Rusty."

Joe nodded, distracted as he glanced back at Shea. Making an instant decision, he closed his mouth. He'd been about to tell Van about Shea, but he didn't want to worry the rest of the family unnecessarily. Not until he knew for certain they had something to worry about. It was enough that he had Nathan at his back.

"Okay, thanks, Van," he murmured.

"You find anything out today?" Van asked.

Joe grimaced. He'd hoped to get out of the topic of his date with Zoe. As if that would happen. He'd been worried about all the wives being up his ass—and Zoe's—along with his mother, but it was his brothers who would probably prove to be the annoying gnats.

"Just that she has zero self-confidence, doesn't think much of herself as a woman and is scared."

"Don't know what to tell you, man," Donovan said. "Until she confides in you there isn't a lot you can do to reassure her. Take it from someone who knows, it's better to forget all that PC bullshit about time and space and respecting boundaries. The first thing you have to do is make sure she can trust you, and that isn't going to happen the very first time you tell her that. But if you combine that with also trying to get her to confide in you about what she's afraid of, then hopefully you'll wear her down. Push but don't be an asshole. And in the meantime, shower her with as much personal attention as possible. She'll figure out you aren't going to hurt her."

"You sound so sure about that," Joe said dryly. "I don't know that I ought to constantly be in her space. That could be sending her all the wrong signals, and I don't want that to happen."

"Don't have your head stuck so far up your ass that you don't recognize the one when she's right under your nose,"

Donovan chided. "If you insist on living in denial and end up hurting her because you were just being a stubborn horse's ass, you'll never forgive yourself for rejecting her. Not to mention, if you make it clear after trying so hard to get her to trust you that you have no interest in her, then she's going to leave and you'll never get her back."

A knot formed in Joe's stomach and he found his fingers clenching into tight fists at the very thought of Zoe leaving and him never seeing her again.

"I'll bear that in mind," he said before ending the call.

He walked back over to where Nathan and Shea were sitting. He slid onto the couch on Shea's other side and rubbed his hand over the top of his head.

"I had Van do some checking up on Zoe, and he didn't turn up anything."

Shea stirred, her eyes swimming with seriousness as she stared up at him. "I wasn't wrong, Joe. She's terrified of someone or something."

"I know, honey," he said, squeezing her knee.

"I don't want to intrude," she continued. "I'd rather just stay away from her unless I have advance warning so I know to steel myself better. I wouldn't feel right divulging something if she hasn't trusted one of us enough to tell us."

"I agree," Joe said. "She'll tell me when she's ready."

"You sound certain of that," Nathan said, one eyebrow arching in question.

Joe shrugged. "I'm not going to give her much choice."

"I didn't think you were ready for something like this," Shea murmured.

"She's the one not ready," Joe countered, realizing in that instant that it was true. "I was ready the minute I laid eyes on her."

This was also true. He just hadn't wanted it to be. Then.

Now? He couldn't remember a single argument that had rolled off his tongue in the past as to why he should remain single. The only problem was, this wasn't a slam dunk. Far from it. Zoe wasn't going to fall right into his arms, and neither was she going to accept that a man she'd only met twice wanted forever.

Hell, he was having enough problems accepting it for both of them. No, the problem wasn't him accepting—he accepted it just fine. The problem was in believing that it had come this easy when for so long he'd fought the very idea. As much as he hated to admit it, his brothers had all been right.

He would know when the one entered his life. Well, now he knew, and what scared the shit out of him was that knowing was one thing. Making it happen was an altogether different fight. One he had no intention of losing.

CHAPTER 12

THE next morning, Joe awoke with a single purpose. He hadn't slept much. Anticipation and nervousness had crowded his mind and vied for equal attention until the two swam together and blurred. He formed and reformed his plan of attack a dozen times, but each time, it came down to a single objective. Spend another day with Zoe no matter how he had to make it happen.

Knowing what time his mother always prepared breakfast, Joe got up after dozing for a couple of hours, showered and dressed, a sense of urgency beating down on him. As he walked into the cool morning air, he felt invigorated. His skin prickled and his blood surged hotter than ever before. Anticipation of seeing her again, of unveiling more of the mystery that was Zoe Kildare, nagged incessantly at him until it became all consuming. An obsession.

The few minutes it took to drive into the compound and

park outside his mom's door gave him no time to formulate his thoughts any better than the entire night had. He didn't even know what he was going to say yet.

He let himself in the front door and sniffed appreciatively at the air. Pancakes and bacon unless his nostrils told him wrong, and they were rarely ever wrong when it came to pinpointing what his mother was cooking. Lord knows he'd had years to perfect his guesses using only his nose and his growling stomach as his guide.

"Joe!" his mom exclaimed when he entered the kitchen.

"Got enough for one more?" he asked hopefully.

She rolled her eyes. "Don't I always? I never know who will pop in for breakfast so I always make plenty. Your father keeps grousing that I waste too much food, but he never complains when it means he gets seconds. Of course I only serve him half of what he's allowed so he thinks he's getting away with something when I agree to give him seconds."

He laughed and hugged his mom. Ever since his dad's heart attack several years earlier, his mom had taken the reins of his diet and his physical activity, forcing him to work fewer hours at the hardware store, which inevitably meant hiring part-time help or relying on a family member to pick up the slack.

"So what's on your agenda today?" Marlene asked as Joe sat down at the bar. "I didn't think I'd see you again for at least a week."

Heat rose up his neck and he avoided her steady gaze. "I stopped by to see what the girls had planned for the day. I thought I might take Zoe out again. We didn't get to do everything I had planned yesterday."

Marlene studied him for a moment, and evidently approving, she smiled and returned to mixing the pancake batter.

For a moment the only sound in the kitchen was the sizzle of bacon and the *whop whop* of her beating the mix with a wooden spoon.

"She's not going to come easily," his mom said in a quiet voice. "She's one to be handled with care."

"I know," he said just as softly. He didn't bother denying the subtle question in her voice. He was through denying his attraction to Zoe and what she was to him.

"I have every faith that you'll get her to come around," Marlene said with a soft smile that warmed her eyes and entire face. "I like her, Joe. She's perfect for you."

"You'll get no arguments from me," he returned. "But you and I aren't the ones who need convincing. It's going to take a lot more to get her to open up to me and trust me with her heart."

She shook her head, her eyes suddenly awash with unshed tears. "You have no idea how long I've prayed for the day when my last son was spoken for. It's all a mother can ask for. For her children to love as she and her husband have loved for over forty years and to be blessed with families of their own."

"I guess now you'll have to set your sights on Rusty," he said lightly, to shake her from her sudden nostalgia.

She snorted. "That child is going to prove more stubborn than all you boys put together."

"Which child are you referring to?" Rusty piped up as she entered the kitchen.

"Morning, baby," Marlene said, beaming at her youngest chick. "Have a seat. Is Zoe coming down for breakfast?"

Rusty plopped onto one of the stools next to Joe and elbowed him in the ribs as she levered herself down.

"She'll be down in five. I got up and showered before she did, but I told her you were cooking pancakes and how awesome they were, and I think her mouth was watering already."

Joe reached over and hooked his arm around Rusty's neck, pulling her down so he could rub his knuckles over the top of her head.

"Better watch it, squirt. I'm bigger than you. Remember that when you're trying to abuse me. I'll eat your share of the bacon if you don't shape up and show proper respect."

She snorted. "Mess with my bacon and die, old man. I suppose I should be nicer to you. Ma always did preach about respecting my elders."

"You little heifer. I'll get you for the age remark," he said in a voice that promised retribution.

"So what brings you over so early this morning?" Rusty asked, as if just realizing his out-of-the-blue presence.

He shifted uncomfortably, watching her carefully for her reaction. "I was going to ask Zoe if she wanted to have part two of our outing. We didn't get to everything on the list."

Rusty's eyes widened as she stared wordlessly up at him.

"I won't hurt her, Rusty," he said quietly. "She'll always be safe with me."

"Wow. I mean, holy heck. When did this happen?" she asked incredulously.

He shrugged. "I can't tell you when or even how. I just know what is."

"Holy crap," she breathed. "She's never going to believe I didn't set her up for this."

"Would it be so bad?" he asked, still watching his younger sister carefully. "I would never hurt her. I'd never let anyone hurt her again."

To his surprise, her eyes filled with tears. She turned her head and wiped quickly with the back of her hand.

"Hey," he said softly. "What's that for?"

She turned back to him and smiled. "I'm just happy for you. For her. Even if she has no clue yet. In other circumstances it would be a hell of a lot of fun to watch when she figures out resistance is futile."

His eyes narrowed as he stared into Rusty's. "What other circumstances are we talking about here?"

"She's my friend, not just some woman who caught your eye. My loyalties are divided. So I can't, in good conscience, be completely on your side on this one. Besides, she's going to need an ally. In this family it will be a foregone conclusion that she's done for. I can't let her think she has no one at her back."

Rusty's tone was teasing, but there was something in her eyes that worried him. He couldn't quite put his finger on it. Maybe he was trying to see more than there was. At any rate, he'd already decided that Zoe would be the one to tell him her secrets. Not anyone else. He wouldn't have Donovan checking up on her further, and now that Shea was prepared, she'd be better fortified when she came into contact with Zoe again.

"Good morning," Marlene sang out, shooting a quick warning glance at Rusty and Joe. "Did you sleep well, dear?"

Joe turned to see Zoe standing in the doorway to the kitchen, her gaze shy and hesitant.

"I did. Thank you, Mrs. Kelly."

"Come on in and take a seat. The first batch of pancakes will be served up in less than a minute. And how many times do I have to tell you to call me Marlene or Ma? Anything you'd like except Mrs. Kelly. You're family, and we can't have you being so formal. I feel like an old woman when someone calls me Mrs. Kelly!"

Zoe started to hedge around Joe to take the stool on the other side of Rusty, but he caught her hand, rubbing his thumb over the jumping pulse at her wrist. He gently pulled her down to sit at his side so that he was positioned between her and Rusty.

She blushed to the roots of her hair and she looked so damn adorable that it was all he could do not to kiss her right then and there. Casting him furtive glances from the side, she eased onto the stool, her hand still captured by his. He pulled it over to rest on top of his thigh and continued to rub his thumb in gentle circles on her baby-soft skin.

"I came over to invite you out with me again today. There's still a lot I didn't get to show you yesterday. And if I'm a good boy, I hoped you'd give me a rematch in skipping stones since you kicked my ass yesterday."

Her eyes widened and her mouth fell open in obvious surprise. "Why would you want to spend the day with me again?" she asked in astonishment. Then she lowered her gaze as more color rose into her cheeks. "You don't have to put your day on hold to be nice to me."

He had to suck in several steadying breaths as rage filtered through his system. The idea that she somehow didn't think she was good enough for him to want to take out, that she was some sort of pity case, infuriated him. He wanted to track down the son of a bitch who'd made her doubt her self-worth and take off his balls.

"Actually, I was hoping you'd be nice to *me*," he said as lightly as he could given how pissed off he was.

He wasn't the only one who'd caught the way she'd phrased her statement or her embarrassment. Both Rusty and his mom were visibly upset, though they quickly schooled their features. His mom went back to beating the batter for the next batch of pancakes but her jaw was tight and she put a little more strength in her movements.

"I want to spend the day with you, Zoe," he said in a low

tone so it wouldn't carry to the others. "I know I don't have to do anything, but it would make me very happy if you'd agree to spend the day with me."

She finally lifted her gaze to meet his and what he saw damn near broke his heart. Her eyes were hopeful and yet sad at the same time. Almost as if she'd resigned herself to being insignificant and unworthy of his or any man's notice.

He lifted her hand to his mouth and pressed his lips against each of her fingertips. Her eyes immediately widened and a shiver erupted over her body. Thank God she felt the same chemistry he did. He wasn't flying solo, nor was his attraction a one-sided thing.

"Say you'll put me out of my misery and agree to spend the day with me," he coaxed.

Her lips parted and he nearly groaned at the unconscious invitation. If only they were alone. Then he'd take advantage of her silky-looking lips and devote the better part of an hour to exploring the fullness and softness of her mouth.

Her smile was adorably shy, but it slowly spread warmth to her eyes until her entire face was alight with pleasure and excitement. He felt savage satisfaction that she was starting to get it.

"I'd like that," she whispered. "But—"

He pressed a finger to her lips, the same lips he was dying to taste. "Shhh. No buts. You and me, and today is ours. What do you say we make the best of it?"

Finally, she nodded, and he realized he'd been holding his breath when his chest started to burn. He slowly let the trapped air out of his lungs, feeling as weak and unsteady as a newborn colt as relief hit him right where he lived.

One hurdle overcome. Only a dozen more to go before he knew each and every dragon his lady needed slaying.

CHAPTER 13

"**YOU** have to help me," Zoe squeaked as she all but dragged Rusty into the bedroom they shared.

"Calm down, sister," Rusty said. "You know I'll do anything I can. What do you need help with?"

"Everything? What do I wear? And by that I mean something that doesn't scream *desperate* or that I'm trying too hard. Casual. I mean we went wading and skipped stones on the lake yesterday so I have to be prepared for anything, but not too casual. I don't want to look horrible or anything."

Rusty laughed. "Leave it to me. Simple, casual and not desperate. I think I can handle that." She went to her closet and a few seconds later stuck her head back out. "Are the legs and pits shaved?"

"What?" Zoe gasped.

"Shaved," she explained patiently. "I have a pair of shorts that would look awesome on you and a tank top that would be perfect, but I wouldn't want to show those legs if they're hairy, you know."

Zoe closed her eyes in mortification. "Yes, I've shaved. But are you sure? Shorts?"

Rusty sent her a patient look filled with love. "Zoe, you have killer legs and a to-die-for ass. You'll fill out my shorts like I've never been able to. I had hoped my scrawny teenage years were just that, teenage years that I'd grow out of. Unfortunately, my body didn't get that memo, and as a result I have no hips, no ass and no boobs. I've seen sticks with a better shape than me."

"That's so not true!" Zoe protested. "You're gorgeous, Rusty. I wish I was as tall as you are. You're the one with killer legs, and your breasts and hips, not to mention your behind, are in perfect proportion."

Rusty rolled her eyes. "Not that I don't appreciate the observations, but it's you we need to focus on. Now, are you going to trust me?"

Zoe sighed. "You know I do. I just wish I weren't so nervous. It's not like he has any interest in me as a woman."

"Lord save me from oblivious women," Rusty said with an exaggerated sigh. "Now come on. We don't want to keep him waiting."

Ten minutes later, Zoe was dressed, her hair up in a messy bun and makeup lightly applied in a natural look that highlighted her features in a way that even she had to admit made her feel . . . pretty.

"Come on, I'll walk you down," Rusty said with a smile.

Zoe shoved her feet into a pair of sparkly flip-flops, checking the fresh coat of toenail polish she and Rusty had applied just the previous night while Rusty had gotten the lowdown on her first date with Joe. Hot pink wasn't a shade she would have usually gone for, but it made her feel a little daring and ultrafeminine.

"You look gorgeous," Rusty assured her.

"I must be out of my mind," Zoe murmured as she allowed Rusty to herd her down the stairs.

"Honey, you know this. God knows I've said it enough times. But you can't let that asshole control the rest of your life, and you damn sure can't give him the power over your self-confidence. Can you imagine if it was me thinking and saying the things you are? You'd be all over me like a bad rash. Now stop overthinking everything and go have fun. It's not a crime, you know."

Zoe's head came up and with it a surge of realization. "You're right. I've been letting him control me for too long. Enough is enough."

"Thata girl," Rusty said approvingly. "Now have fun and we'll dish about it later."

"Yeah, well, don't forget that we're going to dish about Sean too," Zoe said in a warning tone.

Rusty's expression immediately soured. "Nothing to dish about except an obnoxiously arrogant male with his head stuck up his ass."

Zoe laughed. "Girl, you just described half of the male population."

"Only half?" Rusty asked innocently.

Another peal of laughter rolled off Zoe's lips just as they rounded the corner into the living room, and Joe immediately looked up. His eyes warmed with approval as his gaze raked up and down her. Her skin prickled and goose bumps rose and raced down her bare arms all the way to her fingertips.

Heavens but the man was sex on a stick. Heat swamped her cheeks as mortification struck her. She was disgustingly transparent for the most part and she just prayed he missed that particular thought that had surely been reflected in her eyes.

Judging by the way his expression hardened and his gaze smoldered and grew darker, she didn't think he'd missed anything. Nor did it appear he had any objection to that train of thought either.

Get it together, Zoe. Nothing can happen. Nothing will *happen.*

She was reading far too much into what Rusty deemed southern hospitality. She'd been told over and over how warm and welcoming Rusty's family was, and all she was seeing was evidence of that fact.

"You ready?" Joe asked, his voice husky and gruff. "Ma packed us lunch again."

"Is it bad that as stuffed as I am from her pancakes, my stomach just growled in anticipation?"

He chuckled. "You aren't human if Ma's cooking doesn't have that effect on you."

He leaned over and kissed Rusty's cheek and then pulled her into a quick hug. "I'll have my cell if you or Ma needs anything. Have a good day, sweetheart."

"You take good care of her," Rusty warned.

Joe tangled his fingers with Zoe's and pulled her to his side so that she settled beneath his shoulder. "Only the best," he said sincerely.

A soft smile curved Rusty's mouth, and for a moment, Zoe thought she saw raw emotion reflected in the deep green of her eyes. Puzzled by the brief interaction, she glanced up at Joe only to see deep seriousness reflected in his gaze.

He lifted the picnic basket with his free hand and then guided her to the door and then out to the waiting truck. Once he had her in the passenger seat, he walked around and stuck the picnic basket in back before sliding in behind the wheel.

"I thought I might take you out in the boat and do a little fishing while it's still cool out," he said as they backed out of the driveway.

"Really?" Zoe asked, excitement threading through her veins.

He smiled at her, his eyes glowing with the warmth she'd grown accustomed to when he looked at her. "Yeah. Really. I have a smaller boat at my house but I also keep a larger platform boat docked at the marina. We use it when there's a group of us and we go out swimming or to have a day in the sun. We can fish, swim or both. We don't even have to leave the lake until this afternoon if that's what you'd like. We can fish while it's cool, take a break for lunch and then swim to cool off."

Her face fell. "I didn't bring anything to swim in, though."

He flashed a triumphant grin. "I may have told Rusty to pack one of her bathing suits for you, and I wore my swim trunks under my jeans. Always pays to be prepared."

"I can't change on a boat in the middle of the lake!"

"There's a changing curtain that boxes you in on all four sides," he said, not losing his smile. "I'd never put you in a situation you weren't comfortable with."

"Oh, okay then."

She was momentarily lost for words.

"Well?" he prompted. "What'll it be? Fishing then swimming, or you just want to fish and head back in?"

"Uh, well, I'd like to swim. I mean, that is unless you don't want to."

"And miss out on seeing you in a bathing suit?" he asked in mock horror.

Her face flushed crimson. It had to be bright red, as hot

as it was burning. She cursed the fact she was a redhead and had the fair skin to go with it. It meant she never got away with an embarrassing thought, and that those embarrassing thoughts were always prominently on display.

"It's nothing to write home about," she mumbled as she glanced away.

"You're a beautiful woman, Zoe," he said, all humor gone from his voice. She peeked at him from the corner of her eyes and saw that his face was a picture of absolute solemnity. "I don't give a shit who told you different or that you believe the asshole, but you are gorgeous, and not just on the outside. You're beautiful where it counts."

For a moment it was painful to breathe and she rapidly turned so he wouldn't see the betraying evidence of her tears. If he only knew that she wasn't beautiful inside or out. If he knew who and what she was, the filth she came from, he'd never look at her the same again.

Her heart ached painfully and she closed her eyes as the pain intensified. Anger and betrayal burned like acid and left a foul taste in her mouth. Anger at the choices her father had made and the fact he hadn't cared that his own daughter would be made to pay for them. And anger at her mother for simply leaving and not caring enough about the child she left behind.

What was it about her that was so damned unlovable? Unworthy of love?

When she finally risked looking back over at Joe, he was staring straight ahead, his jaw set tightly in a mask of anger. What had she done to piss him off? Damn it, for just one day could she at least pretend to be the person she'd become with Rusty's help? Just once could she leave behind the mess that was her old life and live a few stolen moments as someone she wasn't but wanted to be with her every breath?

Knowing she'd already made a mess of the day and they

were only just outside the compound, she forced away the taste of despair and made herself inquire lightly, "So what kind of fish are we fishing for? And do you eat what you catch or do you throw them back?"

He reached for her hand before answering, the reassuring warmth and strength of his fingers as they laced through hers easing the tightness in her chest.

"I fish for anything I can catch and I definitely eat them. In fact, if we manage to catch enough for a meal, I thought I could fry them up for you for dinner. I won't even make you help clean them," he teased.

She couldn't control the shudder at the thought of what cleaning fish entailed. She had a firm policy on never eating anything at a restaurant that wasn't completely beheaded already so that no eyeballs stared lifelessly back at her.

"Thanks," she said dryly.

He chuckled. "As to what kind of fish we'll try for today, I thought I'd start you out on something that's not only easy but fun as hell. I'll set you up with a Zebco rod and reel and a bobber and we'll see if we can catch a bream or two. Nothing more fun than watching your cork start to bounce in the water right before it disappears. For such a small fish, they fight like hell. There's nothing like it."

She wrinkled her nose in thought. "How small? If they're so small, how can you eat them?"

He smiled indulgently at her. "Leave the sizing to me. You'd be surprised what constitutes a keeper. And there's no better eating. That I can guarantee. You haven't lived until you've had a big ole fish fry with bream and hush puppies."

"Yum," she said, smacking her lips appreciatively.

"That's what I'm thinking," he murmured, his eyes on her mouth, giving her the distinct feeling he wasn't referring to fish.

She flushed again, this time a buzz of pleasure heating her cheeks. His mouth was beautiful, and she wondered how it would feel against hers. Whether he'd be a demanding, passionate kisser or a man who'd be content to let her lead. God, she hoped for the former because something as delicious as surely his kisses would be shouldn't be left up to her guidance.

Whoa. She needed to back the heck up and stop with that line of thought. She was getting so far ahead of herself even thinking about him kissing her. He was being friendly. Hospitable. And it was obvious he felt sorry for her. *Ouch.* That was one way to douse the heady euphoria that had enveloped her the moment she'd begun fantasizing about him kissing her.

Besides, it would only complicate matters, and complicated was the very last thing she needed right now. Especially since she couldn't stay here indefinitely. Or even for much longer. She was becoming complacent. Already the fact that Sebastian hadn't just used her but had planned to kill her was growing dimmer in her memory. How screwed up was that? She needed to wake the hell up and stop fantasizing or she'd not only get herself killed but endanger a lot of innocent people as well.

"Give a mint to know what you're thinking right now."

His statement brought her focus sharply back and she saw that his eyes were narrowed and his lips a tight line as he stared intently at her. *Crap.* She had to quit being a freaking open book when it came to every single thought process she had.

"Was just thinking about how many more fish I'm going to catch today than you," she said lightly.

"Mmm-hmm," he said, clearly not believing her. But he let it drop. Thankfully.

A few minutes later, they pulled into the marina across the lake from where the compound was located, and she stared at the cozy inlet that housed so many boats. It had the beginnings of an absolutely perfect day. The water was calm and serene and a vibrant, deep blue that had her sighing with delight.

"Liking that sound a lot better, so whatever you're thinking now, keep thinking and stop dwelling on that other shit," he said firmly.

Her eyes widened in surprise at how adeptly he read her body language even when her face wasn't a direct reflection of her thoughts. But then considering what he and his brothers did and the fact that Rusty had warned her of their ability to read any situation, it shouldn't shock her that he seemed so in tune with her chaotic mind.

He chose a parking spot and then hopped out, reaching back for the basket and a cooler she hadn't seen until now. Then he walked around before she could clamor out and held up his bended arm for her to hold on to as she slid down from his truck.

"Ready to go put the whooping on a mess of unsuspecting bream?" he asked, his eyes gleaming with amusement.

"Ready to get your ass kicked by a girl again?" she challenged in her sassiest tone.

He threw back his head and laughed. Then to her surprise he dropped a kiss on her upturned forehead. "Yep. And I plan to enjoy every minute of it."

CHAPTER 14

"MY cork bobbed!" Zoe shrieked, nearly dropping the rod and reel she had a death grip on.

Joe smiled as the bobber went crazy over the surface of the water and then suddenly disappeared from view. "Now!" he shouted. "Pull up, but not too hard. Set the hook just like I taught you."

She yanked entirely too hard but thankfully the hook was firmly set, because all she got for her efforts was resistance. Her eyes danced with excitement as she began to frantically reel. Her brow furrowed and she bit into her bottom lip in concentration as she fought the bowed rod.

"That's it. Reel slowly. Not too fast. Get him into the boat."

Suddenly the fish broke free of the surface and dangled haphazardly as the line swung in crazy circles. Joe reached out to snag the line and then brought the fish inside the boat so he could take out the hook.

Zoe stood over him, a frown dimming her earlier enthusiasm. "That's it?" she asked skeptically. "He felt so much bigger! We're supposed to eat that?"

He laughed at her bemusement and then held up the freed fish for her inspection. "That's a very nice size catch," he pointed out. "Larger than average. Definitely a keeper."

"Seriously? You're not putting me on?" she asked as he opened the live well and tossed the fish inside.

"Nope," he returned. "You catch us a few more like that and supper is guaranteed."

"Oh. They just seem so . . . *small.*"

"Sometimes the best things in life come in small packages," he said, allowing his gaze to drift meaningfully over her sun-kissed body.

She flushed but pleasure shone in her eyes. "Think I'll catch another one in the same spot or should I fish somewhere else?"

"Oh hell no. Throw your bait right back where you had it. Where there's one, there's usually at least a dozen."

"What about you?" she asked, staring back at him as he perched on one of the seats to watch her.

"I'm having a good time right where I am. No better view on the lake," he said lazily.

She snorted. "You're so full of it, Joe Kelly."

He grinned. "Nothing but the truth, ma'am. My mama taught me never to lie."

At that, her expression sobered and she turned quickly around as she cast her line in the general vicinity of where she'd just caught the first fish. Joe shook his head, impatience flaring. She was no closer to opening up to him and trusting him than she had been the first time they'd met. In fact, if anything, it seemed that she'd only tightened her reserve around him as if she'd firmed her resolve not to let anyone in. Had she confided nothing in Rusty or was Rusty as clueless as the rest of them were? More and more he wondered if his sister had been telling him everything when she'd related what Zoe supposedly told her about her ex-boyfriend screwing her over. But even if Rusty did, he couldn't ask her to betray Zoe's confidence. Not when it would likely send her running as fast and as far in the opposite direction as possible.

Frustration beat at him. At a time when he should feel as if he had all the time in the world to explore a relationship with a woman he could very well see forever with, instead he felt as if he were working against the clock and time was fast running out. He couldn't explain the persistent edge of panic that assailed him. Just that it was eating a hole in his gut and if he didn't make his move fast, he could lose her. However, if he made his move too fast or came on too strong, he lost her anyway.

Hell of a position to be in.

Suddenly all the times he'd given his brothers so much shit over their women came to mind and he grimaced. If they had felt even half of his fear and frustration when he was busy giving them shit, he was surprised they hadn't beat his ass on the spot. He would have deserved it. He had a bad feeling he was going to owe one hell of a round of apologies before it was all over with. But he could eat humble pie with the best of them as long as it meant coming home to Zoe every night.

"Joe!" she cried as she grappled with her pole. "I've got another one! Oh my God, you were right! There's more!"

This time when he unhooked the fish, Zoe was staring at him, her eyes glowing with pleasure and excitement and with such a rapt expression that he had to physically control the urge to kiss her senseless and keep on kissing her until fishing was all but forgotten.

Her lips were moist from her repeatedly running her tongue

over them in abject concentration. Even now, her tongue darted out frequently in an endearing nervous gesture. He was having some serious fantasies about what she tasted like and doing his own exploration of her lips, nibbling over every delicious inch. God knew she smelled good enough to eat. When, *not* if, he got his mouth on her, he might spend the better part of a week just tasting her delectable skin from the top of her mussed hair right down to those dainty, feminine, hot pink–painted toenails.

"Joe?"

Shit. She'd totally caught him out with his head in the clouds. Or rather with his mind solidly focused on her and those groan-worthy fantasies he was torturing himself with.

"Yeah, honey?" he asked absentmindedly as he continued to watch her work her lower lip with her teeth. He focused on baiting her hook again, praying his thoughts weren't as transparent as they felt.

He had to shift position because his balls were aching and throbbing like a son of a bitch and his dick had already pushed past the opening in his swim trunks and was pressed so tightly against his zipper that the marks were going to be a permanent tattoo.

"Is this one a keeper too?" she asked.

He smiled at her anxious question. "Yeah, honey. It's definitely a keeper too."

Just like you are.

He damn near said the last aloud and clamped his lips shut to prevent his thought from escaping.

She clapped her hands together in satisfaction. "How many more do we need?"

"We fish until you get tired of catching them or they stop biting," he said in amusement. "The more we catch just means the more people I have to invite over for a fish fry." Then he paused and pretended to give the matter great consideration. "On second thought, let's quit at a dozen. That way I don't have to invite anyone over and I'll have you all to myself for dinner. I'll be a gentleman and wait until I drop you back by Ma's this evening to clean them so you don't have to help. Then I'll head home, clean and ice down the fish and I'll fry them up for you for dinner tomorrow night. How does that sound?"

She had a complete deer-in-headlights look going on. Her eyes were wide and panicked, but more than that, her mouth was open in apparent shock that he'd invited her to spend time with him again. Anger stirred within him, making him restless and edgy. Why the hell it should surprise her that he—or any man—would be interested was beyond him. She had to see her own beauty and appeal. But that was just it. She *didn't*. She didn't see what he and everyone else saw. Her vision of herself in the mirror was flawed. Marred by some selfish, unthinking dickhead's perception of her, and worse, he'd apparently taken every opportunity to knock her down a few notches. To remind her just what *he* thought about her and to make her feel like less of a woman and more insecure.

He wanted . . . Hell, Joe had no idea what the asshole wanted. What more could he have wanted when he had Zoe? She had been his. Though the idea left a bad taste in his mouth, he had to accept that she had once belonged to a bastard who hadn't appreciated her, hadn't realized what a treasure he had. But that didn't mean that Joe wouldn't now move heaven and earth to make her realize that he would never make the same mistakes her ex had. He'd never squander the beautiful gift she'd once given another man. Herself. If he were blessed enough for her to ever entrust herself to his care, he'd never give her a single reason to doubt him or the fact that he'd spend every single day showing her just how fortunate he believed himself to be.

He roused himself from his dour thoughts and regarded her solemn features. "Is that a no?" he teased lightly, bringing the topic back to his dinner invitation. "Or is it that you're just dying to help me clean the fish and would prefer we do that together?"

She shot him a startled look over her shoulder and then a giggle escaped her.

"Zoe! You've got one on!"

She nearly dropped her pole as she scrambled back around, her feet tangling as she sought purchase. She yanked upward on the rod and let out a sound of jubilation when the tip bowed and the cork disappeared even farther from view.

"I've got it!" she yelled. "Holy crap, Joe. This one must be huge!"

He moved quickly behind her and pressed his chest against her back, reaching around her to steady the pole. "Like this," he murmured close to her ear. "Hold the tip upward at all times. Don't let him have any slack. As you pull up, reel in every bit of slack. Keep the line tight at all times."

He rested his hands over hers, guiding her movements as the pole wiggled and danced against her palms. He inhaled the sweet scent of her hair and wrinkled his nose when the wind blew soft strands over his nostrils, tickling them slightly.

She felt warm and so very soft in his arms. Like she belonged. Like it was where she'd always belonged. Though she was concentrating fiercely on reeling her fish in, he could see that she was very aware of his close proximity. Her tongue darted over her lower lip and then her teeth sank into it as if to steady her nerves. Or perhaps disguise her reaction. He smiled to himself. He hoped like hell she wasn't immune and that he wasn't flying solo here. It would suck if his attraction wasn't returned, but that clearly wasn't the case. She may not want to feel the sexual tension between them but it was there, acknowledged by them both.

His hand cupped over hers, he helped her reel in enough line that the fish came sliding free of the surface of the water and he reluctantly let her go so he could retrieve her catch. He snagged the line and then expertly slipped the hook from the fish's mouth.

"Yep. You were right, Zoe. This is a huge one. One of the biggest I've ever seen, for sure."

"Really?"

Her eyes danced with delight and she wiggled in her excitement, causing his smile to grow even more affectionate. Lord but she made it easy for someone to love her. How could anyone not?

"I'm definitely taking pics of this one before he gets cleaned, and I plan to measure and weigh him too. Who knows? Maybe you caught a record breaker."

And he didn't think it was possible for her smile to get any bigger or for her to light up any more than she already was. He busied himself dropping the fish in with the others and then he turned back to her.

"Well, Zoe, what's it going to be? Fish fry for the entire family or dinner for two tomorrow night at my place? At the rate you're catching them, you'll have a dozen in the boat in no time flat."

She flushed and ducked her head in embarrassment but her lips twitched upward in a smile. "Well, I'd hate for you to be up late cleaning more than a dozen," she said.

He chuckled. "That's generous of you, sweetheart. All right then. Three down and nine to go. You ready to go again?"

She wrinkled her nose as he put a cricket on the hook

and was careful to keep her bobber plenty distant from her body as she swung it out over the water.

"I thought people fished with worms and such. I've never heard of using crickets. Not that I'd want to touch a worm either," she said in distaste. "I'm not sure which is worse. Slimy or creepy, crawly legs." She shuddered. "How come you got the raw end of this deal anyway? I get the fun of catching them all while you get stuck baiting the hook, taking the fish off the line and cleaning them afterward."

"I assure you that at no time have I gotten a raw deal," he drawled, a smile twisting his lips. "In fact, if putting a few creepy-crawlies on a hook, taking a few slimy fish off a hook and cleaning them afterward is the price I have to pay for an afternoon with a fun, cute-as-hell woman who's made me laugh more than I've laughed in longer than I can remember, then sign me up for more."

This time she didn't look away nor did she seem to deny that anyone would think any such thing. She looked at him with honest bemusement as if she couldn't quite figure out his angle.

He took a step closer to her as he guided her line toward the spot where she'd caught the first several fish. He stopped just inches from touching her and stared down into her eyes.

"I'm not hard to figure out, Zoe," he murmured. "No games. I'm not the flirting type. If I don't mean it, I don't say it. And I never feel obligated to say shit I don't really mean just to make someone else feel better. I think it's best if we get that out of the way right now. You with me?"

She swallowed, her throat working up and down as she slowly nodded. Her gaze was full of wonder as she continued to stare back up at him, as if processing his solemn statement and measuring its sincerity.

"Yeah," she finally whispered. "I think so."

"Then you might want to catch that fish that's messing with your line," he said in amusement.

She whirled around just in time to see her bobber plunge under for the fourth time, and she hauled upward on the pole with both hands, letting out a peal of infectious laughter.

"I'm so fucked," Joe whispered to himself. "And the hell of it is, I'm loving every fucking minute of it."

CHAPTER 15

ZOE stretched lazily and yawned as the sun beat down over her, warming her muscles to the bone. She could so take a nap. She was tired in the best kind of I've-never-had-so-much-fun-in-my-life way, and the sun's rays weren't making it any easier to beat back the lethargy that had taken hold of her the minute she'd changed into the swimsuit Joe had borrowed from Rusty.

She'd been horrified when she'd figured out that the suit Rusty had given Joe was a two-piece bikini, and not a particularly modest one either. She'd kept a towel wrapped firmly around her until finally she'd picked out a place to sun herself. Only when she realized she needed the towel to lie on did she finally allow it to fall from her body as she scrambled to get down as quickly as possible.

Thankfully Joe had given her privacy, busying himself with something else, so he hadn't been witness to the debacle of her in a bikini.

Now that he was done though, it might be a better idea to roll onto her stomach so her boobs weren't falling out of her top. As soon as she'd settled back down on her stomach, she sighed as the heat slid languidly over her back.

She startled when Joe's hand came down on her bare back, and she rose, turning her head to look over her shoulder.

"Sorry to disturb you," he said. "But I don't want you to burn so I'm going to rub sunblock on your back. Just relax and go back to what you were doing. You won't even know I'm here."

She nearly snorted. On what planet would she not know he was there or that his hands would be sliding over her bare skin?

"I can do it," she said uneasily, trying to push herself up.

He put gentle pressure on her back, pushing her back down. "Unless you're an octopus or are extremely flexible, I don't see how you're going to get parts of your back. Besides, I'll need someone to do my back when I'm done with yours."

He said it so innocently, as if it were no big deal whatsoever for them to be rubbing sunblock all over each other. And maybe it wasn't to him, which meant she was just making a huge fool of herself.

With a sigh, she settled back down and closed her eyes. A few seconds later, she nearly moaned aloud when both of his palms pressed down over her skin and he began rubbing in tight, circular patterns. It had to be a crime for a man's hands to feel this good. Everywhere he touched lit up beneath his fingers as if begging and aching for more.

She was about to fidget right out of her skin and she had to bite hard into her lips to prevent sounds of pleasure from escaping her throat. This was torture. Absolute, magnificent, the most amazing torture ever concocted in the history of mankind. Thank God he wasn't asking her any questions because she'd do or say just about anything as long as he didn't stop.

He didn't appear to be in a rush, a fact she was thankful for. She closed her eyes as his hands caressed every inch of exposed skin from the sensitive skin at her nape to the soles of her feet and all parts in between.

When his fingertips massaged perilously close to the globes of her buttocks, she found herself holding her breath until spots appeared in her vision. But he continued with featherlight strokes, merely tracing the boundaries of the bikini bottom and tantalizing her mercilessly with one thought: What if that bottom weren't there?

She was nearing unconsciousness when he finally halted, and this time her moan of displeasure couldn't be held back. He chuckled softly above her but it penetrated the thick fog surrounding her as more of a whisper than a true laugh. Then she felt something else press against her shoulder. Something that felt like his . . . lips? Now she was just hallucinating. There was only so much orgasmic bliss a girl could take, after all.

"You just lie there, sweetheart. I'll put my shirt on so you don't have to worry about doing me."

"Mmmkay," she said dreamily.

Again his amused chuckle penetrated her semiconscious state, but she just smiled and drifted away on a cloud of euphoria. She could swear his fingers then sifted through the stray strands of her hair that had come undone from the messy bun, but she couldn't be bothered to open her eyes to investigate. Besides, as far as fantasies went, this one was pretty damn awesome and she had no desire for it to end anytime soon.

"I wonder if you even know how very beautiful you are," Joe whispered, his voice seemingly miles away.

Now she knew she was definitely asleep and dreaming. For once it was nice to dream about something other than fear and humiliation or to wake with her heart pounding, sweat drenching her hair.

"Never had a better dream," she murmured through unmoving lips. "Are you going to go away when I wake up?"

She heard soft laughter and then a voice that was anything but light and teasing. It was contradictory to the entire setting of the dream. It was firm and filled with gentle yet implacable resolve and sent shivers all the way to her toes.

"I'm not going anywhere, Zoe. Not now. Not ever. I'm afraid you're stuck with me, baby. I'm not sure how much you'll like that when you wake up and figure out this wasn't a dream and is all too real, but I like it a hell of a lot, *you* being stuck with *me*."

"No one ever stays," she said sadly, not liking the turn this dream had taken. She wanted the good parts back. "No one ever loves me back. Everyone always leaves."

There was a long silence and for a moment she relaxed, content to let the dream die after its not-so-great shift from really awesome to not so awesome. And then . . .

"Not this time, baby." That voice again. So achingly familiar, but then it had occupied a solid place in her dreams for the last several nights. "And that's a promise."

Even though she knew no such promise would ever be kept, it still gave her comfort and she clung to it as she drifted further into oblivion.

JOE sat a short distance away from where Zoe slept, his gaze drifting occasionally between the sun and her back, which still glistened from the sunblock he'd now applied twice. The second time he'd gently worked the lotion into her skin, she hadn't so much as stirred, but the tiny puckered frown she wore even while sleeping and the strain evident on her forehead and around her mouth instilled an ache in his chest that wouldn't be assuaged.

Who was the "everyone" she'd referred to in an almost childlike voice that had broken his heart? Her pain went beyond that of one ex-lover. What about her childhood? Donovan hadn't mentioned a family. Parents or siblings. He hadn't said anything at all, and now Joe wondered why. Was she all alone in the world? Surely Rusty knew that much about her. Perhaps it was why Rusty had befriended her and was so loyal and protective of her. He commended his sister for that, but from now on, protecting Zoe from anything that had the power to hurt her was *his* job.

He checked his watch as he watched the sun sink farther down in the sky. As much as he hated even a night's separation from her, it was getting late and she was clearly exhausted. It was time to be getting her back to his mom's for the night. She hadn't eaten much at lunch. She'd been quiet. Almost pensive while they shared the offering his mother had prepared for them. Every once in a while he managed to get a smile out of her when he teased or joked with her, but sadness had clung to her features for most of the afternoon after they'd finished catching the dozen fish he'd told her they needed.

And then she'd fallen asleep while he applied the first coat of sunblock. In her dreamlike state, her reactions had been honest and sincere. She'd greatly enjoyed his touch, arching into it like a purring kitten. But then sadness had dripped from her voice when she'd quietly told him that no one ever stayed and that no one ever loved her back.

He'd never wanted anything more in that moment than to cradle her in his arms and hold her tightly and vow to never let her go. But he knew it wouldn't be as easy as simply promising her something she had no faith in. It would take time for her to establish trust and be able to fully place it in him. And he intended to give her all the time in the world she needed until the time came that she was with him, in his arms where he intended to prove to her every single day that he wasn't going anywhere but wherever she did.

"What secrets are you hiding, baby?" he whispered as he watched her sigh and tuck her fist beneath her chin. "Will you trust me enough to share them and let me take away their power to hurt you?"

He let out a sigh and then reluctantly stood from where he'd been sprawled on the platform of the boat. He crawled over to where Zoe lay, smiling as he stared down at her closed eyes, the lashes that rested on her skin making her appear so innocent in sleep. She reminded him of an angel or one of those little pixies in fairy tales.

"Zoe. Zoe, honey. I need you to wake up. It's time to go home."

She wrinkled her nose and her lips turned downward. "G'away," she muttered.

He laughed as he lowered his head to kiss the wrinkles from her nose. Her eyelashes immediately fluttered as she came awake.

"Hi," he said, smiling at her befuddlement.

Then she smiled, and it sent warmth through regions of his heart he hadn't even realized had been so shut off before.

"Hi," she said shyly. "Is it time to go?"

She sounded so disappointed that he hated to tell her it was. Instead he nodded.

"Sun's setting. I thought you might enjoy watching the sun go down while we head back to the marina. Ma will have supper on the table soon and she'll wonder where we are."

She yawned, covering her mouth. "I had the most wonderful dream," she said wistfully.

His pulse sped up as he simply watched her, his gaze traveling over every inch of her face, her eyes, even her hair. "Oh? Did you dream about me then?" he teased.

She flushed a deep red and dropped her gaze, though a smile still hovered on her lips.

"Not going to share what this wonderful dream was about?"

She shook her head. "No. Because if I do then it might not come true."

She had his attention there. Was she referring to what she thought she'd dreamed? Or had she dreamed something else in the two hours he'd let her sleep after she'd drifted off?

"And do you want your dream to come true?" he asked casually.

Yearning was evident in her eyes as they became focused on something far away, in another time perhaps.

"If any dream could come true, then yes, more than anything I'd want this one to."

Not that he hadn't already decided his fate and course, but if he hadn't, those words would have sealed it for him. She had no idea that he knew exactly what she was referring to and that he'd been party to what she thought she'd dreamed about. And, well, in a way it was fitting since he planned to make every last part of it come true exactly as she wanted.

"Dreams come true all the time," he said.

Her smile slowly faded. "For some, I guess."

"But not for you?"

She looked away. "I'm not much of a dreamer," she said with forced nonchalance. "I'm more of a realist. When reality continually bites you on the ass, you tend to pay attention."

Joe extended his hand, sliding his thumb under her chin before gently turning her back to face him. "I don't agree."

She looked confused. "What don't you agree with?"

"That you aren't a dreamer."

Her eyes went wide and she blinked several times as if trying to figure out how she wanted to respond.

"There's nothing wrong with being a dreamer, Zoe. The bigger you dream, the bigger the outcome and the happier the ending, wouldn't you say?"

Her eyes filled with tears and she would have turned away again, but he cupped her cheeks with both palms, cradling her face in his hands. He used his thumbs to tenderly wipe away the slip of moisture that trailed down one side.

"One could also say the bigger you dream, the harder you fall when reality bites you on the ass," she choked out.

He laughed softly. "You have an obsession with reality and people's asses."

"This isn't a joke," she said in a pleading voice, as if begging him not to make light of her statements. "This is my reality. It may not be yours, Joe. But it is mine and I'm well acquainted with what dreaming gets you. In my world, it's a big fat nothing no matter how hard I wish it otherwise."

"Baby, listen to me," he said, caressing the silky skin over her cheekbones. "When I said that I believe you are a dreamer, it was the best of compliments. Just because not all your dreams have come true so far doesn't mean they're destined to *never* come true for you at all. We all have a dreamer inside us. You may not think you do, but I see her. I see you. And it just makes me all the more determined to make those dreams of yours come true so you can finally let that beautiful dreamer out for the entire world to see."

Her eyes were glazed with shock as she stared back helplessly at him. "You can't make promises like that to me, to anyone," she denied. "You aren't responsible for making anyone else's dreams come true. Only your own. Only I can make my dreams come true, and if there's one thing I've learned about myself in that area it's that I'm a huge, fat failure."

Joe let out a growl of impatience and anger, though it wasn't directed at her. She jumped and then looked at him with wounded eyes, even as she tried to shrink away from him. He cursed violently under his breath. He was coming on with the finesse of a freight train and he knew damn well she had to be handled with the utmost care, as if she were the most precious of things.

"You forget something about me, baby. I'm in the business of doing two things. Making some people's dreams come true. And making other people's nightmares come to life. So don't tell me what I can or can't do or what I can or can't take on. Because I promise you that if you let me in, if you give me the chance, I'll do my damnedest to make every single one of your dreams come true."

She swallowed hard and her lips parted in shock, and it took everything he had inside him not to haul her across the last remaining inches of distance between them and kiss her until neither could draw a breath without breathing the other's air. That was his dream right now, fuck it all. All the others could wait their damn turns.

"You don't even know me," she whispered. "Why would you even say something like that to me?"

"You're right. I don't know all of you. Yet. But I want to. I will. And when I do, then I plan to keep every last one of my promises. Now, before I finish freaking you out so badly that you jump in the lake and swim your way back to the compound, we need to get going or Ma's going to have my ass in a sling. I need you to put your life vest on and find somewhere to get comfortable for the ride back in. Okay?"

She looked dazed, and he couldn't very well blame her.

He'd rolled over her like a bulldozer and then backed off so quickly he was lucky she hadn't fallen into the lake, much less jumped. But he had to get a grip and keep himself in check before he went way too far way too damned fast and ended up letting her slip right through his fingers.

Jesus, but the mere thought of reaching out only to find her gone nearly paralyzed him with fear. He was a fucking mess and if he didn't get his shit together quick, he was going to fuck everything up before he even had a chance to prove she was safe with him. That he'd never hurt her. That he'd take apart anyone who ever fucking tried to hurt her again.

And right now, maybe the best course of action was to simply keep her off balance. If she was a little unsteady and trying to figure him out, then she couldn't run at the same time. Her running was the possibility that terrified the fucking hell out of him, when not much had ever had the power to scare him in his life. Losing his brother, losing Shea, losing his parents. Those were the only things close to the terror he felt when he thought of losing Zoe.

As soon as he navigated out of the cove where he'd anchored the boat so he and Zoe could swim and sunbathe, he opened the throttle and planed out as they roared over the smooth-as-glass water of Kentucky Lake. The sun was a giant fiery ball of orange in the west inching its way farther down the horizon, and up ahead, the twinkling lights of the marina were starting to flash on.

Zoe sat huddled on the side bench just two feet from where he stood to navigate the boat, her gaze focused sightlessly on some distant object, the strands of hair that had escaped the bun atop her head streaming behind her like splashes of moonlight.

She had a towel wrapped around her slight figure and

wore her safety jacket underneath. He should have allowed her to change back into her clothing before they headed back in, but it would have been dark by the time they set back for the marina. He could give her privacy where the truck was parked and stand on the other side of his open door with his back to her, standing guard to watch for anyone else in seeing distance.

At least now he understood the mischievous twinkle in Rusty's eyes and her innocent grin when she'd given him a bathing suit for Zoe as he'd requested. Rusty was taller and not as rounded in the places Zoe was, and as a result, Rusty's bikini, which covered her modestly enough, was too small for Zoe in places that had given him a permanent erection for the entire afternoon.

Rusty had known exactly what she was doing and precisely how the bikini would fit—or rather not fit—Zoe, and if the devious little heifer didn't think he'd get her back, she was deluded.

Once parked in his slip at the marina, he helped Zoe from the boat and then wrapped his arm around her waist, pulling her into the warmth of his body as they walked to his truck. The early summer mornings and nights still had a hint of a chill to them as spring reluctantly gave way to the hotter days of summer that lay ahead.

These were the best times of the year. Days filled with many a happy memory. Countless trips just like today. Fishing, swimming, horsing around with family, cookouts, campfires, a cooler full of beer, talking about old times and of the days ahead.

Joe had never really been able to participate in the talks of what was yet to come as his brothers looked at their wives and children with love in their eyes and spoke of raising their kids where they'd been raised. He could recount plenty of "good ole days" stories and all of the hell-raising that had been involved, but he'd always gone silent when the conversation turned to the future. Over time, as all of his brothers had finally been accounted for, he had felt an awkwardness he'd never before experienced. Like an outsider looking in at something so beautiful that it hurt his eyes to look at it. He realized now that what he'd felt was loneliness. And envy for what his brothers had that he didn't.

He glanced over at Zoe as he opened his passenger door for her. Who knew such a short time ago that his future would right now be standing beside him and that for the first time he'd truly understand and be able to relate to everything his brothers talked about, shared and related.

"Stand on the other side of the door and I'll turn my back and shield the opening in the doorway so that no one can see you change," he said. "Not that anyone's around that I can see, but just in case, I promise you they won't see a thing. Just hurry before I'm tempted to peek," he teased.

To his surprise and delight she responded by laughing. "You're incorrigible, Joe. But then Marlene said as much. She said you were the evil twin, always into mischief, and that Nathan was the quieter one. I see now what she means."

He gasped in mock outrage and indignation. "I'll have you know that I'm considered the sensitive twin. Nathan's just a caveman with no manners. Did you see how he is with my poor sister-in-law Shea?"

"Yeah," she said in a wistful voice. "It's obvious he loves her a lot. I loved watching them together."

Joe's eyebrow went up. He hadn't realized that she had been watching any one person or couple in particular at the cookout or that she'd even been able to sort through the haphazard introductions to make the connections between names and faces, but it was obvious that Nathan and Shea had at least caught her attention and that she'd spent a lot of time studying them.

"They have a pretty amazing story," he said softly.

"Oh? What do you mean?" she asked eagerly.

He smiled to himself. His Zoe was a romantic. Good to know. At least now he knew a way of winning points in his favor down the road.

"It's a long story, and it's not always pretty. But it's definitely always beautiful."

"Wow," she breathed. "That was beautiful, Joe."

His brow furrowed in confusion. "What do you mean?"

"The way you put it. The way you described it. It was very poetic." There was quiet yearning in her voice, as if she'd always wanted someone to speak to her in such a way.

It took him a moment to realize what she meant and then he smiled. "As much as I'd like to take credit for my philosophical side, I have to confess that I gave no forethought to the wording of that statement."

"That's what makes it all the more beautiful," she said pointedly. "But what did you mean exactly, when you said it wasn't always pretty. Did they argue a lot or something?"

As she said the last, she tapped him on the shoulder to let him know she was finished, and he turned around, smiling down at her. "No, baby. I don't know that I've ever seen them actually argue. Well, unless Nathan is worried that something she's doing is going to be too hard on her."

"Do you know your entire face lights up when you talk about them?" Zoe asked quietly.

He smiled again. "Yeah, I guess it does. You have to understand. Nathan is my twin. We share something most people don't understand. But Shea gets it because she's a part of it. I'll tell you all about it sometime. I promise. But as I said, it's a long story and parts of it are definitely not for the faint of heart. But it was always going to be a happily-ever-after ending. Nathan wouldn't have had it any other way. It just took them a little longer to get there than others. But if I had to guess, it's all the more sweet for just that reason."

"Do you ever listen to yourself?" she asked as they both closed their doors after climbing into the truck. "You have the most eloquent way of phrasing things. I could spend hours just listening to you talk."

He reared his head back in surprise. He stared at her a long moment before he realized she was absolutely serious. Then he laughed. He laughed so hard that he put his arms over the steering wheel and then laid his forehead down on top of them and wheezed until his sides hurt.

Zoe made a sound of exasperation. "What?" she demanded. "What's wrong with you? I take it back. You talk like a jerk."

She made a huffing sound and crossed her arms over her chest, glaring at him from her periphery.

"I'm sorry, sweetheart," he said, still trying to contain his laughter. "You have to understand that according to the rest of my brothers I'm impatient, short tempered and foul tempered to boot. Not to mention foulmouthed. Hmm, they like the word *foul* a lot when it comes to describing me," he said with a grin in her direction. "If they heard you describe anything having to do with me as being eloquent or, God forbid, beautiful, they'd laugh themselves silly. Hell, they'd probably piss themselves from laughing so hard."

"Well, they sound like jerks," Zoe said darkly.

Warmth spread through his chest and slid up his neck until it gripped him fiercely right around the throat. No one had ever defended him to his brothers. Everyone was usually too busy agreeing with his brothers' assessment of him to ever offer any disagreement. And yet Zoe looked like she wanted to wade in and kick their asses for insulting him.

"Don't hurt anyone, honey." He chuckled. "In their defense, I *am* all of that. Well, most of the time. I seem to make exceptions for really beautiful women named Zoe."

She ducked her head and loosened her arms until her hands fell into her lap. She stared down at them for a long moment before she cocked her head to study him once more.

"I forget what you do most of the time."

His smile and ready laughter faded as he tensed.

"How hard it must be to protect and defend people you don't even know at such a great risk to yourself. I'd be shocked if you weren't all those things your brothers call you. But that *isn't* who you are. I haven't seen that person even once. I think I've figured out your little secret, Joe Kelly."

He looked at her in horror. "You're not going to expose me, are you?"

"What you are is a nice guy. A tough guy outside and a completely gooey, mushy softy on the inside."

He damn near choked. He covered his reaction with a cough and then cleared his throat. A softy? Oh wait, not just a softy. It was way worse. A "gooey, mushy" softy. Sweet mother of God. If he thought he was going to get shit from his brothers before, that was nothing compared to the way he'd be laughed right out of the war room if it ever got out that Zoe called him a "gooey, mushy softy."

His expression must have been as appalled as he felt because she burst into laughter and proceeded to laugh so hard that she was wiping tears from her cheeks.

"Oh God, if you could just see your face," she sputtered and choked out.

"Yeah, yeah, have your fun. Kick a man when he's down," he grumbled good-naturedly. "We'll see who has the last laugh."

"Do they also call you a bad sport?" she teased.

"Definitely."

She cracked up again. "No! I can't imagine why."

"Sarcasm doesn't suit you, pretty lady."

"I think it suits me just fine," she said cheekily.

Well, she had him there, but then everything suited her just fine. He couldn't think of a single thing that wouldn't suit her.

"Oh, here we are," she said, sounding surprised—and a little disappointed—as they drove into the compound.

He well understood the feeling. Today had been one of the best days he could ever remember. It was right up there with the day he learned his twin was finally safe and coming home when it wasn't known if Nathan was dead or alive. Or the day when a badly traumatized Shea had finally returned to them after days of being withdrawn completely into herself as the only way she'd survived the worst.

He frowned. Until now, all the best times he could remember revolved around either Nathan and Shea or his other brothers and memorable moments with their wives. Never before had he had anyone to share those kinds of moments with. Until now.

He gazed lovingly at her as he parked in front of his mother's house, knowing she wouldn't see how he was looking at her. She was too busy glancing up at the porch like she expected his mom or dad to walk out at any moment.

"Zoe."

She turned to look up at him. He touched a tendril of hair, tenderly pulling it away from her cheek to tuck behind her ear.

"Thank you for today," he said, brushing his thumb over her chin and jaw.

She looked inquisitively at him. "Shouldn't that be my line?"

"Not unless you're me and you just had one of the best days of your life for the second day in a row," he said with no hint of teasing or jest in his tone.

Her gaze softened and for a moment he saw so much want and need, so much yearning in her eyes, that it was like a punch to the stomach. No longer could he resist the temptation of her pull. Slowly he closed the distance between them in the cab of the truck. He cupped her jaw in his palm, tilting her head in just the right position for her to take his kiss.

He said nothing for fear of breaking the spell. Instead he gently pressed his lips to hers. He swallowed up her breathy sigh, sucking it deep into his lungs, savoring it before reluctantly expelling it once more. He lapped slowly over the surface of her lips, tasting every centimeter, leaving no part untouched or untasted. Then he became a little bolder, flicking his tongue forward, asking her to let him in even as he continued his gentle assault on her mouth.

She gasped, her lips parting and another breathy-sounding noise, almost like a tiny sob, disappeared into his mouth as he slid his tongue inside, rubbing sensuously over hers. Touching, retreating, performing a delicate dance. Careful not to batter her senses or overwhelm her, he merely continued to pour every bit of his love and desire into one precious kiss.

Then suddenly she yanked away, tears filling her eyes as she stared back at him. Grief shone in her gaze. Grief? *What the fuck?*

"I'm sorry, Joe. God, I'm so sorry," she said with an agonized cry. "I didn't mean to lead you on. I know I sent mixed signals. But we can't do this. *I* can't," she whispered in a tortured voice. "Oh God, don't you see?"

"No, I don't see," he said in the most gentle tone he could muster when he was raging on the inside at the blame she was heaping on herself. Misplaced and misdirected blame!

"You deserve so much better than someone like me," she said, tears now streaming down her face. "Please, we have to forget this ever happened."

He almost snorted. Like that was going to happen. And what the fuck kind of bullshit was she spouting about him deserving so much better? He wanted to put his fist through the fucking glass he was so enraged at how a pathetic excuse of a human being could ever tear down a woman as sweet and vulnerable and beautiful as Zoe. He wanted to kill the son of a bitch!

"I'm sorry," she whispered again.

Before he could collect himself and trust himself to speak without roaring and scaring her to death, she flung her door open and jumped down and was gone, leaving him sitting in the truck, staring in frustration, as she ran into the house.

He sat there for a long moment before he realized Rusty had come outside and was now standing at his window waiting for him to acknowledge her.

He quickly rolled it down, and she gave him a look filled with sympathy and answering pain.

"Mom has her," she said quietly before he could demand the answer.

He pounded his fist on the steering wheel and swore viciously. Then he let his hand fall and gave his sister a remorseful look.

"Don't you dare apologize for something I've done myself more than once since I saw Zoe again." Rusty glowered at him.

"What the fuck did he do, Rusty? And don't give me that bullshit answer you gave me before. I'm losing her just after I gained so much ground with her today. I kissed her, and she freaked out. Started apologizing and saying I deserved so much better. What the fuck kind of bullshit is that?"

Rusty's lips trembled and sorrow filled her eyes. "It isn't my story to tell, Joe. Even if I had the whole story. You can't ask me to betray Zoe when everyone else in her life has. I can't do that to her. It would destroy her."

He sighed. "No, of course you can't, honey. I'm sorry. I'm just so frustrated. I can't lose her. I won't lose her," he said more emphatically.

She smiled. "If you sat back and did nothing, then what kind of sorry-ass Kelly would you be?"

"Damn straight," he growled. "Look. She needs you right now. Be a good friend to her, Rusty. I won't ask you to betray that. But damn it, I don't care what you have to say to her or tell her, you make sure she doesn't start hiding from me. We have a date tomorrow night. I'm cooking for her at my place and I expect you to have her ready to go by the time I get here. Can I trust you with her?"

She reached up and covered his arm with her hand. He then took her hand and squeezed affectionately.

"I'll have her ready to go. You just be here when you said you would and leave the rest to me. Okay?"

"I'm trusting you with my future, Rusty," he said quietly. "She's everything to me. You understand that?"

Her smile was oddly sad. "I understand all too well what happens when a Kelly man decides a woman is his. It's too bad the rest of the male population can't take their cues from you. Don't worry, Joe. I'll call you if anything comes up. In the meantime, leave us girls to have our girl time. I'll have her talked around by tomorrow, and then it's up to you."

Then her expression grew serious and she looked him directly in the eyes. "It's not going to be easy, Joe. I hope you know that, and I hope you're prepared for it. You don't live your life under a pile of shit and then have someone dig you out and convince you all in a day that you smell like a rose garden. You're going to have to have patience with her and handle her very carefully."

"You do have a way with words, little sister," he said, shaking his head. Then he snorted. "A rose garden. I've got to remember that one."

She laughed, but the sadness in her eyes still bothered him because he had a feeling what he saw had nothing to do with Zoe and everything to do with something that was making his baby sister look defeated. Because *defeat* was not ever a word used in context with Rusty Kelly.

Until now.

CHAPTER 16

ZOE sat huddled against the headboard of Rusty's bed, knees drawn up to her chest, her arms wrapped tightly around her legs as she rested her chin atop them. She was so embarrassed, and she had only herself to blame after making such a spectacle when Joe had kissed her.

Okay, so it wasn't *just* because he kissed her. It was the *way* he kissed her. It was the promise of love and forever in his kiss that had sliced her open and prompted her meltdown. Here was a guy putting it all on the table, not holding anything back. Everything she'd ever dreamed of in a man, only now she'd found it too damn late to make any difference. There'd been nothing but honesty and sincerity in his kiss, his words and even his actions. No deception or lies. No, that was all her doing. Those things were coming from her and it broke her heart.

Joe was one of the *good* guys. A rare breed she wasn't even sure existed anymore outside of fairy tales and urban legends. He was too *much* of a good guy. Too good for the likes of her and her ilk. Too good to be tainted by her legacy of crime, murder and corruption. Although taking her father's empire down might look good on KGI's résumé.

The hysterical thought rose and died just as quickly as it welled. Tears burned her eyelids and she closed her eyes, refusing to cry any more for all she'd never had and never would. It was fine before when she didn't know what she was missing. Didn't know that what she fantasized about wasn't a mere fantasy but an actual flesh and blood man. A man who seemed interested in her. In Zoe Kildare. And that was the problem. As much as Zoe liked to declare that Stella Huntington was a woman who no longer existed, had never existed, Zoe Kildare was the fictional character. Not Stella. Zoe had no birth certificate. No past beyond what Rusty had fabricated, no matter how expertly it had been done. Zoe was just Stella's imaginary friend, a result of her pathetic, lonely childhood and her refusal to accept reality. Maybe if she'd gotten a good grip on what was real a hell of a lot earlier in life, she wouldn't be such a naïve, clueless twit as an adult. Gullible. That about covered all the bases in a single word. She had to be the most gullible woman on earth.

"Sister, if you beat up on yourself any harder, you're going to have bruises tomorrow," Rusty said as she plopped onto the bed beside her.

"I'm an idiot, Rusty."

To her horror, a fresh torrent of tears welled in her eyes as she spoke.

Rusty wrapped both arms around her and hugged her fiercely. Zoe held on to her as tears slid soundlessly down her cheeks.

"I'm so stupid," she whispered. "I wanted—want—what I can't have so badly it hurts."

Rusty pushed away from her and stared hard, her features drawn into a fierce expression. "Why on earth would you say a dumb thing like that? Do you think he's better than you, Zoe? Do you think this family is better than you? That *I'm* better than you? For fuck's sake, listen to yourself. You know what I came from. The things I did. The things I had to do. How is that worse than your situation? You've done *nothing* except be born to the wrong people, and if that's a crime, then lock me and a hell of a lot of other people up right now and throw away the damn keys."

"My entire life—identity—is a complete lie," Zoe said earnestly. "I've lied to your *entire* family. To *Joe*. Do you honestly think he'd just shrug and say *oh well* if he knew that everything he knows about me, that everything I've told him, is nothing but a fabrication? *I* don't even know who I am right now, so how can I expect someone else to want someone who doesn't even exist?"

Rusty's smile was soft and full of understanding and compassion. "Because that's what love is all about. Love is what's there in the absence of proof. Love doesn't require evidence, and if it does, then it's a fucked-up aberration of love, and personally I wouldn't want anything to do with it. Besides, you didn't lie about what matters. You've never lied about who you are *today*. Right now. Who you were when you stepped into this house. You've been the person you always were but was never *allowed* to be. How is that wrong? I'll tell you what's wrong. It's the people who never allowed you to be anything except the person they wanted to make you into. That's fucked-up, Zoe. You wanting to be free of all that shit, free to be your own person and above all free to be happy, is *not* fucked-up. It's real, it's good, it's precious and it's right. You'll never persuade me differently. You'd never persuade a single person in this family any differently, and it damn sure wouldn't change the way my brother looks at you. Don't you get it yet? You're *loved*, Zoe. *You.* Not the pretend Stella. Not the person you think you are. The real *you.* How much more real do you want to get?"

Zoe went quiet and then frowned as she processed Rusty's impassioned statement. "You act like me lying about who and what I am to everyone in your family and especially Joe is no big deal."

Rusty sighed. "It's only a big deal because you've *made* it one, honey."

Zoe stared at her friend in utter bewilderment. "What do you suggest I do then? Tell Joe the truth?"

She blurted the question that she'd been burning to ask, but she wasn't prepared for Rusty's calm, measured response.

"That's exactly what I think you should do."

"What? Are you *insane*? How does that solve anything? Do you think I want to involve anyone else in the mess that is my life? I don't want him or anyone in your family to get hurt because of me," she burst out.

"Honey, I am not demeaning your situation whatsoever when I say this, but after all I've told you about what my brothers do on an everyday basis, do you think this would even register as a blip on their radar? Do you think hiding for the rest of your life, having no friends, no family, no chance at love, is any real solution to the threat against you? They could help you," Rusty said quietly. "They absolutely *would* help you. And isn't that what you want? For the situation to be resolved so you can sleep at night without worrying if you'll die the next day or never see the next day? Is this the way you want to continue?"

"Of course not," Zoe said, a sob bubbling up from her chest.

She buried her face in her hands, wiping helplessly at the tears sliding down her cheeks.

Rusty's arms went around her once more as the two women hugged in silence. Zoe buried her face in Rusty's shoulder as her body shook with subdued sobs. Rusty stroked her hair, offering comfort and support as Zoe slowly pulled herself together. When the sobs quieted, Zoe pulled back, her hands shaking as she met Rusty's earnest, sympathetic gaze.

"I don't know what to do," she admitted. "I'm so tired, Rusty. Being here with you and your family has been hell for me. The best sort of heaven and the worst kind of hell all at the same time, and it's exhausting. It's like being taunted with everything I ever wanted but can never have."

"Answer me honestly," Rusty said, pinning her with her gaze. "Do you care about Joe? Could you see yourself loving him? And don't offer me reasons why you shouldn't or reasons why you can't. I'm only interested in hearing your honest, heartfelt response."

For a moment, Zoe was paralyzed and unable to formulate a single word. Her lips felt numb and frozen. She closed her eyes and finally whispered what she'd desperately tried not to allow herself to feel but had failed miserably. "I already do love him."

When she opened her eyes, Rusty was smiling at her through her own tears. She squeezed Zoe's hands in hers as a single tear slipped down her cheek.

"Then I think you have your answer. Are you going to give up any chance you have at a happy life with the man you love because you're afraid of all the what-ifs? Or are you going to get off your ass and take a chance and lay it all on the line?"

"You really think I should just . . . tell him? *Everything?*" Zoe asked uneasily.

"Every single word. From your father right down to the shithead Sebastian. Not only can he and my other brothers help you, but honey, they *will* help you. Even if you meant nothing to Joe, and that's clearly *not* the case, they would still help you. It's who they are and what they do."

"You make it sound so easy," Zoe said miserably.

"It is," Rusty said. "It's only hard if you make it difficult. But honey, listen to me. Joe loves you. That much is clear to anyone who has eyeballs. He's going to swear a blue streak and make all kinds of threats against humanity, but listen to me. None of his anger and rage will be directed at you. He'll want to storm off and go kick the ever-loving shit out of Sebastian and then go stomp all over your father, and I'm sure my other brothers will have to sit on him—that is, after they've stopped making their own threats against everyone who's ever wronged you. But he'll be so freaking thrilled that you trusted him and that you gave him that last part of you he knows he doesn't have yet."

"You sound so sure," Zoe said doubtfully.

"I am!" she said in exasperation. "Do you want me to write it out in blood? Or maybe we should make a blood pact between us."

Zoe laughed. "Only if it includes whatever the latest development is between you and a certain hot sheriff named Sean Cameron."

Rusty's expression became murderous, but behind the anger was so much hurt that Zoe winced at the raw emotion flaring in her friend's eyes.

"What happened?" Zoe asked softly.

Rusty sighed and then flopped backward onto the bed, spreading her arms outward.

"He's making me crazy. I told you about The Kiss."

"Yeah."

"Well, ever since The Kiss, he's spared no opportunity to put as much distance between me and him as possible.

The length he goes to to avoid me is ridiculous, not to mention childish and beneath a grown-ass man who's an elected sheriff."

Zoe frowned. "It didn't seem to me like he was avoiding you at the barbecue. In fact, it looked like you were the one doing the avoiding."

"Yeah, well, that's because all of a sudden he stopped avoiding me and I was merely giving him a dose of his own medicine. Turns out he doesn't like it very much. Imagine that."

Zoe burst out laughing. "Oh, I get it. So you'll jump all over me about sacrificing my wants and desires out of misplaced guilt, but you're sacrificing your wants and desires out of petty revenge?"

"It's a good enough reason." Rusty sniffed.

"Okay, I'll give you that one. He *has* been an ass ever since The Kiss."

"Damn straight."

"So, when are you going to let him off the hook?"

Rusty lifted herself up to prop up on her elbows. "Huh? Who said I was doing any such thing?"

Zoe rolled her eyes. "Come on, girlfriend. Like you haven't had serious fantasies about 'the copper' ever since you were a teenager?"

Rusty flushed and ducked her gaze. "I seriously regret ever telling you just how long I've had this stupid crush on Sean," she muttered.

"Crush? I'd think you were well beyond that stage by now," Zoe said gently. "Admit it. You're in love with him."

Rusty grimaced. "You ever tell anyone that and I'll kill you myself. Joe may never forgive me, but I can live with that."

"It seems to me that you need a dose of your own medicine," Zoe pointed out.

"What's that supposed to mean?" Rusty grumbled.

"You're over here giving me advice on not letting go of love and just putting it all on the line. So take your own advice. He's decided to stop avoiding you. Aren't you curious as to why? Stop avoiding him and confront him in a place at a time where he can't possibly back away from you and lay it out. Don't take no for an answer or let him dodge the question. What have you got to lose?"

"Everything," Rusty said softly. "Right now I can imagine all kinds of reasons why he's avoided me at every turn after giving me the most scorching, toe-curling kiss of my life. But imagining and knowing are two different things. What if he doesn't feel the same way about me?"

"I'd like to point out here that you may think you know how Joe feels but we don't know for sure, and yet you want me to put everything out there and risk getting shot down. And that's what you're afraid of, isn't it? Him shooting you down."

"Bingo," Rusty said, her voice so low Zoe could barely hear her.

"I get it," she said, reaching for Rusty's hand. "But wouldn't you rather know one way or the other? That way if he does give you the brush-off then you can close that door for good. Move on with your life and get over him and find someone who will appreciate you for the wonderfully awesome, insanely intelligent, beautiful woman you are."

"It's hard to imagine ever feeling for another man what I feel for Sean," Rusty said, tears forming in her eyes again. "Oh God, Zoe. If he rejects me again, it'll crush me, and nothing has *ever* been able to crush me and keep me down in my life. Not my bitch of a mother. Not my shithead of a stepfather. None of the other assholes who tried to take advantage of a barely teenaged girl. But him rejecting me *could*."

"What do you plan to do if you *don't* confront him? Make

him talk to you and make him acknowledge you?" Zoe asked sympathetically.

"Grow old, become a cat lady, paper the entire property with 'no trespassing' signs and run everyone off my property with a shotgun," Rusty mumbled.

Zoe snorted. "You're way too young and far too smart, talented and gorgeous for that. No man's worth that kind of life."

Rusty sighed. "You're right. I know you're right. As much as it pains me to admit that, since I'm the one who's supposed to be on your ass about shit like this."

"Then maybe we both ought to put it all on the line, and if we both get shot down then we can become old cat ladies together, but I'll leave the handling of trespassers and the shotgun to you."

Rusty burst out laughing even as she wiped a stray tear from her cheek. "God, I love you, Zoe. You honestly are the sister I never had but always wanted. And I have a gazillion sisters-in-law, not to mention all of Mama Kelly's adoptees, and I love them all dearly, but I could never share with them everything I've shared with you."

"Same goes for me," Zoe said quietly. "I love you, Rusty, and no matter what happens with Joe, you'll always be my sister in my heart. I hope you know that."

Rusty leaned up and the two women hugged again, just holding tightly to each other.

"So . . . about Sean?" Zoe ventured.

Rusty sighed. "I'll make you a deal. You go to dinner with Joe as planned tomorrow night and tell him everything. Sean works tomorrow night; however, I happen to know how to get into his house. His security system is total shit considering he's a cop. And maybe I'll just be waiting on him when he gets home after work."

Zoe's eyes widened. "Seriously?"

Rusty nodded. "I can't let you one-up me. We sisters have to go for the gusto. Go get our man. Or some other schmaltzy saying like that. If I sit around and wait on Sean's stubborn ass, I *will* end up growing old with only dozens of cats to keep me company."

"No matter where I am, what I'm doing or who I'm with, you have to swear to call me the minute it's done with Sean," Zoe said adamantly.

"Same goes for you after you spill to Joe. Deal?"

Zoe smiled and then hugged Rusty one last time. "It's a deal, sister. I love you, you know."

Rusty smiled. "Back atcha, Zoe. If we're lucky, Joe and Sean will never know what hit them."

But doubt—and fear—were both reflected in their eyes as they drew away.

CHAPTER 17

"SHE'S here!" Shea Kelly squealed as she dashed for the door.

Nathan shook his head, smiling as he followed his wife to greet her sister Grace; Grace's husband, Rio; and their adopted teenage daughter, Elizabeth. Though the two sisters could speak telepathically at will, on a daily basis, they didn't see each other in person all that often because Rio lived in Belize in a fortified compound, away from the prying eyes of the public. More importantly, off the government's radar, since Grace had been declared dead a few years earlier.

When he got to the door, he saw Shea and Grace in a mad hugging marathon while Rio stood to the side with an amused look on his face. Rio exchanged glances with Elizabeth and then they both rolled their eyes.

"Hey, man," Nathan called out as he ambled down the steps of the porch. "Hey, Elizabeth. God, girl, look at you! I swear, every time I see you it's like looking at a stranger.

Rio, are you sure you don't need a team assigned to you just for her protection? You probably have a boy problem around the clock."

Elizabeth blushed, but she looked pleased with Nathan's teasing compliment.

Rio put his arm around his daughter's neck and hauled her into his side in a headlock. "I've had to kill two just this week," he growled. "Pretty soon I'm going to need a new dumping sight if she keeps attracting them like flies."

"Da-ad!" she complained, drawing the word out into two whiny syllables.

Rio grinned at her but Nathan didn't miss the warmth that entered his eyes at her manner of address. Elizabeth had been left an orphan at twelve after her father, the ruthless head of a worldwide criminal empire, had been killed by the same man who'd kidnapped Grace so she could heal Elizabeth, who at the time was dying from a pervasive form of cancer.

It had taken time and Rio and Grace's constant, unwavering love for Elizabeth to adjust and come to terms with what her father was, her own guilt and the worry that Rio and Grace couldn't possibly love her after her father had nearly caused both of their deaths. For a few years after they had taken her in, she had always called them by their first names. And then one year earlier while eating dinner, she had quietly asked Rio if he minded if she called him Dad.

Grace had sent Elizabeth a tearful, knowing look, as the two had discussed Rio's probable reaction earlier in the day when she had first approached Grace about calling her Mom. Rio had later confided in his KGI teammates that next to the day Grace had become his, it was the single best day of his life.

Finally, the sisters pulled away, both wiping tears from

their faces. Nathan winced, because even though it was obvious the tears were of joy, he hated to see Shea cry. It was a well-known fact he was useless if she shed so much as one tear. A lot of women would take advantage of that, but Shea didn't. But then she didn't have to resort to manipulation to get what she wanted. Nathan would give her the moon if she asked.

"Hello, Nathan," Grace said, moving in to hug him as Shea exchanged hugs with Rio. "I'm so glad you're taking such good care of Shea."

"More like she takes care of me," Nathan said with a grin. "But I'm happy to take the credit."

Grace laughed.

"You ready to shove off?" Rio asked Nathan.

Nathan nodded and pulled Shea into his arms. "You girls have fun. We won't be long. Standard meeting and check-in."

Grace, Elizabeth and Shea waved as Nathan jumped in with Rio and the two drove the short distance from Nathan's house to the war room.

Shea dropped her hand then turned to her sister and niece. "Come on in, you two. We have so much to catch up on. I don't see you two enough."

Grace smiled. In fact, she was all but beaming. And glowing like a star. She looked like she'd swallowed the sunshine and her smile was so happy that tears pricked Shea's eyelids. Not so long ago the two sisters had been desperate and running for their lives, unsure if they'd ever see each other again. Now everything was perfect.

They plopped down on the couch and Shea bit her lip to suppress her own goofy grin. Sometimes? Life just kept getting better. She peeked up at Grace to see Grace looking kind of funny at her. Shea licked her lips just as Grace's lips parted.

"I—"

"Have—"

"News!"

Both women stopped then stared back at each other in shock and then they burst into laughter. Elizabeth rolled her eyes, but Shea noticed how close she stayed to Grace and the fact that she'd slipped her hand into Grace's and held it tightly.

"Okay, so we both obviously have news," Shea said as she finally gained her composure. "You go first."

Grace was fidgeting with excitement. She glanced at Elizabeth, and Elizabeth gave her an encouraging smile. Grace's return smile was soft and full of love. Then she turned glowing eyes on Shea.

"I'm pregnant," Grace said in a tear-clogged voice.

Shea's mouth dropped open. "Are you serious? Really?"

"Really!"

Shea fell back on the couch, holding her stomach as she laughed. She struggled to right herself but was wheezing when she tried to say something.

She wiped her eyes with the back of her hand and grinned like a fool over at Grace and Elizabeth. Then she shook her head. "It would seem we really do share everything. I'm pregnant too," she confessed shyly.

Grace looked thunderstruck. Elizabeth squealed and dove for Shea, latching on to her and hugging as she shook with excitement.

"Oh my God! Two babies!" Elizabeth said, clapping her hands when she pulled away from Shea.

"Shea?" Grace asked in a concerned voice. "Are you happy about this? I thought you and Nathan were waiting awhile."

Shea sent her a smile that couldn't be construed as anything short of absolute delirium. "We did wait, silly. It's just that in the past several months, we've started talking about it. It's something Nathan wants more than anything, but I think he's worried about pressuring me and that it's not what I want, so he doesn't say much about it *now*."

"So you being you, you took matters into your own hands," Grace said dryly.

Shea grinned. "If we waited around on our men to get things done, we'd wait forever."

Grace sighed. "This is true. So you're happy, Shea? Really happy? And this is what you want?"

"Oh, yeah," Shea breathed. "It's been a regular baby factory around here the last few years. I swear I'm the only one who hasn't been popping babies out. But one thing I have noticed is that it does seem to be catching. I wouldn't be surprised if there wasn't a sudden rash of pregnancies in all the wives. Maren's already pregnant, so we can blame it on her if anyone tries to blame us for an oops baby."

Grace sucked in her breath. "She is? Oh, that's wonderful! Steele with two babies. God, I have to have a picture of that."

"You and me both." Shea giggled. "Nathan said he was all out of sorts the day he found out. Said he was freaking out at a KGI meeting."

Grace smothered her laughter with a hand. "Poor guy. Oh well, this is Rio's first rodeo, so that should take the heat off the Ice Man. They'll have fresh blood to torment now that Rio will be drowning in diapers and bottles and sleepless nights. Maybe I shouldn't tell him for a while. That would keep everyone off his case for a few extra weeks anyway, right?"

Shea held up her hand. "Whoa. Wait a minute. He doesn't know? You haven't told him?"

Grace made a face. "I only just found out. Yes, I could

have told Rio before we left the house in Belize, but if I had, he probably wouldn't have let me come. In fact, he'd likely keep me under strict lock and key for the duration of my pregnancy."

"He so would too," Elizabeth muttered.

The two women laughed.

"Well, I haven't told Nathan either, but I only found out this morning and didn't want to tell him two minutes before you guys got here and then shove him out the door. The poor man wouldn't be able to remember his own name after news like that."

Grace nodded. "This is true. So I guess we'll both be giving our husbands some news tonight, huh?"

"Looks that way," Shea said with a grin.

Grace smiled at her, tears shimmering in her eyes. "I can't believe we get to share this. I can't think of anything more perfect."

JOE strode into the war room hoping no one looked too closely at him. He looked—and felt—like shit. He hadn't slept worth a fuck the previous night despite gaining Rusty's assurance that Zoe would be at his house tonight. He was too focused on the one hundred and one other things that could go wrong, resulting in him not having a chance in hell with Zoe.

A day ago he would have said he was only two inches from pathetic. Today? He'd long since surpassed *pathetic* and gone straight to *desperate*.

He nodded at his older brothers but didn't stop to talk as he made his way to where his team was standing.

"Hey, hold up a sec," Donovan called.

Joe stopped and turned around to see Donovan jog to

catch up with him. He had a concerned look on his face. *Fuck.*

"What's up, Van?" he asked lightly.

Donovan's eyes narrowed in a don't-feed-me-that-line-of-bullshit manner. "Everything okay with Zoe?" he asked, lowering his voice so they weren't overheard. Joe appreciated that at least.

"I don't know. Yet," Joe added. "I'm getting there, though. I should know what I need to know tonight," he added vaguely.

Donovan frowned, studying his younger brother a long moment. "Anything I can do?"

Joe sighed. "Did you dig anything up on her family? Parents? Siblings? That sort of thing? You didn't mention them so I assumed she didn't have any, but I didn't verify that with you."

Donovan slowly shook his head. "She was an only child. According to my report, her parents died in a car accident when she was seventeen years old. Didn't find anything about foster care, but it's not unusual for a seventeen-year-old to be emancipated by virtue of being ignored instead of a court order. Could be she didn't pursue help and just went it alone. The hell of it is, she was likely smarter to do that. There are a lot of great foster care providers out there, but there are also a fuck ton of leeches in it for the check every month too. It appears she was smart and resourceful and made it on her own. She has grit, and that's admirable."

"She shouldn't have had to go it alone for so fucking long," Joe said around his tightly clenched jaw. "Admirable or not, it sucks not to have anyone to lean on or be there to help pick you up if you fall."

"You planning to be that person in the future?" Donovan asked casually.

"Bet your ass, I am," he snapped.

Then he realized just how neatly his brother had baited the trap and how quickly he'd fallen right into it. He scowled darkly at Donovan and stepped into his space, his finger up and pointing.

"You say one fucking word or smile even one fucking smug smile and I'll rearrange that smile for you," Joe growled. "Furthermore, you say shit to anyone, and that includes the other clowns I call brother, and it gets back to Zoe or it causes a problem for her, then there's going to be a serious problem between you and me. The last thing I need right now is yet another reason for her to push me away, not let me in or run the hell as fast and as far away from me and everyone here as possible. You got me?"

Donovan barely managed to stifle his laughter but it was there, gleaming in his green eyes. But instead of needling Joe any further, he surprised him by dropping the smirk and adopting a look of complete seriousness.

"Meant what I said, man. You need anything, anything at all. Don't care what time of day it is, where I am or where you are, you call me. I'll be one pissed-off big brother you ignore me on this. We clear?"

Joe nodded, not trusting himself to speak around the knot in his throat.

"How'd you get Eve to trust you? In the beginning, I mean," he said when he'd regained his composure.

Donovan's gaze softened at the mention of his wife. "I didn't give her any choice," he admitted. "I was an ass, if you want to know the truth. But I was a desperate ass. She was going to—hell, what am I saying—she *was* running. From me, from everyone else. And there wasn't a damn thing I could do about it other than to press my advantage and use every tool available to me, including coercion and manipulation."

He winced but continued on. "Not proud of the way I handled it, but neither do I regret it, because however I accomplished my goal, Eve is here. Travis and Cammie are here. Safe. Loved. Taken care of. Not out there still running or, God forbid, if her bastard stepfather hadn't been taken out and she were still on the run, she could, right this minute, be in his hands, under his control." Donovan shuddered, his eyes going dark with anger and . . . stark fear and pain. "So no, I don't have any regrets, because at the end of the day, they're all safe. Sometimes . . . well, it has to be said. Sometimes the caveman approach really does work the best."

Joe burst into laughter. "This is rich. You, who always lectured me and the rest of our brothers on the correct way to treat a woman. Who was always critical of our caveman, knuckles-dragging-the-ground methods and the fact that we weren't sensitive enough to women's needs. And now suddenly when it's your woman we're talking about, you're practically beating your chest while grunting and growling *my woman*. I'm surprised you don't drag her around by the hair. Or that you allow me and the rest of the men in the family to even look at her, much less talk to her."

Donovan shot him a disgruntled look. "I may have strongly considered not letting any of my boneheaded brothers so much as breathe the same air as my wife, but she informed me that my Neanderthal thinking, however endearing, simply wouldn't fly with her. And then she threatened to withhold sex from me until I saw the error of my ways."

Joe choked and sputtered, his eyes watering as he hooted with laughter. He pictured quiet and sweet Evie glaring at Donovan and refusing to have sex with him, and he doubled over, holding his stomach as he howled.

"You mock my pain," Donovan said in a wounded voice. "Just wait, Mr. Sensitive. Your time is coming. Laugh it up now. Enjoy it while you have the chance. Your time is so limited it's not even funny. The hell of it is you won't mind one fucking bit. You'll be walking around meek and ball-less with a big ole smile on your face, swearing you love it."

Joe grinned. "As long as the right woman is in possession of my balls, then nope, I won't mind one damned bit."

Donovan's lips twitched and he slapped him on the back, ending the torture session. "Jesus, man, you take all the fun out of mocking you into oblivion. Geesh. You're pathetic. You were supposed to be more of a challenge than this. It was your duty as last man standing."

Joe gave him a two-finger salute and then joined his team, who were all looking at him strangely. Except Nathan, who knew all too well how much his twin's life was changing—had already changed. He sighed. He only prayed he'd be able to make an announcement to his team soon. That would mean that Zoe was on board and that his relationship with her was a sure thing.

"Everything okay?" Nathan asked under his breath.

Joe sighed and ran his hand through his hair. "Yeah. I think so. I hope so. Hell, I have no fucking clue, and I won't until tonight."

"What happens tonight? Anything I can do to help?"

"Made a date with Zoe to have dinner at my house. Then I kissed her when I took her back to Ma's yesterday afternoon. You know, after we'd already made dinner plans for tonight."

Nathan cringed. "Uh-oh. This doesn't sound good."

Joe let out his breath. "Yeah. Tell me about it. She freaked. Started babbling a bunch of shit about not being good enough for me. That I deserved better. That she'd been sending mixed signals and that it was all her fault. Fuck. Even worse, she kept apologizing over and over. Every other statement was

I'm so sorry. I felt about two fucking inches tall, man. And before I could correct that load of crap, she bolted and ran into the house. Jesus."

"Damn," Nathan said quietly. "Y'all still on for tonight?"

"Oh yeah," he muttered. "Rusty promised me no matter what she had to do she'd have Zoe ready to go when I got there. I'm taking her at her word. Speaking of Rusty. You know of anything going on with her?"

Nathan sent him a puzzled look. "What the hell are you talking about? What makes you ask that?"

Joe sighed. "Just asking. I can't put my finger on it, but something's up with her. She's not herself. Not acting like herself. But that's all I know and I didn't want to raise the alarm when it could just be my overactive imagination. I'm so mind fucked over this thing with Zoe that who knows what the hell I'm seeing."

Sam called for attention, interrupting his conversation with Nathan. It was just as well since there wasn't anything more to say, and if he had to speculate or worry any further on Zoe's state of mind or on the state of their relationship, or lack thereof, he was going to lose his fucking mind and start barking at the moon.

"Allie's got the floor for the next hour," Sam announced. "She'll be going over the steps in defusing three of the most common bombs used in domestic terrorist threats and attacks. Pay attention, boys and girls, because there will be homework, and there will be a test on this in a few days," he said with undisguised amusement. "And we'll meet back up tomorrow for the field lecture and demonstration part of this exercise. I'm being easy on you, cupcakes. Oh nine hundred sharp. It won't take long, and yes, this is mandatory. You miss and your salary gets docked and you get sidelined. Just in case anyone is thinking of giving it a pass."

There was a series of grumbles, flipping the bird and name-calling, and curses echoed through the war room. It was probably one of the very few times Garrett wasn't threatened over his use of an F-bomb—or rather repeated uses of the F-bomb. For that matter, it was hard to separate out who was dropping the most since it came from so many directions.

"Jesus, what got up his ass?" Ryker grumbled. "I don't remember him being such a tight-ass. I may be rethinking my employment."

"Oh, I've got a good idea what got up his ass," Skylar muttered, casting a look guaranteed to shrivel a man's balls on contact in Allie's direction.

Joe stifled his laughter and tried to adopt a stern look befitting a team leader. He failed. Miserably.

"He's probably worried about Allie sticking around since we haven't exactly had a lot of action in the last four weeks," Edge murmured, interjecting his opinion. "So maybe this is his attempt to show her how *serious* we are. You know, because we can't be cracking jokes when we have downtime. That would be highly improper."

Swanny choked and then covered the sound with a cough, covering his mouth to also hide the not-so-straight face behind it. Nathan pressed his lips together but they still twitched suspiciously. Skylar snorted and rolled her eyes. Ryker emitted a chuckle that got him looks from the rest of the room.

"Oh for fuck's sake," Skylar muttered. "Give me fifteen minutes in the ring with her and I'll show her how fucking serious I am."

Ryker's eyes widened and he looked like he was about to drop to his knees and worship at the altar of Skylar. He even put one hand over his heart as if reciting his pledge of allegiance to his teammate.

"Holy fuck, that would be hot," Edge breathed, his eyes

widening in exaggerated fashion. "Oh wait, my sincerest apologies for my unfortunate, extremely inappropriate response, Ms. Watkins. The *more* appropriate response would be, that would be very educational and an excellent example of just how serious-minded this *extremely* serious organization of serious special forces operators is. And of course how serious we take the serious matter of opening up a can of whoop ass, er, uh, I mean the matter of seriously training our new recruits, how seriously we take respect, particularly when it comes to the serious issue of humor. We, of course, have no senses of humor and take serious offense to the supposition that the nonexistent senses of humor are in any way inappropriate."

Skylar lost it, bursting into laughter and shaking so hard that she began wheezing. She held her ribs, choking each time she tried to form a word. Swanny's eyes were huge as he stared in shock at the big man who'd just spoken more words in a minute than he had in the entire time he'd been a member of KGI. Nathan and Joe exchanged amused glances, each shaking his head.

"Wow," Ryker whispered. "That was righteous. Shit, I had no idea what an irreverent bunch I had fallen in with. I think I'm in love. In a completely platonic, heterosexual way, of course."

"Jesus," Nathan muttered. "We've got mutiny on our hands. We've got a temper worse than P.J.'s, with more than enough to back up the bravado, and then we have a guy who makes my other brothers look like two-year-olds in the sarcasm department. And then the new guy over here egging them *all* on. You deal with them, Joe."

Joe snorted. "I'm kind of scared of Skylar. I think I'll just stand here and keep my mouth shut or she might decide to give me fifteen minutes in the ring. I like my good looks just the way they are. But Edge, dude, gotta say, that's the funniest fucking shit I've ever heard in my life. Will you write that up for me so I can hang it up in the team room? I'm thinking about making it our new mantra. And something to aspire to, you know? We should all strive to be more . . . serious."

The others groaned. Swanny rolled his eyes. "Leave the humor to Edge, man. You just killed the buzz."

"Which one of you cares to share what's so funny?" Sam asked tersely.

"Uh-oh," Edge murmured so only his team could hear. "The *serious* nanny is about to give time-outs because somebody laughed while school's in session."

Skylar and Swanny made choking sounds again, Ryker had his face turned up toward heaven while mouthing *thank you, God*, and Nathan looked frozen in place while Joe fought with his lips as they tried to fidget right off his damn face. Ah fuck it. Edge was right. Skylar was right. This serious bullshit was just that. Shit. If the rookie couldn't deal with a little morbid humor, then she didn't fucking belong on any KGI team to begin with.

"Things were getting a little too . . . serious," Joe said, causing his teammates to groan as they fought another round of laughter. "Just trying to break up the monotony. Anyone got a problem with that?"

He scanned the room as he made the challenging statement, his gaze lingering on Allie a little longer than the others. Yeah, he was calling her out. It was obvious, but his team was right. Everyone needed to lighten the fuck up. When his gaze found Allie again, she flushed and then glanced down, realizing his team's pointed message. Joe felt a twinge of guilt. He didn't want to embarrass her, but for fuck's sake, she'd embarrassed herself enough at the last meeting when every single person had tried to make her feel more at ease in her surroundings.

"Not like you to let someone other than Sophie keep your balls for you, Sam," Joe drawled. "Any particular reason why you're allowing it now?"

Sam's glare was murderous. Garrett looked like he was about to burst a blood vessel as he fought to keep a straight face. Donovan didn't even try. He covered his face with one hand and looked upward as if praying for guidance, deliverance or strength. Joe couldn't tell which. Or maybe he was praying for Joe to disappear before Sam *did* burst something. One thing was clear, though. Joe's team wasn't the only one that had problems with Allie's judgment and disapproval. They were just the only ones who'd had the guts to say anything.

Sam crossed his arms over his chest and then leaned back against the planning platform as he stared Joe down. "What exactly is that supposed to mean?" he asked in a dangerously quiet voice.

Skylar cleared her throat. "He doesn't mean anything, Sam. He's covering for comments I made, and while you'd probably find those comments inappropriate, I stand by them."

Joe held up his hand. "Stand down, Sky. And that's an order."

Skylar lifted one eyebrow but went quiet. She shot Edge an inquisitive look. Joe couldn't blame her. He and Nathan didn't give orders and they definitely didn't voice one in the way he had, like he was on some power trip. They were a team. A well-organized, well-oiled and damn efficient group that did what was needed, no questions asked.

"My *team* stands by statements and opinions expressed by my *team*," Joe said, an edge to his voice. "We wouldn't be having this conversation had you not butted into what was clearly team communication in an attempt to micromanage and suppress any hint of a goddamn sense of humor. Get a clue, Sam. No one on my team is offended by humor or opinions, so look somewhere else for your problem. Now if we can get this over with, I'd appreciate it, and I'm sure everyone else would too."

Allie's lips were pressed together and guilt shadowed her eyes. Rio didn't look pissed nor did he look pleased. He was as unreadable as ever, though he said something, obviously to Allie, because she nodded and faded back into the stronghold of her team. Fine. Let her team protect her. That's what they were there for. And let her team deal with the stick up her ass while they were at it. Her issues didn't mean that the entire KGI organization had a problem, and Sam needed to get that memo pretty damn quick before P.J., who was more outspoken than Sky, peeled an inch of hide off Allie's ass.

Joe's gaze darted over to where Steele's team was posted to get their reaction, but he didn't even bother looking at Steele. The man wore the same expression twenty-four-seven. Except when learning his wife was pregnant, Joe mentally amended. P.J.'s eyes were dancing with laughter and she was staring at Sky. When Sky glanced in P.J.'s direction, P.J. gave her an exaggerated wink and a thumbs-up behind Cole's back so it wasn't witnessed by the entire room.

Cole met Joe's expression with a pained one as he dipped his head toward P.J. and then gestured subtly in Sky's direction. Joe nearly laughed. Cole was clearly praying for mercy. He'd probably had to bear more than one of P.J.'s pissed-off diatribes after both P.J. and Skylar had gone to great lengths to smooth things over with Allie the first time Allie had demonstrated concerns with levity in the workplace. Allie obviously hadn't been appeased, judging by the way the next meeting had gone and her ever-increasing ire. And after today? And Sam being a giant-ass stick-in-the-mud to match

Allie's brand of stick up the ass? Joe was very glad he didn't have to go home with P.J. or Skylar. Or Edge for that matter. Edge didn't get pissed at much. He was too much of a live-and-let-live guy, short on words but big on action. But it was obvious Allie had rubbed him the wrong way and equally clear which side his loyalty was aligned with, given that Sky was his best friend, roommate and coworker.

"You and I will talk later," Sam said icily.

Fuck no they wouldn't. Joe had bigger fish to fry than listening to a goddamn lecture from his big brother. Besides, Sam really didn't want to fuck with him right now. His temper was on a short fuse and his patience was in shreds. One wrong word from Sam and he would tell him where he could shove KGI and his job.

Not the best idea to enter a new relationship unemployed.

Joe turned back to his team and rolled his eyes, but Skylar looked at him with big, blue, unhappy eyes that shone with apology. Edge looked worried, and Swanny was just staring strangely at him. Nathan was the only one who seemed to be relaxed and unworried, but then he was the only one who knew the source of Joe's short fuse and hot temper.

"Let's just suck it up and get through this," Joe said in a low voice. "I don't have time to deal with Sam or any of this bullshit right now, but I *will* deal with it, I swear."

"I'm sorry I ever opened my mouth," Skylar said miserably, as she and the rest of the team tried to look like they were paying attention to Allie drone on about defusing bombs. "It was childish of me, and I won't have you take the fall for my pettiness, Joe. You're a great team leader and you don't deserve this crap."

He smiled gently at her. "You don't think everyone else here is thinking exactly what you said, but you were the only one willing to give voice to it? Look, if Rio wants to let her ruin the chemistry of his team, that's Rio's business, not ours. I doubt he or any of his men have a sense of fucking humor anyway, so they likely don't give a shit about her uppity, holier-than-thou attitude. But she's not fucking with or intruding on my team. And no one on my team is going to be given time-outs like a fucking preschooler for speaking his or her mind. Jesus, do you know how insane that is? When has anyone in this organization ever been censured for speaking his or her mind? Hell, until now, it's always been encouraged. And who in this organization has ever bitched about cracking jokes at 'inappropriate times' or criticized this organization for not being serious or whatever the fuck she has up her ass?"

"I'm not even navy, but that gets a serious hooyah from me," Edge muttered. "Stupid serious pun intended."

"Gotta say, couldn't have said it better," Swanny murmured out the side of his mouth.

Skylar's lips quirked and her eyes sparkled with amusement. "We going rogue?"

Joe covered his laughter with his hand, rubbing over his lips until the sound in his throat diminished.

Ryker looked excited. "Man, have to say, my life was as dull as fuck before I joined up with you all. I'm guessing a normal day on the job is an alien concept to you folks."

Nathan leaned forward, pretending interest in the diagrams Allie was pointing to, eliciting another round of snickers from his team. "We're not going rogue," Nathan said, impressively keeping his lips still as he continued his act of ventriloquism. "Sky will challenge Allie to a bikini Jell-O wrestling match, and Joe will challenge Sam to a thumb-wrestling, best-of-three match."

"Oh *hell* yes," Ryker said, his eyes hopeful.

Edge snorted. "I was hoping for a P.J./Allie throw down.

Mud wrestling. Clothes optional. Sky's like my sister, man. I'd have to bleach my eyeballs if I saw her naked or mostly naked."

"I'm oddly offended by that," Skylar drawled. "God, y'all sound like assholes. Y'all know that, don't you?"

Joe grinned. "Of course we do. You didn't think we were serious, did you? Jesus. And risk not only your ire but yours, P.J.'s *and* Allie's? One of you is bad enough, but all three of you on my ass or anyone else's ass? Like I said, I prefer my good looks intact. Not rearranged along with my balls."

"Besides, he's practicing for the next time we're all grouped together and not having to watch a boring as fuck bomb presentation," Nathan offered. "He figures if he says all that shit in front of Allie, then anything else any of us says or laughs at will pale in comparison."

"An unexpectedly devious plot," Skylar said admiringly. "I approve. Gotta admit, though, I had a moment of flash rage when you started spouting all that sexist-pig shit. You're lucky you're far enough away from me that I didn't insta-react and put you on your ass and serve up your balls in my palm."

"And she wonders why I keep my mouth shut," Joe muttered. "Well, most of the time."

The rest of his team's laughter, snorts and snickers were muffled by a variety of measures, eliciting suspicious looks from the rest of the assembled KGI members.

Joe?

Joe was immediately alert, all earlier signs of laid-back and joking vanishing instantly. He struggled for a brief moment, trying to coordinate and direct all his focus down the narrow mental pathway that connected him and Shea.

What's wrong, sweetheart? Even as he asked the question, he glanced at Nathan in his periphery, but Nathan was completely relaxed, arms crossed over his chest as he watched Allie wrap up her instructional lecture. *Do you need help?*

Her soft laughter set him at ease and he *felt* her hug of reassurance. He never could quite wrap his brain around how she did that. The communicating was weird enough by itself, but how the hell could she make it feel as though she were physically touching him when they were not even in viewing distance? It was as mind-boggling as her ability to not only block pain from the person she was telepathically connected to, but to also take it on herself, redirecting not only the injury but the actual wound and pain that ensued.

I'm sorry. I tried to think of the best way to talk to you without you thinking the worst but, well, there just wasn't any. But I'm fine. I promise. I just wanted to know if you could do something for me?

She sounded uncertain and a little hesitant as she said the last, causing Joe to frown.

Of course I will, honey. You have to know that. You know, or you should know, that all you have to do is ask. Now what's the problem and what do you need me to do?

He felt as well as heard her little sigh of relief. Crazy woman. He was going to have a serious come-to-Jesus meeting with her later about coming to him when she needed something. No matter what it was.

Her soft laughter invaded his mind again. *You do know I can read your mind when we're connected like this. You may as well have said it. Thinking and saying are the same thing.*

He mentally rolled his eyes. God help him with smart-ass women. It seemed he was plagued with them today.

She giggled again. He glowered, making sure she was on the telepathic receiving end of it in the process.

Nathan said he was going to be held up after the meeting

for a while. Something to do with digging you out of a mess so you could go home and focus on your female problems. His words, not mine, she hastily amended. *Anyway, any other time you know I wouldn't mind, Joe, but I need him to come straight home. I have something . . . special . . . planned. There's something I need to tell him, and I wondered if you could maybe make sure he didn't hang around after y'all's meeting today?*

With her words came a flash of insight, or rather a view into her thoughts. He felt her smiling and joy flooding him, or rather he was feeling her joy, and then the image of Shea with a protruding belly, her hand resting protectively over the swell as she whispered softly to her unborn child.

Holy fuck. He glanced sideways at his brother again, barely able to contain the smile from taking over his face. Nathan was going to be a father! His twin was having his first child. Holy shit, this was epic!

Then he sobered. *Honey, are you happy about this? Was this planned? Were y'all trying?* Left unsaid was the fact that Nathan had said nothing to Joe about the possibility and eventuality of Shea becoming pregnant. Wouldn't Nathan have shared something that momentous with the person he was closest to on earth next to his wife?

He didn't tell you because it wasn't final, Shea said gently. *It's difficult to put into words.* She laughed at the unintended joke. *Or rather thoughts, I suppose. We have talked about it, yes. But he was worried that I wasn't ready and that he was projecting his own desires onto me, so he stopped talking about it completely. But he definitely wants a child—I want a child,* she said, conviction lacing her words.

I just want to make sure you're both happy, Joe said warmly. *After all, you're my two favorite people on earth. Congratulations, little mama. I'm so happy for you and my brother. And yes, I'll make sure he gets his ass home right after we finish up here, which should be in the next two minutes.*

Thanks, Joe. You're the best. You're going to be this baby's godfather, you know.

His heart swelled with a myriad of emotions. Love. Gratitude. Pride. And hope. So much hope. Not only for his brother and sister-in-law but for him as well, that in the not-so-distant future, this would be his life. With Zoe.

You'll get there, Joe. You have to believe that. If you love her, then never doubt her or you or the eventuality of a life with her.

Thanks, baby girl. Thank God he wasn't having to hold this conversation by speaking or he'd never be able to get the words out around the huge knot in his throat. *Gotta run now. We're wrapping up now so you have about ten minutes to prepare.*

Love you, Joe.

Love you too, sweetheart. Take good care of yourself and my niece or nephew.

On cue, Allie wrapped up her session and then stepped back, indicating to Sam that the floor was his. Already everyone else was shuffling, picking up stuff they had with them and starting to inch in the direction of the doorway. Sam sighed and merely said, "Dismissed. We'll readjourn at oh nine hundred tomorrow morning."

Nathan hesitated, and Joe clapped him on the shoulder. "Don't bother, man. I can read you like a book. You're not taking on Sam in my place so I can get home and figure out my game plan for tonight. We're *both* going out the back way. Fuck Sam. He can wait until fucking tomorrow."

Nathan grinned. "That's not a bad plan. Shea said she had a surprise for me when I got back, and her surprises usually involve sexy new lingerie."

Joe groaned. "Dude, really? Can we not go there?"

"Gladly," Nathan said in satisfaction. "You are not getting any intel on how my woman looks in Victoria's Secret shit."

Joe cast him a baleful look. "It was you who brought up her lingerie to begin with. Remember?"

CHAPTER 18

ZOE'S stomach was full of butterflies as she finished apply-
ing the sheer lip gloss and smacked her lips together as she
surveyed her reflection in the mirror. No messy bun tonight.
Instead she'd brushed out the long strands, leaving them
loose down her back. Despite her earlier concerns about
lengthening her hair, she had to admit she liked it. A lot.

When this was all over with and the extensions came out,
she had a goal to grow out her hair just as long as it was
now. Embarrassment forced her gaze downward as she
was unable to even meet her own eyes in the mirror. It was
humiliating to admit that she'd worn her hair to a precise length because that was what her father had required.
He was very exacting in his requirements. Right down to
manner of dress, precise wardrobe, hair, makeup and even
jewelry and accessories.

"What you are is a wuss," she accused the reflection staring back at her. "A spineless jellyfish who's scared of her own shadow and possesses absolutely no gumption."

"You're awfully hard on jellyfish," Rusty commented dryly from the doorway.

Zoe spun around, horrified that she'd been overheard talking to herself.

"Relax, Zoe. You look frozen stiff. You have to relax, and for God's sake, cut yourself some slack."

Zoe sighed. "My life is a mess. It's always been a mess, and the fact that I've never done a single thing to correct that or stand up to my father is beyond mortifying."

Rusty lifted an eyebrow. "Is that not what you're doing now? I'm pretty sure dear old dad doesn't have a clue where you are, what you're doing or who you're doing it with."

A smile glimmered on Zoe's lips. She fought it but it continued to tug at her mouth until she let out a laugh. "Very true." Then she giggled harder. "Can you imagine bringing Joe home to meet my dad? My dad would be all pompous and condescending and Joe would be like, 'I don't really give a fuck what you think.'"

Rusty broke into laughter, her eyes sparking in merriment. "What's bad is I can totally see it. I could see it with any of my brothers. Especially Garrett."

"Is it also bad that I suddenly feel one hundred percent better about tonight's date?"

Rusty grinned. "You have a liking for rebellion, do you?"

"I guess," she murmured. "Who knew I'd become such a wild child. I swear for the entirety of my life until now I was a study in obedience and subservience."

"You had reason," Rusty said gently. "It's not a crime to want love and acceptance. Especially from the people who are supposed to give it freely and without condition. I'm not too ashamed to admit that I would have done anything to please my mother and even my shithead stepfather until I finally realized it was pointless and the only thing that had been successful was the deterioration of my self-respect."

"I know that feeling," Zoe said glumly.

Rusty checked her watch. "Joe should be rolling up any time now so you need to finish up and head downstairs. If you make him wait tonight, I'm worried he'll come up the stairs and carry you out over his shoulder. Cut him some slack, Zoe. He was all out of sorts when you had your melt-down after he kissed you. The poor guy was too pitiful even for me to give shit to."

Zoe rolled her eyes but hurried to complete her makeup. A few minutes later, she stepped back from the mirror.

"That's as good as it's going to get."

"You look perfect," Rusty said warmly. "And I hear Joe, so not a moment too soon. Let's go."

Zoe allowed herself to be herded down the stairs, but she refused to meet Joe's gaze. It was too embarrassing after freaking out on him the night before. She whispered good-bye to Rusty, Frank and Marlene and then walked out to Joe's truck with him. He opened her door for her and helped her up before walking around and getting in the driver's seat.

He cranked the engine but didn't immediately drive away. He reached over and curled his hand around hers then picked her hand up and pulled it to his mouth to kiss each finger. She stared at him in shock.

He smiled. "Finally. I wasn't sure if you were going to avoid looking at me all night."

She blushed furiously and ducked her head. But he tucked his fingers underneath her chin and nudged it back up so their gazes met again.

"Don't do that, beautiful. Whatever you're thinking or feeling, let it go. Can you do that for me tonight?"

She smiled, slowly relaxing in his presence. "Yeah, I can do that."

His eyes were warm and tender and his smile was gentle. His smile broadened with her agreement.

"Yeah? Good deal. Let's go eat then. Fish are all cleaned and prepped and ready to fry. Even the hush puppies are mixed."

"Sounds good. I've never been able to eat fish I've caught myself," she said ruefully.

"Well, thanks to you, we both get to eat tonight," he said, giving her a warm smile again.

She found herself seated on a bar stool at the kitchen counter where Joe poured her a glass of wine before instructing her to sit back and relax and keep him company while he cooked.

She sniffed appreciatively as the smell of frying fish and hush puppies soon filled the air. She'd been so petrified about this evening after the debacle of last night, but she felt none of the unease she'd imagined. It was as if last night hadn't even happened. Joe was still . . . Joe. The same guy he'd been over the last three days. He was funny and sweet and unfailingly conscientious of her every need. And the way he looked at her sent the already present butterflies into flight mode as they scuttled round and round in her belly and chest.

When he was finished taking out the last of the fish and hush puppies, he set the tray down on the counter before refilling her wineglass and filling his own, and then he walked around to slide onto the stool beside her.

He reached for one of the headless fish—thank God it was headless—and put it on her plate but held on to it.

"There's a little trick to eating it but nothing difficult," he assured. He pinched his thumb and forefinger over one of the fins while holding the rest of the body steady. Then he lifted and easily removed the fin, creating a horizontal dividing line in the meat of the fish. Then he turned the fish over and repeated the process with the lower fin as well. "Now you're ready to peel off one of the filets," he said triumphantly.

He carefully pulled down with his thumb, sliding a thin slice of meat that was breaded on one side but bare on the inside. Steam rose from the white flesh and Zoe noticed little tiny black squiggly markings through it.

"Now, just because I peeled away the filet doesn't mean there might not still be a few tiny bones around the edges, especially toward the top where the ribs were located. You have to chew carefully and if you feel anything hard or sharp, maneuver it onto your tongue and simply reach in and pluck it out or spit it into a paper towel," he added with a grin.

Her eyes narrowed suspiciously at him. "Is this an attempt to dupe me into some fish-out-of-water city-girl trip where I do or say something completely ridiculous that results in you laughing yourself silly over how totally out of my depth I am?"

His brow furrowed and he looked confused at first. A rush of shame and regret washed over her, heating her skin and reddening her cheeks until they felt like they were on fire. He stared intently at her, his eyes seeming to penetrate right through her barriers so he saw to the heart of her. As if he saw how much she feared being the butt of his—or anyone's—joke.

"Zoe, sweetheart, that seriously pisses me off," he said in a growl-laced voice. "Not that you questioned my intentions. You're absolutely allowed to do that anytime you want. I'll always be honest with you about my intentions. I swear it. What pisses me off is whatever bastard trained you to expect the worst from people. And it pisses me off even more that you're speaking from personal experience."

She shifted uncomfortably, fingering the still-hot piece of meat she hadn't even tasted yet. The last thing she wanted was his pity. And she had a feeling if she apologized it would only piss him off all the more, so she said nothing and instead gingerly bit into the fish, blowing around the edges of her mouth so it didn't burn her tongue.

Paying heed to his warning, she chewed carefully, feeling for anything that felt like a piece of bone. The delicious flavor burst onto her taste buds and her eyes instantly widened.

"This is really good," she blurted.

He smiled. "Would I lead you wrong?"

She took another bite, chewing quickly. Then she picked up one of the hush puppies, noticing that Joe was dipping his into ketchup. She frowned, but he hadn't been wrong yet. So she followed suit, dipping her hush puppy into his ketchup since she hadn't poured any onto her plate yet, and then tentatively took a small bite of the fried cornbread.

Again she was stunned.

"Good?" Joe asked in amusement.

But she was already stuffing the rest of the hush puppy into her mouth, waving him away imperiously with her free hand.

He burst out laughing and then quickly deboned a few more pieces of fish and piled them onto her plate along with several hush puppies. He even squirted a generous amount of ketchup onto her plate and then sat back, watching as she continued to eat with enthusiasm.

She halted when she realized he wasn't eating. He was just staring at her. She paused in the act of putting more into her mouth and turned to look at him.

"What? Why aren't you eating?"

He smiled that bone-melting, heart-wrenching smile that made her want to cry and smile all at the same time. It was a smile that had the most confusing effect on her. Her knees went weak and her nipples immediately puckered. How could he make her think of sex simply by smiling?

He was dangerous to all women. God, if this was all it took, he had to have women in his bed every freaking day, or at least anytime he wanted them. A man like him didn't need to settle down with one in particular and embrace a life of monogamy. He could play by any set of rules he wanted, and Zoe doubted women would even care.

So why was he focusing so much of his attention and charm on . . . her? It didn't make any sense. Zoe wasn't being pitiful or woebegone. She was matter-of-fact about her assets, features and appearance. She was just mediocre. She wasn't ugly, but she was far from beautiful. Definitely average. Someone who blended with a crowd, never standing out. She wasn't the type to ever stop traffic, and she was grateful for that fact. It had enabled her to disappear and remain out of notice thus far, so she had to be doing something right.

"What the hell are you torturing yourself about now?" Joe murmured, stroking his fingertip lightly down the curve of her cheek.

Such a simple caress had the power to rob her of speech and make her completely forget herself and what she was doing. What *had* she been doing? Other than staring at him like an idiot. She opened her mouth to respond but found she couldn't think of a single thing to say.

"I have no idea," she finally admitted. "Every time you look at me that way or touch me, my mind goes to mush."

Oh God, had she just admitted that? Could the floor open up and swallow her . . . like now?

But he didn't laugh or make fun of her. No, he was as serious as someone could get.

"I'm glad I'm not the only one in way over his head here," he said quietly. "It would suck if I was the only one feeling that way about you looking at or touching me."

Her mouth fell open as she gaped at him. Then she snapped it shut and quickly returned to her meal. Eat. Just eat and pretend he hadn't said something that outrageous or that the result of him saying that had her heart fluttering so wildly that she couldn't catch her breath.

She ate robotically, afraid to glance his way again in case he had any other mind-blowing revelations guaranteed to tilt the earth on its axis. But he remained quiet until she had finished. She pushed her plate back with a sigh and then flashed him a smile without directly looking at him.

"That was fantastic, Joe. I really enjoyed it."

"I'm glad," he said simply.

He lifted one leg over the stool and grabbed their plates before heading to the sink to dump them. Then he simply returned to where she was sitting and laced his fingers with hers before pulling her up and guiding her toward the living room couch.

He settled her onto the plump cushions and then eased beside her, pulling her into the crook of his shoulder. She tensed for a long moment before gradually relaxing into his embrace. His arm was wrapped around her shoulders, resting on her opposite arm, his fingers lazily tracing lines up and down her skin.

He was seducing her with nothing more than the lightest of touches. Already she was ready to squirm off the couch, and she could kick herself for overreacting so badly the night before when he'd kissed her. Now, he'd never kiss her again. But she could kiss him, couldn't she?

She licked her lips before realizing what she was doing. He groaned softly and closed his eyes, strain evident on his forehead. He sucked in a deep breath and then turned his head toward her, their noses just inches apart.

He reached up to touch her face, tracing her cheekbone with the gentlest of caresses.

"Tell me something, Zoe," he said quietly. "If you could have anything you wanted in the world, have any wish granted, what would you wish for?"

She swallowed nervously. If that wasn't a loaded question destined to get her into huge trouble, she didn't know what was. But maybe he was tired of being the one making all the overtures. Was this his plea for her to meet him halfway? Had she sent the wrong message after all?

Closing her eyes, she sighed and gathered her courage tightly around her, her hands trembling as she tried to work the knot from her throat. Then finally, she was able to form actual words.

"You," she whispered. "You, Joe. I'd wish for you."

Satisfaction and so much relief blazed in his eyes, telling her that she hadn't in any way just made the worst mistake of her life. He cupped her cheek as he lowered his face to hers, his eyes half lidded and heavy with desire.

"Then make both our dreams come true, Zoe," he said in a gruff voice. "Make love with me. Let me make love to you. Let me show you how very perfect it would be between us. I've never wanted anything so much in my life. I've never wanted anyone as much as I want you."

She bit her lip as her heart hammered thunderously against her chest wall. Her mouth went completely dry and she had to unstick her tongue from the roof of her mouth so she could speak.

"Do you really mean that?" she asked hoarsely.

"If you give me the chance, I'll show you," he vowed.

"Then make love to me," she said in the softest whisper. "Please."

"That is something you never have to ask me for," he breathed past her lips as their tongues met hotly.

He delved deep, stroking his tongue over hers and then exploring the deepest recesses of her mouth until she was breathing him. Smelling him. Utterly intoxicated by his taste and touch. She shivered as his fingers danced lightly over her shoulders and then skated down her arms until they circled her wrists like bracelets.

He entwined their hands as he pulled her to her feet and then began walking her backward toward another room. Even as she backstepped through the open doorway, one of his hands flipped the light switch while the other slid beneath her shirt, pulling the ends free from her pants.

The hand that had left her ever so briefly returned, cupping and molding her breast through her bra and shirt, his fingers coming together to lightly tug at the rigid peak. She gasped, and he swallowed up the sound and then slid both hands beneath her shirt, lifting upward and urging her arms above her head so he could pull the shirt over her head.

Wanting to touch him as badly as he seemed to want to touch her, she gave him the same treatment, sliding her palms over the light smattering of hair at his midline, pushing his shirt as she continued upward until he voluntarily lifted his arms and helped her free him completely of it.

They went for each other's pants simultaneously, fumbling, hands bouncing off denim, the rasping sound of zippers as each frantically tried to free the other. Then Joe went still, reaching for Zoe's wrists and holding them as he slowed the pace.

"Let me savor this moment—you," he murmured, his

eyes glowing warmly with need and desire. "This will be the most perfect night of my life, guaranteed, and I want to make sure it's damn perfect for you too."

Her heart melted even further at the gravity in his tone, utter seriousness etched into his expression as he made love to her with his eyes alone. Heat crept up her neck and into her cheeks as he stood back, his gaze solidly fixed on her as he gently unfastened the clasp of her bra. He gave the straps a gentle tug and allowed it to flutter downward, landing on the floor between them.

Then he turned his attention to finishing the job of sliding her jeans off, bending to one knee as he freed first one of her legs and then the other. She felt utterly exposed and vulnerable, standing before him in just the lacy panties she'd worn. His eyes once more fastened on hers, he hooked his thumbs in the thin band, resting his hands at her hips, and then tugged downward until finally she was completely bared to his gaze and his touch.

She shivered at the predatory gleam in his eyes, at the heated way his gaze slid so sensuously over her skin. Palming her shoulders, he once more walked her back until the underside of her legs met the mattress of his bed.

He coaxed her downward and then knelt in front of her, his lips closing over her nipple. Chill bumps erupted over her flesh and she quaked under the onslaught of his mouth as he tongued and sucked each nipple in turn, repeating several times before returning to her lips, his fingers thrust into her hair, angling her head downward to meet his mouth while he remained on his knees.

"You're so damn beautiful," he rasped.

His hands continued to roam freely, touching and caressing every inch of exposed flesh he could find as he kissed her and fed on her lips, sucking the tip of her tongue into his mouth. Her hands flew to his shoulders when he started upward, levering her back as he moved up and over her.

He left her for only as long as it took to free himself from his pants and underwear, and she boldly stared down the length of his body, taking in his highly muscled physique, broad shoulders, rigid six-pack and sizable erection. Her eyes widened and she made a uniquely feminine sound of appreciation.

Unable to resist, she reached to slide her fingers down the length of him as he climbed onto the bed between her legs. He went utterly still, closing his eyes as he groaned in pleasure. If possible, he grew even harder and larger as she stroked and then went lower to cup his sac, running her fingers over the slightly rougher skin there.

Moisture beaded the broad head and she wiped her finger over it, collecting it before bringing her hand to her mouth to slowly insert the digit between her lips, sucking before releasing her finger with an audible pop.

Joe moaned again, the muscles in his neck and chest rigid and straining as he lowered his body carefully onto hers. His heat was a shock as he blanketed her, all the masculine hardness making her feel dainty and feminine. Desirable even. This was no man who found having sex with her to be a chore.

Though the thought was triumphant, it also held a discordant note, but she refused to allow thoughts of Sebastian to intrude on the beauty of this moment with a man who made him look and sound like a complete wuss.

His mouth crashed down on hers, hot, urgent, so passionate it took her breath away. His body covered hers, molded her softness to his much harder frame, and yet he cradled her protectively, making her feel more cherished than she'd ever felt in her life.

His mouth moved hotly down her jaw to her neck, stopping to nibble and graze his teeth lightly over her ear before switching to the other side and starting all over again from the top. This time when he reached her ear, he swept downward, centering his lips and tongue on the hollow of her throat before kissing a path down her midsection, from the valley of her breasts to her navel.

He licked the shallow indention before beginning a torturous path back up, this time veering to one breast, toying and teasing her nipple before finally sucking it firmly between his teeth, nipping with just enough bite to have her awash in pleasurable agony of the sweetest kind.

Not having had much experience in the sex department, Zoe had no idea a man could be as patient as Joe. As undemanding and unselfish. It seemed he spent hours on her breasts alone until she was arching helplessly beneath him, responding to the exquisite sensations. The breathless pants and moans that filled the air were coming from her.

"Joe!" she gasped.

"Easy, honey," he crooned, giving her nipple a long, lazy swipe just as his hand slid slowly between her splayed legs.

She went rigid, her mouth forming an O as his fingers gently parted her folds, baring her ultrasensitive clit to his touch. He made her wait, stroking through her wetness, petting and teasing her opening, then moving ever closer to the pulsating, swollen nub.

If he didn't touch her soon, she was going to die. If he touched her, she was going to die. Either way she was going to explode.

She whimpered deep in her throat. "Joe, please."

He rewarded her by stroking his thumb in a circular motion while sliding his middle finger just inside the mouth of her pussy. She went rigid, her mouth opening in a silent cry.

He grew bolder, exerting more pressure on her clit and sliding his fingers deeper inside her, stroking her walls as she clutched greedily at them, clenching and spasming as he increased the speed and intensity of his movements.

His head lifted from her breast, and for a moment, he fondled her and playfully teased her with only his fingers as he watched her every reaction.

"God, you're so beautiful," he said, pressing a kiss to her navel as he slowed the rhythm of his fingers.

She was so on edge, so *close* to the edge, that if he so much as breathed on her in just the right place, she'd see fireworks. And yet at the same time, she didn't want it to end. She wanted to prolong it until she was crazy with anticipation. Who was she kidding? She was already mindless with an insane need for completion.

She gazed at him with heavy-lidded eyes, loving the absolute focus she saw in his. Focus on her and her pleasure. She lifted her hand and slid it through his short cropped hair, stroking, allowing her fingers to drift down the chiseled line of his jaw. He captured her index finger with his lips, sucking it and laving his tongue over the tip.

"I need you now," she whispered huskily.

His hand eased from her pussy as his body slid sensuously up hers until his mouth aligned perfectly with hers. He kissed her deeply, thoroughly, outlining the bow of her lips before pulling away to stare intently at her.

"Let me get a condom, sweetheart."

She watched in a dreamlike state as he leaned over her body to open the drawer of his nightstand. He pulled out a packet and tore open the foil, for now leaving the condom still in the opened wrapper. Then he returned to kissing her with renewed vigor, his body moving to position himself above her, his knee nudging her thighs apart.

He reexplored his earlier route down her body with his mouth, this time teasing her with his hand at the same time, pushing gently inward, stretching her in preparation for his possession.

She grew restless, writhing beneath him, her legs moving wider apart, her ankles hooking over the backs of his calves, silently urging him to take her. Holding his weight off her with one hand, he reached with the other for the condom and deftly rolled it over his straining erection. Then he grasped the base and rubbed the tip up and down her cleft, circling her clitoris before easing downward to circle her opening repeatedly.

She was nearly to the point of mindless begging when he finally, *finally* positioned the broad tip at the mouth of her entrance and pushed barely inside, stilling as he stared down at her, watching intently for any sign of discomfort.

Her response was to tighten her ankles around his legs, urging him downward as her hands flew to his shoulders, her nails digging into his flesh, marking and branding him in the same way he'd marked her repeatedly the entire time with his mouth.

He inched forward, and she sighed as she stretched and re-formed around him to accommodate his size. Every centimeter of flesh he touched was highly sensitized and it was like receiving an electric shock each time he moved the slightest bit.

She clutched at him, desperate for release and yet wanting it to last forever. His name was a litany on her lips and it seemed to make him more dominant, more forceful and possessive. He levered his body lower until it was flush with hers and put his elbows down on either side of her head so she didn't bear his full weight and then he fused his mouth to hers as he began surging deeper, harder, faster.

Her eyes fluttered shut but he nipped at her chin, and when she opened her eyes, he was staring at her with an intensity that set her ablaze.

"Keep your eyes open, baby. I want to see you when you come."

The words were demanding—not a request but a command—and only heightened her desire and added a sharper edge to the building inferno deep within her. She did as he asked and locked her gaze with his, fascinated by the fierce pleasure burning so brightly in his eyes, surely a mirror to her own.

"Want you with me," he said with a ragged breath. "Come with me, baby. Let's go together."

To ensure the outcome he desired, he slid one hand between them just as he increased the speed and force of his thrusts. His fingers performed a tight circle around and over her clitoris and she gasped for breath as the storm blew out of control.

"Joe, I can't—I can't . . ."

"Breathe, honey. Ride the wave with me. See how beautiful we are together." He smoothed her hair from her forehead and then pressed his lips in a line across her brow as his face creased in an expression of sweet agony. "Now," he whispered. "Now, Zoe. Let go. Step off and let yourself fall."

The tender words so filled with genuine emotion and need as urgent as her own catapulted her into free fall. She spiraled downward like a leaf in autumn, spinning crazily until she was dizzy and so filled with pleasure that she feared bursting with it. The edge grew sharper and sharper still until she could no longer bear the strain. Every muscle in her body tensed and coiled to the point of delicious pain.

And then the world exploded around her and she lost all sense of time and space. She tried valiantly to obey Joe's command to keep her eyes open, but they were so weighted down that it was a struggle to keep them even half lidded. He didn't chasten or rebuke her. He seemed to understand— and share—her experience. He kissed each eyelid sweetly and reverently as he tensed inside her, his body shaking uncontrollably.

He roared her name and then gathered her tightly in his arms, sliding them beneath her body until they were locked together in every possible way. He buried his face in her neck, inhaling her scent as if permanently imprinting himself with her essence. She let her head fall back, giving him free access to imprint all he wanted, simply enjoying the feel of his touch and tenderness in the aftermath of the most explosive orgasm she'd ever experienced in her life.

Several long minutes passed, Joe atop Zoe, alternately kissing and nibbling her neck and her lazily running her palms and fingers up and down his back as he went completely limp, sated and satisfied, as was she.

"That was the most beautiful thing I've ever experienced," she whispered against his ear.

His arms tightened around her, and for a moment he was silent, as if collecting himself after such an earth-shattering event.

"*You're* the most beautiful thing I've ever experienced," he said softly. "I never want it to end, baby. Never had anything as precious as you, and never will."

CHAPTER 19

ZOE slowly woke, remaining perfectly still as she absorbed the simple comfort not waking up alone gave her. Joe was wrapped so tightly around her that there was no space between them. She closed her eyes, reliving the beauty of his lovemaking. Tears surged and despite her best effort they leaked from underneath her eyelashes and trickled down her cheeks. She turned her head away from where it rested on Joe's chest, praying he was still sound asleep.

No such luck.

He stirred and rolled so they faced each other, his eyes bright with worry and fear.

"Hey," he said softly, reaching to wipe away her tears. "What's wrong, baby? Did I hurt you? Are you okay?"

Emotion clogged her throat, nearly rendering her incapable of speech. "It was beautiful," she whispered, echoing the words she'd used the night before. "I've never experienced anything so . . . *perfect*."

No longer able to bear his scrutiny, she buried her face against his shoulder and sucked in steadying breaths in an effort to gain control over her scattered emotions.

He said nothing, just caressed up and down her back in a soothing motion. "Did I scare you, Zoe? Did I come on too hard and fast?"

He sounded so worried and disgusted with himself that she lifted herself from the warm haven of his body so that she could stare down at him, hoping her expression reflected all she could barely put into words. How could you explain such exquisiteness with mere words?

Her eyes glittered with tears and frustration. What had she done to give him the idea that he'd been anything but gentle, loving and so very tender?

It was when fire blazed in his eyes and a flood of emotion swamped his face and he pulled her back down until their mouths were just a breath away that she realized, to her complete mortification, that she had voiced her last question aloud.

"Honey, you did *nothing* wrong," he said, smudging away the remnants of tears that had collected in the corners of her eyes. "As it is, I've wondered more than once if I've died and gone to heaven, because having you here, in my bed after giving me the honor and privilege of making love to you, is nothing short of God's glory. I'm pretty sure I heard angels singing the 'Hallelujah Chorus,' or maybe that was me, in which case I probably did scare you to death," he teased.

"Or maybe we should do it all over again, you know, just so you're sure," he added in a husky whisper.

Zoe's body came to life, her nipples forming rigid points and a pulse beginning low in her groin.

"Maybe you're right," she whispered.

"I like the way my woman thinks," he said, kissing her,

his tongue plunging inside her mouth as he licked and dueled with her tongue.

"Am I?" she asked breathlessly. "Your woman?"

He drew away, a deep frown on his face. "That's the dumbest question I've ever heard. Was it not you I was so deep inside that I could feel your every movement?"

She blushed.

"You *are* mine, Zoe. Make no mistake in that."

"We need to talk, Joe," she said in a quiet, somber voice.

"And we will. Just as soon as I convince you beyond a shadow of a doubt that you belong to me heart, body and soul."

"But—"

He shushed her with a gentle finger and then followed it with his lips. His words thrilled and scared her at the same time. And they released a pent-up longing for things she'd never dared to dream of.

His hands drifted up and down the curves of her body, caressing, making lazy patterns on her skin, dipping lower and lower until she thought she'd go mad with wanting. Her nipples strained upward as if begging for his mouth, and he readily complied, taking one taut peak deeply into his mouth and sucking in rhythmic motion, then turning to give equal attention to the other.

Her fingers delved into his hair, her nails digging into his scalp before lovingly cradling his head to her breast as his fingers worked their magic over her most delicate, quivering flesh. He inserted one long finger inside her channel, causing her to cry out and arch her hips upward, seeking more.

"Please, Joe, don't make me wait," she pleaded softly. "I need you right now."

He added another finger, stretching the swollen, slick passage, and then eased them out, raising them to his mouth to suck her moisture from each digit.

"You taste delicious," he said in a new growl.

"Now, Joe," she urged, twisting and rolling her head from side to side as urgency continued to mount until she feared going mad with it.

"Shhh, my darling," he said tenderly.

He laced their fingers together and then pressed the backs of her palms against the mattress as he positioned himself between her legs.

"Are you ready for me, baby?"

She moaned and arched upward, trying to force him inside her. And then he slid deep, causing her to gasp at the sudden fullness. He stopped withdrawing when he was barely inside, concern flashing in his eyes.

"If you stop now, I'll be forced to kill you," she said in a ragged breath.

Joe chuckled but he thrust deeply, eliciting a groan from them both. Zoe's nails scoured his back as she held tightly to him, arching upward to meet him. Where the night before had been long, sweet and languid, an exploration of something new and so very precious, this morning was borne of desperation to renew that connection. Hurried. A tangle of arms and legs, passionate kisses and breathless sighs and moans of pleasure from both of them.

"Fuck," he breathed. "Damn it, I'm sorry, baby, but this is going to be fast. I can't hold back."

"Who asked you to go slow?" she growled.

He slammed into her and her nails tightened in his shoulders. He was likely going to bear marks, but she didn't care. She liked the idea of marking him, of making her ownership known.

His face was a wreath of agony as he hammered his way into her, rocking her against the headboard in unrelenting thrusts.

"Want you with me, baby. How close are you?"

"If you'd stop asking me how I was, I'd be there already," she wailed.

He smiled, dropping a kiss on her lips that soon turned into a ravenous exploration of her mouth. She felt him swell inside her just as she felt the sharp rise of her orgasm, suddenly explosive and all consuming.

"Joe!" she cried.

"I'm here, baby. Always here. Come with me. Be with me."

She shattered just as he shouted and thrust home one last time, their release flashing like a lightning storm crashing wildly in the night sky. He slumped against her and she wrapped her arms tightly around him, refusing to allow him to move his weight.

"Honey, I'm going to crush you," he said, his voice thick with amusement.

"Don't care," she said, her voice muffled by his chest.

He buried his face in her neck and lay there a long moment. Then he let out a groan.

"Shit."

"What's wrong?" she asked, suddenly worried.

He rolled off her and flopped onto his back. "Damn it! I forgot all about the mandatory KGI meeting this morning."

She sat up, pulling the sheets to cover her chest. She looked anxiously at him. "Should I go, then?" she asked in a hesitant voice.

He leaned forward and kissed her, cupping her cheek and deepening the kiss.

"What I want is for you to stay *here*," he said softly. "This won't take long, and when I get back I'll make you breakfast in bed. Please stay, Zoe. Give me something worth coming home to."

Her heart fluttered out of control as she stared at the sincerity etched in his features.

"Okay," she whispered. "But Joe, when you get back . . . we have to talk."

"We'll talk about whatever you want, baby."

"Promise?"

He pressed one more kiss to her trembling lips. "Promise," he whispered.

JOE walked into the meeting five minutes late, ignoring Sam's sharp look of reprimand. Nathan and Donovan, however, grinned broadly while Nathan arched an inquiring eyebrow.

"Later, bro," Joe murmured to Nathan. "How long is today's sermon supposed to last?"

"However long it takes us all to ace this candy-ass final exam that Allie is under the impression will make fools of us all," Skylar muttered, overhearing Joe's question.

"Need y'all to run interference for me if big brother wants to hold me after for time-out in the corner," Joe said so only his team could hear.

Skylar smiled. "We have your back. We're well aware you have better things to be doing. And Joe? For what it's worth, I wish you the best," she said sincerely.

He smiled warmly at his teammate. "Thanks, Sky. I really appreciate that."

Allie had set up a station where each team member would disable and dismantle an explosive device, and it had to be done in under two minutes.

"Jesus," Dolphin, one of Steele's men, muttered. "A fifth grader could disarm this pansy-ass thing."

Chuckles went up, causing Allie to frown and look in their direction.

"Time to get serious, y'all," Edge drawled. "As our esteemed colleague is so fond of saying, giddyup, let's rope the goats and get the hell out of here."

This time laughter broke out and P.J., who was within earshot, rolled her eyes. "Y'all are never going to let me live that one down."

"Hey, it was a damn good mantra at the time," Dolphin said, grinning like an idiot.

"If I could have your attention, we can get started," Allie said in a voice that could freeze the fires of hell.

"I'll go first," Joe volunteered. If it got him out first, he'd gladly be the sacrificial lamb.

"I was going to go by team," Allie replied.

Joe shrugged. "Works for me. My team will go first, and as coleader of my team, that means I go first. Nathan will follow. Got any problem with that?" he asked sweetly.

She motioned him to the first station, and he wanted to laugh. He could do this with his eyes closed. Did she really think KGI was this stupid? If she did, then why bother joining?

She started to drone on with instructions, but before she could finish, Joe snipped the final wire, checked for any remaining traps that would detonate the bomb if the primary trigger were disabled then stood back, holding his hands up.

"Done. Satisfied, ma'am?"

She had a stunned look on her face. She stepped forward with a frown and did a thorough check of the device and then shook her head.

"That was amazing," she said, a hint of admiration creeping into her voice. "I think that's the fastest time anyone's ever registered in any of my classes."

Joe smiled. "I'm not even the best. We like to give Baker shit about explosives, but he's the man when it comes to setting, dismantling or detonating any device known, and well, quite a few classified ones that we aren't supposed to know about."

Allie looked like she had no idea what to do with that information.

Joe turned to his twin. "You're up, bro. Try not to show me up too badly."

The others laughed, but Allie was now giving them all thoughtful looks, and something that resembled guilt and embarrassment shadowed her eyes.

Joe made a subtle gesture to pull Donovan to the side.

"What's up?" Donovan asked quietly.

"I need you to cover for me with Sam. I'm sure he's still pissed about me ducking out yesterday, but I have to go. It's important or I wouldn't ask."

Concern shone in his brother's eyes. "Is everything okay?"

Joe smiled. "It will be, Van. It will be just as soon as I can get back home."

Donovan grinned with sudden understanding. "Don't worry about Sam. I'll handle things here."

Joe didn't waste any time, striding out of the war room as Sam called for him to hold up. Ignoring the request, he hopped into his truck and headed out of the compound back to his cabin. He was out of his truck heading to the front door when he noticed it was ajar.

Alarm prickled up his spine. He hadn't left the door open. Had Zoe taken off despite her promise to stay? He rushed inside, hastily looking in the living room and kitchen before running to the bedroom. It too was empty, but what made his blood run cold, his heart nearly stopping, was the utter chaos there.

There were obvious signs of a struggle. Knocked-over lamps. The covers and sheets were off the bed and strewn all over the floor, and Zoe's clothing was still where he'd tossed it the night before when he'd undressed her.

But what sent terror blazing through his heart and mind were blood spatters on the bed, the floor and even the wall.

Someone had taken Zoe while he'd left her alone. Without protection. Outside the safety of the compound. Oh God, this was his fault. All the Kelly women were safely ensconced within the walls of the compound, and yet he'd left Zoe to fend for herself. He'd never forgive himself if he didn't get her back safe and unharmed, and so help him, if it was the last thing he did, he'd track down every last fucker who'd dared to put their hands on the woman he loved. Who'd shed her blood. He'd kill every last one of them.

CHAPTER 20

RUSTY crept through Sean's house, and then realizing how absurd she was being, she rolled her eyes and made her way into his bedroom. It wasn't as though anyone was here, and Sean's security system was an embarrassment for a law enforcement officer.

She paused in the doorway of his bedroom, heat suffusing her cheeks as she imagined being in that bed with Sean. It was humiliating to acknowledge just how long she'd had that particular fantasy. But she was no longer a young girl with adolescent fantasies about kissing Sean. Her fantasies were of the adult variety now. The naked kind that involved Sean making love to her and admitting he wanted her every bit as much as she wanted him.

Well, in for a penny, in for a pound. She hastily undressed before she lost her nerve and then pulled back the covers of the neatly made bed and slid underneath sheets that smelled like him. She buried her face in his pillows, inhaling his wholly masculine smell that had driven her crazy for more years than she'd like to admit.

She heard the front door open and shivered. Boy, she hadn't been a minute too soon. She heard his light step through the house, pausing at intervals, and then his pace slowed and she could no longer hear his footfalls. She frowned, wondering what was going on.

Then suddenly the bedroom door burst open and she was looking down the barrel of Sean's pistol. She shot upward, forgetting that she was naked underneath, and the sheet fell, baring her breasts to his startled gaze.

"Rusty, what the hell?" he demanded. "Are you just *try-ing* to get shot? What the fuck are you doing? And put your damn clothes back on," he said in a strangled voice.

She smiled to herself. His gaze had been trained to her body ever since discovering who was in his bedroom—or bed, to be more exact—and his eyes were focused on her breasts to the exclusion of all else.

"Well, if you insist," she said innocently, throwing back the sheet to fully uncover her nudity.

Sean looked as if he had just swallowed his tongue, and then he closed his eyes, his jaw tight, and she could see it tic in agitation. His hand shook as he replaced his gun in his holster. Well, at least he wasn't unaffected, which had been her worst fear.

"For God's sake, Rusty, what the hell are you doing in my bed? For that matter, how the hell did you get in?"

She smirked. "Your security system sucks."

Sean rubbed a tired hand over his face. "What's really going on here, Rusty? And why are you . . . naked . . . in my bed?" He almost choked over the word *naked*.

"If I have to spell it out for you then there really is no hope for you."

He sat on the end of the bed, torment and clear indecision reflected in his eyes. He suddenly seemed so unsure when he was always nothing if not certain of himself.

"What is it you want?" he asked softly.

"You," she said bluntly. "We've been dancing around each other for years, Sean. I refuse to believe my attraction is one sided. And it's obvious you aren't going to make the first move, so I did. This seemed to be the best way to get your attention, and judging by your reaction, I'd say it worked."

"You know this can't happen, Rusty," he said gently.

"Do I? Do you, for that matter? Your words say one thing but your eyes say something quite different," she said quietly.

"You're a beautiful woman, sweetheart. No man with a dick is going to ignore you."

"Except you, apparently," she said, suddenly feeling the need to yank the covers back over her. But she'd be damned if she'd back down now. "You kissed *me*, remember? Because I remember every second of it. I've never forgotten it, Sean. Did you? Can you look me in the eye and tell me you forgot? Maybe it meant nothing to you, but it meant *everything* to me. And I never got to kiss *you*."

She crawled to the end of the bed, ignoring the alarmed look on his face, focusing instead on the blaze of desire that sparked in his eyes. She wrapped her arms around his shoulders, noting the rigidity with which he held himself in check. Then she pressed her lips to his and sighed, melting against him, her breasts pressing to his hard, muscled chest.

He let out a groan that sounded like a mixture of protest and raw desire, and she took the opportunity to trace the inside of his mouth with her tongue. To slide the tip over the rough edges of his. For one glorious moment, he gave in and took control of the kiss, and the mastery in it made her quiver from head to toe. Then he abruptly grasped her shoulders, setting her firmly away from him, his expression hard. A quick glance down confirmed he was hard elsewhere too.

"This can't happen, Rusty. Damn it. Just *stop*."

"You can't deny your response to me," she whispered.

"I think it's safe to say that I'd have the same reaction if any beautiful, *naked* woman wrapped herself around me," he snapped.

She flinched as if she'd been slapped, recoiling and ducking her head to hide the sudden surge of tears. Never had she felt as devastated as she did in this moment. Not the torment of her childhood. The humiliation heaped upon her by her mother and then her stepfather or the constant mockery and shame leveled at her in high school.

She'd sworn when she was little more than a child that no one would ever see her cry again.

"Rusty, honey," he said gently.

"I'm nothing to you, not good enough for you," she said tonelessly. "You've made that abundantly clear for years. I guess I'm just too dumb and too fresh from the trailer park for someone of your standing. Apparently I needed someone to beat me over the head with it. Well, you just did. Congratulations. I get it."

Sean swore long and viciously. "Goddamn it, Rusty, that is not what I meant. Would you listen to me, please? The last thing I want is to hurt you."

"Too late," she said, choking back tears.

She wrapped the sheet around her and then scrambled to retrieve her clothing, ignoring his repeated pleas for her to listen. She was done subjecting herself to rejection and being treated like a fucking charity case. Sean Cameron could go fuck himself because she was finished putting herself on the line when he was too big of a coward to do the same.

Sean's cell rang and he swore as he picked up his phone. "Cameron," he clipped out. *"What?"*

The way he said *what* sent a prickle of apprehension down Rusty's spine.

"I'm on my way. I'll get Rusty and bring her. Give me five minutes."

He closed his phone, his face a wreath of concern. "Get dressed," he said tersely.

"Sean, what's wrong?" she asked, hating the fact that her voice trembled.

"Zoe's gone missing and it doesn't look good. You're going with me because it would seem you're the only one who has any real answers."

She went pale and her lips trembled. "Oh God," she whispered. "No. He couldn't have found her. He couldn't have," she moaned.

"Save it for Joe, who's out of his fucking mind," Sean snapped. "You've got a hell of a lot of explaining to do, like the *he* in question finding her, but none of which entails me finding you naked in my bed."

"Oh, don't worry, Sean. I'd never humiliate myself any more than I already have. You have my promise that will *never* happen again."

CHAPTER 21

THE last of the testing had just been completed and Allie was visibly stunned that every single KGI member had not only passed but had done so with speed and accuracy she clearly wasn't expecting. She also seemed surprised that there seemed to be little doubt among her team members that they *would* pass so easily. She'd fully expected them to rub it in her face, but she'd been wrong about that as well. She was puzzled by the entire situation.

Shame swept through her, through every judgmental bone in her body. She'd been so convinced that her position in the KGI organization was provisional, that somehow she was a second-class citizen, the rookie who had to prove what a badass she was so she'd fit in with all the other badasses that surrounded her. Worse was the fact that there were already two female warriors who were obviously as qualified as their male counterparts and treated as equals. She'd seen nothing but respect leveled at P.J. and Skylar. She wanted that same respect and yet had done nothing to earn it except act like a bitch with an ax to grind and a bad attitude. Hardly the team player she professed to wanting to be. It was she who had a hell of a lot of learning to do, not the others.

It embarrassed her that she had been the one coming in with preconceived notions, not her new teammates. She was the one with a chip on her shoulder and she'd made a complete ass of herself when she had nothing to prove to anyone.

Was it any wonder the others weren't exactly extending their friendship? Loyalty? Absolutely. Backup? She had no doubt there. But camaraderie, friendship and a true sense of belonging? Not so much, and that was on her.

A loud buzz interrupted her somber thoughts and she glanced sharply around as the entire room came to attention, gazes intent and tense, ready for action. A few curses rent the air and someone muttered, "All good things must come to an end."

Donovan was the first to reach the phone she realized was the secure line, which never meant a social call or someone calling for a friendly chat. It was a call to arms.

"Kelly here," he said tersely.

There was a long pause.

"What the *fuck*? Slow down, Joe. Tell me what happened."

The entire room surged closer to Donovan, concern etched on every single person's face, most especially that of Nathan, Joe's twin.

"Fuck!" Donovan exploded. "Keep your cool, man. We'll be there in two."

He hung up amid a chorus of demands to know what the hell was wrong. He ignored the outcry and began issuing orders.

"Nathan's and Steele's teams with me. Rio, your team stays here to organize communications and act as backup.

Until we know what we're up against, I need every available man at the ready."

Allie frowned. "He's one of our own. Shouldn't we all be going?"

Nathan and his team turned to Allie, their expressions not the friendliest. Even P.J., Cole and Dolphin closed ranks with Nathan and the rest of his and Joe's team.

But it was Sam who held his hand up to silence the others before they had time to respond.

"We live and die as a team, and thus far you haven't proven to be a team player. And this concerns one of our own, so I only want those who are committed one hundred and ten percent to this *family* to be involved in this mission. Because we *are* family, not just some fucking organization that collects a paycheck and calls it a day. Now, we've wasted enough fucking time while my brother obviously needs our help. Donovan can give a report on what he knows on the way. Now move out. Double time."

"I was unfair to you all," Allie said in a low voice. "I owe you all an apology, but as you said, right now one of our own needs our help, and my wrongs can be righted later if I'm given that opportunity."

"Rio? It's your call," Sam said to the team leader.

Rio simply nodded. "Fall in and let's get the fuck out of here."

Ninety seconds later, four vehicles roared to a stop outside Joe's cabin. Nathan led the charge inside and his heart sank when he saw Joe sitting on the couch, his face buried in his hands. He looked up when he heard the others enter and Nathan winced at the raw agony and grief reflected in his twin's eyes.

Nathan sank onto the couch next to him while the others stood by, tense and ready to go to fucking war if that's what it took.

"What happened?" Nathan asked softly.

"I left her here," Joe said painfully. "I left her here un-protected. I told her I wouldn't be gone long. Asked her to stay and we'd have breakfast when I got back." He gestured at the living room that looked as though a tornado had hit it. "This is what I came home to. And the bedroom . . ." He broke off, choking on the words, once more burying his face in his hands

Sam gestured to Dolphin and Baker to check the bedroom.

"What was in the bedroom?" Nathan pressed quietly.

"She fought hard," Joe said painfully. "Her blood is on the floor, Jesus, even the wall. Splattered like some asshole hit her hard enough to spill her blood. I left her here, god-damn it!"

"You couldn't have known, Joe," Skylar said gently, tak-ing the seat on his other side.

She slipped her hand into his, holding tightly.

"No, but if I hadn't dragged my fucking heels about build-ing inside the compound, if I had my house already built, she would have been there, safe, inside the compound where some asshole couldn't get to her."

"The question is who?" Sam said.

"I think Rusty probably has the answer to that question," Sean said grimly from the doorway as he propelled Rusty inside.

Joe was on his feet immediately, his expression pleading. Rusty rushed into his arms, tears running down her cheeks. He crushed her to him, holding her tightly.

"You have to help me, Rusty. You have to tell me what you know. Everything. Don't leave anything out. Someone has her. She's hurt. Her blood is all over my bedroom."

Rusty drew away and hugged her arms around her mid-dle as she faced the room full of people all staring at her for answers. She closed her eyes as more tears leaked down her cheeks.

"Her real name is Stella Huntington."

"What the fuck?" Joe demanded.

Donovan held his hand up. "Let her explain, Joe. We don't have much time."

Rusty closed her eyes once more and her voice quavered as she made her next revelation. "Her father is Garth Huntington."

The room went utterly silent as shocked looks came at her from every direction. Then an explosion of responses echoed over the room. Joe was torn between shock and betrayal. He didn't understand any of it. Zoe—Stella—whoever the fuck she was . . . Her father was a crime lord who headed one of the biggest criminal empires in North America?

Rusty hurried back to Joe and hugged him tightly before leaning back and staring earnestly into his eyes. "She didn't use you or betray you, Joe. She was running for her life. I created a new identity for her. An airtight one. One that couldn't possibly link her to Stella Huntington. She had no idea who or what her father was until some asshole played her in an effort to get to her father, a father who never gave a shit about her, who spent her entire life telling her what to do, how to be, *who* to be, how to dress. He dictated every aspect of her life."

She sucked in a deep breath before anyone could say anything because everyone looked like they were about to erupt. She continued on breathlessly, the words tumbling out so fast even she had a hard time following her train of thought.

"Sebastian, the bastard who got close to her, used her and played on her insecurities and her need to be loved for the first time in her life, did so in an effort to get to her father.

When he realized her father didn't give one fuck about her, his plan changed. Zoe overheard him on the phone with someone saying that she was no longer of any use because the old man didn't give a shit about her, so using her as a pawn was pointless, and he planned to kill her."

A round of curses went up and Joe's face tightened to the point of fury.

Rusty put her hand on his arm, feeling the coil of muscles tense and spasm beneath her touch. "Please, let me finish," she begged.

"She panicked. She knew no one and had no friends. Except . . . me. We did meet when we were in college. That much is true. She attended UT. She came to me because she had no one else to turn to, and thank God she did. After a lot of hacking and long hours of mind-numbing work, I created an entirely new identity—a new life—and Zoe Kildare was born. It was the name of the imaginary friend she had growing up because she had no one else," Rusty whispered painfully. "I created her entire life from birth to the present, complete with social media presences and contacts, an Amazon account with a history of purchases that matched her new persona. I got her a birth certificate issued in her new name, Social Security card and driver's license as well as recorded attendance and graduation from DePaul University in Chicago.

"We laid a lot of false trails to separate parts of the country, even opening a bank account on the East Coast. And since most people trying to disguise themselves can only cut, not grow, their hair, I not only dyed her hair from its original red color, I meticulously layered in extensions so they looked as natural as possible so her hair appeared a good six inches longer than her actual length. I created an entirely new look for her, so much so that her own father wouldn't recognize her."

"Holy shit," Donovan said in awe. "You managed all of

that, Rusty? Shit, even I came up with nothing except what you created when I did some digging on her."

"Why the hell didn't either of you tell me?" Joe asked painfully. "I would have never left her alone and unprotected. This would have never happened. I understand why Zoe wouldn't—couldn't—trust me, but why didn't *you*, Rusty?"

Her eyes filled with tears. "I couldn't betray her, Joe. How was I to know you'd fall for her or even take an interest in her? If I betrayed her, if she even suspected I had confided the truth in any of my family, she would have run and she'd be dead right now."

Sam cleared his throat to get Joe's attention. "I'm sending Rio and his team to gather the wives and hole up at Ma's. We have no way of knowing what this asshole has planned, if he's still in the vicinity or off to parts unknown, but we'd be dumbasses if we took anything for granted. No one goes anywhere until we get this figured out. Steele, I need you to go pull surveillance footage of the cabin and surroundings, including the outside perimeter of the compound, but leave P.J. and Cole to provide cover here just in case."

Joe shook himself from his terror long enough to issue orders to his team as well. "Sky, you and Swanny do a complete sweep of the bedroom and be careful not to contaminate any potential evidence. Edge, I need you and Ryker on the lookout around the cabin and search for any tracks, footprints or tire marks."

Then he turned back to Rusty, trying to wrap his head around the deception he'd become unwittingly mired in.

"What was this asshole's name again? The one who fucked her over in order to get to her father?"

"Sebastian, but I doubt it's his real name," she said bitterly.

"Damn it, Rusty, you should have come to us with this," Sam said in frustration.

His other brothers voiced the same nearly in unison.

Rusty turned from Joe, but he saw the flicker of pain and betrayal in her eyes as she did and as she saw the accusation written on every one of his brothers' faces. Even Nathan looked angry, which seemed to be the final straw for Rusty.

She fisted her hands at her sides and exploded with rage and grief, lashing out at the people who considered her family and who she considered to be her family.

"I was only doing what any one of you would do—what you *always* do—for complete strangers, much less someone you love and consider family or a close friend. If all of you would stop viewing me as a fuckup without brains, responsibility or regard for anyone but myself, you'd realize that *everything* I've done has been to overcome the stigma of my past so Mom and Dad could be *proud* of me. So all of you could be proud of me. So I could be *worthy* of being a Kelly. So I could be part of something I never had before. A *family*.

"You're such fucking hypocrites," she raged in a voice that sounded like she was precariously close to tears. "Donovan lets all the wives help with his charitable foundation, which often necessitates one or more of them to be in contact with the person or persons who need help, and all of the victims they aid, that they help get out of shit situations, help move after getting new aliases, papers, money, housing and a new life in a new city, are involved in dangerous, often life-threatening situations. Have you ever stopped to consider the danger you're putting *your* wives in? Your *children*? Your entire *family*?

"What if one of these victims was found by the assholes they're running from? The ones your wives help them hide from? Don't you think that asshole might be a little interested in knowing how the victim was able to pull off something that elaborate? Where they got the money, the job, the new name and everything else you give them? If their lives were threatened, don't you think those victims would throw every single person under the bus if it was the only way they'd survive? The only way their children would survive?

"And don't you ever stop to consider the possibility that one of these abusive bastards would want revenge against the people who helped their *property*, particularly other *women* who'd stuck their noses into his goddamn business and given *his* woman the idea that she was better off without him? Are you seriously going to stand there and lecture me in such a hypocritical manner when one of your wives could be seriously injured, raped or even killed in retaliation?

"And if you don't think it can happen then you're fucking naïve, and men who do what you do and who've seen the shit y'all have seen shouldn't damn well be surprised by anything.

"If there's one thing I've learned in this family, it's that you're all about doing the right thing and you're all about family, and yet you don't spare any opportunity to remind me that I'm *not* family, and furthermore you all lash out at me for doing exactly what you all do on a daily basis, but I suppose it's different because apparently in this organization it's *do as we say, not as we do.*"

Tears coursed down her cheeks as she broke into sobs. The room was stunned into complete silence as the brothers exchanged remorseful looks. Oddly, Sean looked . . . pissed. Rusty wiped angrily at the tears and her blotchy face and then started toward the door.

"Rusty," Joe called.

She stopped only long enough to look back, more tears escaping from her swollen eyes. "Don't worry about me. Your focus needs to be on finding Zoe. I'm going home—to Frank and Marlene's," she amended. "Provided I'm still welcome," she finished bitterly.

A round of curses echoed in the room as she hurried away. When Donovan and Garrett would have followed, Sean, who had been standing silently in the back, held up his hand to stop them.

"I'll make sure she gets home safely," he said quietly. "I'll be back shortly. It goes without saying that you'll have the full resources of the sheriff's department to help in any way we can."

Sean stomped out of Joe's cabin and then ran to catch up to Rusty, who was walking down the winding highway that led to the compound.

"Rusty, goddamn it, hold up," he shouted.

She visibly stiffened, her spine going ramrod straight as she stood rigidly while he strode up. When she turned, he winced at the coldness in her eyes, but his anger was hot enough to melt any ice she managed to erect.

"Were you just *trying* to get yourself killed?" he seethed. "You endangered not only yourself and Zoe but your entire family by not telling them the truth from the very start. Grow the hell up, Rusty, and stop acting like the world is still out to get you. That chip you've got on your shoulder has gotten so heavy that you're staggering under its weight."

"I just have two words for you, copper," she said in a voice so quiet and defeated that it sent chills down his spine. "Fuck off."

"Damn it, Rusty! Haven't you figured out yet that there are people who love and care about you? You're so convinced the world's out to get you that you can't see what's right under your nose."

"Oh, I see what's under my nose," she said softly. "I see it very well. I'm sure you have better things to do than taunt me with my childish, adolescent whims, so why don't you go make yourself useful and help clean up my fuckup while I see myself the rest of the way to Marlene's."

"It's home, Rusty," he said in frustration. "Your home. And whether you choose to believe it or not, there are a hell of a lot of people who love you if you'd just let them."

She shrugged. "It doesn't really matter what I call it now, does it? I believe the saying goes 'home is where the heart is,' and let's just say my heart isn't here anymore. And if the one you love doesn't love you back, there isn't much point, is there?"

She turned and began running at full sprint, and Sean watched helplessly as she reached the gates of the compound. He closed his eyes and curled his fingers into tight fists at his sides.

It was always that way with Rusty. Like trying to hold water in a hand with fingers spread open. And he'd fucked up any chance he'd ever had of being able to prevent her from sliding even further away because she had him twisted in so many knots that nothing he ever said or did came out the way he intended.

CHAPTER 22

"**WHAT** the fuck am I going to do?" Joe demanded, despair filling his voice. "God, I didn't even have the chance to tell her I loved her or that I wanted forever."

"Stop it," Garrett said harshly. "You can't talk like that. We've all been there. We've all felt exactly what you're feeling. You have to have faith, man. We'll get her back."

"The question is, who the hell has her?" Ethan muttered. "We've got two angles to explore. Asshole number one—her father. Or asshole number two—this Sebastian dickhead who used her and then planned to kill her."

"Or a third angle—any number of the many enemies her father has made over the years," Donovan added. "If Sebastian didn't realize at first that Zoe's old man didn't give a shit about her, chances are a lot of other people didn't either."

God, the possibilities seemed endless, and Joe felt like beating his head against the wall. Why hadn't he made the time to talk when Zoe had wanted to? She'd looked so hesitant and worried, and now he knew, goddamn it, he *knew* what she had wanted to tell him, and he'd blown her off for a fucking meeting that was so unimportant in the scheme of things that he wanted to hit something.

"She tried to tell me," Joe said hoarsely. "This morning she said we needed to talk and she was so nervous and hesitant, but I put her off because of that fucking meeting. I asked her to stay, said we'd have breakfast and then talk about whatever she wanted. Fuck me! Why didn't I just put her first?"

Sam's phone rang and he snatched it up, putting it to his ear. "Talk to me."

After a moment of silence, he said, "We'll be right there."

"Steele pulled all the surveillance. He has something we need to take a look at," Sam said. "Y'all go on. I'll round up the others and we'll be right behind you."

Joe was already running for the door, his brothers right behind him. They roared into the compound, skidding to a halt outside the war room.

"What you got?" Joe demanded as soon as they entered.

Steele punched in a series of commands and brought up surveillance footage of Joe's cabin. A few seconds into it, Joe froze when he saw an unconscious, bloody Zoe being hauled out of his cabin by a man, closely followed by an accomplice. Rage boiled in his veins and he pounded his fist into the planning table.

Sam burst in, followed by the rest of the KGI team members minus Rio's team, who were guarding the rest of the family at Frank and Marlene's house. They all watched in horror as Zoe was tossed without care into the backseat of a black SUV while one man climbed in the back with her, the other getting into the driver's seat.

"Freeze that," Donovan ordered. "Back up one frame and

hold. Can you zoom in and get a clear read of the license plate?"

Joe held his breath as Steele zoomed, and then impatiently, Donovan took over the controls and cleared the image until finally the numbers were visible and more easily read. Sean walked into the war room and Joe immediately barked a command to the sheriff to call in the plates and put out a BOLO for the entire state of Tennessee. The bastards couldn't have gone that far yet. Unless they were flying Zoe out.

"Contact all local landing strips or any location a chopper could take off from," Joe added.

To the shock of everyone present, the war room door opened again, admitting Rio and Diego, but the room exploded in chaos, with Nathan losing his fucking mind when it was realized that Shea was tucked solidly between them, their bodies forming a protective barrier around her.

"What the fuck?" Nathan demanded.

His furious gaze found Rio, demanding without words an explanation as to why his wife wasn't safely ensconced with the other wives.

Shea pushed forward, rushing to Joe, throwing her arms around him and hugging him tightly. "I'm so sorry, Joe. I had to come." She cast an apologetic look in her husband's direction, pleading silently with him to understand. "I think I can help," she said quietly.

For a moment Joe couldn't breathe as hope seized him by the throat. Tears burned his eyelids at his sister-in-law's unselfish act. An act he knew could cost her dearly.

"No! Damn it, Shea. No! You aren't doing this. I forbid it," Nathan said heatedly. "You're pregnant, baby. You can't take that kind of risk!"

The others were clearly at a loss as they stared back and

forth between Nathan, Shea and the sudden hopefulness and relief that spilled into Joe's eyes.

"Will someone tell me what the hell is going on here?" Garrett demanded.

"You all know my telepathy, or rather my ability to connect to people, is random," she said, not meeting Nathan's furious, panicked eyes. "The day of the barbecue, the first time Zoe met us all . . . I heard her. Or rather I felt her," she quickly amended. "Her fear was overwhelming. It nearly suffocated me. For a long moment I couldn't breathe, it was so gut-wrenching. I thought I would pass out."

"Jesus," Donovan muttered.

"And you think you can connect to her now?" Sam asked gently.

"I don't want her to even try it," Nathan snarled. "You have no idea what's going on with Zoe, what her situation is, what you'd be exposing yourself to. I won't allow this, Shea. You're already fragile enough with this pregnancy kicking your ass on a daily basis. I don't even want to contemplate what this might do to you or our baby."

Part of Joe agreed with Nathan. The risk was great. But the other part wanted to scream at his brother that if the roles were reversed and it was Shea enduring God knows what and someone might be the key in finding—helping—her, he'd be just as adamant about doing whatever was necessary to help her.

It's exactly why I'm going to do everything I can to help her—and you, Joe.

Shea's soft voice echoed in Joe's mind and he gathered her close, hugging her tightly as he buried his face in her hair.

You'll never know how much this means to me, baby girl. I love her so damn much. I can't lose her now that I've finally found her.

Joe saw Nathan sigh in resignation and realized that he and Shea had been having their own telepathic conversation.

Everyone looked at Shea in concern and a flush turned her cheeks pink at being the object of so much scrutiny.

"You tell us how you want to do this, Shea," Garrett said gently. "If you prefer to only have Nathan and Joe with you, then the rest of us will clear out until you give us the all clear."

Shea smiled shyly. "That's sweet of you, Garrett, but I think everyone should be here. I'm not always cognizant of what I relay, and if we have everyone's ear then we run the least risk of missing important details."

"Promise me," Nathan said fiercely. "If this causes you any pain or distress, promise me you'll break away."

Shea pulled away from Joe and went into her husband's arms. "I'll be fine, Nathan. Promise. I need to get started. We're wasting time Zoe may not have."

Joe stiffened, his face spasming in pain. Shea sent him a look of apology but he shook his head. "You're only speaking the truth. We don't know what we're up against—what she's up against, so yes, we need to hurry. Just tell me what you need. Anything at all."

"Just be here and try to be calm so I can give my entire focus to trying to establish the link between me and Zoe. It may take a while because it's a lot to grasp that you can suddenly hear someone talking in your head, and she'll wonder if she's going crazy."

Nathan led Shea over to one of the couches in the war room and sat down next to her. She reached her hand out to Joe to pull him down next to her and then sat between the two men, their hands clasped in hers.

She sucked in a deep breath and closed her eyes, her brow

puckering with strain. The entire room fell silent as all attention was focused on her.

Shea blanked everything from her mind as she closed off every path except the narrow, faint fingerprints that led her to Zoe.

CHAPTER 23

ZOE lay numbly on the floor, her hands tied behind her back, her ankles bound so tightly together that the rope cut into her skin, which was smeared with blood. She blinked in an effort to clear her vision, obscured by blood and swelling, but her head had incurred the most injury. The pain was so overwhelming that nausea was ever present, and she swallowed rapidly to prevent vomiting.

Sebastian stood a short distance away with two accomplices she couldn't identify. He wore a smug expression of victory, and every so often he leered openly at her, seemingly amused at the damage he'd inflicted.

"The old man really *doesn't* give a fuck about you," he said with a laugh. "He sounded quite bored when I listed my demands. I wonder if he'll say the same when I call his bluff and send him footage of his daughter's head being blown off."

He bent down and ran his fingers suggestively over her

breasts, and she shrank away, nearly moaning at the pain the motion caused her. He laughed and then backhanded her across her already bruised cheek.

"I plan to have a taste of that pussy again before I hand you back over to Daddy. If you give me any trouble, I'll let my partners have a turn as well, so if I were you, I'd be a very good girl."

Tears trailed down her cheeks, mixing with fresh and drying blood from her nose and mouth. There was no hope for rescue. No one knew where she was, and even if Rusty told Joe and his brothers everything, Joe wouldn't want her anyway. Her father didn't give a shit about her—he never had. Once . . . before her mother left, he had been a different man. He'd been an actual father. She had vague memories of a loving family, of his tossing her into the air as she squealed in delight. Him tucking her into bed at night after reading her a bedtime story.

All of that had come to an end after her mother had left without so much as a good-bye, a letter or an I love you. One day she was there and then she wasn't, and her father had turned into a cold, heartless man she didn't recognize. Did he blame her for her mother leaving? Did he hate her for that? What kind of father placed blame on a five-year-old child? And even if he didn't blame her, didn't he realize she was hurting every bit as much as he was? She hadn't only lost one parent. She'd lost both the day her mother left them behind.

And now Sebastian was taunting her, knowing full well her father didn't give a shit about her. She knew she wouldn't come out of this alive. She'd heard the phone call and his plan to kill her that had prompted her to flee in the first place. What kind of monster toyed with her when she knew the eventuality of her fate? It seemed Sebastian and her father were cut from the same cloth.

She closed her eyes, replaying every single moment with Joe, Rusty, the Kelly family. For a short period of time she'd known what it was like to touch the sun, to understand what unconditional love and loyalty felt like.

And Joe, how she wished she'd told him she loved him. If only she could have that beautiful night back, the most wonderful night of her entire life.

Pain assaulted her again when Sebastian slapped her bruised cheek, causing a fresh trickle of blood to leak from the corner of her mouth.

"Open your eyes, bitch. Yeah, that's right. Look at the man who's going to fuck you while Daddy listens."

He rubbed his hands in glee and she looked at him in horror. The man was insane. A complete sociopath. To her relief, one of his accomplices called him over and the two conversed across the room out of the range of her hearing. She had no desire to hear more of the atrocities he had planned for her. She closed her eyes, biting into her abused lip in a futile attempt to staunch the flow of tears and the vicious grip of helplessness that besieged her.

Zoe? This is Shea, Nathan's wife. Please don't react in any way. I know you likely think you're crazy. You're not. I'm telepathic and I can talk to some people this way over great distances. Joe is with me and he's scared out of his mind. He's desperate to find you. We're all desperate to find you, but I need you to help me help you.

Zoe shook her head, hysteria rising fast. Oh God, she was losing her mind.

No, Zoe. You're perfectly sane. I don't have time to explain it all but I swear to you your mind isn't playing tricks on you. I know you're in pain and you feel hopeless, but I can help you. Please let me help you. Don't shut me out,

*and don't speak aloud. Just think of what you want to say.
I'll hear you.*

Shea?

Zoe's tentative response convinced her that she really
was out of her mind. But she was so numb that even if her
mind was playing tricks on her, it beat the alternative, which
was living in reality.

I'm here, came Shea's soothing response.

What do I do? What am I supposed to do? Fear edged
the desperate pleas. *Oh God, I'm crazy, aren't I? I've lost
all touch with reality. I really am going to die.*

The oddest thing happened. She felt Shea's concern and
compassion. She had a pathway into Shea's mind and it was
consumed with fear for her. For Joe. She could even sense
Shea trying to calm Joe down and had to swallow back the
sob that welled in her throat.

*No! Zoe, please, I'll explain everything to you later, but
I swear, this is very real and I can help you. Do you understand? I can help you. We can save you but you have to help
me. Can you do that?*

After a long hesitation Zoe whispered a mental *yes* even
as tears pooled in her eyes. What did she have to lose? She
was going to die, and if there was even the slimmest of chances
that she wasn't hallucinating, she had to take it.

*Can you tell me where you are? Where they're holding
you? Any detail no matter how small. What do you remember? What have they said? Anything you can give us that
would help in locating you, Zoe. Don't leave a word out.*

*It's not that far from the compound, or at least I don't
think I was out that long. It's a silly name, the town, I mean.*
Frustration beat along with the ache in her head, and she
felt Shea dig her fingers into her temples and forehead in an

effort to ward off the pain. Was Zoe causing her pain? Was she able to feel what Zoe felt? The temptation to break away, to ignore Shea's offer of help, was strong.

No! Zoe, I'm fine. You can't give up and you can't ignore me.

And then the oddest thing happened. The pain that was so prevalent in Zoe's battered body simply faded as if it were never there. But she felt Shea's suffering, and it brought tears to her eyes.

No! If you do this I won't tell you anything, Zoe said fiercely. *You won't suffer this for me. I won't let you.*

She felt Shea's sigh of frustration and oddly the faint trail of Nathan's anger and fear for Shea.

What did you do? Zoe asked in wonder. *How did you make the pain stop?*

I don't have a lot of time, Shea said weakly. *Holding a pathway like this saps my strength, and soon I'll be insensible. You have to tell me how to find you before it's too late.*

I saw a sign that said Bucksnort. Am I crazy? I was woozy and just coming to consciousness but we turned off an exit that said Bucksnort. I swear that's what it said.

How many of them are holding you, Zoe? What are we up against and what are they waiting for?

My father. They think he'll care that they have me, she added sadly. *They have no idea how wrong they are. If he doesn't come, they're going to kill me. If he does come, they'll kill me. It doesn't really matter.*

She didn't tell Shea of the other threats Sebastian had made. That he planned to rape her regardless of whether her father came or not. But then she realized how ridiculous it was since Shea was in her head and knew exactly what Sebastian had threatened and what he'd done already.

That's not going to happen, Shea said fiercely. *Do you*

hear me, Zoe? You hold on and do whatever you have to do to stay safe and survive. The men will be there. They'll get you out of there just like they once did for me.

They're coming back, Zoe said fearfully. *What do I do?*

I'll stay with you, Zoe. I'll be here the entire time. I won't leave you.

Shea's quiet vow comforted her as she stared up into the eyes of her captors that gleamed with triumph.

Shea? Joe, I mean they, need to know there are more than just the three men inside the room they're holding me in. There are more. A lot more. Outside, keeping guard, and they're heavily armed.

Do or say nothing to raise their ire, Shea whispered into her mind. *Be meek and mild. Don't tip your hand. Let them think you're terrified. Be brave and wait for us, Zoe.*

Shea? Can you do something for me, please?

Anything, Zoe.

If . . . if I die, will you please tell Joe that I'm sorry. Tell Rusty and the rest of your family I'm sorry. I never meant to endanger you all. And tell Joe . . . She paused a moment, battling a fresh surge of tears. *Tell him I love him and that he was the best thing that ever happened to me.*

Shea was fierce, power surging into Zoe's mind, giving her a burst of strength and a reprieve from the relentless pain in her head.

Don't even think it, Zoe. Don't you dare give up. We're coming for you. Joe's coming for you.

Zoe held tight to Shea's firm vow. Maybe she was losing her mind, but the conviction in Shea's voice was not imagined. Shea—and Joe—were her only hope.

CHAPTER 24

THE entire KGI organization converged on the small, rural town of Bucksnort, Tennessee, crawling like ants over the entire terrain, investigating every possible hiding place. Shea had insisted on going and wouldn't back down. Her connection to Zoe was integral to the rescue operation, and so in the end, they had no choice but to include her as the point of contact with Zoe.

Shea kept in constant communication with Zoe, though with each session Zoe seemed to grow weaker, a fact Shea kept to herself so Joe wouldn't completely lose his already thin hold on his own sanity. But she worried for Zoe, because she knew that in addition to the abuse heaped on her by the asshole in charge, Sebastian, she had also suffered a head injury. While Shea could buffer her from the constant barrage of pain, she couldn't heal the wound. Only Grace could do that, and Shea would never drag her pregnant sister into a situation where she or her baby could be seriously harmed by taking on the wound herself.

By following the hazy images picked from Zoe's mind, she was able to identify certain road markers and excitedly directed the way when she recognized one of the paths from Zoe's memory.

None of the KGI members liked that Shea, being pregnant, was even remotely involved in the situation, but had little choice in the matter when Zoe's life hung in the balance. Allie had remained conspicuously quiet, absorbing the oddity of what she was witnessing with wonderment, not the skepticism one might expect.

"Shit," Shea murmured when she directed the convoy of vehicles to stop. A worried frown tugged at her lips and she looked at Nathan and Joe in alarm.

"What is it, baby?" Nathan asked.

"The place they're holding her is a veritable fortress. I told you what Zoe said about there being many armed men guarding the perimeter of the building where they're keeping her. She was in and out of consciousness when she was carried in, so the memories were jumbled and confusing to her. But I'm reading what she did see as more comes back to her, and it isn't good. The outside is heavily fortified. There's no way to get in there quietly or without a fight," she added in a worried tone.

Joe smiled and squeezed Shea's hand in comfort. "Fighting our way in and out is what we do, sweetheart. Besides, we have a secret weapon. You."

She tried to smile, but it wavered and her face fell completely. "I don't want any of you to get hurt," she pleaded.

Nathan kissed her softly. "Promise me you'll stay back and out of the way. If I have to worry about you *and* covering my team, then I do you both an injustice."

The members of KGI all assembled a half mile from the abandoned factory where Zoe was being held prisoner.

"Allie, I need you and Baker to set explosives around the most heavily reinforced sections of the building, away from where Zoe is being held so she isn't caught in the blast. I don't particularly care who else gets caught in it. And I need it done fast," Sam ordered tersely.

"Yes, sir," Allie said, motioning for Baker to follow as they melted away, each carrying a pack with enough C-4 to bomb a small city.

"P.J., Cole, Diego and Dolphin, I need y'all on sniper duty covering north, south, east and west wings. Take out any targets in your sights. Signal when it's all clear."

Sam's gaze wandered over Nathan, as if he knew his brother wasn't going to like his next order. "I need you to fall back and stay with Shea."

"Now wait a damn minute," Nathan protested.

"She has to be protected at all costs," Sam said quietly. "This isn't about taking you out of action. She's our only means of communication with Zoe. If she's hurt or captured, we're fucked. I need you to make sure that doesn't happen. Plus, if things go bad, you're our best chance at reaching Shea before she's too far gone."

Nathan reluctantly conceded the point.

"The rest of you split up. We'll converge from all directions, gain access as soon as Allie and Baker have set off the explosives. It needs to be a quick in and out, and I don't give a fuck about casualties unless they're our own. I don't want there to be so much as a scratch on any of you."

"Donovan, Garrett, you're with me. The rest of you fan out. Joe, Shea believes Zoe is being held underground in a cellar. Rio, Ryker and Terrence will take your six and go down with you. As soon as we achieve our objective, we're out of here. We have ten minutes, starting now."

"We're ready when you are," Sam said softly into the mouthpiece to Allie and Baker. "Time to show us what you're made of, girl."

In response, a series of explosions rocked the earth, shaking it like an earthquake. Outcries and yells erupted as men started scrambling from the building.

"They always gotta make it so easy," P.J. grumbled as she began picking them off one by one.

"Hey, save some for us and don't be a hog, Mrs. Coletrane," Cole complained.

Joe ignored the typical banter he usually enjoyed on their missions. Never before had one been this personal to him. He didn't know how his brothers had survived the times when it had been the women they loved that they were going in to save. His heart couldn't take it.

Rio and Terrence flanked him, with Ryker falling in behind, taking out any threat as soon as it appeared, and Joe flipped on a floodlight to illuminate the hallways that looked like something out of a sixteenth-century dungeon. Jesus but it was dank and musty and smelled of death and human decay down here. Imagining Zoe—his Zoe—imprisoned in this nearly sent him right over the edge.

How's she doing, Shea?

His anxious call to his sister-in-law was more to keep him from losing his mind than anything else.

She's gone quiet, Joe. She's scared out of her mind and is more worried about all of you than she is herself. She's resigned herself to not surviving this and it breaks my heart.

You tell her we're coming for her and you tell her not to give up, Joe demanded, the knot in his throat and the ache in his chest nearly paralyzing him. *You tell her I'm getting her the hell out of here and to do whatever she has to do to survive until I get to her.*

Joe! They're moving her! Shea's anxious intrusion into

his mind caused him to freeze. *She's so terrified that her thoughts are in complete chaos. I've lost my connection to her. I don't know if she shut me out or if she's just so panicked that she's incapable of reason.*

Rio, Ryker and Terrence automatically held up when Joe halted abruptly, gazes warily scanning the area for any possible threat.

"What's up?" Rio asked in a low voice.

"Shea says they're moving her but can't get a good read on Zoe because she's fucking scared out of her mind. For us, goddamn it. She's more worried about us and has resigned herself to dying but doesn't want any of us to be killed."

"Fuck," Terrence rumbled. He wasn't a man of many words, but he always managed to cut to the heart of the matter.

"That's fucked-up," Rio growled. "Jesus, she doesn't deserve the shit life she's had when she represents everything good in this world."

"You don't have to tell *me* that," Joe bit out.

Gunshots erupted in the distance, and yelling and the sounds of physical fighting could be heard.

"Zoe's on the move," Joe barked into his mouthpiece. "Use extreme caution when targeting. Make sure she's not caught in the cross fire."

"Spread out," Sam barked. "I want a complete perimeter check. No one gets on or off this property until Zoe is found."

Radio communications went silent. Then suddenly P.J. came over the radio. "I've got a bead on two men. One is carrying Zoe, I'm sure of it."

"Where?" Joe demanded.

But their communication was interrupted by gunfire, and then a round of curses filled Joe's ear and terror seized him.

He began running, forgetting his training, caution, everything but getting to the woman he loved.

"Get down, Joe!" Ryker barked, flattening him with a tackle.

"What the fuck?" Joe roared.

Bullets peppered the wall just where Joe's head had been moments earlier.

"Don't be stupid," Terrence growled. "You dying does nothing for Zoe."

"Man down," P.J. said urgently. "East wing. Double time. Get a chopper in the air, STAT."

Chaos ensued. Rio went pale as he received a transmission, and then he and Terrence sprinted away, leaving Joe and Ryker to follow behind.

Allie was sprawled on the concrete helipad, blood pooling beneath her. Diego was tending her as Donovan ran up with a field kit to start an IV and attempt to stop the bleeding.

P.J. rushed up, a grim expression on her face. "She took a bullet meant for Zoe," she said quietly. "The assholes panicked when they figured out they weren't getting out alive, so they were going to shoot Zoe, leave her on the helipad and take off in the chopper. Allie came out of nowhere, drawing their fire and telling Zoe to run like hell."

Terrence knelt beside Allie, and Diego and Donovan worked on her. "You hang in there, Allie girl. We aren't letting you off that easy. You have to get shot at least twice before you get special treatment around here."

Allie tried to laugh but ended up coughing, the movement causing her pain. "Did I ever tell you guys how wrong I was about you?"

"No, but you'll get around to it, I'm sure," Rio teased.

"How bad is it?" she asked, pain creasing her forehead.

Diego grinned. "Nothing that will keep you out of any beauty pageants."

"Allie, which direction did Zoe go?" Joe asked gently. "I have to find her."

"She ran for the woods. I told her to get out, that someone would find her but to get as far away from the gunfire as possible."

"You saved her life. Thank you," Joe said gravely.

"Just doing my job," she said faintly. "Provided I still have one after the ass I was to you all."

"You'll do, Allie," Rio said with a smile. "You'll do."

ZOE ran in no clear direction, cringing and ducking when she heard distant gunfire. She wiped at the blood smearing her vision and kept running, but then she stepped in a hole and painfully twisted her ankle, going down in a painful heap on the ground. She tried to push herself up but her strength was utterly sapped. She curled into a ball, moaning as the pain she'd tried so valiantly to suppress hit her with a vengeance.

She huddled there, shaking violently, tears mixing with the blood smeared on her cheeks and mouth. The metallic taste sickened her and she dry-heaved, her stomach rebelling at the violence that surrounded her like a thick fog.

This was who she was. Her legacy. How could Joe possibly want this—her? She'd never even been able to tell him the truth herself, and now it looked as though she had used him, purposely deceived him and his entire family. Dragging them all down with her to her level of subhumanity.

"Zoe! Zoe! Where are you, honey?"

The unfamiliar voice made her tense all over and she held her breath, praying she was hidden among the dirt and rubble she was lying in. And then . . .

"Zoe! Honey, are you all right? Don't be scared. I'm one of the good guys."

She opened her eyes to see an unfamiliar set of ice blue eyes belonging to a tall, imposing man with blond hair and hard features. She shivered at the intensity in his eyes and shrank back involuntarily.

"My name's Steele, ma'am. I work with KGI. I'm one of the team leaders like Joe. My team is made up of P.J., Cole, Baker and Renshaw. I'm here to take you back to Joe. How badly are you hurt?"

Tears filled her eyes as he gently wiped some of the blood away from her face.

"I can't go back there," she whispered. "I don't belong there. I'm not your kind."

He cocked his head, obviously confused by her statement. "And what kind is that, honey?"

"The good kind," she choked out. "I'm . . . dirty. Tainted. My entire life I've been surrounded by corruption and filth. My father heads a vast criminal empire. *That's* who I am, what I come from, the kind of person I am. My mother didn't even love me enough to take me with her when she left my father. Please, just let me go. I can't go back there. Not like this. Please just let me go. I'm begging you."

Steele's hard face softened with lines of understanding. He cupped her cheek, dabbing at more of the blood seeping from the cuts on her face, his expression going cold as he examined the damage done to her.

"How about I bring you to my wife. She's a doctor and she can see to your injuries. You need medical attention, Zoe. You'd like her. She's one in a million."

"You won't let Joe see me like this?" she asked fearfully.

His face softened again. "No, Zoe. I won't make you do anything you don't want. But I need to take you now. We

don't know how badly you're hurt or if you broke anything.
I'll call ahead to Maren and let her know we're coming in
so she'll be waiting to examine you. Deal?"

"O-Okay," she said shakily. "Do you . . . do you have a
blanket? I don't want anyone to see . . ."

She broke off, ducking her head in shame.

Steele reached into the pack he was carrying and pulled
out a blanket. Then he simply wrapped it around her, lifting
her into his arms so he could tuck the corners up around her
chin so that only her face was visible.

"I'm bringing Zoe in. Have the chopper ready for trans-
port. I'm taking her to the infirmary to see Maren," he said
into his mic. "And tell Joe to stand down," he said in a warning voice.

Zoe closed her eyes and buried her face against Steele's
chest to avoid the scrutiny of the others as Steele strode
toward the waiting chopper. She heard the distant protests
of Joe and his brothers arguing with him to stand down.
Only when she was safely inside the helicopter with Donovan and Steele and it took off into the air did she give in to
the overwhelming pull of unconsciousness.

CHAPTER 25

"I think you should bring Rusty into the exam room," Maren said quietly to her husband. "Zoe's severely traumatized to the point I think she's had a break with reality. She's borderline catatonic, and at the mere mention of seeing Joe, she gets hysterical."

"Fuck," Steele said, rubbing the back of his neck. "You should have seen her when I found her. She was so goddamn ashamed, and for *what*? Genetics? She's convinced that she's a bad seed because of who and what her father is. She's shouldering enormous guilt for involving all of us when if she *hadn't* gone to Rusty, she'd be dead."

"She's refused to see anyone else. Even Marlene. I think Rusty is our best chance at getting through to her."

"She's in the waiting room, silent and not talking to anyone. She's shouldering as much guilt and blame as Zoe is, and that's just bullshit. What her family did to her is unforgivable," he said in disgust. "And I'm worried the damage can't be undone."

"Go get her," Maren said softly. "Tell her Zoe needs her. Rusty would never turn her back on anyone who needed her."

Steele gathered his wife in his arms and kissed her long and sweet. His hand automatically went to her still-flat belly as it always did when he held her. As terrified as he was at the prospect of her going through another pregnancy, he couldn't imagine life getting any better. His wife and daughter were his entire world, and now they'd be adding another tiny life. It scared and awed him in equal measure.

"I love you," he said, because he took every opportunity to tell her so.

She smiled. "Back at ya, Ice Man. Now go get Rusty so we can try to break through to Zoe. I'm worried about her."

He stole one more kiss and then left the exam room to where all the KGI members were assembled except for Allie and the rest of Rio's team, who were with her at the hospital in Murray, Kentucky, where she was undergoing surgery to remove the bullet that had ricocheted off one of her lower ribs—breaking it—and embedded in her appendix, requiring it to be removed.

Joe surged to his feet, but Steele shook his head as a signal to stand down and then walked over to where Rusty was huddled in the corner, knees drawn to her chest, gaze downcast, refusing to look at the rest of her family.

Steele hunkered down and nudged her chin up in a gentle motion so she was forced to meet his eyes.

"Maren wants you to go back with Zoe. She's not doing well, Rusty. She needs you."

"I'm the one who got her into this situation," she said bitterly. "I hardly think it's me she needs."

"That's where you're wrong," Steele said softly. "You're

a good friend, Rusty. You did the right thing. I don't care what anyone says. You saved her life."

She looked stunned as she stared back at him, her eyes watering at his support. He simply rose and extended his hand down to help her up. She tentatively took it and allowed him to pull her to her feet. Ignoring Joe's desperate demands to know what was going on, Steele guided her into the exam room, where Maren was carefully cleaning the blood from Zoe's face.

As soon as Rusty saw Zoe, she burst into tears and ran to the bed, carefully wrapping her arms around Zoe in a gentle hug. Maren discreetly stepped back and motioned Steele to follow her out of the room.

Zoe stirred, some of the dullness receding from her eyes, and then tears began leaking down her cheeks as she pulled Rusty to her, hugging fiercely.

"Thank you for coming," Zoe whispered, clinging desperately to her friend.

"Why would you thank me?" Rusty asked bitterly. "I almost got you killed. As it is, I got you kidnapped and abused."

Zoe reared back in shock, her mouth falling open, and then winced at the pain in her swollen mouth and jaw.

"What are you talking about?" she asked hoarsely. "You saved me, Rusty. I'd be dead if it weren't for you."

"Not according to my family," Rusty said as a fresh torrent of tears flooded her eyes.

"What? They're blaming you? That's bullshit," she said vehemently. "What are they thinking? You're the only friend I have in the world. You risked so much for me. I could have gotten you and your entire family hurt or murdered. I should have never asked you to do what you did and agreed to all you did for me."

"If I hadn't lied to my family, you would have been better protected," Rusty said in a dull voice. "You wouldn't have been left alone even for a minute. They're furious with me. And Sean . . ."

Rusty broke off, her face crumpling. Zoe leaned up and wrapped her arms around her once more.

"What happened?" Zoe asked quietly.

"The better question is, what didn't happen?" Pain and betrayal were bright in Rusty's eyes. "I made an absolute fool of myself the morning I waited for Sean to get home. And if that wasn't bad enough, he got the call that you'd been kidnapped right in the middle of my humiliation and then dragged me to the war room and had to tell everyone everything I'd done. After my family raked me over the coals, Sean spared no opportunity to tell me I was a selfish child who needed to grow the fuck up and that everything wasn't about me and I needed to learn to be more responsible."

"And to think I liked him," Zoe said angrily. "I'm going to kill him for that. How could they, Rusty? How could they say those things to you? You risked your life for me. You helped me when I had no one else to turn to, and you never asked for anything in return. And they're angry with you for that?"

"Sean's pissed. The rest are disappointed, I think. I'm not sure which is worse. The idea that I would ever purposely do anything to place the parents who adopted me, the only people who ever loved and accepted me, in danger makes me sick. I'd do anything for them. Anything," Rusty said, choking back a sob.

"It's my fault. Not yours, Rusty. I won't have you blame yourself. You're the most selfless, caring person I've ever known."

Rusty smiled tearfully at her. "I had to see you. I had to tell you how sorry I was while I still had the chance. It's the only reason I've sat with the entire family for the last several hours while Maren examined you."

Zoe frowned. "I don't like the sound of this, Rusty. It's too close to a good-bye, and I won't let you leave."

Rusty gave her a sad smile. "I can't stay. At least not right now. I have to get away. Get myself together. Get over Sean and move on. Figure out what I'm going to do with my life."

"Rusty, no," Zoe choked out. "Don't go. Please don't go. I'll go with you. I can't stay here any more than you can. We can go together."

Rusty's smile was genuine this time. "If you think Joe's just going to sit back and let you walk away, then, sister, you don't know the man very well. He's about to lose his mind because he hasn't been able to see you. To see for himself that you're okay. He went through hell and he blames himself for leaving you unprotected."

Another tear slid down Zoe's cheek. "I'll never fit in here," she said sadly. "It was foolish of me to dream. I've lived in my own head, creating my own fantasy my entire life, refusing to face reality. I can't continue doing that."

"I need to ask you for a favor," Rusty said, ignoring her statement.

"Anything. We're sisters, and time and distance will never change that."

Rusty's lips trembled and she briefly looked away. Then she turned back to Zoe and grasped both hands in hers. "Don't tell anyone that I'm going. I'm not just going to disappear. I'd never worry Marlene and Frank like that. I'm going to leave a letter for Marlene explaining everything— well, not *everything*. But it's time to start living my life and stop wishing for the impossible. I need time to sort myself out and figure out what I want."

"Promise me you'll stay in touch," Zoe said, gripping Rusty's hands tightly as tears rolled down both their cheeks. "No matter what. I'll never betray your confidence, but please stay in communication."

Rusty nodded, shaking too badly to respond verbally.

"And I have a favor to ask in return," Zoe said, grief consuming her.

"Anything," Rusty said, echoing her vow.

"Can you ask Marlene to come get me? I don't want to see Joe—or anyone. I just need time. I guess, like you, I need some time to figure my life out. I just hope she's not so upset with me that she won't want me in her home."

Rusty hugged her again. "Consider it done. Marlene doesn't have a judgmental bone in her body. And if I tell her you need her, then she'll be here, and trust me, no one crosses her. Especially her sons. Joe may not like it, but he respects her word as law."

"Make me one more promise," Zoe said, gripping Rusty's hand once more. "Don't leave without saying good-bye and without giving me a way to contact you."

Rusty smiled. "I won't. Love you, sister."

"Love you too," Zoe whispered.

"I'll go get Marlene for you now."

The fact that Rusty hadn't once referred to Marlene as Mom or Ma wasn't lost on Zoe. It broke her heart that she had brought so much pain to this family. Irreparable damage. She couldn't change what was, but she could at least make sure of what was to be.

"On your way out, could you ask Shea if she would talk to me?" Zoe asked hesitantly.

Rusty squeezed her hand then hugged her in farewell. "Will do. Then promise me that as soon as you get to Marlene's you'll get some rest."

Zoe's smile was faint. "That's one promise I won't have any trouble keeping."

CHAPTER 26

RUSTY walked out of the exam room and felt every eye on her. She refused to meet anyone's gaze, seeking out Shea only. She walked to the other woman and stiffly said in a low voice, "Zoe would like to see you."

Shea's eyes were full of compassion and sympathy, so much so that it made Rusty squirm in discomfort. By now, the entire family would have heard of her betrayal. Nathan's anger hurt the worst, though, because of all the brothers, he'd been the most accepting of her from the start. He'd been kind when she'd been an abrasive, defensive fifteen-year-old, afraid that Rachel's "return from the dead" would displace her in Marlene's affection. As a result, she'd always had a closer bond with him than with any of the other Kelly brothers.

"How is she doing?" Shea whispered.

Rusty grimaced. "Not good, but then what else could be expected? She's been shit on at every stage of her life."

She very nearly winced because it sounded as though she

were speaking of herself and not of Zoe, and Shea picked up on it.

"It will all be okay, Rusty," she offered.

Rusty tried to smile but failed miserably. "It will never be okay again, Shea. But thank you."

She turned to walk out, ignoring Joe's call to her. She quickened her step and, once outside, she all but ran to her vehicle and hurriedly got in, keying the ignition and reversing as Joe frantically waved at her to stop.

Joe dragged a hand through his hair and closed his eyes in despair. The entire goddamn world had turned upside down. And he was helpless to do a fucking thing about it. He walked back into the infirmary determined to check on Zoe. He hadn't been able to get close enough to even get a good look at her much less touch her, hold her, comfort her and tell her how much he loved her and that his heart was breaking for her.

Enough was enough. This time he wasn't taking no for an answer.

When he returned, he noticed Shea was no longer beside Nathan, and he immediately sent his twin a questioning look.

"Zoe asked to see her," Nathan said quietly. "I'm sure she's confused and has a lot of questions."

"I'm going in there," Joe said, turning toward the exam room only to find Steele standing in front of him, barring his way.

"You need to calm down," Steele said. "The only way I could get Zoe to cooperate and allow me to take her to Maren to get the medical attention she desperately needed was if I swore you wouldn't see her. I gave her that and I'm not breaking my promise."

"Give her some time, Joe," Donovan warned softly. "She's been through hell. She's not herself right now, and who can blame her? Be patient. You'll see her soon."

"But why won't she see *me*?" Joe asked, agony in his voice. "Rusty's been in there. Now Shea. Is it because I failed her?"

"Sit down before you fall down," Sam ordered.

Steele sighed. "She doesn't think she's good enough for you."

Joe stumbled back toward one of the chairs and sank down, burying his face in his hands. He was worried out of his mind. A dozen reasons had floated around in his head as to why Zoe was so adamant that he—or anyone else—not see her, the worst of which was that more had happened to her than they were aware of. Never in a million years had he dreamed that she would have the fool-headed notion that she wasn't good enough for him. *He* was the one who'd failed to protect her. It was *him* who'd left her vulnerable to kidnapping and being terrorized by those assholes.

Steele's jaw was tight with anger. "Look, Zoe's thinking some pretty fucked-up shit right now, and it has nothing to do with you failing her. Just the opposite. She believes she failed you—all of us. She begged me not to let you see her."

Joe flinched, unable to breathe through the pain.

"She was ashamed," Steele said, his expression one of fury. "That woman is convinced that she's damaged goods. Tainted. Not good enough for you or anyone in this family or organization. The only way I could convince her to let me get her medical help was to promise to take her to Maren. I had to wrap her in a blanket because she was shamed by what some asshole did to her, the bruises and blood on her body and face. I have to tell you, man. I've pretty much seen it all during my time in the military and with KGI, but this . . . This makes me fucking sick. You're going to have to be very careful with her, but at the same time you can't let her go on thinking that messed-up shit in her head."

Joe stared at him in shock and in answering fury.

"Not *good* enough for me? This family?" he choked out. "What the fuck?"

"Look at it from her perspective," Steele said. "She's been surrounded by and used by assholes her entire life. Rusty was her first and only friend, and through her, she met all of us and for the first time learned what acceptance—and love— was like. And she thinks that she brought all of this down on our heads. She doesn't realize if Rusty hadn't done what she did that she'd be dead. None of you seem to realize that."

Joe's brothers exchanged worried glances but remained silent, their expressions ones of regret.

Joe's eyes narrowed. "I don't blame Rusty for anything."

"Not the way it appears to me. More importantly, it's not the way Rusty sees it either."

"Fuck!" Joe exploded. "I wasn't angry at Rusty for helping her. Or even for not breaking Zoe's confidence. I knew Rusty knew more than she'd let on. We even talked about it. I just wish that she had confided in me once she knew what Zoe was to me, because other than Zoe, she was the only one who knew the kind of danger Zoe faced."

"All I know is that two women are suffering because both feel like failures and that they aren't good enough, and *that* is fucked up and we both know it."

Steele turned and walked back to where his team was standing, effectively ending the conversation. Joe closed his eyes and reached out to Shea.

Shea, honey, I have to know. How is she? How is she really?

There was a brief pause and then, *She's broken, Joe. She's despondent and bears the blame for things she had no control over.*

Joe could hear the tears in Shea's voice and it gutted him. He wanted to tell Shea to tell Zoe he loved her, but Zoe deserved to hear those words for the first time from him.

If he could only have the chance.

I don't know that I ever thanked you for what you did for her, baby girl, but I love you for that.

You have to know I'd do anything for you, Joe. I love her too. She's good for you. I've prayed for someone exactly like her for you. You look good happy and in love.

Keep praying then, Shea. Because I don't have her . . . yet.

CHAPTER 27

JUST when Joe thought things couldn't get more difficult in his hope to gain access to Zoe, his mom hurried into the infirmary and was greeted by Maren, who'd just come from the exam room.

His frustration must have been evident because when his mother saw him, her features softened with sympathy and love and she rushed over to enfold him in a hug. He held on to her for a long moment, grief enveloping him like a fog.

"Don't worry, baby," his mom whispered. "It's going to be okay. I promise. I'm taking Zoe home with me. Just give her time. What she needs most right now is time, patience and above all else, love."

"I do love her, Ma," he said in an aching voice.

"I know you do. And she loves you. Believe in that and hold on to it. Don't give up."

"I'll never give up on her," he said fiercely. "Take care of her, Ma. Please."

She pulled away and patted him on the cheek. "You know I will, and I'll update you often. I give it a day or two at most. I'll smother her with so much love and acceptance that she'll forget all this nonsense about not being good enough for this family. She's just what this family—and you—needs."

"I couldn't agree more," he said gruffly.

"Now listen, son. I know you want to see her—you need to see her. I get that. But she's not in a good place right now. I think you should go so I can bring her home. She's horrified over the thought of you seeing her right now. You'll only make it more traumatic for her if you stay."

Tears burned the edges of his eyelids. He wanted to do more than just see her. He wanted to cradle her in his arms and never let go, but he didn't want to put her under any further stress. His shoulders sagged and he knew the bleakness he felt was reflected in every part of his body.

"I'll go, Ma. But can you please just call me and let me know how she's doing and when or if she'll agree to see me?"

Tears shone in his mother's eyes as well. "Of course, baby. Now go get some rest if you can. I hate to see you in so much pain. I'll cover her up with love until you get the honor of doing so yourself."

He hugged her again. "Thank you."

"Go now so I can get her home so she can rest. She has to be in terrible pain."

He didn't think it was possible to feel more tortured than he already did. Slowly, feeling a hundred years old, he turned and trudged toward the door. Donovan followed him out.

"Come on. I'll give you a ride," Donovan said quietly. "I've got an errand I need to run anyway."

Joe sent him a questioning look as they walked out to

Donovan's SUV. "I figured you'd be in a hurry to get back to Eve and Cammie."

"I need to go talk to Rusty first," Donovan said grimly. "I owe her an apology."

Joe's heart ached a little more because he and Zoe weren't the only two people suffering.

"Give her my love, will you?" Joe asked softly.

"Will do. Now let's get you home so you can get some sleep. You look like hell."

"I feel like hell."

DONOVAN pulled up to his parents' house and got out, heading to the door. Rusty's Jeep was there so he didn't bother knocking. He wasn't sure how well a visit from any of his brothers would be received at the moment. Rusty had every right to be pissed. And feel betrayed.

He let himself in, noting the silence within. His dad would have ridden over with his mom to get Zoe, and after a quick check of the downstairs, he knew Rusty must be upstairs in her bedroom. Not wanting to barge in and invade her privacy, he instead stood at the foot of the staircase and called up to her.

"Rusty?"

There was prolonged silence, and just as he was about to call her name again, she appeared at the top, her expression inscrutable.

"Donovan? What are you doing here?"

"Can we talk?" he asked.

She hesitated but then slowly descended the stairs, and it was then he could see the grief dulling her usually vibrant, mischievous eyes.

"What's up?" she asked nonchalantly when she reached the bottom.

"Come into the living room and let's sit," he said, cupping her elbow in a gentle grasp.

"Is Zoe all right?" she asked anxiously.

"She's fine, honey. Or at least she's doing as well as can be expected. Ma is bringing her over shortly."

She shot him a confused look. "What do you want to talk about then?"

"Have a seat," he said, motioning toward the couch and taking the space next to her. "I owe you an apology, honey. I—we—were way out of line, and we had no right to say the things we said to you."

She shrugged. "I deserved it. I lied to all of you."

"No," he said emphatically. "You did the right thing. You were a good friend and you saved Zoe's life. Hell, I was flabbergasted at all you managed to pull off. You even fooled me, and my ego took one hell of a beating. You're a genius. I never suspected a thing when I did a background check on her. You impressed the hell out of me, Rusty. I always knew you were brilliant. I just didn't realize the extent of your tech skills."

She stared down at her hands, not responding to his compliment.

"I'm sorry for what happened, Rusty. I'm not going to offer excuses. It never should have happened. You're family, and that's not how family should be treated. But offering you an apology isn't the only reason I came to see you, though it's the primary one. I want to offer you a job."

Her head came up at that and her forehead furrowed in confusion. "What?"

"You know about the foundation and that the wives help

out to the best of their ability, but the technical aspects are handled by me. New identities, documents, birth certificates, basically everything you did for Zoe, only you did a far more superior job than I ever pulled off. I want you to take over and manage the foundation. The wives would still help, but you'd head everything up and take over the technical aspects. And don't think this is a pity offer or an apology of sorts. The foundation is my baby and I take it very seriously. If I didn't know for sure you could do the job and do it well, I wouldn't ask you to take it over."

Her smile was sad and didn't reach her eyes. "Actually, I've had other job offers. I was taking the summer off and spending it here at home to decide which opportunity I want to pursue. I've narrowed it down to two and plan to make my decision soon."

Something in her tone and expression made Donovan hesitate to believe her, but he'd never call her on it. She'd already been given too much disrespect by her family.

"Are you sure I can't persuade you to turn to the dark side?" he teased. "Not only would you be paid a very generous salary, but it would be a load off for me. Eve and I are talking about having a child, and with KGI already being a full-time job, the foundation would take even more time away from my family and eventually a baby."

"I think Eve would make a great director of operations," Rusty countered. "She knows what it's like. She would be a great advocate for these women because she's been where they've been. And if not her, what about Eden? She rarely takes modeling assignments anymore."

Donovan was frustrated by the subdued Rusty sitting beside him. Conversing as if they were strangers. He had a sinking feeling but couldn't put his finger on what bothered him. Maybe she just needed time to get over the hurt his brothers had inflicted when emotions had been so volatile in the wake of Zoe's disappearance. And he didn't know what to do and he hated that kind of helpless feeling of not knowing how to repair the damage done.

She obviously hadn't said anything to Ma or Pop or they both would have torn a strip off all their sons' hides. But then Rusty wasn't malicious. She'd been greatly misunderstood all those years ago when she'd first entered their lives, but she had the biggest heart of anyone he knew.

Knowing he wouldn't get anything else out of her, he forced a grin and reached over to ruffle her hair affectionately.

"Okay, well if you change your mind, you know where to find me. Or if you're holding out for a bigger salary, I'm sure we can come to a mutually satisfying agreement."

She smiled faintly and for a moment he could swear her eyes glistened with moisture, but it was gone so quickly he must have imagined it.

"Thanks, Van. If the other possibilities don't pan out, you'll be the first person I call."

Again, he had the feeling she wasn't remotely telling the truth but rather saying whatever she had to in order to get him to back off. Impulsively, he stood and pulled her to her feet and enfolded her in a huge hug.

"Love you, girl. Hope you always remember that."

She hugged him just as fiercely for a moment and then carefully disentangled herself from his embrace. He could swear he saw relief in her features when they heard the sound of a car pulling up outside.

"That'll be Zoe," she said. "I'd better go help get her settled."

Just like that he was summarily dismissed. As he watched her hurry to the door, something inside him twisted just a little tighter and he frowned, worried about what his gut was trying to tell him.

CHAPTER 28

ZOE sank into the fluffy, overstuffed reading chair in the room she shared with Rusty, which afforded her a prime view of the lake that spread out over the horizon. She wrapped the old quilt more firmly around her, one that Marlene had given her, stating that it had belonged to her mother.

Zoe had objected to the gift, asserting she had no right to a family heirloom. Marlene had merely hugged her and informed her that she *was* family.

An entire week had passed since the day she'd escaped certain death at the hands of a man whose purpose she never knew exactly. Other than to wrest power from her father. It was laughable that he'd actually believed, even for a minute, that her father would sacrifice anything for her, when that knowledge had been what prompted him to end the farce of his relationship with her what seemed a lifetime ago.

In many ways, it had been a lifetime. Or at least another life. One that she realized she'd never truly lived but had simply survived. She hadn't known what it was to live, laugh and love until Rusty, Joe and their family. Especially Joe.

She closed her eyes against the sudden surge of emotion, determined not to be weak. Not to break. Somehow she had to learn to survive all over again after two decades of surviving.

The house had been eerily silent since her return. Marlene and Frank were exceedingly respectful of her privacy and her care. Zoe and Rusty still shared a room and they conversed, but Rusty was distant and wounded, her devastation as evident as Zoe's own.

As thick as her own grief was, she wasn't blind to Rusty's, and each morning, she feared she would wake up to find Rusty gone.

It was as if the entire community and network in the small Tennessee county adjoining Kentucky Lake was holding its breath in trepidation. Zoe purposely sought refuge in her bedroom, rarely leaving and only doing so when Marlene became insistent enough that guilt weighed too heavily on her.

She felt . . . dirty. As if her very presence in a family like the Kellys was offensive and she sullied their name by association. Intellectually she knew how screwed up her thinking was. She knew her father's sins were not her own. And yet she simply couldn't get beyond the fact that she *represented* every single thing the Kellys risked their lives for on a daily basis to defeat. How could she ever expect to hold her head up in a family whose sole ambition was to make the world a better place? When *her* family was one of the very ones who polluted it?

Was it any wonder her mother had left without ever look-

ing back? She tried to feel sympathy for a woman she held
such scant memories of, but she couldn't consider a single
circumstance in which she'd ever willingly leave her child,
especially in the care of someone whose level of success
was measured by how intimidating and feared he was.

Anger welled in Zoe's chest, bubbling like a cauldron.
Not only at her mother, whom she'd resented ever since she'd
been old enough to understand that she'd been deserted, but
at her father, who could have—who should have—made
different choices. Someone who should never have had
a child if he wasn't willing to sacrifice everything for him
or her.

It sickened her to her soul that she carried that bloodline
and legacy. That was what tainted her. Springing from a
gene pool of not one but two self-absorbed, irresponsible
people who had no business procreating.

*Genetics don't influence decision making. Only the peo-
ple making the decisions do.*

The words of one of her college professors fluttered in
her mind. She'd never really paid them much attention until
now. It was all well and fine to say she could and would
make different choices than her parents, but what of her
offspring? Would they be influenced and shaped by nature
or nurture?

Zoe frowned. If either was worth a damn as a scientific
argument, then she herself would be a complete miscreant.

She stared moodily into the distance, watching as the
sun dipped lower, seemingly sliding right into the lake in
the distance. She was so lost in her thoughts that she didn't
hear Rusty come in. Didn't realize she was even in the room
until she quietly sat on the edge of the bed, the motion detected in Zoe's periphery.

Like Zoe, Rusty had holed up in Marlene's house, refusing to venture out, especially after the third day when Sean had apparently decided he'd been patient long enough and had begun coming by the house, asking to talk to Rusty. Rusty, who'd never hidden from anything in her life, had feared that if she left the compound Sean would immediately corner her. Zoe felt so bad for the embarrassment Rusty had suffered, and she was furious for the way Sean had handled the entire situation. He was obviously an ass who didn't deserve Rusty anyway.

She turned and offered a half-hearted smile, not even bothering with an attempt at faking one. It still hurt too damn much to move her lips enough for a convincing smile. Today had been the first day she'd been able to tolerate chewing solid food after six days of broths and soups, eventually graduating up to pasta dishes and chicken and dumplings. She'd been convinced her jaw had been broken, but Maren had confirmed via X-ray that it was just severely bruised and no fracture was evident.

"Hey," Zoe said softly, when Rusty didn't speak.

For a long moment, Rusty didn't respond. She simply looked back at Zoe, her eyes suspiciously bright. Zoe's stomach lurched and then tightened.

"No," Zoe whispered, shaking her head.

Rusty attempted a watery smile that resulted in more of a grimace. Then she lurched off the bed and bent down, enfolding Zoe in a tight hug. Tears ran unabashedly down Zoe's cheeks as she held on to Rusty as tightly as she could.

"Don't go," Zoe pleaded. "Or at least don't go alone. I'll come with you."

Rusty disentangled herself from her arms and slid onto the wide chair so that she faced Zoe, and her legs were angled away. Tears were streaming down Rusty's cheeks as well as the two stared wordlessly at each other. Finally, Rusty broke her silence.

"I have to go," she choked out. "I can't be here right now. Maybe in time. But right now it just hurts too damn much. I've got to move on with my life. Prove something to myself if to no one else."

Zoe gripped her hand, squeezing as she struggled for breath around the huge knot forming in her throat.

"Where will you go?" she asked.

Rusty shrugged. "For now? Away. Wherever the road takes me. Who knows? Maybe I'll find myself out there." She touched Zoe's hair, stroking one long strand and then tucking it behind her ear. "Give Joe a chance, Zoe. I know you're scared. I know you think you're not good enough, but that's so fucked up that I don't even know where to begin. Promise me you'll allow yourself to be happy for once. You deserve that much."

"And you don't?" Zoe challenged, lifting her chin defiantly.

Rusty's eyes went bleak. "That's why I'm going. Because I'm never going to find what I'm looking for here, and I don't want to spend the rest of my life staring at what I wanted but could never have."

Zoe leaned her forehead into Rusty's until they touched, tears running silently down both women's cheeks.

"I'll never be able to repay everything you did for me," Zoe whispered.

Rusty's hand tightened, reversing Zoe's hold on her hand so that she now held Zoe's.

"You can repay me by being happy and making my brother happy."

Zoe swallowed and then swallowed again, her nose and throat aching from the weight of so much heartache and tears.

"I love you, Rusty. You'll always be the sister of my heart no matter where life takes us."

Rusty smiled as her tears splashed onto Zoe's knee and then she closed her eyes, her forehead still touching Zoe's.

"And you're the sister I never had but always wanted. I once wished for brothers with all my heart, and that wish was granted. Then I realized how much I'd missed out on by not having a sister. Now I'm missing nothing," she said softly.

"You'll call?" Zoe asked in a strangled voice. "You'll keep in touch?"

"You know it," she said. Then she pulled Zoe into a hug, her arms wrapped firmly around her neck. "Be happy, Zoe. Don't do it for me or anyone else. Do it for you. You're only who you want to be, not what others say or think. Never let anyone make you believe any different. That's a lesson I learned the hard way but one I won't ever forget."

Zoe bit into her lip as Rusty pulled away and then rose from the chair. The two women stared at each other for a long moment before Rusty finally smiled.

"I'll call you soon. Promise."

Zoe pulled the quilt tighter around her, needing to clutch something so she didn't hang on to Rusty as she tried to leave. Rusty was the first friend she had ever had, the first person she'd trusted and who had trusted her, and in no way would she betray her now if leaving was what she felt she had to do.

As soon as Rusty closed the door softly behind her, Zoe buried her face in the quilt so her sobs wouldn't be heard.

* * *

RUSTY snuck out the back door and down the winding, shaded path to the rocky edge of the bluff overlooking the lake. It was her favorite spot to come when she wanted to be alone, because no one had ever discovered it but her. A grove of trees offered a barrier between the large, smooth boulders that jutted outward and the back of Frank and Marlene's house, so she didn't have to worry about being detected. She eased down into the hollowed-out crevice formed by two huge stones that anchored the cliff's edge, an awesome place to sit, relax and watch the sun go down and reflect.

She let out a sigh. All her reflection had been done and her decisions made. So why did it hurt so damn much, and why did it feel like she was bleeding to death on the inside? Tears obscured her vision and she wiped defiantly at her cheeks with the back of one hand.

Her cell phone rang, and she glanced down, prepared to ignore the call, but she hesitated when she saw Joe's name appear. Sucking in a steadying breath, she picked up the phone and hit the accept button.

"How're you doing?" she asked quietly with no preamble, taking charge of the conversation before he could start asking questions about *her* or how *she* was doing.

"Fucking miserable. I'm about to lose my goddamn mind. You have to help me, Rusty. What the hell can I do? How can I talk to her when she doesn't leave her room, much less the house?"

Grief was thick in his voice and Rusty's own voice matched the ache in his. "I can do you one better," she said, after a brief battle to force herself to sound normal. "If she won't leave her room, then I suggest you do a little B and E and meet her on her own turf."

There was a long pause. There was a hitch in his voice and she couldn't tell if it was the sound of excitement, disbelief, fear or doubt.

"You're giving her up to me?" he asked doubtfully.

"You make her sound like a chew toy," Rusty said dryly. "And I'm not betraying her by wanting her to have some fucking happiness for once. I want her to be happy more than anything in the world," she added in a sad whisper.

"Hey, are you okay?" he asked sharply. "Where are you anyway? I just talked to Ma, and she said she wasn't sure where you were, but you haven't left the house for the entire week either."

"Around. But if you're going to stage a B and E, then I'll need to be elsewhere tomorrow night," she drawled, hoping to diffuse his concern.

"You seriously think I should break into my own parents' house?" he asked skeptically.

Rusty rolled her eyes. "Duh? Let's see, I have a big-ass window, a good-sized tree that happens to reside just outside this big-ass window, but if you have issues with climbing trees, there's always a ladder. The window will be unlocked. You're welcome, by the way."

"Smart-ass," he said with no heat. Then his tone grew serious. "I hope you know I was never angry with you, Rusty. I'm grateful Zoe had you and even more grateful for all you did to protect her. I love you, and you better damn well wear a dress to my wedding."

Rusty smiled through a wash of tears and then she had to turn the phone downward so the receiver didn't pick up the sound of her crying. She sucked air in through her nostrils and tried like hell to be cool and keep Joe's mind occupied with what it should be on: Zoe. And making her happy.

"If you get her to marry you, I'll even wear heels," she said lightly.

"I'm gonna remember that," he said gleefully. "And thanks, Rusty. Love you, girl."

She leaned back, resting her head against the rock, focusing on the shimmering surface of the water as tears carved harsh lines down the sides of her face.

"Love you too," she choked out. "Gotta go. Be happy, Joe."

CHAPTER 29

MARLENE was up at her usual hour to shower before waking Frank and leaving him to use the bathroom while she prepared breakfast. She sighed as she made her way into the kitchen. The house all but groaned under the weight of so much pain and sadness. Her girls were hurting, and it broke Marlene's heart that she couldn't fix things and make everything all right.

She walked by the counter to open the fridge when she saw an envelope with her name on it. Frowning, she retraced her steps and picked it up, feeling that it was fairly thin. She studied the handwriting, noting that it was awfully similar to Rusty's. But why would Rusty leave an envelope for her?

With shaking hands, she tore open the seal and pulled a single folded sheet of paper out. As she read the first few lines, her vision blurred with tears and she sank heavily down onto one of the stools.

Dear Mom,

I have so much to thank you for that it would take an entire ream of paper and an entire day to list everything, so I'll thank you for the single most important thing you and Dad ever gave me. Love. I never knew what love was, what it felt like, and I never loved anyone until you let me into your lives. You gave a young, vulnerable, teenaged girl something more valuable than all the money in the world. You gave me a sense of value. Of self-worth. The knowledge that I could have and deserved better. You believed in me when nobody else did. I'll never forget that. You saved my life. I hope you know that. I wouldn't be who I am and what I am today if it weren't for you.

I just wanted to say how sorry I am that I lied to you and Dad and deceived the family and brought danger to you all. I wouldn't hurt any of you for the world. Y'all are my world. I have to go away for a while. I need to figure out my place in the world, what I want out of life, what kind of life I want to have. I have a degree and job opportunities, and it's time I took advantage of them. Please don't worry about me. I'll stay in touch and I'll call you as often as I can. And please don't be angry over my decision or that I didn't say good-bye. It was hard enough to write this letter. I would have never been able to tell you all of this in person.

I'm young, and as a result, I did something foolish, and now I have to suffer the consequences, but it's also time to close that chapter of my life and move on and try to forget. I know I don't have the right to ask anything of you, but I would ask that you not let the others know where I am or what I'm doing. Just know that I'll be just fine. You and Dad taught me how to be the kind of person I can be proud of and that y'all can be proud of.

I'll be in touch as soon as I'm able. Tell Dad that I could have never asked for a better father. The second greatest gift you both gave to me was the Kelly name, and I'll do my best to do that name proud.

Love you,
Rusty

Marlene clasped the paper to her chest as sobs welled in her throat. Then she leaned over, folding her arms on the counter, and buried her face against them as grief overwhelmed her.

SEAN pulled into the compound in his personal vehicle, his hands clenched tightly around the steering wheel. He could feel sweat forming at his nape and trickling down his back. Jesus, he was as nervous and as jittery as a rookie participating in his first big bust. He hadn't been this unsettled when he *had* been a rookie and had gotten shot in his first year as a deputy.

That was what she did to him, though. She had him so twisted up in knots that he never knew if he was coming or going, and as a result, everything that came out of his mouth came out horribly wrong.

As he pulled to a stop in front of Frank and Marlene's house, he briefly closed his eyes, regret consuming him. He'd hurt her. He'd done more than hurt her. He'd fucking devastated her. Had ripped her to shreds, said shit he didn't even mean, all because of the thought of what could have happened to her, what he had no way of protecting her from because he had no clue what she'd done.

Well, he finally knew exactly what he wanted to say, damn it. Figures that he finally got it worked out and she hadn't so much as stuck her head out of her damn house in a week. He refused to wait a minute longer. Refused to allow her to think the absolute worst a minute longer. He'd make her listen to him, and this time, he'd get his fucking mouth and tongue to work in unison so he could say everything he wanted to say.

He trudged up the steps and rang the doorbell, his stomach tightening with dread. He'd treated her horribly. She probably hated him now. What if she wouldn't listen to him? No. He wasn't taking no for an answer. If it meant handcuffing the little hellion and hauling her out of the house over his shoulder and over to his, where he'd secure her to one of his chairs, he'd make her listen.

The door opened and Marlene stood there, deep lines of sadness in her face, her cheeks blotchy, nose and eyes swollen. What the fuck? His stomach bottomed out as concern for a woman he considered his adopted mother pushed to the forefront.

"Marlene, is everything all right?" he asked sharply.

Her lips tightened but she didn't reply. Instead she quietly asked, "What can I do for you, Sean?"

It wasn't like Marlene to be so . . . private . . . but maybe it was a personal matter and he needed to butt out. Besides, he'd just drag it out of Rusty after he got everything else off his chest.

"I'd like to talk to Rusty," he said in a grim tone. "I won't take no for an answer either. She can come downstairs or I can go up, but either way, she's going to talk to me."

Marlene wiped hastily at her eyes. "She's gone," she said tearfully.

Sean flinched, feeling as though he'd suffered a vicious body blow. For several long seconds, he couldn't breathe.

"What do you mean, she's gone?" he asked hoarsely.

"She was so upset and feels she let everyone down," Marlene said in a grief-stricken voice. "Donovan apologized and even offered her a job heading up the foundation. She impressed him greatly with all she managed to do creating such an elaborate, foolproof background for Zoe, but she told him she had other job offers and that she was just home for the summer before deciding which job to take."

She pulled a tissue from the pocket of her skirt and dabbed at her eyes and nose.

"She blames herself for what happened, and she was so hurt by how her brothers reacted. I believe she feels as though she failed them—us, me—and now she needs time to regroup and prove herself worthy. God, Sean, of what? Of whom? She is so very loved, and I couldn't be more proud of her if she was of my own blood."

Sean put a hand to the back of his neck, sick to his very soul. *He* was the reason Rusty had left, not her family. He was the one who'd ripped her to shreds, rejected her and humiliated her. Not her family. And he'd been too damn angry and scared out of his mind at the time over what could have happened to her to make her understand *why* he'd been so furious.

Oh God, she'd never forgive him. How could she when he'd never be able to forgive himself?

"When will she be home?" he choked out.

Marlene gave him a look so sad that it ripped his heart right out of his chest.

"I don't think she's coming back this time," she whispered.

She covered her mouth with her hand and briefly looked away before directing her gaze back at Sean.

"I'm sorry. I have to go now. Zoe is so upset and she needs me. I've already failed Rusty. I'm not going to fail Zoe now."

She quietly shut the door, leaving Sean standing there, utterly sick at heart.

Dear God, what had he done?

He closed his eyes against the sudden stinging in his eyelids, remembering coming home to find her naked. In his bed. Just like he'd always dreamed of. Fantasized about. How much courage must it have taken her to put her heart on the line like that when for so long she'd been convinced he hated her and he'd given her no reason to believe otherwise?

You fucking coward.

He hadn't even been able to get his shit together enough to simply tell her, to admit to her everything that was in his heart. She scared him shitless. She always had. How could anyone expect to hold on to her? To capture her when she was a free spirit, larger than life, with more courage and heart than anyone he'd ever known?

And now she was out of reach. As elusive as trying to catch a shooting star. What if she didn't come back?

His jaw became hard and he was seized by rigid determination. He refused to give up. Not when she'd done so much to reach out to him. She deserved far better than he could ever give her, but he'd be damned if he ever let her go again.

He'd give her time, but he wasn't waiting. Not anymore. He'd only give her so long before he dragged her back, kicking and screaming the entire way if he had to.

CHAPTER 30

JOE stood in the shadow cast by the tree against the moonlight and stared up at the window to the bedroom where Zoe was sleeping. His fingers curled and uncurled as nervousness assailed him. Grief was a heavy blanket over the Kelly family. They'd lost Rusty. The possibility that he could lose Zoe as well was unbearable.

With Rusty now gone, it was very possible that Zoe would no longer feel comfortable remaining in his parents' house. She already blamed herself for what had been done to her and considered herself a burden. God, a burden!

She was the most precious gift he could have ever hoped to have been given. A burden? No fucking way, and he wasn't going to let her go on thinking that bullshit a second longer.

Nothing had ever been this important in his life. Nothing ever would be. This was his life, or rather the future of it. He wiped his hand over his suddenly dry mouth and swallowed back the paralyzing fear of losing her. Of not spending the rest of his life with her. Of her not loving him back. Of her not wanting him as desperately as he wanted her.

He sucked in a steadying breath and then stared at the window with renewed purpose.

"Here I come, Zoe," he murmured. "I guess I'll have to be the prince to your Rapunzel."

He hastily scaled the lower trunk until he was able to get a foothold on branches strong enough to support his weight. Gaining speed, he went higher until he was within reaching distance of the windowsill.

Not wanting to scare her to death, he slowly and very quietly slid the window upward, holding his breath in fear of a sudden creak or groan, but the night remained cloaked in silence.

He ducked inside, his gaze immediately seeking her out. He softened all over as he saw her lying on the bed on her side facing the window, her small hand tucked beneath her cheek and the pillow. He swallowed back his fury as he took in the bruises that, while fading, were still evident even when only illuminated by moonlight.

Wanting—needing—to touch her, to just be near her, he crossed the distance and slid onto the bed so his back rested against the headboard, his hip just a few inches from her face. He reached down to run his fingers through stray strands of hair that rested over her forehead and exposed cheek, and then he followed his hand down with his mouth, pressing his lips to her temple.

She stirred beneath him and opened her eyes just as he drew away and flipped the lamp on so she'd know who he was. Her eyes widened in recognition and then in panic.

"It kills me that you look at me with such fear," Joe choked out, no longer able to contain the tidal wave of suppressed emotion. So much emotion. "Don't you know how much I love you? That I'll always love you? That I'd do anything in the damn world for you? That I want forever with you?"

He was pleading with her, for all practical purposes on his hands and knees begging for his future. Her love.

Zoe sat up, moisture rimming her eyelids, her hand fluttering in a helpless motion toward her throat as if she were suddenly incapable of speaking. At the moment, so was he. He was too busy soaking up the sight of her. Hoping . . . praying . . . for a miracle. She was *his* miracle.

"How can you want forever with someone like me?" she asked in a husky voice laced with shame.

Her gaze wouldn't even meet his. She was looking everywhere except his face. He reached out and cupped her chin, gently tipping it upward until he knew she was finally looking at him.

"You mean someone as beautiful, compassionate, brave, sweet, loving and loyal as you?" he said in a tender voice.

She closed her eyes as tears sloshed over the rims, colliding with his fingers as he swept them from her skin.

"You know who and what my father is," she choked out. "My own mother left him—*me*—before I was even able to remember much about her. Is that the kind of person you want? Someone who is the antithesis of every single thing you believe in and fight for?"

Joe leaned down, still cupping her face in his palm, and silenced her with a kiss. He infused the wealth of his love for her, holding her with the most tender of touches, as though she were the most precious person in the world. In his world, she *was*. Absolutely. He'd never been more certain of anything in his life.

"You keep referring to the kind of people I am and the kind of people you are," he said gently. "Let me ask you something, baby. What do you think of Sam's wife, Sophie?"

Zoe's brow furrowed in obvious confusion. "She's wonderful and so nice and beautiful. Why would you ask such a question?"

"What about Garrett's wife, Sarah?"

"Joe, why are you asking me if I like your sisters-in-law? They're *good*. They're everything I'm *not*."

"And Eve, Donovan's wife?" he persisted.

She shook her head in confusion. Unable to contain himself a second longer, he pulled her into his arms, feeling the rapid beat of her pulse against his own.

"I think there are some things you need to know about some of my brothers' wives. Then maybe you'll finally get what I'm trying to make you understand."

She frowned again as she waited for what it was he had to say.

"Sophie's father, when he was still alive, was the second or third—I forget where exactly he ranked—most wanted man by the CIA." He watched as she processed that information, her eyes widening in surprise. "And Sarah? Her half brother was also someone the U.S. wanted to take down very badly, and he shot Garrett when Garrett was still in the Marines. In fact, Garrett and Sarah met because at the time, Garrett was using her to get to her brother and bring him down for good. And then there's Eve's father. He was an abusive pedophile, a complete monster who murdered Eve's mother and was making creepy-as-fuck overtures toward Eve's half sister, who at the time was only four years old. For that matter, neither one of Rusty's biological parents were worth a damn, and I know you don't think she's tainted or unworthy and that you love her as much as she loves you."

Zoe stared at him in utter bewilderment, her expressive eyes flashing a rapid-fire exchange of hope versus defeat.

Much the same war he'd been waging since the day she'd been taken from him.

"But most of all, *I* love you," Joe said, emphasizing each word. "I want forever with you and no one else. I don't give a shit who and what your mother and father were. You're who I care about. You're who I love, and I'll never love anyone else. You're who I want to marry and have children with."

He cupped her cheeks with both hands, framing her beautiful face with his palms as he stared down into her eyes. "Love me back," he whispered. "Take a chance with me—on me. I won't let you down, Zoe. I'll never let you down. I'll spend the rest of my life loving you if you'll let me."

She reached up and curled her fingers around his wrists and held on as she bowed her head in his grasp. He felt the dampness of her tears against his thumbs and he ducked down so he could meet her gaze once more.

"Hey, what's this?" he asked softly.

"I love you too," she said on a sob. "I love you so much. I want forever too. I want it more than *anything*. I'm so tired of dreaming, Joe. Just once I want something real that's mine. *You*."

Sweet relief swept through him with so much power that it momentarily weakened him. He closed his eyes and then pressed his mouth to the top of her head.

"Thank God," he whispered. "Thank God."

She slid her hands up his arms and over his shoulders, wrapping her slender arms around him. He caught her to him and held on tightly, burying his face in her hair, savoring holding everything that was important to him in his arms.

"I want to be better than my parents were," she said tearfully. "I want my children not to just feel loved but for them to *know* they're loved. And I want their father to be you."

He smiled, tugging her hair gently, pulling her away so that their noses nearly touched.

"It's a damn good thing, honey, because I wouldn't be very tolerant of another man fathering your children."

He trailed a finger down the bruise on her right cheek and then traced the split in the corner of her mouth that was still red and tender looking.

"How are you doing?" he asked quietly. "I'm so goddamn sorry I left you unprotected. It'll never happen again, baby. I'm starting construction on our house inside the compound just as soon as you pick out the plan you want. And until it's finished, when I'm not around, you'll be inside the compound where I know you'll always be safe."

"It was my fault—"

He pressed his finger over the uninjured side of her mouth. "Shhh. It was not your fault, and I don't want you saying it. Ever. Deal?"

"Only if you never apologize to me again," she said, tilting her chin upward in defiance.

He chuckled and pressed his lips to hers again, eager to taste her, to glory in the simple act of finding the woman he'd spend the rest of his life with and to be so blessed as to have her love him back.

"Only if you marry me as soon as it can be arranged," he challenged in a husky tone.

Her eyes went glossy again as she stared silently into his. Then sadness replaced her earlier joy.

"What's wrong, baby?"

"Rusty's gone," she said, a sob escaping. "I love her and miss her so much. It's my fault. It is!" she insisted when he issued a soft growl. "I got her into this mess and as a result it damaged her relationship with her family, and I hate that.

She's the best friend I'll ever have and I'm the reason she couldn't stay."

Joe sighed and brushed his fingers over her cheek. "No, honey. You didn't fail her. We did. Her family. That's on us. We completely crossed the line when every single one of us would have done the same damn thing."

She scowled. "Sean's the main reason she left."

Joe looked at her in confusion. "Sean? What the hell does he have to do with anything?"

Zoe rolled her eyes. "I swear, men are so thick. You're incredibly dense, all of you."

"You lost me, baby."

"Never mind," she said in exasperation. "She'll be okay. She's strong and she's a fighter."

"Yes, she is, but so are you," he said, kissing her. Then he ensured she was looking directly at him as he became serious. "Zoe, you are not to blame or responsible for Rusty leaving, and she'd be the first to tell you so. I spoke to her the day before she left."

He couldn't control the spasm of pain that rippled over his face and he had to stop talking momentarily because of the knot in his throat.

"You did?" Zoe asked. "You knew? I don't understand."

He shook his head, awed by his sister's selflessness. "I didn't know what she was doing. I called her because I was desperate and I was lost without you. I had to know how you were doing. Anything, any information, whatever crumbs she could give me. She had me completely fooled. Joked and teased then suggested I break and enter through your bedroom window and that she would make sure she wasn't around tonight."

He glanced down briefly, the ache in his voice more pronounced. "She wanted you—and me—to be happy when she was desperately unhappy herself and knew she'd be going away."

"She's pretty special," Zoe said.

He nodded but didn't say anything as quiet descended around them. Zoe wrapped her arms around him and rested her cheek against his chest.

"I love you," she said, a soft ache to her voice when she finally broke the silence. "You were what I was searching for all along but never figured it out until I thought I'd lost it all."

As she had just done to him, he wrapped his arms tightly around her, anchoring her firmly to his body, and rained kisses down on her hair. "Hush, baby. You'll never lose me. You couldn't if you tried. I'm afraid I'm resigned to tagging along behind you for the rest of my life and soaking up every crumb of love and attention you feed me."

She smiled against his chest and squeezed him despite the fact he was being so mindful of not holding her too tightly after the injuries and bruises she'd incurred.

"I hope you're hungry then," she said, tilting her head up to grin broadly at him. "Because I've got a lot of crumbs for you."

"Say it again," he whispered.

She smiled, not misunderstanding his request at all. And it was the most beautiful thing he'd ever seen in his life. Followed by the most beautiful words in existence.

"I love you," she said.

EPILOGUE

WITH construction to complete on their house, plus three pregnant members of the bridal party, Joe and Zoe made the decision to wait until the house was finished and furnished and Maren, Grace and Shea had all delivered their babies to get married.

Of course Zoe had to have a little fun torturing Joe when Rachel announced *she* was pregnant two months before the wedding day by pouting in an exaggerated fashion and saying that now they had to put off the wedding until Rachel had *her* baby.

Joe failed to see the humor in the situation, citing that if they had to wait for every pregnant Kelly woman to deliver their babies they'd never get married, because in a family this large, someone was *always* pregnant.

And when Sarah glowingly announced that she was pregnant with her second child just a week before the wedding, Zoe had laughed and conceded the point to Joe.

When the day finally arrived, Zoe was beside herself with joy and excitement. The entire contingent of Kelly wives had accompanied Zoe to Nashville to pick out her wedding dress, and that shopping trip had turned into an entire weekend marathon as they looked for *the one.*

As Zoe carefully stepped into the cloud of satin and pulled the dress up so one of the other women could begin fastening the tiny pearl buttons in the back, she stared in awe at her reflection in the mirror, unable to believe the woman who looked like a princess was actually *her.*

"Don't you dare cry," Shea warned. "Your makeup took an hour to do, and plus, if you start crying then I'll start crying and then everyone will start crying, which means seven more hours of reapplication."

Laughter went up and Zoe smiled, her lips spreading so wide that she thought she might burst from happiness. Her entire face glowed and the light shimmer from the sparkly eye shadow added to the shine in her gaze. She felt like a fairy princess. Like royalty. Her hair, which was now extension free but nearly the length it was when the extensions were in, was coiled loosely atop her head with curled tendrils floating down her neck.

The tiara the other women had insisted she wear sparkled atop her head, but what she loved the most, aside from the ginormous engagement ring Joe had given her, were the diamond chandelier earrings he had gifted her with the night before, after the rehearsal.

He'd leaned in and whispered in her ear, "Every princess needs kick-ass earrings to wear with her tiara."

She managed not to burst into tears on the spot. Barely.

A light knock on the door sounded and Zoe looked up, her brow furrowing. Everyone who should be in the bridal room was present and the men had been banned, so who on earth would be knocking?

The other women exchanged huge grins and were practically jiggling with excitement. Zoe just shook her head, wondering what on earth they'd cooked up now.

But when the door opened, Zoe forgot all about makeup, hair, her tiara or whether everything was perfect. Tears gathered in her eyes and then she ran, nearly tripping over the long train. She wobbled drunkenly and then hurled herself into Rusty's arms.

The two women hung on to each other, laughing and crying all at the same time.

"I'm glad I told the makeup artist we'd be needing a major touch-up before go time," Sophie said dryly.

But all of the women had tears in their eyes as they surrounded the two hugging women and then converged on them until it was one giant group hug. Finally Zoe pulled away long enough to examine her friend.

"You came," she said tearfully.

Rusty waved a hand down the gorgeous dress and then pointed out the heels.

"I'd never let my girl get married without me standing up for her," Rusty said teasingly. "And . . . Joe made me promise to wear a dress to his wedding, and I told him I'd even wear heels if he actually got you to marry him, so here I am."

Zoe hugged her again. "I'm so glad you're here. This day couldn't be any more perfect now. I wanted you to be here so much. You'll be my maid of honor, of course."

Rusty hugged her back. "You don't think I'm wearing this getup for my health, do you?"

"You look beautiful," Zoe said truthfully as she examined Rusty closely.

It had been eight months since Rusty had left, and she looked . . . different. She'd always been beautiful, but now she was gorgeous. Her hair was longer and fell in waves of soft curls down her back. She'd gained a little weight, filled out more, her curves more pronounced. A consistent complaint that Rusty voiced was that she had no hips, ass or boobs, but evidently she was an extremely late bloomer because her figure was absolutely lush now.

Rusty blushed, and to someone who didn't know her well it would appear she was happy, content, in a good place. But sorrow was engraved deep in her eyes. She was quieter and more resigned, a direct contradiction from the sarcastic, irreverent, ever-teasing girl who had somehow disappeared during her absence.

Zoe squeezed her hand, trying her best not to do further damage to her makeup by crying again.

"Does everyone else know you're here? Oh my God, they're going to be so happy to see you, Rusty!"

Rusty looked away, guilt flashing in her eyes. "Mom knows," she said quietly. "And Dad. And of course all the women," she said, smiling in their direction. "But I swore them to secrecy and threatened not to come if they told anyone else."

She sobered as she once again took in the faces of all the women gathered. "I'm sorry for putting y'all in that position, but I just couldn't . . ." She broke off, flushing with embarrassment.

Rachel, who was perhaps the sweetest, most empathetic woman in the group, wrapped her arm around Rusty's shoulders and squeezed.

"Don't apologize, Rusty. Let's face it. Men are morons. Granted, some of them are bigger morons than others, but they're all dense as a fog."

Laughter rang out, breaking the awkwardness. Even Rusty smiled and gave Rachel a grateful look.

"There's one other thing before we get this started," Rusty hedged. "I have a favor to ask of all of you."

"Name it," Zoe said with no hesitation.

"I'll stay for photos right after the ceremony, but then I want to make my exit as quickly as possible and I need you all to help act as a buffer."

Left unsaid, but understood by all, was that the buffer was meant for Sean. Since he wasn't part of the actual wedding party, he wouldn't be in the church while pictures were being taken, which granted Rusty the opportunity to dodge him as soon as the photo session was done.

"Leave Sean to me," Rachel said smugly. "We're pretty tight and all I'll have to do is pretend to feel a little ill because of my pregnancy and I'll have his full attention. You can make a run for it while I try not to vomit on him."

The image was so hilarious that they all began laughing again, many wiping tears from their eyes, prompting groans as they realized the makeup artist was going to be very busy if they were going to start the ceremony on time.

"Come sit with me while I get my makeup redone," Zoe urged. "I want to know everything that's gone on for the last eight months."

Rusty rolled her eyes. "Trust me, it's boring."

Zoe snorted. "As if you could ever be boring."

SEAN sat in the pew and shifted uncomfortably as he loosened his tie. He checked his watch, frowning, as were the men standing up for Joe and especially Joe himself, because it was already ten minutes past time to start. Joe looked nervous and edgy. Hell, he appeared to be sweating.

He wanted to give Joe shit for being such a nervous wreck but he could well imagine his fear of Zoe changing her mind or something happening at the last minute that would cause him to lose her. He knew that feeling all too well. Joe would get his happy ending, though. Sean was still holding out for his.

Relief was tangible in the sanctuary when the music began and the doors leading from the vestibule were opened. One by one, the Kelly wives plus Maren glided down the aisle, each holding a bouquet of purple irises. For the first time in his life, Sean envied his friends for the lives they had. The wives they came home to. The children they doted on.

Being several years younger than the Kelly brothers, he'd been more concerned with establishing his career and remaining single than establishing families like his older mentors. But now he was the age they had been when they'd all started getting married. There was only one woman he was remotely interested in settling down with, and he'd fucked up his chance with her time and time again.

There was a pause as Sophie took her place in line with the other attendants and Sean turned, expecting Zoe to make her appearance at any moment. But when he saw who walked down the aisle, back straight, eyes focused straight ahead, his stomach bottomed out.

Rusty?

He was bombarded by a host of contradictory emotions. Elation. Relief. Anger. Excitement. Betrayal. He sent accusing stares toward the Kelly men but they looked as shell-shocked as he did. Obviously they had no more forewarning of her return than he did. How could they not know? She was acting as Zoe's goddamn maid of honor and even Joe looked flabbergasted.

His eyes narrowed when his gaze shifted to the women,

who didn't look at all surprised. They looked ecstatic. And just as he was witnessing it, the men were also making the same observation.

He turned rapidly as Rusty neared the pew where he was seated right next to the aisle. Her gaze flickered for the first time, dropping from the pulpit to where he was seated.

"Rusty," he said in a low voice. "Where the hell have you been? I've been worried out of my goddamned mind!"

"Not here!" she hissed, lengthening her stride and nearly stumbling in the ridiculous heels she wore.

His Rusty never wore toothpicks disguised as shoes. She was a flip-flop, combat boot, tennis shoe–wearing woman who didn't give one fuck about makeup and girly froufrou shit and she rarely wore her hair in any way except a ponytail or a messy bun, and yet tonight . . . she looked so beautiful his teeth ached.

She was different—looked different—and yet she was still his Rusty. Nothing would ever change that.

As she increased the distance between them, he called out to her, uncaring of the scene he was making.

She immediately halted and whirled around, bitterness burning brightly in her eyes.

"I will *never* forgive you if you ruin Zoe's wedding," she said, emotion thick in her voice.

Sean grimaced and then sent Joe an apologetic look. Goddamn but he could never say or do the right thing. He bowed his head, unable to look at Rusty, because if he did, he wouldn't be able to overcome the urge to haul her out of the church, wedding be damned, and handcuff her to his bed for however long it took for her to listen to him. Or for him to finally get it right.

Joe's heart swelled with love and gratitude as he stared over at Rusty. Uncaring of protocol, since he planned to break it in just a few moments anyway, he walked over to where she had taken her place and pulled her into his arms, hugging her fiercely.

"Thank you for being here for Zoe—and for me," he whispered in her ear. "I love you, baby sister, and I've missed you so damn much. I hope this means you're coming back where you belong."

Rusty smiled and returned his hug, mindful of the flowers she carried. "Love you too, big brother. Now get on with it before Zoe has a meltdown thinking you've changed your mind."

"Oh shit," he breathed.

Hurriedly he went to the microphone stand and nervously cleared his throat as he motioned for the doors to be opened. Once opened, they revealed Zoe, looking so beautiful that it hurt to look at her. She was clearly confused and her gaze found his in obvious question.

He smiled tenderly at her and then spoke into the microphone for the entire gathering to hear.

"I wanted to do something special for my bride to be. Something to let her know how very much I love her and how much I cherish the honor she's bestowed on me by agreeing to spend the rest of her life with me. I know it's typical to play the wedding march for the bridal procession, but I chose a song as my gift to her, as my message to her as she walks to me, escorted by my father."

Zoe's watery gaze lifted to Joe's dad, whose arm hers was firmly tucked under as he prepared to walk her down the aisle and give her away.

Once again he motioned, and the song he'd picked—"I Swear" by John Michael Montgomery—began to play. He'd instructed his father to walk her very slowly, and when Zoe and his father reached the spot where Joe stood waiting, he'd take over.

His gaze was riveted to her. He couldn't look away if he tried. She was the most beautiful thing he'd ever seen in his life. And she was *his*.

As Zoe absorbed the lyrics to the song, a thin trickle of tears tracked down her cheeks and her smile was so big that it lit up the entire room. But what nearly brought Joe to his knees was the overwhelming love shining in her eyes for all to see.

It felt as though he'd waited for this moment forever. The time it took his father to escort her to where he waited for her was interminable. When his dad finally stopped just in front of him, his heart was thudding so violently that he was convinced the beats could be heard over the music.

Frank leaned down and kissed her on the cheek, his own eyes tearing up. "Welcome to the family, my girl."

Zoe squeezed his hand and released a shuddering breath in her effort not to completely break down into sobs. Then he formally transferred her hand to Joe's and looked him in the eye, his expression one of utter gravity.

"Take care of her well and love her always."

"I will," Joe said, his voice cracking.

His father stepped back to join his mother, who was openly crying and wiping her face repeatedly with a tissue. Joe captured both of Zoe's hands in his and turned so they faced each other and were sideways to the congregation.

He simply watched her, allowing all of the love he felt for her to flow from every part of his body, heart and soul. The only sound was the music and the lyrics, and Zoe was listening intently, moisture welling as the song told of the promises he was making to her.

I love you, she mouthed, her eyes watery but shining with absolute joy.

I love you more, he mouthed back.

And then he silently mouthed the last of the song, standing with his bride and serenading her in front of his entire family. A family made up of blood and love. A family that wasn't defined by genetics, DNA or birth. A family that Zoe now belonged to and would call her own. He knew that the gift of that alone was the most precious thing she'd ever been given.

And when he gave her children—a family of her own—he knew her bliss would only increase tenfold. That he was the one to get the privilege and honor of making her happy, of making all her dreams come true and of being granted her love, was all he'd ever ask for and nothing more.

The song died and he realized that both their eyes were wet. Once again, forgoing custom, he lifted her hands that he still held firmly in his to his chest so they lay directly over his heart and leaned forward and pressed a gentle kiss on her lips.

Now that the music had ended, he could hear sniffles and suspicious sounds of clearing throats arising from multiple locations—even from *his* side, where all his brothers stood behind him. No one was unaffected by the absolute beauty and perfection of this moment in time. If he could make it last forever, he would. But no, she still wasn't his. They had a ceremony to get through.

He turned to the minister, who'd married most of his family members. He'd been pastoring the old whitewashed country church for the last forty years so he was quite accustomed to the Kellys not exactly following the usual protocol.

Even his eyes glimmered and his smile was soft, making

the weathered wrinkles in his face more pronounced. His hair was stark white but he had the bluest, most gentle eyes and the most caring, generous soul of any man Joe knew. He'd supported the Kelly family through some of the best and worst moments, dating back to when his parents had been young and Sam was the only child.

"Feel like getting married today, son?" he asked in amusement.

"Yes, sir," Joe said emphatically.

Zoe smiled and nodded her agreement.

They turned to face the preacher and solemnly recited their vows, never once looking away from each other or breaking physical contact, their hands entwined the entire time. Even when Joe slid the wedding band on the ring finger of her left hand, his left hand still clung to her right.

Just before pronouncing them man and wife, the older man put one hand on Joe's shoulder, his expression serious as he focused his attention on Joe.

"Son, a good woman is hard to find and a priceless treasure. Never forget God's gift to you or His grace, and always turn to Him in times of hardship. Be her friend, her biggest fan and supporter, and always, always take out the trash, and if you want brownie points, offer to do the dishes."

Laughter scattered throughout the church.

"It is my honor to pronounce you man and wife. Son, not only may you kiss your bride, but I highly recommend it."

Joe needed no urging. He turned and pulled Zoe close, wrapping his arms around her and holding her until there was no space between them and her softness molded to his harder frame. For just one precious moment, he stared into her eyes, committing to memory the way she looked, knowing he'd remember it to his dying day and play it back often.

Then he lowered his mouth and took her lips, savoring their first kiss as man and wife. Uncaring that they had an audience or that his mom and dad were sitting a few feet away watching the entire time, he teased the line of her lips with his tongue, coaxing her to open for him.

With a breathy sigh, she capitulated and he delved within, tasting her and sipping at her sweetness. The kiss went on for so long that they were both gasping for breath. Cheers, applause and ribbing broke out from the wedding party and those sitting in the pews.

"If you'll turn around and face your family, I'll present you and your wife," the pastor said with an amused grin.

Joe tucked Zoe into his side as they turned and faced the people they loved.

"Ladies and gentlemen, I give you Mr. and Mrs. Joseph Kelly."

Those who'd been sitting stood and everyone started clapping—when they weren't wiping tears from their cheeks. His mother had amassed a pile of tissues on the pew beside her while his father merely had his arm around her, a soft smile on his face as he gazed tenderly down at his own wife.

Joe smiled down at Zoe. "Shall we, Mrs. Kelly?"

She laughed. "There's an awful lot of Mrs. Kellys, you know. How in the world do you not confuse the heck out of everyone?"

He threw back his head and laughed. "Honey, as long as you're mine, I don't care who we confuse. I can guarantee that I'll never be confused over who *my* wife is."

He propelled her forward and they walked back down the aisle, smiling at the offered congratulations and the obvious joy shared by everyone in attendance. When they got to the vestibule, Joe hurriedly pulled her into another long, breathless kiss. He reluctantly pulled back to see her eyes laughing up at him.

"Well, I only have a few seconds before they follow us," he grumbled. "It's not a crime to take every opportunity to kiss your wife on your wedding day."

She leaned up and brushed her mouth across his. "Indeed not," she murmured.

Then the doors opened as attendees began flooding out of the sanctuary. They stood and smiled until those not in the wedding party had exited, heading toward Marlene and Frank's house where the reception would be held. Sean, however, stood in the vestibule, his expression brooding as he stared into the church.

"Come on," Zoe whispered, tugging at Joe's hand. "We have to take pictures."

Joe sent Sean a curious look as he and Zoe walked by, wondering what was up and why he looked as though he were about to explode. Then something Zoe had said the night he'd climbed through her window registered, and the veritable lightbulb went off.

"Holy shit!" he whispered in Zoe's ear as they walked through the doors and down the aisle. "Rusty and *Sean*?"

Zoe halted in midstep and turned, looking up at Joe, her expression pleading. "Please, Joe, you can't say anything to anyone. I'll explain later. I promise. But you can't say anything or you'll just make things worse for Rusty, and they're already bad enough."

"Is he why she left?" he asked harshly.

He had the sudden urge to walk back through the doors and beat the shit out of the man responsible for causing his sister so much pain that she'd left her own home, but Zoe was silently begging him to let it go, and he wasn't about to do anything to mar her wedding day.

"I'll tell you *later*," she hissed.

He leaned down and kissed her so the others would think that was the reason for their hesitation.

"Later," he agreed. "And I'll want to know if I need to beat the county sheriff's ass when it's over."

Zoe rolled her eyes and shook her head. Then she let go of his hand and hurried to where Rusty was being hugged and mauled by all his brothers. She sent him another pleading look and this time he understood that she wanted him to shield Rusty from inquisition from his five brothers.

Man, was he going to get shit for throwing in with the women, but hell, ask him if he gave a fuck.

He waded into the middle of his brothers and wrapped Rusty up in a huge bear hug as if he was thrilled she was here. And he was. But he maneuvered her away from the others, amid questions being asked by Sam and Donovan.

Still hugging her, he turned so his mouth was not visible to his brothers and whispered in her ear, "Don't worry, sweetheart. Stick close to me and Zoe. We'll keep the heat off you. And just a heads-up, Sean is in the vestibule and he's got a massive brood going on."

Rusty pulled away, her desperate tears diminishing as surprise and gratitude replaced them. "Thank you," she said in a ragged voice.

Joe tugged gently at her hair. "You look beautiful in that dress and heels by the way. I kept my end of the bargain. I'm glad to see you did as well."

She laughed and then impulsively hugged him, squeezing the breath out of him. "I miss you," she whispered.

"Miss you too, baby girl. I know you're not ready to come home yet, but remember one thing for me, will you? This will *always* be your home, and when you are ready, we'll be waiting for you with open arms."

"Damn it, don't you dare make me cry in front of everyone," she said fiercely.

The photographer interrupted and for the next hour, there was no time for questions as the poses were run through, groups were formed and dozens and dozens of photos were taken.

Toward the end, Zoe pulled Rusty to her side and then turned to the photographer, asking him something in a voice too low to be heard by anyone. Then she and Rusty walked to the steps that led to the platform where the pulpit, baptismal and choir section were situated and turned to face the back of the church while the photographer issued instructions.

But for the last picture, Zoe held up her hand to the photographer and said, "One more."

Then she wrapped her arms around Rusty's waist, turning them both outward to face forward and she pressed her cheek to Rusty's. Rusty was visibly emotional as she wrapped her arms around Zoe, so the two were connected, cheek to cheek, and smiling so big that the faces of everyone watching softened.

Zoe turned and kissed Rusty's cheek and the photographer quickly snapped a shot before the two separated. Zoe held Rusty's hands in front of her, and Joe knew this was her silent good-bye. Sadness gripped him even in his happiest hour. He hated the idea of Rusty being so unhappy, and he knew that Zoe would be sad in the coming days, but he would be right by her side to put a smile on her face every time.

He walked over, ready to lend his support in any way possible. He glanced between the two women. "What do I need to do?" he asked in a low voice.

Zoe smiled at him, the love in her eyes glowing like the brightest star in the night sky.

"Tell everyone we're done here and are heading to the reception, then herd everyone out front, and if they ask, tell them I wanted a moment alone with Rusty."

Rusty squeezed Joe's hand, her face contorting to keep her emotions at bay.

"Just stay in touch, honey," he said quietly. "And don't be a stranger. If you ever need anything, I'm just a phone call away. I'll come, no questions asked."

"That means more to me than you'll ever know," she said. She squared her shoulders. "Okay, let's do this."

Joe sauntered back toward the group and announced that it was time to head to the reception. He motioned toward the front as he began moving everyone in that direction. Donovan frowned and glanced back at Rusty, but Joe nudged him.

"Zoe asked for a moment alone with her. I told her we'd wait out front."

Seemingly appeased, Donovan looked back one more time and then followed the rest out of the church.

Zoe waited until the doors closed and then she turned back to Rusty, swallowing several times in an effort to clear her throat.

"It means the world that you came and stood for me."

Rusty smiled. "I'll always stand for you, sister. And hey, don't worry about me, okay? I'm fine. Really. And I'm making it on my own. It's been . . . liberating in a way."

"Just be careful and remember I love you."

Rusty leaned in to hug her. "Love you too. Now go on. Your husband is waiting for you and you have a kick-ass honeymoon to go on."

"Call me soon?"

"I will. *After* you get back from your honeymoon."

Rusty glanced nervously toward the front and Zoe turned her toward the back. "Hurry before Sean loses his patience and barges in anyway."

Rusty's eyes saddened a brief moment and then she shook it off and gave Zoe a jaunty wave before disappearing through the door leading into the social hall, which in turn would give her an exit to the back of the church.

Zoe waited a few moments to give Rusty enough time to make her escape and then she turned, gathering the folds of material in each hand, and walked up the aisle, her lips curving into a dreamy smile.

She was married. She'd found her Prince Charming, only he wore camo and combat boots and it was sexy as hell. Regret no longer found a pathway into her heart. Not for anything. Even Sebastian. Because if not for that debacle, she would have never gone to Rusty for help and would never have met and fallen in love with Joe.

No, she wouldn't change a single thing even if she could go back and do it all over again. Because if she did then she wouldn't be where and what she was today. And what she was . . . was *happy*.

As she reached the door, it opened to reveal Joe standing there and she stopped, struck by the gorgeous image of him in the black tux looking at her with so much love that it still bewildered her every time she caught him doing it.

Without saying a word, she launched herself the remaining distance and he caught her, hefting her up his chest. She wrapped her legs around him as best she could with so much material between them and planted her lips hungrily on his.

He groaned as his hand cupped her behind and lovingly caressed it. "Do we have to go to the reception?"

She laughed. "Well . . . we do have a honeymoon to see about. Don't you have a plane?"

His eyes gleamed and a slow smile spread over his face. "As a matter of fact . . . I do." He turned, hoisting her higher in his arms as he carried her through the church doors and into the midday sun. "Want to check it out, Mrs. Kelly?"

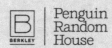